ARE YOU
THERE
AND OTHER STORIES

I0661699

OTHER BOOKS BY JACK SKILLINGSTEAD

The Whole Mess and Other Stories
The Chaos Function
Life on the Preservation
Harbinger

Praise for Jack Skillingstead and Are You There

"Jack Skillingstead's stories are smart: smart in the sense of intelligent, savvy, stylish, biting, and succinct. And they all have heart. Choose any tale in *Are You There*—the Ellisonian "The Avenger of Love," the tersely convolute "Life on the Preservation," the Shirley Jacksonesque "The Tree," the poignant "Stranger on a Bus," or any of the gems in between—and that story will flash upon you like a memory, with a light at once familiar and uniquely brilliant. I am not only a reader of these pieces, but a devout admirer of their art."

—Michael Bishop, author of *Brittle Innings*

"Jack Skillingstead is fearless. No one in SF writes about death, sex, loneliness, and love with such searing honesty."

—Daryl Gregory, author of *Afterparty*

"Jack Skillingstead writes the noir of the future, dark and cool and literate. I loved these stories so much that I worried I'd finish the book and run out of stories. But Jack, thinking ahead, has written more books."

—Eileen Gunn, author of *Questionable Practices*

"Edgy and dark . . . readers braced for powerful emotions will find this collection more than worthwhile."

—*Publishers Weekly*

"A generous collection! Skillingstead makes elegant use of classic SF tropes. The wonder is sharp-edged, the dreams disturbing, and the human relations hard and real in ways you won't find anywhere else!"

—Richard Bowes, author of *If Angels Fight*

"Protagonists with ruptured childhoods fight solipsism on near-future mean streets tingling with avatars and ghosts and parallels and deaths. Each tale, taken individually, is brilliant."

—John Clute, *Strange Horizons*

"A master of the many worlds of science fiction, Jack Skillingstead is also one of our most humane writers."

—James Patrick Kelly, author of *Wildlife*

ARE YOU THERE

AND OTHER STORIES

JACK
SKILLINGSTEAD

FAIRWOOD PRESS
Bonney Lake, WA

ARE YOU THERE

A Fairwood Press Book
July 2024
Copyright © 2009 Jack Skillingstead

All Rights Reserved

Fairwood Press
21528 104th Street Court East
Bonney Lake, WA   98391
www.fairwoodpress.com

Cover illustration by
John Picacio

Book design by
Patrick Swenson

ISBN: 978-1-958880-24-1
First Fairwood Press Edition: July 2014
Second Fairwood Press Edition: July 2024
Printed in the United States of America

For My Parents

CONTENTS

13	•	*Reading Jack Skillingstead*, by Nancy Kress.
17	•	Dead Worlds
31	•	Life on the Preservation
49	•	Double Occupancy
61	•	The Chimera Transit
71	•	Overlay
83	•	Scatter
94	•	Bean There
107	•	Girl in the Empty Apartment
124	•	Rewind
133	•	The Apprentice
143	•	Everyone Bleeds Through
152	•	Reunion
160	•	Strangers on a Bus
177	•	Free Dog
192	•	Thank You, Mr. Whiskers
205	•	The Tree
215	•	Are You There
239	•	Transplant
259	•	Here's Your Space
265	•	Cat in the Rain
281	•	Alone With an Inconvenient Companion
295	•	What You Are About to See
311	•	Rescue Mission
326	•	Two
332	•	Scrawl Daddy
349	•	Human Day
362	•	*Introduction to* The Avenger of Love
367	•	The Avenger of Love
387	•	*Author's Notes*
391	•	*Thermalling*

This is a reprint of a reprint. The publisher and I wanted to re-design and reformat *Are You There* so that my two story collections, which already share complimentary cover art, will match. We've shuffled a couple of stories, corrected a few errors, and added an introduction to "The Avenger Of Love," the story inspired by my two year experience trying to collaborate with Harlan Ellison. Other than the changes mentioned here, the book is essentially the same as the first Fairwood edition.

These stories represent my first professional expression as a writer. Many of them are what I call *wound* stories. As such, they form a picture of a particular type of character. I call him an outsider. My wife refers to him as "tortured lonely guy." Well, you get the idea. Anyway, this book means a lot to me. The writing of these stories preserved my sanity and led me to the far shore. It is no exaggeration to say *Are You There and Other Stories* changed my life. May you discover your own far shore.

—Jack Skillingstead
June 2024

Reading
Jack Skillingstead

Why does anyone write science fiction? Or read it? There are probably as many answers to that as there are writers and readers. Some like the wide-lens adventure of zipping around the galaxy, free of gravity and Terran law. Some like all the nifty gadgets, from smart clothing to doomsday machines. Some like the Cassandra role, peering into the future of science and crying, "If we go *there*, we might end up *here*—Beware! Beware!" Some like comforting tales of clashes between Good and Evil, in which Good eventually wins and everyone can draw a deep breath, close the book, and say, "Now *that* was a rattling good yarn!"

Other writers, however, have different motives. Jack Skillingstead, for one. Skillingstead is a terrorist.

Not, of course, that he will say that, if you should happen to ask him why he writes. He blinks his eyes and says slowly–to a New York ear, Jack says everything slowly—"I always wanted to be a writer. Since I was about twelve years old." He first succeeded in 2003, and has been publishing steadily ever since. If you push on and ask him why he chooses to write science fiction, he says, "The question presumes it was a choice. But actually, I'm just attracted to the weird and strange."

Well, all right—most SF writers are attracted to the weird and strange. (If they weren't, they'd be writing about suburban angst or growing up in Iowa or suburban angst in Iowa.) But not all SF writers are terrorists. What Jack does is set up a situation—plausible, interesting, sometimes even conventional—and then throw an emotional and philosophical grenade into the middle of it. When the dust settles, situation, characters, and reader are all shattered.

How, exactly, does he accomplish this?

Most often, it is by peering around the edges of reality, staring unflinchingly at what lurks there, and then making us peer at it, too, with the kind of mixed fascination and horror of witnesses at a train wreck. The scene thus illuminated isn't what usually passes for re-ality. It's what lies below the surface, behind the veil, in the closed trunk of the mental attic.

"I was gradually becoming an Eye again, a thing of the Tank. But no matter what, I was through with pills. I wanted to know if there was anything real left in me."
—*from "Dead Worlds"*

Skillingstead characters are always looking for the real, even when they would really prefer to be doing something else. (Some-times, anything else.) They find it in places both expected and unexpected, welcoming and horrific. And when they do find it, or it finds them, the Skillingstead reality is not the sentimental, one-dimensional, comforting reality of inferior fiction. Jack is af-ter truth, and truth is never simple.

"I noted the flavor of lemon and the feel of the icy liquid sluicing over my tongue. Sensation without complication."
—*Robert, in "Dead Worlds"*

Robert doesn't get to keep his simplistic sensation without complication. His creator knows better. Skillingstead characters know—or must learn—that there are always complications. For Robert, who thinks he wanted to explore distant planets but learns that interstellar exploration is more complicated than he thought. For Kylie ("Life on the Preservation"), who thinks she wants to de-stroy Seattle but learns that destruction is more complicated than she thought. For John ("Everyone Bleeds Through"), who wants to end his affair with a married woman but learns that love is more layered than he ever imagined. For Brian ("Are You There"), whose job is to solve murders but who learns that not even death is a sim-ple binary state.

"We were all bigger than what we appeared."
— *"Everyone Bleeds Through"*

However, I don't want to give the impression that these stories merely uncover complicated anguish. They do that, certainly, but they also do much more. After my sister Kate read a selection of Jack's stories, I asked her for her opinion. She said, succinctly, "Not an easy writer. His specialty is pain. But do not be afraid!"

She was absolutely right. Unlike most terrorists, Jack has a redemptive side.

Nearly seventy years ago, Albert Camus wrote, "There is but one truly serious philosophical problem and that is suicide." Camus then explored the reasons why one should not choose suicide—in other words, the reasons to choose life, despite the anguish that living often entails. A Skillingstead story does the same thing. It dismisses the easy and sentimental reasons to choose life, in order to find the real, complicated, sometimes hidden reasons. To do that, you sometimes need to blow things up: pretty conventions, superficial answers, comfortable complacency. That's how you find out what lies underneath.

"She punched through, and the sudden light shift dazzled her."
—"Life on the Preservation"

These are pretty dazzling stories. Not always easy or comfortable; the sudden light shift can be disorienting. But your eyes will get used to it, and you will see things you never expected to see, and you will be very glad you did, in fact, let Jack Skillingstead punch you through.

—Nancy Kress
December 2008

DEAD WORLDS

A week after my retrieval, I went for a drive in the country. I turned the music up loud, Aaron Copland. The two-lane blacktop wound into late summer woods. Sun and shadow slipped over my Mitsubishi. I felt okay, but how long could it last? The point, I guess, was to find out.

I was driving too fast, but that's not why I hit the dog. Even at a reduced speed, I wouldn't have been able to stop in time. I had shifted into a slightly banked corner overhung with maple—and the dog was just there. A big shepherd, standing in the middle of the road with his tongue hanging out, as if he'd been running. Brakes, clutch, panicked wrenching of the wheel, a tight skid. The heavy thud of impact felt through the car's frame.

I turned off the digital music stream and sat a few moments in silence except for the nearly subaudible ripple of the engine. In the rearview mirror, the dog lay in the road.

I swallowed, took a couple of deep breaths, then let the clutch out, slowly rolled onto the shoulder, and killed the engine.

The door swung smoothly up and away. A warm breeze scooped into the car, carrying birdsong and the muted purl of running water—a creek or stream.

I walked back to the dog. He wasn't dead. At the sound of my footsteps approaching, he twisted his head around and snapped at me. I halted a few yards away. The dog whined. Bloody foam flecked his lips. His hind legs twitched brokenly.

"Easy," I said.

The dog whimpered, working his jaws. He didn't snap again, not even when I hunkered close and laid my hand between his ears. The short hairs bristled against my palm.

His chest heaved. He made a grunting, coughing sound.

Blood spattered the road. I looked on, dispassionate. Already, I was losing my sense of emotional connection. I had deliberately neglected to take my pill that morning.

Then the woman showed up.

I heard her trampling through the underbrush. She called out, "Buddy! Buddy!"

"Here," I said.

She came out of the woods, holding a red nylon leash, a woman maybe thirty-five years old, with short blond hair, wearing a sleeveless blouse, khaki shorts, and ankle boots. She hesitated. Shock crossed her face. Then she ran to us.

"Buddy, oh Buddy."

She knelt by the dog, tears spilling from her blue eyes. My chest tightened. I wanted to cherish the emotion. But was it genuine, or a residual effect of the drug?

"I'm sorry," I said. "He was in the road."

"I took him off leash," she said. "It's my fault."

She kept stroking the dog's side, saying his name. Buddy laid his head in her lap as if he was going to sleep. He coughed again, choking up blood. She stroked him and cried.

"Is there a vet?" I asked.

She didn't answer.

Buddy shuddered violently and ceased breathing; that was the end. "We'd better move him out of the road," I said.

She looked at me and there was something fierce in her eyes. "I'm taking him home," she said.

She struggled to pick the big shepherd up in her arms. The dog was almost as long as she was tall.

"Let me help you. We can put him in the car."

"I can manage."

She staggered with Buddy, feet scuffing, the dog's hind legs limp, like weird dance partners. She found her balance, back swayed, and carried the dead dog into the woods.

I went to the car, grabbed the keys. My hand reached for the glove box, but I drew it back. I was gradually becoming an Eye again, a thing of the Tank. But no matter what, I was through with pills. I wanted to know if there was anything real left in me.

I locked the car and followed the woman into the woods.

She hadn't gotten far. I found her sitting on the ground crying, hugging the dog. She looked up.

"Help me," she said. "Please."

I carried the dog to her house, about a hundred yards. The body seemed to get heavier in direct relation to the number of steps I took.

It was a modern house, octagonal, lots of glass, standing on a green expanse of recently cut lawn. We approached it from the back. She opened a gate in the wooden fence, and I stepped through with the dog. That was about as far as I could go. I was feeling it in my arms, my back. The woman touched my shoulder.

"Please," she said. "Just a little farther."

I nodded, clenched my teeth, and hefted the dead weight. She led me to a tool shed. Finally, I laid the dog down. She covered it with a green tarp and then pulled the door shut.

"I'll call somebody to come out. I didn't want Buddy to lie out by the road or in the woods where the other animals might get at him."

"I understand," I said, but I was drifting, beginning to detach from human sensibilities.

"You better come inside and wash," she said.

I looked at my hands. "Yeah."

I washed in her bathroom. There was blood on my shirt and she insisted I allow her to launder it. When I came out of the bathroom in my T-shirt, she had already thrown my outer shirt, along with her own soiled clothes, into the washer, and called the animal control people, too. Now wearing a blue shift, she offered me ice tea, and we sat together in the big, sunny kitchen, drinking from tall glasses. I noted the flavor of lemon, the feel of the icy liquid sluicing over my tongue. Sensation without complication.

"Did you have the dog a long time?"

"About eight years," she said. "He was my husband's, actually."

"Where is your husband?"

"He passed away two years ago."

"I'm sorry."

She was looking at me in a strange way, and it suddenly struck me that she knew what I was. Somehow, people can tell. I started to stand up.

"Don't go yet," she said. "Wait until they come for Buddy. Please?"

"You'll be all right by yourself."

"Will I?" she said. "I haven't been all right by myself for a long, long time. You haven't even told me your name."

"It's Robert."

She reached across the table for my hand and we shook. "I'm Kim Pham," she said. I was aware of the soft coolness of her flesh, the way her eyes swiveled in their wet orbits, the lemon exhalation of her breath.

"You're an Eye," she said.

I took my hand back.

"And you're not on your medication, are you?"

"It isn't medication, strictly speaking."

"What is it, then?"

A lie, I thought, but said, "It restores function. Viagra for the emotionally limp, is the joke."

She didn't smile.

"I know all the jokes," she said. "My husband was a data analyst on the Tau Boo Project. The jokes aren't funny."

The name Pham didn't ring any bells, but a lot of people flogged data at the Project.

"Why don't you take your Viagra or whatever you want to call it?"

I shrugged. "Maybe I'm allergic."

"Or you don't trust the emotional and cognitive reality is the same one you possessed before the Tank."

I stared at her. She picked up her ice tea and sipped.

"I've read about you," she said.

"Really."

"Not you in particular. I've read about Eyes, the psychological phenomenon."

"Don't forget the sexual mystique."

She looked away. I noted the way the musculature of her neck worked, the slight flushing near her hairline. I was concentrating, but knew I was close to slipping away.

"Being an Eye is not what the public generally thinks," I said.

"How is it different?"

"It's more terrible."

"Tell me."

"The Tank is really a perfect isolation chamber. Negative gravity, total sensory deprivation. Your body is covered with transdermal patches. The cranium is cored to allow for the direct insertion of the conductor. You probably knew that much. Here's what they don't say: The process kills you. To become an Eye, you must literally surrender your life."

I kept talking because it helped root me in my present consciousness. But it wouldn't last.

"They keep you functioning in the Tank, but it's more than your consciousness that rides the tachyon stream. It's your *being*, it's who you are. And somehow, between Earth and the robot receiver fifty light years away, it sloughs off, all of it except your raw perceptions. You become a thing of the senses, not just an Eye but a hand, a tongue, an ear. You inhabit a machine that was launched before you were born, transmit data back along a tachyon stream, mingled with your own thought impulses for analysts like your husband to dissect endlessly. Then they retrieve you, and all they're really retrieving is a thing of raw perception. They tell you the drugs restore chemical balances in your brain, vitalize cognitive ability. But really it's a lie. You're dead, and that's all there is to it."

The animal control truck showed up, and I seized the opportunity to leave. The world was breaking up into all its parts now. People separate from the earth upon which they walked. A tree, a doorknob, a blue eye swiveling. Separate parts constituting a chaotic and meaningless whole.

At the fence, I paused and looked back, saw Kim Pham watching me. She was like the glass of ice tea, the dead weight of the dog, the cold pool on the fourth planet that quivered like mercury as I probed it with a sensor.

Back in the car, I sat. I had found the automobile, but I wasn't sure I could operate it. All I could see or understand were the thousand individual parts, the alloys and plastics, the wires and servos and treated leather, and the aggregate smell.

A rapping sounded next to my left ear. Thick glass, blue eyes, bone structure beneath stretched skin. I comprehended everything, but understood nothing. The eyes went away. Then: "You better take this." Syllables, modulated air. A bitter taste.

Retrieval.

I blinked at the world, temporarily restored to coherence.

"Are you all right? Kim was sitting beside me in the Mitsubi-shi.

"Yes, I'm all right."

"You looked catatonic."

"What time is it?"

"What time do you *think* it is?"

"I asked first."

"Almost seven o'clock."

"Shit."

"I was driving to town. I couldn't believe you were still sitting here."

I rubbed my eyes. "God, I'm tired."

"Where are you staying?"

"I have a charming little apartment at the Project."

"Do you feel well enough to drive there?"

"Yeah, but I don't want to."

"Why not?"

"They might not let me out again."

"Are you serious?"

"Not really."

"It's hard to tell with you."

"Did they take care of Buddy okay?"

"Yes."

I looked at her, and saw an attractive woman of thirty-five or so with light blue eyes.

"You better follow me back to my house. Besides, you forgot your shirt."

"That's right," I said.

I parked my car in the detached garage and stowed the keys under the visor. The Project had given me the car, but it was strict-ly for publicity purposes and day trips. We Eyes were supposed to have the right stuff.

There was a guest room with a twin bed and a window that admitted a refreshing breeze. I removed my shoes and lay on the bed and listened to hear if she picked up the phone, listened for the sound of her voice calling the Project. She would know people there, have numbers. Former associates of her husband. I closed my eyes, assuming the next face I saw would be that of a Project security type.

It wasn't.

When I opened my eyes the room was suffused with soft lamplight. Kim stood in the doorway.

"I have your pills," she said, showing me the little silver case.

"It's okay. I won't need another one until tomorrow."

She studied me.

"Really," I said. "Just one a day."

"What would have happened if I hadn't found you?"

"I would have sat there until somebody else saw me, and if no one else happened by, I would have gone on sitting there until doomsday. Mine, at any rate."

"Did you mean it when you said the Project people wouldn't let you leave again?"

I thought about my answer. "It's not an overt threat. They'd like to get another session out of me. I think they're a little desperate for results."

"Results equal funding, my husband used to say."

"Right."

"My husband was depressed about the lack of life."

I sat up on the bed, rubbing my arms, which felt goosebumpy in spite of the warmth.

"How did he die?" I asked.

"A tumor in his brain. It was awful. Toward the end he was in constant pain. They medicated him heavily. He didn't even know me anymore." She looked away. "I'm afraid I got a little desperate myself after he died. But I'm stronger now."

"Why do you live out here all by yourself?"

"It's my home. If I want a change there's a cottage up in Oregon, Cannon Beach. But I'm used to being left on my own."

"Used to it?"

"It seems to be a theme in my life."

It was also a statement that begged questions, and I asked them over coffee in the front room. Her parents were killed in a car accident when Kim was fourteen. Her aunt raised her, but it was an awkward relationship.

"I felt more like an imposition than a niece."

And then, of course, there was Mr. Pham and the brain tumor. When she finished, something inside me whimpered to get out but I wouldn't let it.

"Sometimes, I think I'd prefer to be an Eye," Kim said.

"Trust me, you wouldn't."

"Why not?" She was turned to the side, facing me on the couch we shared, one leg drawn up and tucked under, her face alive, eyes questing.

"I already told you: Because you'd have to die."

"I thought that was you being metaphorical."

I shook my head, patted the case of pills now replaced in the cargo pocket of my pants.

"I'm in these pills," I said. "The 'me' you're now talking to. But it isn't the me I left behind when I climbed into the Tank." I sipped my coffee. "There's no official line on that, by the way. It's just my personal theory."

"It's kind of neurotic."

"Kind of."

"I don't think you really believe it."

I shrugged. "That's your prerogative."

For a while we didn't talk.

"It does get lonely out here sometimes," Kim said.

"Yes."

Her bedroom was nicer than the guest room. With the lights out, she dialed to transparency three of the walls and the ceiling, and it was like lying out in the open with a billion stars overhead and the trees waving at us. I touched her naked belly and kissed her. Time unwound deliciously, but eventually wound back up tight as a watch spring and resumed ticking.

We lay on our backs, staring up, limbs entwined. The stars wheeled imperceptibly. I couldn't see Tau Boo, and that was fine with me.

"Why did you do it, then?" she asked.

"Because it felt good. Plus, you seemed to be enjoying yourself as well."

"Not that. Why did you want to be an Eye."

"Oh. I wanted to see things that no one else could see, ever. I wanted to travel farther than it was possible for a man physically to travel. Pure ego. Which is slightly ironic."

"Worth it?"

I thought of things, the weird aquamarine sky of the fourth planet, the texture of nitrogen-heavy atmosphere. Those quicksilver pools. But I also recalled the ripping away of my personality, and how all those wonders in my mind's eye were like something I'd read about or seen pictures of—unless I went off the pill and allowed myself to become pregnant with chaos. Then it was all real and all indistinguishable, without meaning.

"No," I said, "it wasn't worth it."

"When I think about it," Kim said, "it feels like escape."

"There's that too, yes."

In the morning, I kissed her bare shoulder while she slept. I traced my fingers lightly down her arm, pausing at the white scars on her wrist. She woke up and pulled her arm away. I kissed her neck, and we made love again.

Later, I felt disinclined to return to the Project compound and equally disinclined to check in, which I was required to do.

"Why don't you stay here," Kim said.

It sounded good. I swallowed my daily dose of personality with my first cup of coffee. In fact, I made a habit of it every morning I woke up lying next to Kim. Some nights, we fell asleep having neglected to dial the walls back to opacity, and I awakened with the vulnerable illusion that we were outdoors. Once, I felt like I was being watched, and when I opened my eyes, I saw a doe observing us from the lawn.

I began to discover my health and some measure of happiness that I hadn't previously known. Before, always, I'd been a loner. Kim's story was essentially my story, with variations. It was partly what had driven me to the Tau Boo Project. But for those two weeks, living with Kim Pham, I wasn't alone, not in the usual sense. This was something new in my world. It was good. But it could also give me that feeling I had when I woke up in the open with something wild watching me.

One morning, the *last* morning, I woke up in our indoor-outdoor bedroom and found Kim weeping. Her back was to me, her face buried in her pillow. Her shoulders made little hitching movements with her sobs. I touched her hair.

"What's wrong?"

Her voice muffled by the pillow, she said, "I can't stand anymore leaving."

"Hey—"

She turned into me, her eyes red from crying. "I *mean* it," she said. "I couldn't stand anymore."

I held her tightly while the sun came up.

At the breakfast table I opened the little silver pill case. There were only three pills left. I took one with my first cup of dark French roast. Kim stared at the open case before I snapped it shut.

"You're almost out," she said.

"Yeah."

"Robert, it's not like what you said. Those pills aren't you. They allow you to feel, that's all. You can't always be afraid."

I contemplated my coffee.

"Listen," she said. "I used to be envious of Eyes. No more pain, no more loneliness, no more fear. Life with none of the messiness of living. But I was wrong. That isn't life at all. This is. What we have."

"So I'll get more pills." I smiled.

Only it wasn't like a trip to the local pharmacy. There was only one place to obtain the magic personality drug: The Project. I decided I should go that day, that there was no point in waiting for my meager supply to run out.

Kim held onto me like somebody clinging to a pole in a hurricane.

"I'll come with you," she said.

"They won't let you past the gate."

"I don't care. I'll wait outside then."

We took her car. She parked across the street. We embraced awkwardly in the front seat. I was aware of the guard watching us.

"You've hardly told me anything personal about yourself," she said. "And here I've told you all my secret pain."

"Maybe I don't have any secret pain."

"You wouldn't be human if you didn't."

"I'll spill my guts when I come out. Promise."

She didn't want to let go, but I was ready to leave. I showed the guard my credentials and he passed me through. I turned and waved to Kim.

"She's a pretty one," the guard said.

I sat in a room. They relieved me of my pill case. I was "debriefed" by a young man who behaved like an automaton, asking questions, checking off my answers on his memorypad. Where had I spent the last two weeks? Why had I failed to communicate with the Project? Did I feel depressed, anxious? Some questions I answered, some I ignored.

"I just want more pills," I said. "I'll check in next time, cross my heart."

A man escorted me to the medical wing, where I underwent a thorough and pointless physical examination. When it was over, Orley Campbell, assistant director of the Tau Boo Project, sat down to chat while we awaited the results of various tests.

"So our stray lamb has returned to the fold," he said. Orley was a tall man with a soft face and the beginnings of a potbelly. I didn't like him.

"Baaa," I said.

"Same old Bobbie."

"Yep, same old me. When do I get out of here?"

"This isn't a jail. You're free to leave any time you wish."

"What about my pills?"

"You'll get them, don't worry about that. You owe us one more session, you know."

"I know."

"Are you having misgivings? I've looked over your evaluation. You appear somewhat depressed."

"I'm not in the least bit depressed."

"Aren't you? I wish I could say the same."

"What time is it? How long have I been here, Orley?"

"Oh, not long. Bobbie, why not jump right back on the horse? If you'd like to relax for a couple of weeks more, that's absolutely not a problem. You just have to remember to check in. I mean, that's part of the drill, right? You knew that when you signed on."

I thought about Kim waiting outside the gate. Would she still be there? Did I even want her to be? I could feel my consciousness spreading thin. Orley kept smiling at me. "I guess I'm ready," I said.

A month is a long time to exist in the Tank. Of course, as an Eye, you are unaware of passing hours. You inhabit a sensory world at the far end of a tachyon tether. I've looked at romanticized illustrations of this. The peaceful dreamer at one end, the industrious robot on the other. In between, the data flows along an ethereal cord of light. Blah. They keep you alive intravenously, maintain hydration, perform body waste removal. A device sucks out the data. It's fairly brutal.

I recouped in the medical wing for several days. I had my pills and a guarantee of more, all I would require. I had put in the maximum Tank time and could not return without suffering serious and permanent brain damage.

My marathon Tank session had yielded zip in terms of the Project's primary goal. The fourth planet was dead.

Now I would have money and freedom and a future, *if* I wanted one. I spent my hours reading, thinking about warm climates. Kim Pham rapped on my memory, but I wouldn't open the door.

A week after my retrieval, I insisted on being released from the medical wing, and nobody put up an argument. I'd served my purpose. Orley caught up to me as I was leaving the building. I was hobbling on my weak legs, carrying my belongings in a shoulder bag. Orley picked up my hand and shook it.

"Good luck to you," he said. "What's first on the agenda, a little 'Eye candy'?"

I wasn't strong enough to belt him. He looked morose and tired, which is approximately the way I felt myself. When I didn't reply he went on:

"Cruising a little close to home last time, weren't you? That Pham woman was persistent. She came around every day for two weeks straight. Nice-looking, but older than the others. I guess you would get tired of the young ones after a while."

The smirk is what did it. I found some ambition and threw a descent punch that bloodied his nose.

A cab picked me up at the gate. On impulse, I switched intended destinations. Instead of the airport, I provided sketchy directions, and we managed to find Kim's house without too much difficulty.

The house had an abandoned look, or at least I thought so. A mood can color things, though, and my mood was gloomy. The desperation of the Tau Boo Project had rubbed off on me. There was no life on the fourth planet, no life on any of the planets that had thus far been explored by our human Eyes. When the receiver craft were launched decades previously, it was with a sense of great purpose and hope. But so far, the known universe had not proved too lively, which only made our own Earth feel isolated, lonely—doomed even.

The windows of Kim's house were all black. I knocked, waited, knocked again. I knew where she hid the spare key, on a hook under the back porch.

The house was silent. Every surface was filmed with dust. I drifted through the hollow rooms like a ghost.

Gone.

I pictured all the ways, all the ugly ways she might have departed this world. Of course, there was no evidence that she had done anything of the sort. An empty house did not necessarily add up to a terminated life. Probably I was giving myself too much credit. But the gloom was upon me. I could see the white scars on her wrists.

I sat on the carpeted floor of the master bedroom, still weak from the Tank. Hunger gnawed at me, but I didn't care. I let time unravel around the tightening in my chest, and, as darkness fell, I dialed the walls and ceiling clear, and lay on my back, and let exhausted sleep take me.

Lack of nourishment inhibits the efficacy of the pill. In the morning, I opened my eyes to dark pre-dawn and a point of reference that was rapidly growing muddy. The pills were in my bag, but my interest in digging them out was not very great. Why not let it all go? Become the fiber in the rug, the glass, the pulse of blood in my own veins. Why not?

I lay still and began to lose myself. I watched the dark blue sky pale toward dawn. At some point, the blue attained a familiar shade. Kim cradling her dead dog, the fierceness of her eyes. *I can manage.*

A sharp bubble of emotion formed in my throat, and I couldn't swallow it down. So I rolled over. Because maybe I could manage it, too. Maybe. I reached for my bag, my mind growing rapidly diffuse. The interesting articulation of my finger joints distracted me: Bone sleeved within soft flesh, blood circulating, finger pads palpating the tight fibers of the rug. Time passed.I shook myself, groped forward, touched the bag, forgot why it was so important, flickeringly remembered, got my hand on the case, fingered a pill loose onto the rug, belly-crawled, absently scanning details, little yellow pill nestled in fibers, extend probe (tongue), and swallow.

One personality pill with lint chaser.

I came around slowly, coalescing back into the mundane world, an empty stomach retarding the absorption process. Eventually, I stood up. First order of business: food. I found some stale crackers in a kitchen cabinet. Ambrosia. Standing at the sink, gazing out the window, I saw the garage. I stopped chewing, the crackers like crumbled cardboard in my mouth. I'd thought of ropes and drugs and razors. But what about exhaust?

I walked toward the garage, my breathing strangely out of sync. I stopped to gather my courage or whatever it was I'd need to proceed.

Then I opened the door.

There was one car in the double space. My Mitsubishi, still parked as I'd left it. I climbed into the unlocked car and checked for the keys under the visor. They fell into my lap, note attached. From Kim.

It wasn't a suicide note.

LIFE ON THE PRESERVATION

Wind buffeted the scutter. Kylie resisted the temptation to fight the controls. Hand light on the joystick, she veered toward the green smolder of Seattle, riding down a cloud canyon aflicker with electric bursts. The Preservation Field extended half a mile over Elliot Bay but did not capture Blake or Vashon Island or any of the blasted lands.

She dropped to the deck. Acid rain and wind lashed the scutter. The Preservation Field loomed like an immense wall of green, jellied glass.

She punched through, and the sudden light shift dazzled her. Kylie polarized the thumbnail port, at the same time deploying braking vanes and dipping steeply to skim the surface of the bay.

The skyline and waterfront were just as they'd appeared in the old photographs and movies. By the angle of the sun she estimated her arrival time at late morning. Not bad. She reduced airspeed and gently pitched forward. The scutter drove under the water. It got dark. She cleared the thumbnail port. Bubbles trailed back over the thick plexi, strings of silver pearls.

Relying on preset coordinates, she allowed the autopilot to navigate. In minutes the scutter was tucked in close to a disused pier. Kyle opened the ballast, and the scutter surfaced in a shadow, bobbing. She saw a ladder and nudged forward.

She was sweating inside her costume. Jeans, black sneakers, olive drab shirt, rain parka. Early twenty-first century urban America: Seattle chic.

She powered down, tracked her seat back, popped the hatch. The air was sharp and clean, with a saltwater tang. Autumn chill in the Pacific Northwest. Water slopped against the pilings.

She climbed up the pitchy, guano-spattered rungs of the ladder.

And stood in awe of the intact city, the untroubled sky. She could sense the thousands of living human beings, their vitality like an electric vibe in her blood. Kylie was nineteen and had never witnessed such a day. It had been this way before the world ended. She reminded herself that she was here to destroy it.

From her pocket she withdrew a remote control, pointed it at the scutter. The hatch slid shut and her vehicle sank from view. She replaced the remote control. Her hand strayed down to another zippered pocket and she felt the outline of the explosive sphere. Behind it her heart was beating wildly. *I'm here*, she thought.

She walked along the waterfront, all her senses exploited. The sheer numbers of people overwhelmed her. The world had ended on a Saturday, November 9, 2004. There were more living human beings in her immediate range of sight than Kylie had seen in her entire life.

She extracted the locator device from her coat pocket and flipped up the lid. It resembled a cellular phone of the period. A strong signal registered immediately. Standing in the middle of the sidewalk, she turned slowly toward the high reflective towers of the city, letting people go around her, so many people, walking, skateboarding, jogging, couples and families and single people, flowing in both directions, and seagulls gliding overhead, and horses harnessed to carriages waiting at the curb (so *much* life), and the odors and rich living scents, and hundreds of cars and pervasive human noise and riot, all of it continuous and—

"Are you all right?"

She started. A tall young man in a black jacket loomed over her. The jacket was made out of *leather*. She could smell it.

"Sorry," he said. "You looked sort of dazed."

Kylie turned away and walked into the street, toward the signal, her mission. Horns blared, she jerked back, dropped her locator. It skittered against the curb near one of the carriage horses. Kylie lunged for it, startling the horse, which clopped back, a hoof coming down on the locator. *No!* She couldn't get close. The great head of the animal tossed, nostrils snorting, the driver shouting at her, Kylie frantic to reach her device.

"Hey, watch it."

It was the man in the leather jacket. He pulled her back, then darted in himself and retrieved the device. He looked at it a moment, brow knitting. She snatched it out of his hand. The display was cracked and blank. She shook it, punched the keypad. Nothing.

"I'm really sorry," the man said.

She ignored him.

"It's like my fault," he said.

She looked up. "You have no idea, *no idea* how bad this is."

He winced.

"I don't even have any tools," she said, not to him.

"Let me—"

She walked away, but not into the street, the locator a useless thing in her hand. She wasn't a tech. Flying the scutter and planting explosives was as technical as she got. So it was plan B, only since plan B didn't exist it was plan Zero. Without the locator she couldn't possibly find the Eternity Core. A horse! Jesus.

"*Shit.*"

She sat on a stone bench near a decorative waterfall that unrolled and shone like a sheet of plastic. Her mind raced but she couldn't formulate a workable plan B.

A shadow moved over her legs. She looked up, squinting in the sun.

"Hi."

"What do you want?" she said to the tall man in the leather jacket.

"I thought an ice cream might cheer you up."

"Huh?"

"Ice cream," he said. "You know, 'You scream, I scream, we all scream for ice cream'?"

She stared at him. His skin was pale, his eyebrows looked sketched on with charcoal and there was a small, white scar on his nose. He was holding two waffle cones, one in each hand, the cones packed with pink ice cream. She had noticed people walking around with these things, had seen the sign.

"I guess you don't like strawberry," he said.

"I've never had it."

"Yeah, right."

"Okay, I'm lying. Now why don't you go away. I need to think."

He extended his left hand. "It's worth trying, at least once.

Even on a cold day."

Kylie knew about ice cream. People in the old movies ate it. It made them happy.

She took the cone.

"Listen, can I sit down for a second?" the man said.

She ignored him, turning the cone in her hand like the mysterious artifact it was. The man sat down anyway.

"My name's Toby," he said.

"It's really pink," Kylie said.

"Yeah." And after a minute. "You're supposed to lick it."

She looked at him.

"Like this," he said, licking his own cone.

"I *know*," she said. "I'm not an ignoramus." Kylie licked her ice cream. *Jesus*! Her whole body lit up. "That's—"

"Yeah?"

"It's wonderful," she said.

"You really haven't had ice cream before?"

She shook her head, licking away at the cone, devouring half of it in seconds.

"That's incredibly far-fetched," Toby said. "What's your name? You want a napkin?" He pointed at her chin.

"I'm Kylie," she said, taking the napkin and wiping her chin and lips. All of a sudden she didn't want any more ice cream. She had never eaten anything so rich. In her world there wasn't anything so rich. Her stomach felt queasy.

"I have to go," she said.

She stood up, so did he.

"Hey, you know the thing is, what you said about not having tools? What I mean is, I have tools. I mean I fix things. It's not a big deal, but I'm good and I like doing it. I can fix all kinds of things, you know? Palm Pilots, cellphones, laptop. Whatever."

Kylie waved the locator. "You don't even know what this *is*."

"I don't *have* to know what it is to make it go again."

Hesitantly, she handed him the locator. While he was turning it in his fingers, she spotted the Tourist. He was wearing a puffy black coat and a watch cap, and he was walking directly toward her, expressionless, his left hand out of sight inside his pocket. He wasn't a human being.

Toby noticed her changed expression and followed her gaze. "You know that guy?"

Kylie ran. She didn't look back to see if the Tourist was running after her. She cut through the people crowding the sidewalk, her heart slamming. It was a minute before she realized she'd left the locator with Toby. That almost made her stop, but it was too late. Let him keep the damn thing.

She ran hard. The Old Men had chosen her for this mission because of her youth and vitality (so many were sickly and weak), but after a while she had to stop and catch her breath. She looked around. The vista of blue water was dazzling. The city was awesome, madly perfect, phantasmagoric, better than the movies. The Old Men called it an abomination. Kylie didn't care what they said. She was here for her mother, who was dying and who grieved for the trapped souls.

Kylie turned slowly around, and here came two more Tourists. No, three.

Three from three different directions, one of them crossing the street, halting traffic. Stalking toward her with no pretense of human expression, as obvious to her among the authentic populace as cockroaches in a scatter of white rice.

Kylie girded herself. Before she could move, a car drew up directly in front of her, a funny round car painted canary yellow. The driver threw the passenger door open, and there was the man again, Toby.

"Get in!"

She ducked into the car, which somehow reminded her of the scutter, and it accelerated away. A Tourist who had scrabbled for the door handle spun back and fell. Kylie leaned over the seat. The Tourist got up, the other two standing beside him, not helping. Then Toby cranked the car into a turn that threw her against the door. They were climbing a steep hill, and Toby seemed to be doing too many things at once, working the clutch, the steering wheel and radio, scanning through stations until he lighted upon something loud and incomprehensible that made him smile and nod his head.

"You better put on your seatbelt," he said. "They'll ticket you for that shit, believe it or not."

Kylie buckled her belt.

"Thanks," she said. "You came out of nowhere."

"Anything can happen. Who were those guys?"

"Tourists."

"Okay. Hey, you know what?"

"What?"

He took his hand off the shifter and pulled Kylie's locator out of his inside jacket pocket.

"I bet you I can fix this gizmo."

"Would you bet your soul on it?"

"Why not?" He grinned.

He stopped at his apartment to pick up his tools, and Kylie waited in the car. There was a clock on the dashboard. 11:45 A.M. She set the timer on her wrist chronometer.

Twelve hours and change.

They sat in a coffee bar in Belltown. More incomprehensible music thumped from box speakers bracketed near the ceiling. Paintings by some local artist decorated the walls, violent slashes of color, faces of dogs and men and women drowning, mouths gaping.

Kylie kept an eye open for Tourists.

Toby hunched over her locator, a jeweler's kit unrolled next to his espresso. He had the back off the device and was examining its exotic components with the aid of a magnifying lens and a battery-operated light of high intensity. He had removed his jacket and was wearing a black sweatshirt with the sleeves pushed up. His forearms were hairy. A tattoo of blue thorns braceleted his right wrist. He was quiet for a considerable time, his attention focused. Kylie drank her second espresso, like the queen of the world, like it was nothing to just *ask* for coffee this good and get it.

"Well?" she said.

"Ah."

"What?"

"Ah, what is this thing?"

"You said you didn't need to know."

"I don't need to know, I just want to know. After all, according to you I'm betting my immortal soul that I can fix it, so it'd be nice to know what it does."

"We don't always get to know the nice things, do we?" Kylie said. "Besides I don't believe in souls. That was just something to say." Something her mother had told her, she thought. The Old Men didn't talk about souls. They talked about zoos.

"You sure downed that coffee fast. You want to go for three?"

"Yeah."

He chuckled and gave her a couple of dollars and she went to the bar and got another espresso, head buzzing in a very good way.

"It's a locator," she said, taking pity on him, after returning to the table and sitting down.

"Yeah? What's it locate?"

"The city's Eternity Core."

"Oh, that explains everything. What's an eternity core?"

"It's an alien machine that generates an energy field around the city and preserves it in a sixteen hour time loop."

"Gotchya."

"*Now* can you fix it?"

"Just point out one thing."

She slurped up her third espresso. "Okay."

"What's the power source? I don't see anything that even vaguely resembles a battery."

She leaned in close, their foreheads practically touching. She pointed with the chipped nail of her pinky finger.

"I think it's that coily thing," she said.

He grunted. She didn't draw back. She was smelling him, smelling his skin. He lifted his gaze from the guts of the locator. His eyes were pale blue, the irises circled with black rings.

"You're kind of a spooky chick," he said.

"Kind of."

"I like spooky."

"Where I come from," Kylie said, "almost all the men are impotent."

"Yeah?"

She nodded.

"Where do you come from," he asked, "the east side?"

"East side of hell."

"Sounds like it," he said.

She kissed him, impulsively, her blood singing with caffeine and long-unrequited pheromones. Then she sat back and wiped her lips with her palm and stared hard at him.

"I wish you hadn't done that," she said.

"*Me.*"

"Just fix the locator, okay?"

"Spooky," he said, picking up a screwdriver with a blade not much bigger than a spider's leg.

A little while later she came back from the bathroom and he had put the locator together and was puzzling over the touch-pad. He had found the power button. The two inch square display glowed the blue of cold starlight. She slipped it from his hand and activated the grid. A pinhead hotspot immediately began blinking.

"It work okay?" Toby asked.

"Yes." She hesitated, then said, "Let's go for a drive. I'll navigate."

They did that.

Kylie liked the little round canary car. It felt luxurious and utilitarian at the same time. Letting the locator guide her, she directed Toby. After many false turns and an accumulated two point six miles on the odometer, she said:

"Stop. No, keep going, but not too fast."

The car juddered as he manipulated clutch, brake, and accelerator. They rolled past a closed store front on the street level of a four story building on First Avenue, some kind of sex shop, the plate glass soaped and brown butcher paper tacked up on the inside.

Two men in cheap business suits loitered in front of the building. Tourists.

Kylie scrunched down in her seat.

"Don't look at those guys," she said. "Just keep driving."

"Whatever."

Later on they were parked under the monorail tracks eating submarine sandwiches. Kylie couldn't get over how great everything was, the food, the coffee, the damn *air*. All of it the way things used to be. She could hardly believe how great it had been, how much had been lost.

"Okay," she said, kind of talking to herself, "so they know I'm here and they're guarding the Core."

"Those bastards," Toby said.

"You wouldn't think it was so funny if you knew what they really were."

"They looked like used-car salesmen."

"They're Tourists," Kylie said.

"Oh my God! More tourists!"

Kylie chewed a mouthful of sub. She'd taken too big a bite. Every flavor was like a drug. Onions, provolone, turkey, mustard, pepper.

"So where are the evil tourists from," Toby asked. "California?"

"Another dimensional reality."

"That's what I said."

Kylie's chronometer toned softly. Ten hours.

Inside the yellow car there were many smells and one of them was Toby.

"Do you have any more tattoos?" she asked.

"One. It's—"

"Don't tell me," she said.

"Okay."

"I want you to show me. But not here. At the place where you live."

"You want to come to my apartment?"

"Your apartment, yes."

"Okay, spooky." He grinned. So did she.

Some precious time later the chronometer toned again. It wasn't on her wrist anymore. It was on the hardwood floor tangled up in her clothes.

Toby, who was standing naked by the refrigerator holding a bottle of grape juice, said, "Why's your watch keep doing that?"

"It's a countdown," Kylie said, looking at him.

"A countdown to what?"

"To the end of the current cycle. The end of the loop."

He drank from the bottle, his throat working. She liked to watch him now, whatever he did. He finished drinking and screwed the cap back on.

"The loop," he said, shaking his head.

When he turned to put the bottle back in the refrigerator, she saw his other tattoo again: a cross throwing off light. It was inked into the skin on his left shoulder blade.

"You can't even see your own cross," she said.

He came back to the bed.

"I don't have to see it," he said. "I just like to know it's there, watching my back."

"Are you Catholic?"

"No."

"My mother is."

"I just like the idea of Jesus," he said.

"You're spookier than I am," Kylie said.

"Not by a mile."

She kissed his mouth, but when he tried to caress her she pushed him gently back.

"Take me someplace."

"Where?"

"My grandparent's house." She meant "great" grandparents, but didn't feel like explaining to him how so many decades had passed outside the loop of the Preservation.

"Right now?"

"Yes."

It was a white frame house on Queen Anne Hill, sitting comfortably among its prosperous neighbors on a street lined with live oaks. Kylie pressed her nose to the window on the passenger side of the Vee Dub, as Toby called his vehicle.

"Stop," she said. "That's it."

He tucked the little car into the curb and turned the engine off. Kylie looked from the faded photo in her hand to the house. Her mother's mother had taken the photo just weeks before the world ended. In it, Kylie's great grandparents stood on the front porch of the house, their arms around each other, waving and smiling. There was no one standing on the front porch now.

"It's real," Kylie said. "I've been looking at this picture my whole life."

"Haven't you ever been here before?"

She shook her head. At the same time her chronometer toned.

"How we doing on the countdown," Toby asked.

She glanced at the digital display.

"Eight hours."

"So what happens at midnight?"

"It starts up again. The end is the beginning."

He laughed. She didn't.

"So then it's Sunday, right? Then do you countdown to Monday?"

"At the end of the loop it's *not* Sunday," she said. "It's the same day over again."

"Two Saturdays. Not a bad deal."

"Not just two. It goes on and on. November ninth a thousand, ten thousand, a million times over."

"Okay."

"You can look at me like that if you want. I don't care if you believe me. You know something, Toby?"

"What?"

"I'm having a really *good* day."

"That's November ninth for you."

She smiled at him, then kissed him, that feeling, the taste, all of the sensation in its totality.

"I want to see my grandparents now."

She opened the door and got out but he stayed in the car. She crossed the lawn strewn with big colorful oak leaves to the front door of the house, stealing backward glances, wanting to know he was still there waiting for her in the yellow car. Her lover. Her boyfriend.

She started to knock on the door but hesitated. From inside the big house she heard muffled music and laughter. She looked around. In the breeze an orange oak leaf detached from the tree and spun down. The sky blew clear and cold. Later it would cloud over and rain. Kylie knew all about this day. She had been told of it since she was a small child. The last day of the world, perfectly preserved for the edification of alien Tourists and anthropologists. Some people said what happened was an accident, a consequence of the aliens opening the rift, disrupting the fabric of reality. What really pissed everybody off, Kylie thought, was the dismissive attitude. There was no occupying army, no invasion.

They came, destroyed everything either intentionally or accidentally, then ignored the survivors. The Preservation was the only
thing about the former masters of the Earth that interested them.

Kylie didn't care about all that right now. She had been told
about the day, but she had never understood what the day meant,
the sheer sensorial joy of it, the incredible beauty and rightness
of it. A surge of pure delight moved through her being, and for a
moment she experienced uncontainable happiness.

She knocked on the door.

"Yes?" A woman in her mid-fifties with vivid green eyes, her
face pressed with comfortable laugh lines. Like the house, she was
a picture come to life. (Kylie's grandmother showing her the photographs, faded and worn from too much touching).

"Hi," Kylie said.

"Can I help you?" the live photograph said.

"No. I mean, I wanted to ask you something."

The waiting expression on her face so familiar. Kylie said, "I
just wanted to know, are you having a good day, I mean a really
good day?"

Slight turn of the head, lips pursed uncertainly, ready to believe this was a harmless question from a harmless person.

"It's like a survey," Kylie said. "For school?"

A man of about sixty years wearing a baggy wool sweater and
glasses came to the door.

"What's all this?" he asked.

"A happiness survey," Kylie's great grandmother said, and
laughed.

"Happiness survey, huh?" He casually put his arm around his
wife and pulled her companionably against him.

"Yes," Kylie said. "For school."

"Well, I'm happy as a clam," Kylie's great grandfather said.

"I'm a clam, too," Kylie's great grandmother said. "A happy
one."

"Thank you," Kylie said.

"You're very welcome. Gosh but you look familiar."

"So do you. Goodbye."

Back in the car Kylie squeezed Toby's hand. There had been
a boy on the Outskirts. He was impotent, but he liked to touch

Kylie and be with her, and he didn't mind watching her movies, the ones that made the Old Men sad and angry but that she obsessively hoarded images from in her mind. The boy's hand always felt cold and bony. Which wasn't his fault. The nicest time they ever had was a night they had spent in one of the ruins with a working fireplace and enough furniture to burn for several hours. They'd had a book of poems and took turns reading them to each other. Most of the poems didn't make sense to Kylie but she liked the sounds of the words, the way they were put together. Outside the perpetual storms crashed and sizzled, violet flashes stuttering into the cozy room with the fire.

In the yellow car, Toby's hand felt warm. Companionable and intimate.

"So how are they doing?" he said.

"They're happy."

"Great. What's next?"

"If you knew this was your last day to live," Kylie asked him, "what would you do?"

"I'd find a spooky girl and make love to her."

She kissed him. "What else?"

"Ah—"

"I mean without leaving the city. You can't leave the city."

"Why not?"

"Because you'd just get stuck in the Preservation Field until the loop re-started. It looks like people are driving out but they're not."

He looked at her closely, searching for the joke, then grinned. "We wouldn't want that to happen to us."

"No."

"So what would *you* do on your last day?" he asked.

"I'd find a spooky guy who could fix things and I'd get him to fix me up."

"You don't need fixing. You're not broken."

"I am."

"Yeah?"

"Let's drive around. Then let's have a really great meal, like the best food you can think of."

"That's doable."

"Then we can go back to your apartment."

"What about the big countdown?"

"Fuck the countdown." Kylie pushed the timing stud into her chronometer. "There," she said. "No more countdown."

"You like pizza?" Toby said.

"I don't know. What is it?"

After they made love the second time Kylie fell into a light doze on Toby's futon bed. She was not used to so much rich stimulation, so much food and drink, so much touching.

She woke with a start from a dream that instantly disappeared from her consciousness. There was the sound of rain, but it wasn't the terrible poisonous rain of her world. Street light through the window cast a flowing shadow across the foot of the bed. It reminded her of the shiny fountain at the waterfront. The room was snug and comforting and safe. There was a clock on the table beside the bed but she didn't look at it. It could end right now.

She sat up. Toby was at his desk under a framed movie poster, bent over something illuminated by a very bright and tightly directed light. He was wearing his jeans but no shirt or socks.

"Hello," she said.

He turned sharply, then smiled. "Oh, hey Kylie. Have a nice rest?"

"I'm thirsty."

He got up and fetched her a half depleted bottle of water from the refrigerator. While he was doing that she noticed her locator in pieces on the desk.

"We don't need that anymore," she said, pointing.

"I was just curious. I can put it back together, no problem."

"I don't care about it." She lay back on the pillows and closed her eyes.

"Kylie?"

"Hmmm?" She kept her eyes closed.

"Who are you? Really."

"I'm your spooky girl."

"Besides that."

She opened her eyes. "Don't spoil it. Please don't."

"Spoil what?"

"This. Us. Now. It's all that matters."

Rain ticked against the window. It would continue all night, a long, cleansing rain. Water that anybody could catch in a cup and drink if they wanted to—water out of the sky.

Toby took his pants down and slipped under the sheet next to her, his body heat like a magnetic field that drew her against him. She pressed her cheek to his chest. His heart beat calmly.

"Everything's perfect," she said.

"Yeah." He didn't sound that certain.

"What's the matter?"

"Nothing," he said. "Only—this is all pretty fast. Don't you think we should know more about each other?"

"Why? Now is what matters."

"Yeah, but I mean, what do you do? Where do you live? Basic stuff. Big stuff, too, like do you believe in God or who'd you vote for president?"

"I want to go for a long walk in the rain. I want to feel it on my face and not be afraid or sick."

"What do you mean?"

"You're spoiling it. Please, let's make every second happy. Make it a day we'd want to relive a thousand times."

"I don't want to live *any* day a thousand times."

"Let's walk now."

"What's the hurry?"

She got out of bed and started dressing, her back to him.

"Don't be mad," he said.

"I'm not mad."

"You are."

She turned to him, buttoning her shirt. "Don't tell me what I am."

"Sorry."

"You practically sleep walk through the most important day of your life."

"I'm not sleep-walking."

"Don't you even want to fall in love with me?"

He laughed uncertainly. "I don't even know your name."

"You know it. Kylie."

"I mean your last name."

"It doesn't matter."

"It matters to me," Toby said. "You matter to me."

Finished with her shirt, she sat on the edge of the bed to lace her shoes. "No you don't," she said. "You only care about me if you can know all about my past and our future. You can't live one day well and be happy."

"Now you sound like Hemingway."

"I don't know what that means and I don't care." She shrugged into her parka.

"Where are you going?"

"For a walk. I *told* you what I wanted."

"Yeah, I guess I was too ignorant to absorb it."

She slammed the door on her way out.

She stood under the pumpkin-colored light of the street lamp, confused, face tilted up to be anointed by the rain. Was he watching her from the apartment window, his heart about to break? She waited and waited. This is the part where he would run to her and embrace her and kiss her and tell her that he loved, loved, loved her.

He didn't come out.

She stared at the brick building checkered with light and dark apartment windows, not certain which one was his.

He didn't come out, and it was spoiled.

A bus rumbled between her and the building, pale indifferent faces inside.

Kylie walked in the rain. It was not poison but it was cold and after a while unpleasant. She pulled her hood up and walked with her head down. The wet sidewalk was a pallet of neon smears. Her fingers touched the shape of the explosive in her pocket. She could find the building with the papered windows. Even if the Tourists tried to stop her she might still get inside and destroy the Eternity Core. It's what her mother wanted, what the Old Men wanted. But what if they caught her? If she remained in the loop through an entire cycle she would become a permanent part of it. She couldn't stand that, not the way she hurt right now. She didn't know what time it was. She didn't know the *time*. She had to reach her scutter and get out.

A horn went off practically at her elbow. Startled, she looked up. A low and wide vehicle, a boy leaning out the passenger window, smirking.

"Hey, you wanna go for a ride?"

"No."

"Then fuck you, bitch!" He cackled, and the vehicle accelerated away, ripping the air into jagged splinters.

She walked faster. The streets were confusing. She was lost. Her panic intensified. Why couldn't he have come after her and be sorry and love her? But it wasn't like the best parts of the movies. Some of it was good, but a lot of it wasn't. Maybe her mother had been right. But Kylie didn't believe in souls, so wasn't it better to have one day forever than no days? Wasn't it?

Fuck you, bitch.

She turned around and ran back in the direction from which she'd come. At first she didn't think she could find it, but there it was, the apartment building! And Toby was coming out the lobby door, pulling his jacket closed. He saw her, and she ran to him. He didn't mean it and she didn't mean it, and this was the part where they made up, and then all the rest of the loop would be good—the good time after making up. You had to mix the good and bad. The bad made the good better. She ran to him and hugged him, the smell of the wet leather so strong.

"You were coming after me," she said.

He didn't say anything.

"You were," she said.

"Yeah."

Something clutched at her heart. "It's the best day ever," she said.

"I give it a seven point five."

"You don't know anything," she said. "You got your spooky girl and you had an adventure and you saved the whole world."

"When you put it that way it's a nine. So come on. I'll buy you a hot drink and you can tell me about the tourists from the fifth dimension."

"What time is it?" she asked.

He looked at his watch. "Five of eleven."

"I don't want a hot drink," she said. "Can you take us some place with a nice view where we can sit in the Vee Dub?"

"You bet."

The city spread out before them. The water of Elliot Bay was black. Rain whispered against the car and the cooling engine ticked down like a slow timer. It was awkward with the separate seats, but they snuggled together, Kylie's head pillowed on his chest. He turned the radio on—not to his loud noise music but a jazz station, like a compliment to the rain. They talked, intimately. Kylie invented a life and gave it to him, borrowing from stories her mother and grandmother had told her. He called her spooky, his term of endearment, and he talked about what they would do to-morrow. She accepted the gift of the future he was giving her, but she lived in this moment, now, this sweet inhalation of the present, this happy, happy ending. Then the lights of Seattle seemed to haze over. Kylie closed her eyes, her hand on the explosive sphere, and her mind slumbered briefly in a dark spun cocoon.

Kylie punched through, and the sudden light shift dazzled her.

DOUBLE OCCUPANCY

C ab Macarron left his patrol car at the state barracks but he didn't bother to change out of his trooper's uniform. He picked up Joe Rodriguez at the Penny Diner in Goldbar and they headed straight to the Soams's place as dusk was descending on the North Cascades. If there was going to be trouble Cab wanted backup. He had played football with Joe in high school. Back then, only five years ago, they had called Rodriguez "The Monster." He was still a big son of a bitch. Cab and Joe had always stuck together, pulling a three-year hitch in the Marines and then going for troopers.

Cab's Jeep Cherokee handily negotiated the county road. The snow was like wedding cake frosting marred once by somebody's fingers—the narrow tire tracks left behind Nancy's snappy little Honda Civic. The Honda tracks slewed around pretty good. That car was *light*, and Nancy had no business coming up here anyway.

"She called you?" Joe Rodgriguez said.

"I already said she did."

Cab parked behind the Civic. He reached into the Cherokee's glove compartment for his flashlight, a rugged, four-cell job with a steel cast barrel.

Their boots made a crumping noise in the snow. Cab pointed his flashlight through the ice-encrusted window of the Honda. It was like peering through clear water, everything appeared wavy, the suitcases and brown grocery bags. Cab could plainly see the AGA logo on the bags.

"Looks like she's moving in," Joe said.

Cab shot him a glance, measured his friend's innocent observation, and shook his head.

"Nancy's seventeen," Cab said.

"She's got a mind of her own, though."

Only Joe Rodriguez, whom Cab had known since boyhood, could get away with telling Cab anything about his kid sister Nancy.

"I seen it in her before she was twelve," Joe said, pushing it.

"Seen what?"

"That she wasn't going to stay put," Joe said. "Not for you or anybody else, not after your mother passed." Cab's mother had held the three of them together after Cab's father was killed in the Panama invasion. A military funeral and a posthumous Medal of Honor didn't mean a thing to Nancy; she had barely been out of diapers. But for Cab, being handed his father's Medal of Honor was like being presented with the burden of his own premature manhood. A few years later their mother collapsed on the kitchen floor in front of Nancy, hammered by a stroke at the age of forty-five. By then Cab had already enlisted, and Nancy endured life in foster care until he mustered out of the Marines and managed to talk the Department of Social and Health Services into giving him guardianship over his sister for the remaining years of her adolescence. Nancy, who'd run away four times from the foster home, took Cab's guardianship as a ticket to freedom. But Cab regarded his responsibility seriously and let her know it.

"She's a minor and I'm bringing her home," Cab said to Joe Rodriguez.

"Because she called you."

"Yeah, because she called me."

A weird call. The dispatcher had relayed the message to Cab. He was at the end of his shift. He called Nancy from the barracks. She had sounded near hysterics. "Peter's brought something through. I thought he was just talking, but God, Cab, he really did it. The thing *bit* him. I don't know where it is now. Out in the woods. I'm afraid to leave the cabin, but Peter's bleeding. I'm scared, Cab." Then there was some angry shouting in the background and Nancy said she had to go, that she shouldn't have called. A moment later the line had gone dead.

I'm scared, Cab.

Now, standing in the deepening twilight beside Nancy's Honda, Cab looked up the hill to old Neal Soams's fancy cabin. Neal had leased the place out to the wrong guy this time. Naturally Cab had done a background check on Peter Goetz as soon as Nancy mentioned the name. This was no local kid. Cab could scare the town boys off easily enough. What he didn't understand was that if Goetz was such a hot-shot genius then what was he doing out here by himself about as far away from MIT as you could go without getting your feet wet?

"Let's go, if you're with me," Cab said.

"Course I'm with you, old son."

The switch-back path to the cabin was buried. They cut straight up the hillside, and Cab felt it in his knees. He drove himself, his breath fogging out in icy clouds.

"What's this?" Joe had stopped. He was bent over, breathing hard, big shoulders moving up and down in his black and red Pendelton jacket. He pointed at what looked like a thick, black snake lying in the snow. Cab didn't want to waste time but he slogged back and hunkered next to Joe.

"Looks like a power cable," Cab said. He put his hand on it. "Sucker's warm, too."

Joe pointed his chin at the cabin, now about fifty yards farther up the hill. "You think he's tied into the underground line?"

"Cable this thick would handle a lot of juice." Cab almost smiled. "Illegal as hell."

Joe stood upright and stretched his back. He moved up the hill a couple of strides, but Cab stayed where he was. In the last few seconds the cable had grown perceptibly warmer. Hell, it was practically too hot to touch. The snow was melting around it.

Suddenly white light burst over them. An explosion, utterly silent. Being down low probably saved Cab. A force drove him onto his back, sliding him down the slope with his head toward the road.

Joe Rodriguez screamed.

A bizarre pattern of silvery shimmers fanned out above Cab, as if the air were filled with irregular sheets of tin foil. Joe was right in the middle of it, arms flailing, his upper body actually glowing.

Cab whipped around in the snow, galvanized by a sensation like a million ants crawling over his body. He squeezed his eyes shut against the painfully bright tin foil air. And then, as suddenly as it had begun, it was over. The crawling sensation ceased, and the shimmers faded, leaving deep purple twilight.

Cab pushed himself to his feet and looked around. Rodriguez

was gone. A trail of boot prints led into the trees. From the cabin to the bottom of the hill the black cable lay exposed in a trench of melted snow.

"God *damn*."

Cab had expected to see the cabin blown to flinders, maybe the fieldstone chimney and a few smoking cross beams standing in the dimness. But the cabin appeared unchanged, except it was dark, when moments ago the porch light had been on.

Cab picked up his flashlight, brushed off the lens, and tried it out. The bulb worked fine. He turned to the tracks in the snow. As much as he wanted to get up to the cabin and see about Nancy, he couldn't leave his friend. Joe Rodriguez's scream shrilled through his mind as if it had never stopped.

He didn't have to follow the tracks far. Joe's legs stuck out from under the shaggy, snow-laden bough of a blue spruce. Cab knelt beside him, barking Joe's name. Rodriguez did not respond, and Cab hooked his fingers in a belt loop at Joe's hip, reached under the spruce bough to find his shoulder and roll him onto his back. What he touched in the concealing shadow under the tree made him jerk his hand back—a reflex, as if he'd inadvertently put his hand into something nasty.

Without conscious volition, Cab stood up and backed away. He caught himself and stopped. That was his friend. Whatever had happened to him, it was still Joe.

Cab tucked the flashlight under his armpit, took hold of his partner's boots and dragged him clear of the tree. "God!" He dropped Joe's legs and the flashlight and staggered back, his hand covering his mouth. After a minute he forced himself to pick up the flashlight and point it at the thing that had been his friend. From the waist up it was a nightmare of tapering gray tentacles limply attached to a trunk of the same rubbery flesh. Joe's red and black Pendelton jacket hung in tatters. Only one of his arms remained, and it was twisted, shrunken, a mere vestige.

Cab didn't even try to fit his mind around the impossibility of what he was seeing. His pragmatic nature took over, as it always did, and he hunkered beside the Rodriguez-thing and rolled it onto its back.

Joe was still there—a piece of him. His face rose out of the neckless gray trunk like a death mask of minutely sculpted clay.

Something shifted in the air above Cab. He looked up sharply and saw a clump of snow falling toward him. The branch from which it had shaken loose was still moving. Cab swung his flashlight up. At first he saw nothing. It wasn't until he began to move the light away that it happened to glint on a silver thread. He glimpsed it then it was gone. He had to move the light again, angle it slightly this way and that before he was able to discern an intricate network of silver threads stretching from the blue spruce to the next nearest tree. It was strange, almost as if the network really wasn't there. Even the barest shifting of his light caused the threads to disappear. After only a moment or two he looked away from it, necessarily dismissing it from his thoughts so he could concentrate on the problems at hand.

He fought an almost overpowering urge to charge up the hill to the cabin. But his partner was down, and God only knew what was happening up there. This was more than he could handle by himself.

Cab half fell, half slid to the bottom of the hill, and then he was yanking open the passenger door of the Cherokee. He grabbed the CB's mike, but when he switched the unit on a storm of static burst from the speaker. It was the same on every channel.

Cab racked the mike and started up the hill again, driving his boots into the deep snow, feeling the fire in his knees. He could have taken the Jeep, maybe out-distanced the interference. Then again he might have had to drive all the way to Goldbar, waste as much as an hour.

Cab, I'm scared.

Ten yards from the cabin's front porch the air felt charged with electricity, reminding him of the crawling sensation he'd experienced during the silent explosion.

He pounded on the door but no one responded. At the back of the cabin he shined his light in the kitchen window. Rustic pine cabinets. Dishes piled in the sink. Something moved on the floor near the doorway to the dining area. He caught it in his light. A hand groping out of an unbuttoned flannel sleeve.

Cab drew his 9mm Beretta. He moved to the back door, prepared to kick it off its hinges. But the door was unlocked.

Peter Goetz lay sprawled on the broad plank floor. The left side of his torso looked mangled and burned. But he wasn't burned;

he was *changed*. Like Joe Rodriguez. Only Goetz's transformation had taken a different form. His left arm was thinned out, almost a black bone, with a couple of extra joints thrown in. Three fingers instead of five, and they weren't really fingers. His left leg was violently twisted, erupting out of the hip socket, halted halfway in its transformation between human and something else.

Cab stepped over the inert body. He had to find Nancy. The floor was streaked with a substance like black tar. It was too thick for blood, which is what Cab took it for at first. He followed it to an open door and the smoke-filled room beyond. His flashlight beam swept through gray layers to discover what looked like a miniature broadcast tower. The air smelled of fried ozone. The tower was partially melted, the intricate cross-braces sagging. This was it, ground zero.

Cab started out of the room to look elsewhere, but a barely audible whimpering made him turn back.

"Nancy?"

"Go away, Cab, I don't want you to see me."

"Are you hurt? Where are you?"

The room wasn't that big, nothing in it but the weird tower and a table loaded with electronic equipment. No place for a girl to hide.

"Come on, Nancy."

He swept the room with the flashlight. A stifled sob, low to the floor. Under the table. But there wasn't space for her under there. He holstered his gun, squatted, pointing the flashlight. The beam touched her and she scuttled back. Cab's heart thudded, blood roaring in his ears. It couldn't be, it *couldn't*. He reached for her. It was Nancy's face, mostly, but God the rest of her . . .

She darted away from his hand, scrabbling out the door on multiple legs, insectile.

"Nancy!"

He stumbled after her into the hall, saw her disappear through an open door. Before he could follow a hand closed on his ankle. He jerked around, gasping. It was Peter Goetz. He had dragged himself down the hall, leaving another smeary black trail. Raising his head, he rolled his eyes up to look at Cab. The left one was big as a golf ball, popping from its socket, egg yoke yellow with a red pinpoint in the center.

Cab jerked loose and said, "What have you done, God damn you?"

Goetz started talking, his words coming out in a rocky mumble—a troll's voice.

". . . the Ancient Ones . . . brought it through, then overload, power surge . . . *gar'ne sothoth neg'a geeth!* . . . god . . . two dimensions, objects *can* occupy the same space . . . never thought . . . blended with counterparts across the dimensional interface . . ."

Goetz's words became unintelligible. Syrupy drool leaked from the corner of his mouth. His alien limb twitched and rapped on the floor. Repulsed, Cab started to back away. Peter Goetz's human hand locked on his ankle again, this time with a much firmer grip. As Cab tried to pull free the black bone limb twitched up behind him, the talonlike digits spiking into Cab's leg.

"*Ga'na-soth!*"

Cab cried out in pain, threw himself back with all his weight and strength, breaking loose. He hit the floor hard. The hideous thing Goetz had become dragged itself toward him, the yellow eye with its evil red spot almost glowing in the dark hall. With a quick, practiced movement Cab produced a small canister of mace and discharged it into the eye. Goetz shrieked, and Cab was able to shove himself away. His hand dropped to the butt of his automatic but he left the weapon holstered. If there was a way of reversing this nightmare Peter Goetz was the only one who knew how to do it.

Cab stood up, reached for his handcuffs. He looked for his chance and lunged in, grabbing Goetz by his human arm. He slapped one cuff snug around the wrist and quickly locked down the other cuff on the wide knob of the tower room's door. Goetz thrashed blindly for him with the spiked digits of his alien hand. Cab danced back out of reach. He felt surprisingly steady and in control, even optimistic. After all, if he'd mistakenly thought Goetz was dead he may also have been wrong about Joe. Cab might still put things right again, even in this insane situation. All he had to do was find Nancy. Once he had her under control they could get out of here in the truck, bring back help, somebody who could figure out what Goetz had done.

Cab backed slowly down the hall, his leg throbbing where talons had spiked him. Goetz whimpered and thrashed helplessly on the floor, the cuff rattling loosely on the neck of the doorknob. Cab proceeded to the open door through which he'd seen Nancy disappear. He paused outside the room, his nerve beginning to fray. He could hear her in there, a chitinous scrabble on the wood floor. For a moment he couldn't move. He had to force a rational calm over himself. He counted five deep breaths, and then he strode into the room and kicked the door shut behind him.

There was a window but by now the twilight had failed. He swept the room with his flashlight. She could be anywhere, anywhere. "Nancy, goddamn it." His light touched the closet door, the windowsill, the counterpane, a pillow without a slipcover, the nightstand, the bare floor, the steam radiator with its elaborate scrollwork, sweeping around, back and forth, a nervous searchlight. He couldn't see her, but she *had* to be in the room. Then his light fell on a Coleman kerosene lantern sitting on top of the dresser. He set the flashlight down, dug a book of matches out of his shirt pocket, primed the wick and lit it. The room filled with hissing lantern light.

He heard the scrape of one of her legs on the floor and turned in time to catch a glimpse of her retreating beneath the bed, like some gigantic, loathsome insect. He cursed under his breath, steeling himself. Plenty of times since he'd taken over guardianship of Nancy she had driven him to the brink of rage with her smart mouth and stubborn refusal to obey his reasonable restrictions. But he had never allowed her to see his anger. At the most trying times he mentally cut her off, completely blocked the annoying teenager she was and cast back into memory for a picture of her as she'd been when their father died. The innocent toddler, the little girl who held his hand to cross the street, who begged him to read stories to her and push her in the swing. He had been the man of the house. Now, getting down on his knees with the flashlight, he used the mental trick again, imagining Nancy as a child, remembering how it had felt to look out for her, to be the man.

"Come out of there, Nancy."

Her words, blurred with sobs, nevertheless sounded human. "I can't stand myself like this."

"We'll get you back to normal somehow. I promise."

"You can't."

A hard knot bulged in Cab's throat. He had been the man in

the house but he'd been a child, too, a boy unfairly pushed toward maturity. He had tried, God he had tried. But always, dogging him like a shadow demon, had been the cruel fear of failing his mother and sister—of letting his father down.

"Don't tell me what I can't do," he said.

He moved the flashlight and she cringed back, holding up two of her knobby, triple-jointed arms to shield her eyes.

"Come out," he said. "All I want to do is help you."

She only sobbed louder. Cab had to get her away from here, back to the Jeep, and he didn't want to waste any more time doing it. He stripped the bedspread from the mattress. Nancy shifted nervously under the box springs.

"What are you doing?" she said.

"I'm taking you out of here." He spoke in a flat, no nonsense tone, deliberately purging his voice of emotion. He couldn't afford to waver, not now. He had to concentrate, keep his head. He had made mistakes with Nancy, he could see that with shocking clarity. The horrors he'd encountered this day seemed to have released all his deepest fears, throwing them up in hideous relief. All his life, since the death of his father, he had been so frightened of failing to live up to his responsibility that he had gone overboard, pushing, pushing until he had pushed Nancy out of his life altogether. But it might not be too late to put things right; he had to try.

Cab set his booted foot on the edge of the bed frame and shoved hard. The bed scraped away from the wall. Nancy tried to dart between his legs but he threw down the bedspread and gathered her up. She fought but he had her, wrapping the spread tight around her, confining her movement. "Don't," he said. "Please don't fight me, Nancy."

Her struggles grew less frenzied.

He tucked her under his right arm, hating the sharp little twitches of her alien limbs. Gripping the big flashlight in his left hand he started down the hall.

Goetz, too, had ceased struggling. Shackled by his wrist to the doorknob, his face lowered, Goetz muttered in a strange, contorted language as Cab stepped past him. The atmosphere was suddenly hushed, expectant. He could feel Nancy breathing inside the bedspread.

He opened the front door with the hand holding the flashlight. Something whipped out of the darkness, striking him across the chest like a stiff yard of rubber hose. Cab staggered back, grunting. Whatever it was crowded itself into the doorway, hissing and muttering alien syllables. At once Nancy went wild trying to kick free of the bedspread, responding to the thing in the doorway. Cab brought the flashlight up.

Joe was still alive, all right—or the thing that had been Joe. It lurched toward him, mostly human from the waist down, but from the belt upward it was a writhing Medusa of tentacles. Rodriguez's face clenched and gasped in the dead gray bulk of its torso.

Cab backed away. It was *speaking* to him, though the words were alien. He could barely hold onto Nancy in her frenzy to get away. Her muffled voice called out to the advancing creature in its own language. The Peter Goetz monstrosity swiped at Cab and he dodged out of the way, retreating down the hall.

He switched Nancy to his left arm. It was more difficult to hold onto her and he couldn't direct the flashlight where he wanted it, but it freed up his right hand. He drew his 9mm but didn't shoot. He *couldn't* shoot, not Joe. The Rodriguez-thing waved its tentacles, whacking against the walls in the narrow hallway. Cab backed into the bedroom he'd only moments ago quit, and slammed the door.

Immediately, Nancy wrenched free and hit the floor, frantically disentangling herself from the bedspread. Before he could stop her she skittered up on the bed and launched herself at the window.

"Nancy!"

The glass shattered and she was gone. Snow breezed into the room.

The Rodriguez-thing crashed through the door, shrieking like a banshee, Joe's human mouth stretched impossibly wide. Cab threw the flashlight. A tentacle sent it pinwheeling into the wall. Cab leveled his automatic but hesitated to fire. If there was one chance in a million of restoring his friend . . .

A tentacle lashed out and wrapped around Cab's ankle, another seized him tightly around his left thigh, while a third waved by his neck, seeking purchase. Cab was out of options. The tentacles tightened down. Cab's femoral artery pounded as if to burst under the pressure. He thrust the Beretta forward. At the same moment a flailing tentacle brushed against the lantern, coiled around its fuel tank and lifted it off the dresser.

Pain hazing his vision, Cab cried out, "Joe, I'm sorry," and squeezed off two quick rounds. They splatted into the gray flesh. All the grasping tentacles squeezed in spasmodic reaction. Cab screamed, fired twice more, but it didn't matter. The lantern burst under the pressure, dousing the Rodriguez-thing with flaming kerosene. Instantly it released Cab, and he was able to push himself away and stumble to the window. The monster's many tentacles waved helplessly. Joe Rodriguez's face became more prominent, stretching out of the hot core of yellow fire. And then it began to melt.

Tears streaming from his eyes, the heat baking over him, Cab shoved the wooden sash up, dislodging a rain of broken glass. He clambered over the sill and pitched face down in the snow that had drifted against the side of the cabin.

He lay there for some moments, his face half buried in the snow, his cheek turning numb, breathing hard, trying to gather his will. What a mess he had made of things. It was all coming apart now. Joe was finished, the cabin was burning—and with it the machinery that had created this nightmare.

Now only Nancy was left.

It was just the two of them, like when they were kids. The way she was now she needed him even more than she had back then. In her present form she was helpless in the world. She would have to understand that. She was going to be depending on him a lot. Who else could bear to love her? He wouldn't screw up again. He was all she had now, but first he had to find her.

He got up and began to walk, favoring his left leg. The jumpy glare from the burning cabin revealed Nancy's tracks in the snow, each peculiar impression a tiny cup of shadow in the red light. She was fast and had a good lead; finding her wouldn't be easy. He set his jaw and slogged forward, determined. He wasn't letting anybody down, not ever again.

As he reached the very limit of the firelight he saw her, squatting on a stump as if she had been waiting for him. Cab halted ten feet from the stump, his instinct warning him to approach no closer. She was barely visible in the weak, red glare, but what he could see was terrible. Oh yes, she was going to need him again. And he would handle things differently this time. He wasn't his father and he didn't have to be. All he wanted was to be good, to do the right thing.

"Nancy."

"I don't belong to you, Cab."

Funny. It was what she had said so many times before, since he had taken responsibility for her. To hear the same words in that tortured rasp her voice was becoming, to see her as she now was, a freakish thing. But it wasn't going to be the old battle of wills. He wouldn't let it be that way. He moved closer.

"Let me help you," he said.

"I won't." She turned and sprang from the stump.

Cab lunged after her, but she was right there on the other side of the stump, not really trying to escape. In a moment he knew why. He found himself hung up in a net of invisible threads. Sticky. A trap. The gun, which he'd still been holding, slipped out of his hand. The more he struggled the more entangled he became. Where the threads touched his exposed skin—on his hands and face—they burned like acid.

Not a net . . . a web.

"I pick my own friends now, Cab. *Gah 'Sogoth!*"

There was a vibration in the web. Cab remembered what Peter Goetz had said about bringing one of the Ancient Ones through before his machine overloaded. And Nancy's hysterical call about a *thing* biting Goetz.

Cab pulled wildly at the complex web that ensnared him, but it was useless. Finally he sagged, exhausted, and looked up. A pair of yellow eyes centered with pinpoints of blood glowed in the dark above him. "*Sig na'getha.*" The eyes twitched closer, and Cab strained to reach his automatic. It lay in the snow, just beyond his grasp.

"Nancy help me!"

The gun was right in front of her; she might have pushed it closer to him, but she didn't. And Cab knew it really was too late. Nancy, the creature that had been Nancy, cocked her strange little head and regarded him with cold, inhuman detachment. Cab never looked away from her again. In his final seconds he had to accept it. After all, he was responsible.

THE CHIMERA TRANSIT

After sex the stranger, whose name was Rebecca, cuddled under my arm. I transmitted seretonin—enough to raise my mood above depression without inviting further arousal. The stranger moved against me, her leg slung over my hip, her hand on my chest, breath in my face. She had a mouth like Lynn's, the shape of it. I waited until she was asleep then carefully extricated myself from her body and her bed.

I walked home in the rain. It was past two A.M. The gloom came upon me again. Looking up, rain anointing my face, I transmitted a dopamine and norepinephin brain cocktail. My mood soared, and for a moment I was infatuated with the sky, as I used to be. A distant roll of thunder reminded me of the Outbound shuttle launches I used to watch with my dad when I was a kid, daydreaming stars. My mind felt nimble. Jazzed. City lights underlit the cloud cover. I thought of starships, which led to my father and the Big Bang (weapon discharge in the basement), which led to Lynn, and I wondered what she was to me.

A woman laughed. I looked across the street. She wore a long coat and floppy hat and she was with a man, hanging on his arm, ducking. A green Tinkerbelle Flirt hovered around her, flew away, returned. The man reached out and captured it in his hand. They bent over it together, their faces illuminated by a green flicker. I heard her say, "It's beautiful, I love you!" She moved her face under his and kissed his mouth. I looked away.

What Lynn was to me: gone.

The next evening as I was dressing to go out a fairy light hovered in close to my window. I stared at it, my shirt hanging open. I thought of half a dozen women who knew my name and could access my People Finder code. But none of them possessed a romantically flirtatious disposition. They might call, or pop me an EyeText on my retinal repeater. Fairy Flirts were kid stuff. I whacked the window with a rolled up *New Yorker*. The Flirt drifted back, flimmering wings making a ruby nimbus in the rain.

I sat by the window in a coffee bar on lower Queen Anne, sipping espresso and reading a flashprint copy of a faux Updike novel. The style and plot were perfect Updike (Rabbit in the 22nd century) but thin under the surface, like all A.I. written books. I read the sentences and listened to the words in my head. It improved when I transmitted some phenylethylamine into my limbic system. A boost of joy surged through me. The words glowed. Analog or not, it didn't matter.

A pretty girl sitting alone at the next table suddenly ooo-ed in my direction. Her hair was styled into glossy blue spear points. I tried a tentative smile, but the *ooo* wasn't for me. Ruby light shimmered on the other side of the window.

"You have an admirer," the pretty girl said.

"So it seems."

I stowed the fake Updike in my overcoat and went out of the bar. The Fairy did a couple of loops around my head. I was conscious of people watching me through the window.

"Okay, okay," I said to the Fairy. It darted off. Too fast if it expected me to keep up. The pretty girl inside the bar made a shooing motion at me. It was idiotic but I started after the Flirt.

Really it seemed determined to evade me. I picked up the pace. The Fairy veered down an alley. It was running out of juice, skimming low, ruby flimmer reflected in rain-stippled puddles. I splashed after it in hot pursuit. It tried to soar up the side of the building on my right, winked out suddenly, and dropped like a dead clinker. I caught it in my hand.

I looked up at the lighted and unlighted windows. The little Flirt was warm in my palm but the rain was cold and I'd left my umbrella in the bar. I started to walk out of the alley. A window opened.

"Hey—" Tentative female voice, almost apologetic. A slight figure backlit by the apartment light.

"Yeah?"

"That's mine." Some kind of accent. Eastern European? "Toss it up?"

I could have, maybe. She was on the second floor. But I shook my head. "Nope."

Her name was Anca. Romanian born. She was fluent in three languages—four if you counted an obscure source code imbedded in a thousand or so of the early DAT model implants. The tech in those old implants was so clunky that you couldn't remove them from the host brain without risking serious tissue damage. I knew these facts because I knew Anca, slightly. My partner at Neuro Options, Dario Crow, had one of the old implants. *Dario* was old, that's why he had one. He and my father had been partners. Until dad's single-minded pursuit of a workable neuro-stim device collapsed under the weight of his misconceived approach and bankrupted the first incarnation of Neuro Options. Twenty years or so later I came along, little Jackie all grown up and twice as clever as his old man. Or so I thought.

Anyway, Dario introduced me to Anca who was helping correct a glitch that had occurred between his DAT and his more contemporary retinal repeater. That was weeks ago.

"Hey, I know you," I said when she opened the door to her apartment. She smiled shyly and didn't meet my eyes.

"And I know you too, Jack Porter."

"Ah, here's your Flirt." I handed it to her.

"Thanks. It's not really mine. I borrowed it. How can I afford such silliness? And I asked Dario for your People Finder number, for the little Fairy to know where to go. So you see it's a grand conspiracy."

"You think it's grand, huh?"

She giggled, quirking her lips as if the giggle were a bug that wanted to get out—a bug that she was fond of keeping *in*.

"Would you—?" She opened the door wider.

I stepped past her into the room. I'm no giant at five ten, but Anca was boyishly small, almost frail and no taller than a twelve year old. She looked starved but cooking smells wafted from the efficiency kitchen. Something boily with cabbage. Her apartment was like the rest of the building. Old, run down, reasonably clean, and too dark. It was the brown carpet and all that stained wood. Lamp light absorbed into it. The overall effect was a little depressing. I resisted transmitting.

"Some wine?" she said.

"Sure."

When she handed me the glass she met my eyes briefly then looked away again.

"That Flirt. I'm not for fads, I mean I would never—"

"It's okay," I said.

"Do you want to watch the review?"

"Absolutely."

It was one of those cheap liquid screens. It rippled like wind over a puddle, then a jerky image appeared. Me waving a magazine, being dive-bombed, etc. Anca suddenly turned it off.

"Oh, well," she said.

"What?"

"It's so silly. I liked you, you know. So—"

I touched her hand.

She clung to me in the dark of the bedroom, her boyish chest crushed against me. I could feel her bones. Her fingers were cold. Rain popped on a fabric awning outside her window. *Don't go,* she'd whispered before falling asleep, as though she knew me.

I caused endorphins to occur and eventually slept.

She caught me at it over orange juice the next morning. Caught me adjusting brain chemistry.

"What are you doing when you close your eyes like that?"

"It's a neuro stimulation device." I tapped my forehead with two fingers.

"Oh. Dario told me about that. You're going to make millions, yes?"

"Maybe. We're at the experimental stage. I'm the guinea pig. Just like your old DATS, only this thing can be easily removed. NanoBotz lay a gossamer web over the brain, attaching to axon fibers. Consciously directed electrical microbursts release chemical molecules from the neuron sacks at the end of the fibers, transmitting them to receiving neurons. It's great tech."

"Hmm." She bit into an apple slice and chewed slowly.

"What?"

"How do you know what you really feel?"

"It's not that dramatic. It just allows you to have more of what you already possess."

"It sounds a little terrible, though."

"God I hope not. It was my dad's idea to begin with, only he never really got it off the ground."

"Okay," Anca said. She put down her half-eaten apple slice. "Do you want to see something with me?"

"Sure."

It was a little museum of oddities near The Pike Place Market. She led me to a trembling holo of a Martian desert. A sign with a down-pointing arrow said: LISTEN. Anca nudged me. I leaned into the aural sphere and heard . . . wind. After a moment I drew back and made a question mark face. Anca shook her hands like she was trying to dry them.

"It's the wind on Mars."

"Okay."

"From the first times, before there were any people. From a robot lander. A digital recording. So *old*."

"It's nice."

"Oh you're dense." She giggled, quirking her lips, holding in the happy bug. "It's the idea. The way it was so distant you could never be there, the way the wind was blowing on another planet and there was only a little robot to record it. A whole empty world. It's *romantic*, Jack."

I leaned forward again and listened to the lost romantic wind of Mars.

"Who is she?" Anca said a month later.

"Who's who?"

We were walking in bright October sunlight in an urban park not far from Neuro Options' offices.

"The woman, the one you can't let go," Anca said.

"Whoever said—"

"Shhh."

"Well."

"Of course you don't have to tell me."

The sidewalk was plastered with wet leaves gone an ugly dun color.

"It's irrelevant who she is," I said. "And besides I have let her go. Mostly."

"You haven't."

I scraped some leaf slime off the path with the heel of my shoe.

"Why don't you call her?" Anca said.

"I can't."

"Why not?"

"She's Outbound to Tau Boo."

"Oh." Anca became thoughtful then said, "Oh," again.

"Yeah."

"And you didn't go with her."

"I couldn't. You only get one shot at the qualifying exam."

"I see. And you failed but she passed. How terrible, but why didn't she stay with you if she loved you? Why—"

"Anca. I didn't fail the exam."

"No?"

"No. I haven't taken it yet."

"But why not?"

I transmitted and felt better about not answering.

"But how long?"

"Since she left? Two years, almost."

"Two years," Anca said.

I transmitted until the two years didn't matter.

She came back to bed with two glasses of wine. It was that uncomfortable stage in the relationship. The stage where I wanted to go home by myself even before the sex. Transmitting oxytonin helped by producing hormonal arousal, but on the down side was a concurrent feeling of emotional attachment. Anca handed me my glass and slid under the covers with me.

"I lost mine, too," she said. "But it happened in a different way."

"Lost your—?"

"My beloved. Perhaps I was mistaken and he wasn't my beloved, or supposing I wasn't his is more truthful. He said he loved me, from all our talking and virtual intimacy, while I was in Bucharest. But when I came, at my own expense and using everything I had, things were different. So. I warned him I was not what he might want in a woman. This happened in San Diego. He flew away to Tokyo and stopped calling. I did make a fool of myself but it didn't help. When my money was almost gone I began offering my DAT skills on the Ethricnet. That's how I came to Seattle after my beloved abandoned me."

She had finished her wine. She reached around to put her glass on the end table and it tipped off the edge and fell empty to the carpet. Her reaching arm, the way her shoulder blade slid under the skin, like bird bones.

"Oopsie," she said. And: "Aren't you going to drink that?"

I gave her my glass.

"I challenge you to something," Anca said.

We were drinking Guinness in an Irish Bar called McGerry's and it was a mistake. The bar, not the Guinness. Lynne and I had spent one of our last nights out in this same bar. McGerry's was saturated with her presence.

"What kind of challenge?" I asked.

"I challenge you to spend one entire night with me and not adjust your chemistry to do it."

"Anca."

"Never mind. I know you can't."

I sipped at my second Guinness and resisted an urgent impulse to transmit.

"You are never in the place you are," Anca said.

I smiled. "I'm here right now."

She shook her head. "You are always thinking about someplace else or somebody else or some other time. There is no now for you, I believe."

"That's ridiculous," I said.

"I think you are too afraid of making even one permanent decision. You always want to take it back, whatever it is, or not give it in the first place, so you can think of the possibility of giving it. Oh I'm not making sense, am I? What are you doing giving this black beer to a little person?"

Around three A.M. Anca woke up next to me in bed. I was staring at the ceiling, not transmitting, my arm loosely around her. She rubbed her eyes. "Aren't you going? You always go lately."

"No, I'm staying."

"You don't act like it."

"What do you mean?"

"Whenever you stay you are like this," she said, and she flung herself around on her left side, facing away from me and as near to the edge of the mattress as possible.

"Hey come back here."

"And why?"

"Because I'm not done with you yet."

"You can't make me," she said.

I grabbed at her waist, which must have tickled. Anca shrieked and jerked away but had nowhere to go but the floor. She didn't make a very big crash. She said "Ouch," and we both laughed, and I pulled her back onto the bed.

You aren't allowed any enhancements when you take the Outbound exam. They want the unadulterated best and brightest. So one day an army of NanoBotz disconnected and devoured my neuro-stimulation web and then dutifully dissolved into my blood, eventually to exit in a stream of piss. A month later I arrived at the Outbound Center with a dozen other hopeful-but-not-too-likelies. Exam questions routed directly to our retinal repeaters. Two hundred questions, each set tailored to the individual's specialties, mine being nano technology and biochemistry. At the end my score was instantly tabulated.

I stood on the sidewalk, head craned way back, staring up the copper face of the Outbound Center. The sky was clear and twilight was upon the world. The first stars had begun to appear. I thought of lying on the roof of the house with my father, watching the shuttles go up, their propellant streaking goblin green across the sky. "There are other worlds now," he had said to me, referring to the advent of Kessel's Outbound Drive. "And if you're good enough you can go to them," he added.

If you're good enough.

Almost pathologically self-critical. In dad's view, I guess, he hadn't been good enough to make Neuro Options a success. He poured his heart into it, and when it failed he accounted his life a failure, too, and put an end to it. That was certainly a greater failure as far as my mother was concerned. After a year or so she started dating. Indiscriminately.

So I finished growing up mostly on my own, and eventually I figured out the neuro-stim thing for dad. It's always easier to make someone else's dream work. Insurance money helps, too.

Anca, who didn't have a mouth like Lynn's, sat as near the fire as she could, huddled inside my overcoat. She was always cold. The fire was in a floating bar on Elliot Bay called Aquablue. The flames cycled through a chemically dictated rainbow pallet. Management dialed the walls and floor to vitreous invisibility. Anca and I and the fire and the tan leather sofa thing all seemed to float upon the surface of the bay. Maybe it was that choppy green water and the steely cloud scud that made her feel so cold.

"I've been thinking about your lost one," Anca said.

"Hmmm."

"I think you like her out there where she can't touch you."

"There's some truth to that."

Anca held my hand. Her fingers were ice cold.

I remembered sitting on this same sofa (it was a sunnier day, though) with Lynn. This was where she told me the results of her Outbound exam. Lynn's hands were always warm and they had been that evening, especially warm in the memory of a thousand intimacies. I'm sorry, she had said, but you're stuck in your fear and I can't wait.

Anca was on her third glass of wine. After a while I told her the results of my Outbound exam. Her grip tightened on my hand. And when I looked into her face and told her about my one irrevocable decision I could transmit nothing. Nothing.

Because Outbound was the only truly irrevocable decision. Once Outbound there was no returning. In a peculiar way, Outbound ships are like Ouroboros, self-consuming. They measuredly convert their specialized mass to energy, feeding it into a tachyon funnel, *becoming* the funnel. By the time you arrive in the Promised Land you barely *have* a ship anymore.

There is a longish period while you transit out of the solar system. A period in which there occurs more than enough time to recall and reform the recent past, to come up with stuff like lips that quirk to hold in the happy bug, and to notice that even in the absence of artificial neuro-stimulation, feelings of attachment persist. There is also time to remember the things you tried not to remember otherwise. Things besides the shape of a mouth and the sweetness of a long confessional summer. The way a person abandoned you, for instance, after you surrendered all your secret pain. Even after that. The transit between Earth and the interstellar gulf, then, is the vacuum between Chimeras.

Then the Outbound Drive kicks in. The stars gather into a whirling funnel. A knot tightens under your heart, and the ship begins to devour itself.

OVERLAY

B ad memories haunted me. I kept my good ones in a box under the bed. It was a small box.

Sweating in the coffin-sized apartment *Northeast News Stream Services* provided, I sat in my underwear and fingered listlessly through the meager selection of loops. I was wasted but couldn't sleep. A Passenger had borrowed my body the previous night. Rubbing the back of my neck, I could feel the hard, little button Thixton's people had implanted under the skin at the base of my skull, the portal.

As with everyone else, my deepest memory impressions occurred before my twelfth birthday, and it was only from that rich memory soil that Dreamloops could be readily fashioned. So I had none of my wife, Cynthia. There was a way of altering near-memory engrams to make them more adaptable to loop technology, and I was working on that. But for now I picked out one of my childhood favorites. Long ago when I was little "Scottie" Kriegel I'd gone Halloweening for the first time. Lying back, I dropped the loop into the player and closed my eyes.

Run the spooky shadows, wind-sway of birch branches under arc sodium light. My right fist tight around the handle of my plastic pumpkin bucket. Big brother James holding my left paw. Sweat and rubber stink inside the mask. We approach the door, which has six panels and is swaged with cotton cobwebs. James tells me to ring the bell, which I do.

And that's where it goes wrong.

Because there's another door overlaying the one in my memory loop. It's a slate gray slab with the number 217 stenciled at eye level, and it opens because I've just swiped a key card. It swings in, slightly out of sync with the Halloween door. And then I'm having some kind of schizophrenic mind-split experience. I'm seven years old trick-or-treating my little heart out, and I'm thirty-eight years old stalking into a strange co-op. A woman turns from the window. Her body is barely concealed by a gossamer shadow that clings to her skin and halts at mid-thigh. There's a home-rolled cigarette between her fingers, and smoky light ladders up the half-open blinds to the accompaniment of helicopter chop. Her lips are black, her tightly razored hair gleams like tarnished copper, and Mrs. Henneke from across the street is wearing a pointy witch hat but smiles like my grandmother and says I'm the cutest thing. The woman with black lipstick says, *Did you kill that boy?* and I show her my hands. A miniature Snickers bar drops into my virgin bucket—

The loop ran to the end of its maximum two-minute duration. The player clicked off. I listened to my breath.

Franz Thixton threw his head back and slurped an oyster into his florid, jowly face. He replaced the empty shell on the plate, lips glistening with juice, and wiped his fingers fussily on a linen napkin. Even though we were sitting outside, the smell of the oysters flirted with my nausea switch. Or maybe it wasn't the oysters.

"You don't look good, Scott," he said. "You need to take better care of yourself."

I brushed the backs of my fingers against two day's growth of beard stubble. "I'll start hitting the gym," I said. "You want to buddy up?"

He laughed asthmatically. I didn't like the proprietary way he looked at me, but I guess it made sense.

"In all seriousness," he said.

"Look," I said. "What I wanted to talk to you about was boundaries. Our agreed upon boundaries."

Thixton sopped up oyster juice with a hunk of French bread then pushed the bread into his mouth with his blunt fingers, as if he were loading something. He chewed methodically and looked at me like I was a good suit of clothes that needed pressing. It was the same look he'd given me on the day I met him, at a press function after the dedication of the Thixton Terminal, Back Bay station. He had picked me out of the crowd of journalists. Naively I'd thought I was going to get a private interview. That's how fogged I was in the first months following Cyn's murder.

"What about them?" he said now, referring to boundaries.

"Nothing illegal," I said. "That was the agreement."

"So I recall. And no scars. Did you find a scar?"

"No."

"Then there's no problem."

"Just nothing illegal," I said. "I mean it."

He skinned his upper lip back and pried with an ivory tooth-pick at something green between his teeth.

"Do you have a particular illegality in mind," he said, "or are you simply seeking in your own clumsy way to terminate our relationship?"

"No, no. I don't want—"

"Perhaps you've found yourself the recipient of an unforeseen inheritance."

"No."

"Lottery ticket? A spectacular day at the track?"

I shook my head.

"Too bad," he said. "Luck is a wonderful companion."

"So I've heard."

Thixton picked up his glass of Chablis and drained it off in one greedy draft.

"Then let me set your mind at ease," he said. "As your passenger I haven't incurred any traffic tickets, nor distributed any bribes, nor robbed any banks. I certainly don't *need* to rob a bank, anyway."

He put his empty glass down and stood, the servos of his dead leg's exo-frames whirring loud enough to draw stares from other tables.

"Go home and shave, for God's sake," he said. "Don't you ever look at yourself?"

"Not as often as you, I'm sure."

He grunted and walked away, whirring and clicking, the exo-frames pinching at his baggy slacks. People stared not only because of who he was but *what* he was.

I looked at my crab salad then pushed it away.

Did you kill that boy?

My hands were clean.

*

I returned to my apartment on the ragged edge of the Boston Sprawl, Medford Township. Sleep continued to elude me. Being ridden by a Passenger denies you your REMs, flattens you out, and paradoxically keeps you vibrating above sleep's sweet threshold for two or three days afterward—then you drop into sleep so lightless and abrupt it might as well be a coma. It can also in some cases have the unfortunate consequence of permanently shorting out your sleep centers, which is why passenger arrangements are illegal. That and the inevitable possibility of body jacking for various unwholesome purposes. I was willing to risk the consequences for a chance at seeing my wife again, if only in vivid memory-loop recall. Certain very expensive drugs had already begun to modify my near-memory engrams. Perhaps that's why the overlay had occurred. Thixton paid well for the occasional use of my body.

I picked through some notes and hammered out five hundred words of scintillating prose concerning the "kinder/gentler" Homeland checkpoint makeover, filed the story with NENSS, and crashed with a beer and the TV.

And there she was! The girl with the tarnished copper hair, part of a guerrilla theater group perpetrating some disruptive art on the Boston Common, something to do with black body suits, red paint, and wrist-to-wrist paper chains. It was a quikclip on MSNBC, a disposable eyeflash that cut out right after the cops waded in with their movealongs.

I called a friend, a third banana news director on the network, and asked if he could ID the girl. He could and did, after an hour or so.

Her name was Rhonda Reppo, and her co-op's security was laughable. I paged her room from the lobby.

"Ms. Reppo?"

"Yes. Franz—?"

"My name's Scott Kriegel."

A pause. "And?"

"And I'd like to talk to you."

"Do I know you, Mr. Kriegel?"

"It's about Franz Thixton."

Another pause, this one longer. Then: "What about him?"

"It would be easier if I came up."

"Easier for whom?"

"Look, I'm not interested in any arrangement you might have with Thixton. It isn't about you."

"I don't know what you think you mean by 'arrangement' but I guess you can come up. Bear in mind I don't have all day."

Number 217 on a gray slab door. It opened, and Rhonda Reppo's face morphed through a variety of reactions then settled on stoic neutrality. She wasn't made up as she'd been in the overlay. Her pale lips and unlined eyes verged on wholesome vulnerability. Right. She turned and walked into the room. No clinging gossamer today; jeans and a green silk blouse. I followed her in and closed the door behind me.

Her place wasn't much bigger than mine, though her taste was a quantum leap beyond. And of course the indulgence of such taste isn't usually cheap.

"Drink?" she said.

"I'll have what you're having."

"*I'm* having a joint, and I don't share."

"Beer, then."

"Be serious."

"Scotch?"

She sat on the white sofa and opened a red lacquered box that held her drug paraphernalia. I stood there like any inanimate object you care to name. She grinned up at me. "It's your bottle and you know where it is," she said.

"I don't—"

But I did. I'm not a scotch drinker, and yet standing in the middle of her apartment the word had appeared in my mind naturally and I even experienced a desire for it. Now I breathed out, allowed the tension to relax from my body, and I found myself walking into the tiny kitchen and opening the cabinet over the stovetop. Horse finding his way home. Somatic memory reflex. I reached for the bottle of Lafroaig and poured a couple of amber-gold ounces into a glass.

She was already smoking when I re-entered the room, the air pungent with a melancholy haze of dope. I sat opposite her in a spindly appearing chair, more skeletal artwork than functional furniture.

"You found it," she said.

I nodded, sipped, put the glass down. "It still tastes like mercurochrome."

"Franz loves it."

"I'm sure he does."

She dragged primly on her joint and sat back, looking at me in a peculiar way that made me want to squirm. Instead of squirming, I told her why I was there. I explained the memory overlay and what I'd heard her say. She went on looking at me after I'd finished. The moment became uncomfortably elastic.

"Look," I said. "I want to know what you meant by asking Thixton whether he'd killed someone."

"I didn't mean anything by it."

"I don't believe you. And I wish you wouldn't stare at me like that."

She laughed. "But it's *fascinating.*"

She made me so nervous I found myself reaching for the scotch again, despite the medicinal—to my taste—flavor. It burned down my throat and almost immediately fumed up into my sleep-deprived brain.

"This is quite a study in opposites," Rhonda said. "When it's Franz he—"

"He what?"

She began preparing another joint. "He likes to be in charge."

"In what way?"

She snorted.

"Tell me."

"In a rough way, what do you think?"

"I think the price must be right."

She lit the new joint with a Zippo and drew hard on it, holding the smoke in her lungs before finally breathing out. She slumped back on the cushions and regarded me with moist, drooping eyes.

"The price is right," she said. "For both of us."

I drank some more mercurochrome.

"I know all about you," she said. "Franz laughs. He says you're pathetic, selling yourself for the price of a few memory loops."

I grunted.

"I can get under your skin so easy," she said. "Franz's skin is like Rhino hide."

"What about the murder?" I said.

"You're persistent."

"I'm a reporter. It comes with the job."

"You looking for a story, then?"

I shook my head. "I just want to know."

She pulled her legs up on the sofa. Feline sinuosity. I recalled the gossamer thing and the black lipstick.

"What if he did kill someone while he was riding you, what would you do about it?"

"I don't know."

"But it would make a difference?"

"Yes."

"Why?"

"It just would."

She reached out and dropped the tiny, glowing scrap of the joint in the ashtray on the table, stretched, and stood up.

"You have a car?"

"Yes."

"Let's go for a drive," she said.

She pointed and I turned. We rolled past grimy brick buildings. I knew the area. My skin felt prickly with sweat and nerves. A Boston police cruiser idled at the curb, flashers alternating, a man in the caged backseat staring out the window like he was watching TV while the cop filled in paperwork on a clipboard. A little farther on Rhonda said stop. We were in front of an empty storefront and a green fire hydrant. Across the street there was a nightclub with a red door.

"Franz drove me down here a few weeks ago," Rhonda said. "There was a boy standing on the sidewalk right over there. Only he wasn't just standing; he was advertising. Young, fifteen. Sixteen—maybe. Franz asked me if I thought the kid was good looking."

Something ugly uncoiled in my stomach.

"Yeah?" I said.

"I told him I wouldn't touch the kid with a ten foot pole even if I was wearing a full bio-hazard suit. So Franz said something like, I don't blame you. He's fucking scum and I'm going to kill him."

"And that's who you were asking about in my memory loop overlay?"

"Yes."

"Did Franz kill him?"

"I'm hungry," Rhonda said. "Let's get out of this neighborhood."

We hit a brewpub near Fenway Park, ordered pints of Revolution Ale and club sandwiches.

"What do you think our patron is having for lunch?" I said.

She almost choked on her sandwich. "Our *patron*. You're too funny. Do me a favor?"

"What kind of favor?"

"Kiss me."

"Why?"

"I want to compare. You know, is it what's inside that counts?"

"Let's skip it."

"Chicken."

I bit into my sandwich.

"How did your wife die?"

I chewed, swallowed, and said, "Let's skip that, too."

"Was she a reporter like you?"

I sighed, put down my sandwich. "Yes, she was a reporter. She was murdered. Not too far from the street corner you took me to."

"Was she a good reporter?"

"She was good enough, which in our line pegs you to second rate venues, second rate pay scales, and second rate lives. She had ambition, though. She was chasing some mystery story on her own time when she got killed."

"What did the police say?"

"Random act. No one has been arrested, but it hasn't been that long. Can we talk about something else now?"

"What was the mystery story?"

"Jesus. It was a *mystery*. Even to me. She kept it to herself. She shouldn't have bothered. I'm *not* ambitious."

I reached for my beer but didn't want it and didn't pick it up. Fatigue overtook me like a gray wave. All of a sudden I could barely keep my eyes open, my post-passenger buzz failing with characteristic abruptness.

"I have to sleep," I said.

"You look like somebody just hit you in the head with a hammer."

"Roughly correct."

I paid the bill. In the parking lot I fumbled the keys out of my pocket, dropped them on the ground. I leaned over, but it was Rhonda's hand that picked them up, her nails finely shaped and painted the faintest mauve.

In my dreams Cynthia was real. Not just a memory, or a desire, or a longing, or a regret. Dreams resemble loops, or the other way around. There is no distance. Imagine being able to turn on your favorite dream at will. Imagine the risen dead.

I woke in my apartment, on my bed, in a straggle of blue TV light filtered through layered strata of dope. It was hot. Rhonda Reppo sat with her legs crossed and locked in a Zen lotus. Her legs were bare, and she was wearing one of my sleeveless T's.

"What—" I started, but my throat was too dry to make much more than a croak. She turned her head, and I swallowed a couple of times and tried again: "What are you doing here?"

"I got your address out of your wallet and drove you home. I didn't want to leave you sleeping in your car, so I walked you up here. Every time we stopped, like at the lobby door or the elevator, you started sliding. So I'm not going to carry you, right? I tried to keep you moving. Got your apartment open, but then what? Let you hit the floor and leave you? Then I'm thinking I'm not cabbing it all the way back to my co-op. So you're my ride, but also I was thinking we could kill Franz together, if you're game."

"You better quit smoking that shit." I rubbed my face, stood up like somebody rising out of a sucking tub of mud, and shambled over to the refrigerator. It was mostly empty, except for a few bottles of beer and one of water. It was water I needed. I chugged on the half-empty bottle, letting the cool air from the open refer dry my sweat.

Rhonda touched my bare shoulder. I'd known she was there, and didn't flinch. She trailed her nails down my back. It felt good, but I said, "Don't," and she stopped. I capped the bottle, replaced it on the shelf, swung the door shut and turned. She had stopped touching me but she hadn't retreated an inch. Her breasts filled out my T-shirt, dark nipples visible through white ribbed cotton.

"You're a nice guy," she said.

"I have my moments."

"Loyal."

"To a fault." I moved past her, picked up my keys. "I'll drive you home now."

"You didn't say whether or not you were game. There's this guy in my troupe? He kind of plays at the street theater thing. In real life he's some kind of techie. I asked him once if he could screw with a passenger while he was riding, and this guy, Tony, he said sure. He said he could make a gizmo that would scramble the passenger like breakfast eggs, but you'd have to be right on the portal. And I could be on it, that's not a problem."

"Nobody's killing Thixton. Nobody's killing anybody."

"You're wrong," she said. She still hadn't moved. The TV light pulsed on her legs.

I clutched my car keys, stared at her.

"You're not the only one," she said. "Franz has many rides. He can buy what he wants and he buys lives."

My head hurt. How long had I slept? It was dark, the time stamp in the corner of the TV said 2 A.M., but what day was it?

"With us," Rhonda said, "it's like a seedy romance, almost. He gets off on the artsy-girl bullshit. In some of his other lives he gets darker. You're a nice guy, but you need to know how much your memories cost."

"Get dressed," I said.

"Franz talks to me," she said. "He shows me things, like that boy. He knows I'm scared and he likes it."

"Get dressed, Rhonda."

She did, and neither of us spoke another word.

*

My hands were clean. But somebody else's were dirty. I was able to ignore this fact for a while, though I knew it would eventually claim me. Meanwhile my drug protocol continued apace and I was well on the road to permanently altering my memory centers—I was on the road to having Cynthia back. Then one night, drunk, trying to write a feature about the role of block captains in co-op districts I became suddenly enraged and threw my beer bottle at the wall hard enough to wake up the unknown occupant of the adjoining apartment. He thumped the wall a couple of times, but it was nothing compared to the thumping going on inside my head. And for the millionth time since Rhonda told me about Thixton's other lives, I wondered what story Cyn had been chasing and who had decided to terminate her investigation.

I closed out my newsfile and buzzed Rhonda Reppo's terminal. It was about three o'clock in the morning. After a moment she answered, a dark, grainy image insert opening in the corner of the screen.

"Don't you ever sleep?" I said.

"Don't you?"

"Not much."

A tiny coal brightened and dimmed in front of her face. "So," she said.

"You can't get at a man like Thixton. He has money and he has political connections, police connections. Even with proof you couldn't expose him. Say you have names, particulars. The cops would collar me for participating in an illegal Passenger arrangement and never bother with the rest of it. Or I write the story, fly it by my editor, whom I've never met in person, by the way. He wouldn't run it. I'd be lucky if he didn't fire me. What's more I'd find myself audited, some government agency raping every data point out of my soul until they found something good to nail me with. I'm a threat to security. Isn't everybody?"

"I never said anything about getting Franz that way," Rhonda said. The tiny glow in the dark image, waiting.

"This gizmo," I said. "What will it really *do* to him?"

"In a perfect world, he'll be a drooling vegetable."

"The world isn't perfect."

"Usually not," she said.

"And what do you need me for? Why haven't you just done it when he's over there with my body?"

The ember of dope glowed bright, subsided. After a long while she said, "Maybe there's a chance he won't be the only vegetable to come out of the deal."

"And I'm a nice guy."

"Yeah."

"Okay," I said. "I'm in."

My night came around. I wanted to call it off but didn't. I was nervous, and when I lay down it was with little expectation of sleep. The next thing I knew I was in a strange bedroom, tumbling backward, a bright ceiling light stabbing into my eyes, somebody gasping for air. I fell through a long gap in cognitive reality before I hit the floor, cracking the back of my head a solid blow. But it was the button-locus of pain at the base of my skull that really hurt. I writhed on my back, eyes squeezed shut. A cool hand touched my cheek. Rhonda Reppo's voice, soothing: *No, it's all right, it's all right . . .*

Bad memories haunted me, and not all of them were my own. Now when I slept a nasty residue of Franz Thixton fumed up, and ghosts of his perverted deeds and desires spooked through the night marshes of my dreams. More than once I'd seen Cynthia on those marshes, and it was no longer memory enhancers I craved but a memory suppressant.

A month after we'd scrambled Thixton like "breakfast eggs," in a lost hour past midnight, I turned to my terminal, its flat blue light the only illumination in my apartment. I buzzed Rhonda Reppo and presently a box opened in the corner of the screen.

"Okay," I said. "Let's find out."

"Find out what?" Rhonda said, after a moment.

"Whether what's inside is what counts."

Light streaked when she pulled the joint away from her mouth. She said, "I guess I'm ready for a ride, if you are."

SCATTER

I was enjoying the memory of a single malt scotch I had once drunk in a Las Vegas casino back around ought '49, when I sensed someone enter my office. I let the scotch go (Glenfiddich, $22 a shot) and came forward.

She stood clutching her handbag in front of her. She was wearing a green skirt in an iridescent fish scale design with a matching jacket. The skirt clung to her hips like a second skin. Holy mackerel! And she wore one of those hats that look like neuro netting with feathers.

"Please take a seat," I said.

The only seat in the office placed her in front of a retinal scanner. Before she had her pack of smokeless c's out of her handbag I knew everything about her, from her name (Kari Tolerico), to her yearly Kotex consumption, the brand of coffee she preferred, and her multiple online ID's, and not to mention that unfortunate polyp she'd had lasered out of her most intimate recesses.

She lit up, crossed her legs, and waited. Fairly impressive. Most of my prospective clients, when confronted with an empty office and a disembodied voice, tended to fidget. Kari Tolerico was not the fidgeting type.

I chose to appear behind my desk as Robert Mitchum, circa 1947, the *Out Of The Past* era. Fully colorized for contemporary sensibilities, of course.

"How can I help you, Ms. Tolerico?"

"There's going to be a murder."

"Is there?"

"It's a plot to kill my lover's husband."

"What makes you think such a thing?"

She shrugged, her jacket gleaming like an oil slick.

"Intuition," she said.

"And—?"

"Poison."

"Intuition and poison. It sounds like somebody or other's autobiography."

"Does it? I'm not a reader."

"You're not missing much," I said. "Just the distilled and refined thoughts, art, philosophy, and history of the human race."

"I see."

"Seeing's good, too," I said.

"Are you a reader then, Mr. Frye?"

"I was before circumstances forced me to surrender corporal existence. Now I can only read books that I'd already read, that are in my memory vault. Anything new is scanned, and I can access the text, but it's not like holding a book in my hands and turning the pages."

"What a romantic you are."

"Yeah, I'm Byronesque. Let's get back to the poison, Ms. Tolerico."

"Actually it's more of a viral infection."

"Huh?"

Suddenly the taste of Glenfiddich came forward, burning at the back of the throat I didn't have. With an effort of concentration, I managed to quell the sensation. But another immediately took its place. The sensation of urine-wet sheets gone cold on my little boy body.

"You don't look well, Mr. Frye."

"You don't think so?"

"Not at all. That hound dog face you're wearing is getting all grainy and flickery, too."

Damn it. I shuffled her data, hunting for the clue I must have missed, the thread, the inconsistency. My Mitchum biolo stood, leaned over the desk, and stretched out his arm to point at the woman's betraying eye. Any reasonable person would have flinched. Ms. Tolerico merely grinned and batted her pretty lashes.

"What did you do?" I said.

"I'm sure I don't know what you mean, Mr. Frye."

"I'm sure you do."

The wet sheets went away, and I found myself experiencing a

memorable orgasm. This orgasm had occurred on the same day that I'd enjoyed my twenty-two dollar Glenfiddich. That had been a hell of a lucky day. Accompanying the orgasm was the scent and taste of the woman's perfume. *La Bon Nuit* was the name of the perfume. Molly was the name of the woman. Later she became my wife, and later still she shoved me off a five-story balcony— more or less accidentally—and I suddenly found myself on a new career path.

I cried out, shook the orgasm *off*, but by then my office was empty.

I accessed the broadcaster on 2nd and Vine, planted myself as Richard Widmark, *Kiss Of Death* period, in the middle of the sidewalk in front of my building. Some people walked though me, momentarily scattering the microscopic swarm that allowed me to flirt with physical existence. A few who weren't paying attention sidestepped at the last moment, and I endured the usual taunts from the anti-biolo contingent. I could sympathize. Before I went incorporeal all the glinty crap on practically every sidewalk used to irritate me, too. And I wasn't sad to see the city ban biolos from public restaurants, either. But it's amazing how a five-story plunge followed by a sudden stop can change your perspective on things.

A kid with a fashionably flayed earlobe passed by on his wheel and waggled his hand around in my head. It was several seconds before the nano flakes could gather light in an orderly fashion and transmit it back to my "eyes." I waited, all the while fending off a chaotic assault of memory sensation.

Just as I regained my vision, Kari Tolerico emerged from the building. I stepped in front of her. She walked through me without a word. I scattered, reconstituted, and turned to follow. I felt like tying her to a chair and hurling her down a staircase.

"Hold on," I said.

She ignored me, and for a moment I thought she might be one of the estimated twelve percent of the population who had declined an Aural Wave implant. I had the figures down cold, because my Redmond-based company had coordinated the local advertising blitz. *Catch The Wave!* was our brilliant hook.

"Ms.—"

"Stop bothering me."

"Lady, I haven't *started* bothering you."

"Then don't."

"Who are you?"

"Jesus, you *scanned* me."

"Okay. *Why* are you? As in: Why are you fucking with my upload? And how did you do it?"

She ignored me again. And we were approaching the outside range of the broadcaster. There were plenty of others, and I knew the location of every one in the city, but I was rapidly becoming incapable of holding a coherent thought. I stopped at the flickering limit of the broadcaster, and she walked on.

"Why!" I shouted.

The sensation of numbingly cold surf foamed around my ankles, undermining the sand beneath my feet.

Kari Tolerico threw me a saucy look over her shoulder and said:

"Favor for a friend."

Then I let go.

It smothered me, a blizzard of sensation and memory, facts and fancies, a short-circuited synopsiscopic not-so-merry-go-round.

I fled to a strong memory of sanctuary: the bedroom in my childhood house. Slamming the door, I simultaneously constructed barricades fashioned from the steady sensation of security and acceptance that had prevailed during the period of childhood that I originally occupied this room. The chaos yammered outside the door. It made scratchy rat sounds in the walls, battered softly and insistently at the window.

But it couldn't get in.

Which was great, except neither could I get out. It beat going insane, though. I paced around my little room. The bed was made up with a baseball themed bedspread and pillowcase. My bookshelf was well stocked with prepubescent adventures (I was still a couple of years early for the pubescent adventures that I would download and hide under the mattress.

Downloading porno. That gave me an idea.

I fired up the terminal on my school desk and punched in

the access code for my agency files. Fortunately, dream logic prevailed, and the data began to flow; I had a narrow conduit to the real world. The world outside my scrambled engrams.

I scrolled the Kari Tolerico file. It was slow work. Beyond the barricaded walls of my child's bedroom I could have immersed my being in the file, let it soak through, a filter catching potential clues.

But here it took hours (relative time) to hunt through Tolerico's info, even after dismissing the dross of her grocery bills, library and digi rental, etc. Her insurance and medical records yielded routine mosaics.

Something heavy thumped against the window.

Giving my better judgment a pass, I got up and tilted the blinds open. Fishsticks, my ex-wife's ex-border collie, was mooshed against the glass, blood gouting from his mouth, body heaving. Just the way he looked that day the van hit him in the parking lot of the Seabreeze. Molly had screamed when she saw him. Some start to a vacation. She'd blamed me, of course. Well, I let him off the leash. We had gone to our Seaside condo to try to fix things and instead wound up with a dead pet and a fresh load of recriminations. And later on we wound up with an almost-dead me. I'm the first to admit that one weekend at the seashore is unlikely to retrieve a romance buried under eleven years of estrangement. Standing out in the salty breeze on the balcony, trying to put my arms around Molly who was having none of it, I'd said something stupid like, "You'd rather be up here with Fishsticks." We were both drunk. She shoved me hard, and I tipped over the rail. I guess she loved that damn dog.

I closed the blinds.

Good old Fishsticks. Molly liked goofy names. With that thought, something clicked. I addressed the terminal again, hunted down Ms. Tolerico's net monikers. I *thought* one of them had a familiar ring. Surga Can. A term of endearment, back when Molly and I had shared such things.

I composed a brief message and routed it to every one of Kari Tolerico's mail accounts, work and private. When she opened her primary account from her cell, I nailed her location. Hours if not days may have passed in my bedroom, but out in the real world only minutes had elapsed since I evaporated on 2nd Avenue.

She didn't reply to my message.

If I wanted answers I'd have to brave the storm, only bravery didn't have much to do with it. All things being equal, it was more a matter of abject surrender to a suicidally stupid impulse. But it was either that or spend the rest of eternity in my nine-year-old self's bedroom.

I opened the door—

—and came forward.

Hell's own sensorium awaited me. I slogged through kisses and constipation, the one swat on the ass my father ever gave me—and a few erotically intended ones from a certain female companion in later years as well. The taste of heavily salted yams. Farts and the smell of pickle juice. Headaches, drunken euphoria, sushi, vomit erupting up my throat, tears, falling from the Seabreeze balcony, turning over in midair, drunk, leaving my stomach on the fifth floor.

Before I struck with a paralyzing, tissue-tearing, bone-breaking smack, I side-slipped into a projector two blocks north of the last one I'd used, and as Kirk Douglas (*Bad And The Beautiful*, 1952) I fell into stride with the Tolerico woman. Most of the old time tough guys were out of copyright, fortunately.

"Guess who," I said.

"For Christ's sake."

"Now don't be that way. Surga Can."

She stopped walking. So did I. A skinny teenager on a wheel glided through me. I scattered and reconstituted. Ms. Tolerico and I faced each other across from a micropark. A squirrel, representing the park's contingent of fauna, twitched halfway up a spindly birch and watched us.

"Tell me," I said. "What I already know."

She took a moment to light a smokeless c, while I grimaced under the continuous assault of chaos. I could only take a little more. If I didn't flee back to my safe room, my core personality would shred and join the Madhatter's fucking tea party.

"She wants you dead," Ms. Tolerico said.

"I am dead."

"Then she wants you gone. She can't stand it, you haunting

around like a ghost or something. It drives her crazy."

"Molly."

"You want my advice?"

"Not especially."

"Let it go. Don't fight. Then it'll be over. Rest in peace. Get it?"

"What did you use?"

"Let it all go, Frye. Be happy."

She snapped her c at the squirrel and walked away.

I almost didn't make it back to my room.

Hunkered over my little kid's terminal, I pecked out a message to my ex-wife. In some ways, I had kept in better touch with her since my death. But this particular message was tough. For a long time I got no further than: Dear Molly. Well, there were distractions aplenty. It sounded like a Lovecraftian army of rats in the walls. I got up and pressed my ear to the wall for a few moments. Not rats; voices. Squealy little voices that scrabbled frantically for a way in.

Dear Molly: You pushed me off the balcony and all, but isn't this a bit much? It won't obliterate me, you know. I'll persist and it'll be hell. Worse than Hell. Please help. Call Surga Can off.

I sent it and started waiting. Reduced to a nine by ten foot room, the texture and content of my memory vault was still impressive, if limited. I flipped through a couple of the flashprint books, boy's adventure stuff. And I was like one of those pictures of the guy looking at a picture of a guy looking at a picture, looking . . . Except I was myself a memory, looking at a memory, which was full of memories, etc.

I put the book away.

On my knees I found my baseball glove and ball under the bed. Cool! I threw the ball into the glove a few times. I guess it would have been cooler if I'd had my nine-year-old's sensibilities.

I checked the flatscreen. No message.

I risked another look out the window. It was kind of like looking out the window of Dorothy's house while it careened around that tornado. *Things* drifted across my vision. School buses, hedges, tennis shoes, toys, faces (auntie Em!), and on and on. If I got closer to the glass I picked up smells, closer still and it was flavor ghosts, closer yet and a vibrating stew of emotion made me draw back abruptly.

I turned away, breathing funny. The image of an envelope was tumbling around the flatscreen. I had mail.

Sitting on the kid's chair, my knees halfway to my armpits, I opened the letter. It was succinct:

Huh?— Molly.

Damn it.

In corporeal life I'd been slightly rich and more than slightly bored. The rich part had allowed me to have an incorporeal existence after the plunge. But one thing I wasn't going to do with Daniel Frye's life, Part Deux, was run a business. At least, not a large business with managers and scores of employees and headaches and all that. Almost immediately after my death, I cashed out, disbursed a healthy mini-fortune Molly's way, then built me a detective agency with one employee: Myself. And I was good at it.

So I tried to be good at it now.

I opened the Tolerico file and began rearranging clunky blocks of raw data. I lingered over her retinal scan, over the image of it. After a while I noticed two anomalies. The first was a tiny scar just above the iris, and I had no doubt it had been surgically created. Because the second anomaly was something like a pinhead glint of metal or some highly reflective grain floating *inside* the retina. If I'd had any skin it would have been crawling.

Speaking of skin . . .

I felt a hot breath on the back of my neck. I jerked around, but the room was empty. Somebody at some time or other had breathed like that on the back of my neck, and the memory impression had just come up. Which was a bad sign, because it meant the barricades had been breached.

"*Shit.*"

I looked around the room, a little frantically. First there was nothing. Then Fishsticks was there, sprawled and heaving and vomiting blood.

I looked away, and had an orgasm, immediately followed by a flutter of stomach flu. My hands dotted up with measles, but only for a few seconds.

I concentrated on my barricades and stared into the flatscreen. The room grew crowded. I didn't look up. Indistinct reflections moved on the flatscreen. Visiting memory ghosts, crowding behind me. The air changed to the recycled hiss of a sub-orbital, familiar from scores of flights. I tried to isolate the reflective grain in Ms. Tolerico's eye. A hot shower's needle spray soaked me. My hair (I had hair!) dripped on the touchpad while my fingers worked. It was tough, because my fingers kept changing size now. At one point a baby's chubby starfish digits slapped at the pad, and the data load dumped out and I bawled.

Suddenly my bedroom fractured, and I was everywhere, tumbling in a confetti of memory impressions. I struggled to protect my core being, clinging to a fragment of stable sanity.

Something bright and implacable twisted through it all like a parasitic spaghetti string worm, and I knew that was the source, the virus or whatever it was the woman had set loose in my upload.

It pulsed silver then red, redder, reddest. Then . . . was gone.

I sensed an eye withdrawing from the retinal scanner in my office, but all I could do was luxuriate in the sudden quiet and peaceful drift. The door opened. I stirred myself, came forward, saw Kari Tolerico pulling my office door shut.

Bogart. *Casablanca / Have and Have Not* era, screw the color saturation.

"Thanks for figuring out my message," I said. "Eventually."

Molly wiped her eyes, which had changed from brown to tentative blue with her tears. I hated that phony Mood Wash crap, but didn't say anything.

"Do you have to be like that?" she said.

Passersby gave us looks. Me looks. Hardly anybody went B/W nowadays. We were sitting on a bench in Myrtle Edwards park, facing Elliot Bay.

"Who do you prefer?" I asked.

"Just be yourself."

"I could saturate Bogie."

"Please, Daniel."

I went away, then came forward as Daniel Frye. I guess it was the wrong one, though, because she frowned and looked away.

"What's the matter now?"

"You never looked like that," she said, watching a white gull ride over the breakwater.

"Yes, I did. You just don't remember. I looked like this when we first met. Come on."

"Daniel."

"Okay, okay."

I dissolved into fairy dust once more. When I came forward again, the bench next to Molly glittered in the noon sun like mica.

"Satisfied?" I said.

She smiled sadly. "I'm trying to be."

"Do I detect a subtext?"

I stood before her, the version of Daniel Frye she had last known, an exemplar of male pattern baldness and the moderately inflated spare tire. The faintly ridiculous man she had shoved in drunken anger one night, then screamed and screamed as I fell from her forever and she tried to draw me back. Slipping away with the dread acceleration of gravity, I'd seen her pale arms thrust out after me.

"Daniel, this is the last time for us. This is goodbye for good. It has to be."

"Why? Because your damn girlfriend says so?"

"No. Because I say so. Jesus, Daniel, when you were around you were never around. Now when you're not real, you're always popping up in my ear, or on my computer, or as one of these creepy projections."

"I'm real," I said.

A thirty-foot yacht motored into the chop beyond the break-water. A man and a woman in bulky white sweaters stood in the open cockpit, arms around each other's backs, the man steering one-handed. Dashing.

I turned to Molly.

"You really said that stuff to her, didn't you. About how you couldn't stand me haunting around your life."

She stared at me, her eyes going deep blue at last.

"Quit that," I said.

"I'm sorry, Daniel. Kari took it to heart. I was upset and vulnerable."

"But you meant it."

"I should have told you and gotten it over with. But I couldn't hurt you again. Kari is protective of me. We're intimate, a concept you never understood."

"I guess I don't have to hear the gory details."

"I'm sorry."

"All right, all right."

"I have to go now," Molly said.

"You don't *have* to."

"Yes."

It was a deep blue goodbye, and I watched her walk across the park. Kari Tolerico was waiting for her in the parking lot. They got into a solar pod and rolled off. A jogger ran through me. I scattered, and stayed that way.

BEAN THERE

I fell flat on my ass, stunned, jaw unhinged, gaping at the thing. Implications piled up fast. My gaze wandered briefly off the marble block, then I fell again. Inside, this time, as my interior order shifted—irrevocably, perhaps. It was a light bulb moment, and cravenly I wished I could pull a chain and turn it off. Thanks a lot, Aimee. Happy Anniversary. I sat on the floor and it sat on the wheeled mover's cart, note still taped to the side facing me, a sheet of printer paper with red Sharpie lettering three inches high: THIS IS YOURS, BURT. MY MIGHTY MAN!

Go back two months. Pick a Tuesday in May. A nice spring morning. There might have been birds twittering happily, the way they do. I had the front door of Bean There propped open, plus all the windows on the sidewalk side. Seven A.M. of a twittering fine morning.

Aimee said, "Wow!"

"Wow what?" Slanting sunlight had discovered beaches of dust on the round table tops, and I was wiping them down ahead of the Clamoring Horde.

"A kid in Ashland levitated his bike," Aimee said. "Can you believe it?"

"No."

"Grouch."

"I'm always grouchy before coffee."

She snorted—but charmingly, not like a warthog or anything. "By my count you've already had a cappuccino and two Americanos. You ought to save some for the paying customers."

It was my turn to snort. "Paying customers? Are you trying to be funny? Besides, I meant before I *sell* any coffee."

She hmmm-ed, her attention riveted back on the laptop. She hunched over it, elbows planted on the counter, fingers pronged in her pixie hair, the pert little behind that had launched a thousand or so of my ships aimed in my direction on the black vinyl swivel stool.

"Come on," I said. "Nobody's levitated anything. Not even in Assland."

"*Ass*-land?" She smirked over her shoulder.

"Ashland. Ashland. What are you reading, anyway. The Weekly World News?"

"Reuters."

At which moment The Clamoring Horde entered Bean There. He was wearing a blue, button-down shirt, crisp khakis, and brown loafers, accessorized with a briefcase and gold earring.

"Double-tall-two-percent," he said.

Aimee got behind the bar and pulled it. I took her place on the stool and scrolled through the Reuters story. In front of witnesses adorable Samuel Welch, aged nine, had purportedly swept his BMX bike into the high altitudes of a neighbor's poplar. Never mind that one of the witnesses was an off-duty state patrol officer, six months ago this story *would* have been relegated to the pseudo-news. But with the Harbingers among us anything, any damned thing at all, had seemed to become possible if not explicable.

Aimee kept glancing in my direction, so I tried not to look too interested in the story.

"It's happening," she said, sing-songy on her way to the freshly de-beached table where the C.H. had seated himself.

"Don't get crazy on me," I sing-songed back. I'd had crazy in my life, plenty of it. An alcoholic father and a bipolar sister. Dad had been a maintenance drinker, and not a mean one. But even a happy drunk is still a drunk, and if you live with one, especially if he's your parent, you'd better gird yourself for two levels of life. The level that occurs on the surface and that everyone sees, which is the presentation level. And the private level that occurs mostly behind closed doors and makes you feel like the world is a wobbly and uncertain place. I was fourteen when a stroke killed my Mom, and Dad tumbled over the line into a realm of sodden self-pity and violent outbursts. At this point toss in the bipolar sister, the older sister who up till then had been your rock of stability, and see where that gets you. Lori began to see the world in a very different way, and was vocal about it, veering toward the occult and a perspective two shades to the left of sane.

Yeah, I knew crazy.

Guys like me grow up obsessed with "normalcy" and order. Or we grow up to be little chaos mavens ourselves. As a kid I watched TV obsessively. It was my escape hatch. I liked Disney, especially the old black and white footage they sometimes showed of the early days. That was a world *in order*, and Uncle Walt was like a cool Mr. Rogers. To me he was, anyway. When I grew up I found another safe obsession in my java joint, Bean There. Later, for balance, I found Aimee (though emotionally she wasn't as safe as a coffee bar). Then the Harbingers arrived.

"You call it crazy," Aimee said. "I call it Evolution."

With a capital E. The famous news clip seen around the world. The aliens arrived neither as an invading force nor as beneficent galactic pals. By their own description they were "Harbingers."

Famous network interviewer: "Harbingers of what?"

Alien: "Evolution."

Speaking of trees, the aliens somewhat resembled gnarled and rootless specimens. Those viewers who had devoted their attention to the minute analysis of The Clip liked to assert that after uttering the word "Evolution" the alien had smiled an enigmatic and very zenish smile. Of course the Harbingers mostly communicated telepathically, and there was even debate as to whether they *had* mouths. I guess you could point to the wartish seam midway up the trunk that constantly oozed some kind of thick sap and call *that* a mouth.

Evolution. Capital E.

It had become a movement. Aimee even had one of the ubiquitous "E" T-shirts, not the Ralph Lauren version, though.

"Seriously," she said, laying her arm across my shoulders. "There're stories like that almost every day. You *can't* deny it."

"Look, I'm just a humble businessman in a business that's gotten too humble."

"Burt—"

"Yes?"

"Oh, never mind."

The C.H. finished his latte, folded his *Wall Street Journal* neatly and replaced it in his briefcase.

"The stories are all bunk," he said, smartly snapping chrome latches and standing up. He was a little flushed around the hairline. "And if you ask me there aren't any aliens, either. It's just some kind of—"

"Some kind of . . . ?" Aimee said.

"Mass hallucination, whatever."

It was true that some people claimed they were unable to quite . . . see . . . the aliens. Most notably the senior senator from Ohio. Who could forget his famous "smoke and mirrors" press conference? And everybody commented on the soap bubble quality of their ships.

"In my opinion," the C.H. said, "Everybody has to get back to normal before it's too late."

And then he went out among the twittered, and it was almost an hour before the next customer wandered in.

"People are scared," I said at the other end of the day, standing in boxers by the window of my apartment, only a couple of blocks from my rapidly drowning venture.

"Some people are," Aimee said. "Are you?"

"It wouldn't be manly to admit it," I said. "Besides, I'm not really."

She moved—a silky whisper of girlflesh and sheets. She didn't say anything, and I felt compelled to fill in the gap. Somehow Aimee and I had lost the comfort of easy silences.

"The fear thing, that's just my pet theory. Remember at first there was an uptick in business? People wanted to talk, gather, bond."

"Have a cup a joe," Aimee said.

"Right. But now they're, I don't know, hunkered down. You can only take so much weirdness before you have to shut it off."

"Not everyone has to shut it off," Aimee said. "Maybe some of those hunkering people are busy."

I turned from the window. Aimee was looking at the ceiling, fingers laced behind her head, the sheet about her waist and her breasts so lovely.

"Busy doing what?" I said.

"Evolving."

I had to ask.

We weren't married but we had anniversaries. One arrived in the midst of the consummate weirdness. That pervasive sense of unreality plus the fact that I was furiously dog-paddling in a sea of red ink had conspired to short-circuit my memory.

"Happy anniversary," Aimee said on the phone.

"Oh, shit."

"Sweet-talker."

"Aim, I'm really sorry."

"You can make it up to me."

"Anything."

"Come over now."

She had borrowed a friend's little Toyota pickup. Aimee's apartment building, which was old and consisted of only twelve units, provided each tenant with his or her own mini-garage so narrow and shallow they were really car boxes with barely enough room to open the driver's door. Which didn't matter to Aimee, since she didn't own a vehicle and used her car box for storage.

The door was up and the interior space had been cleaned out. Presumably to make room for the thing in the back of the yellow Toyota.

A block of white marble. That pickup was riding so low on its springs that it was a wonder the rear wheels could turn.

"Isn't it beautiful!" Aimee said.

"Very pretty. Paper-weight?"

"I'm going to sculpt it, silly." She was beaming.

"Cool."

"Your skepticism does *not* affect me."

"I'm not being skeptical. But don't you think it might be easier to start with something less intimidating, not to mention cheaper, like clay?"

"I am not in the least bit intimidated. And I got a great deal at The Quarry Werks. Kind of an installment plan. They didn't seem to care. Everybody's so spaced out."

The block was three feet on a side and weighed approximately twenty-seven million pounds. A couple of guys from Aimee's building helped us muscle it around. Transferring the thing from the Toyota's tailgate (dangerous *skreek* of hinges) to the mover's cart threatened to give us all hernias. Even pushing it into the garage was not easy. Once it started rolling, okay. But getting it started was murder. We three he-men bent at the knees, put our shoulders into it, and made like Sisyphean triplets.

Aimee was like one of those dilettantes I imagine must inhabit old French novels. During our three-year relationship she had "been" a painter, a writer, a juggler, and a chef. Brief enthusiasms that burned bright then dimmed to forgotten clinkers. When I met her she was waiting tables for a living. We hit it off and I hired her to help me with Bean There. After that, one thing led to the inevitable other and we became much more than partners in caffeine. At thirty-two this was the longest relationship I'd ever managed.

When the other guys left, I wiped the sweat out of my eyes and asked, "What put you onto sculpting, anyway?"

"It's funny," Aimee said. "I had a dream about it and when I woke up I thought, Why not? But that isn't the funny part. The funny part is that I hadn't been asleep, I just thought I was."

She hugged me and kissed my mouth. "You're my mighty man," she said.

"Mighty Man could use a cold beer."

"Come up to my lair, then."

I did, but not for beer.

News clippings taped to the wall of Aimee's garage/sculptor's studio:

From the Associated Press, originally reported in the *Memphis_Herald Tribune*, June 15, 2005. Tupelo Woman Teleports: Candace McCoy, a forty-six-year-old housewife from Tupelo paid an unusual visit to Elvis Presley's Graceland mansion yesterday when she unaccountably materialized in the "Jungle Room" before an eyewitness, security guard Joseph Lytel. Says Lytel, "The air got kind of dark and ripply, then she sort of stepped through." Mrs. McCoy, who appeared in a state of shock and was transported to Mercy Hospital, kept saying, "I just love Elvis . . ."

From Reuters, June 17, 2005. Astronaut Claims Moon Walk,

Thirty Years Late: Former Apollo 13 Commander James Lovell today announced that he had at long last walked upon the surface of the moon. Lovell, 77, said he had not required any life-sustaining equipment and his mode of transport was ". . . nothing more complicated than the simple desire to be there." As evidence, Commander Lovell offered his bedroom slippers, the bottoms of which were caked with a gray talc-like powder. Speaking on condition of anonymity, a source at the Jet Propulsion Laboratory in Houston, Texas confirmed that the powder is indeed moon dust, though there is no official word on that conclusion. Lovell, appearing on the front lawn of his Palm Springs home in a white T-shirt with a large black letter "E" on the front, described his journey as an "Evolutionary" experience, apparently referring to the enigmatic statement of the Harbingers. "The view from Fra Mauro was transcendental," said Lovell.

From The Associated Press: Dead Man Singing. Jerry Garcia performed "live" for the first time since his death in 1994. Tom Petty, performing at Washington State's Gorge amphitheater, announced a "special guest." Garcia then ambled onto the stage wearing a tie-dyed "E" T-shirt and an acoustic guitar. There were cheers, but also some screams from those closest to the stage, and at least three concert goers fainted and required medical attention.

I was sleeping over at Aimee's and woke up, terrified. It must have been a nightmare, I don't know. The Madrona outside her bedroom window cast a pale shadow over the bed, and I thought of the Harbingers, the hideous physicality of them. It was two o'clock in the morning. Aim was not in the bed.

I pulled on a pair of jeans and didn't bother tying my shoes. The door of the garage was raised about a quarter way for air. Bright light spilled out. I ducked under the partially raised door. Hot halogen lamps on tripod stands illuminated the marble block. Aim's face glowed with a sheen of sweat.

"Burt!"

"I had a bad dream, or something."

"Poor baby. Well *I've* had a breakthrough."

"Good."

"It's the tools."

"What about them?"

"I was using the wrong ones. Look at this."

She meant the block. I looked. To my eye it appeared pretty much the same as it had the day we off-loaded it from the pickup truck, though I could tell she had hacked at it a little. A few fragments of marble lay scattered around the stool, and the face of the block had been scarred in a minor way.

"Look *through* it," she said.

"I can't look through it, for Christ's sake, Aim."

"But you can," she said. "It's like anything else. Really. I mean, it's even like boxing."

"What?"

"Sure. Same mental thing, in a way. Like you throw the punch through, as if the jaw wasn't even *there*. And it's not. Neither's the marble. I mean it's there, of course. But also it's *not* there. And if it's not, well, then you can throw your punches right on through. You can do anything. *Anything.*"

"Aimee, come on."

"Don't be afraid."

"I'm *not* afraid."

"Honey." She got up and came to me and hugged me. "It's all right."

I fought it, but the mote around my heart filled with tears and I sobbed into Aimee's hair, "I want everything to be normal again."

"Darling, I know. It's okay, it really is."

But it wasn't. The rational world tilted, threatening chaos, and my anchor was talking phantom punches.

"It's accelerated evolution," she said, excited. "You know, all the little grays, and the crop circles and UFO's and synchronicity and deja vu, just *all* of it—those things are projections, the evolutionary psyche of human potential manifesting in consort with the conscious Universe. Do you see? Oh, I'm not saying it right. But listen. You didn't think real aliens looked liked *X-Files* puppets, did you?" She laughed. "The Harbingers are *real*. All the stuff happening now is real. It's to get us going before it's too late, to get as many of us going as possible. Before we completely fuck over the planet and the whole human race."

We were still holding each other, but now it was like we were two separate people and it didn't matter that I had been inside of her countless times and we had spoken every living shred of our lives to each other. She was just somebody I was holding. In her excited voice I heard my sister's delusional rantings while Dad hunted drunkenly for his car keys.

"Don't, Burt," Aimee said. "You're going away. Please don't do that. You could be so close, if you wanted to be."

I continued holding her but the good between us was gone and there wasn't a damn thing I could do about it. I don't think I was afraid. I don't know that fear had anything to do with it.

"It's like being shut up in a little room," Aimee said. "A room with no windows and a closed door. And it's fine because you don't know you're in a little room, you think you're in the middle of the world. But what if you knew? What if all of a sudden there *was* a window and you could see there was a universe of marvels right outside, and all you had to do was open the door, because it's not locked or anything. It's just a door waiting for the person in the room to wake up enough to open it."

All this while she looked earnestly into my face, her eyes shining.

I said, "Aim, I am so tired."

Most people weren't onboard for the Evolution, and things got pretty bad. The End Is Nigh contingent. Economic collapse. Suicides, lots of suicides. By July I had given up opening Bean There. I just wanted to sleep, perchance not to dream.

Then reality snapped back, and I woke one morning with some kind of hangover and—unknown to me—all my recent memory furniture drastically re-arranged. Harbingers? Never heard of 'em.

The natural response to hangover is aspirin and coffee. I dressed, grabbed my keys, and strolled down to Bean There to open the doors, only vaguely recalling that hard times and some kind of throbbing apathy had compelled me to close the place for a few days.

Open it and they will come. I guess I wasn't the only one with a hangover. I worked my ass off that first day, riding a caffeine bullet train to stay *focused*. Aimee was not around, and I sorely missed her. What in hell had we been fighting about, anyway? I closed up at seven, after a nice relaxing twelve hour day. My CLOSED sign depicted a sad little coffee cup with wavy steam hair.

I got on my cell and called Aimee, because whatever we'd been fighting about wasn't worth it. Dimly I seemed to recall some kind of tiff over her latest artistic indulgence. She picked up on the second ring.

"May I speak with Ms. Rodin, please?"

"Funny guy."

"Aim, I'm sorry."

"For what?"

"I, ah, dunno."

She laughed, sounding extra perky and normal and non-pissed-off.

"So how's it going?" I said. "If I come over will you lure me upstairs with promises of showing me your erotic statues?"

"You've got the only erotic stonework I'm interested in, mister."

"I am so *there.*"

And later, during a wine and underwear moment in her kitchenette, I said:

"I could really use you at Bean There, tomorrow."

Teasing: "Like you used me today?"

"With variations, only not as slippery, and you'll have to pull espressos, too. Aim, business is picking up in a major way. I can't even believe I closed down for a while. I must have been nuts!"

She was quiet awhile and easy within herself. I was the one with jitters all of a sudden. On the way over it had occurred to me that I wanted to marry Aimee, that I'd always wanted to. It was nothing other than fear that had kept us in separate apartments, which had allowed our lives to intersect in work and love-*making*, but not in the long sweet haul of committed love itself. My fear, not hers; Aimee was fearless in all things.

So I'd jacked myself up to ask her, but before I could get the words out she dropped a safe on my head.

"Burt, I think I'm going to do some traveling, see some things, maybe do a little good in the world."

"You're joining the Peace Corps?" I didn't know what she was talking about, and I struggled to keep the irritation out of my voice.

"No, silly. More of a private thing."

"I thought we were partners." I couldn't even mention the marriage thing. Suddenly it wasn't irritation I felt. My throat tightened down with emotion.

"We could still be pards," she said, taking my hand. "But you'd have to be unafraid to come with me, Burt."

"I don't know what you're talking about. Where are you going, really?"

"Burt, what if there was no Time or Space, and if you wanted to be somewhere, wherever and whenever, you could just be there? What would you pick, what would make you feel safe and happy?"

It wasn't what she said exactly, it was some upheaval within myself. I wanted to cry but didn't.

"Does opening day at Disneyland count?" I said, thinking I was being sarcastic.

She laughed. "Sure."

"Okay, I pick that. Now can we talk sense?"

"Won't there be a lot of people?" she said.

"Yeah, but it's the happiest place on Earth, so they'd all be happy, right? Aim, come *on*. Don't go. Please."

"I'm sorry, Burt."

She hugged me, and I wanted to melt into her but that wasn't happening.

"I finished my sculpture," she said. "I want to give it to you."

"Going away present? Thanks."

"Shush. Nobody goes anywhere, not really. I love you. Let's call it the anniversary present, okay?"

"Sure, okay."

"Don't be sad."

She had to be kidding with that one.

I called the next day but she didn't answer. After I hung the CLOSED sign out I walked over to her apartment. A white envelope with my name printed on it was taped to the outside of her door. I ripped the envelope open, but all the note said was "Don't forget your present. Love, Aimee."

That damn rock.

The garage was completely bare except for the marble block pushed into the corner on its rolling cart. The air smelled dry and the cement walls held the heat in. The last of the evening sunlight fell short of the block, which, in shadow at least, appeared as unworked and raw as the last time I'd seen it, its blunt face only slightly scarred by Aimee's amateur chiseling.

A sheet of printer paper was taped to the block. The sheet had been written upon, but I couldn't decipher it from where I stood. And I didn't want to get any closer. I just didn't.

The daylight terminator crept across the oil-stained floor, almost to the toes of my shoes before I imagined Aimee whispering *Don't be afraid.*

But I was afraid.

Nevertheless I took a tentative shuffling step into the shadow, then another, and then I was close enough to read the paper. THIS IS YOURS, BURT. MY MIGHTY MAN! And something about Aim's familiar, jokey intimacy took the hex off and impelled me forward.

Close up, Aimee's sculpture was as artless as any random hunk of stone you might happen to stumble upon. Wondering if there was something chiseled into the side facing the wall, I bent my back and braced my feet to pull it around—and instead fell flat on my ass.

Because the thing on that cart weighed no more than a basket of feathers. It kept rolling around after I fell, and stopped with the sheet of paper facing me again.

I sat stunned for a while, then turned my hands up and looked at them. White eggshell-like flakes clung to the sweat on my fingers. I crawled over to the block and reached out with the spread fingers of my right hand. The outer shell of the sculpture fell away with an airy crackle where I touched it.

I brushed my trembling hands over the block like a palsied conjuror, and it collapsed in an avalanche of rice paper-thin marble flakes, as if it had been held together by nothing more substantial than a hopeful thought.

What remained was something like a Christmas ornament.

One fashioned from and held up by polished marble nets of fila-
mentous intricacy, as if spider-spun. Aimee had created this wonder *inside* the block.

Which was impossible.

An impossible artifact from that newly forgotten world of
teleporting housewives and stumpy, non-deciduous aliens, of
Evolutionary human consciousness. Capital E. Bleh.

A worm uncoiled in my stomach. The room seemed to sway,
and I had nothing to hold onto. Kneeling on the hard cement, my
hands clenching, a singlet of sweat oozed out of my body. The object before me was a memory ornament, intended to remind me
of the impossible world of E. And I wanted it to go away.

I squeezed my eyes shut. *Aim.* But I was on my own. Memory
ornament, invitation to the impossible—it was still my choice to
accept or reject it. I knew amnesia was hovering in the foyer of my
consciousness, waiting. The chaos of a world without rules—at
least the rules I was used to—also hovered out there. I opened my
eyes and moved incrementally toward chaos, because that's where
my girl was.

The light changed. Heat lay on my back like a wool blanket
fresh out of the dryer. I didn't have to turn around, I knew that.
But maybe it wasn't chaos out there. Maybe it was Freedom. Freedom from fear. Capital F.

I stood up and brushed the marble flakes off on my pants.
Then I turned.

A vast and eerily silent crowd milled beyond the garage.
Thousands of people, and an ersatz castle, and a high blue sky
without clouds where a dozen or so giant soap bubbles drifted
serenely, unnoticed by the multitude.

All was utterly quiet until I crossed out of the garage, and then
it struck me like a Phil Spector Wall of Sound, the surf roar of the
crowd and brassy clamor of a New Orleans street band. It was *hot*
and dazzlingly bright. A trombone bell flashed the sun at me. I
shaded my eyes. Mickey Mouse was working the crowd. Then I
saw Aimee, waving. I felt a big goofy grin on my face, which was
appropriate. "I'm going to Disneyland," I yelled and ran to her.

GIRL IN THE EMPTY APARTMENT

Someone was going to die.

My name is Joe Skadan. These were the days of phantom invaders, unexplained disappearances, and Homeland insecurities. I stood in the back of the Context Theater on Capital Hill, Seattle, nursing a few insecurities of my own; the bottle of crappy Zinfandel hung loosely in my left fist, demolished over the duration of the third act. Me and the bottle. Free tickets guaranteed there were only two empty seats in the house. Mine and the one my girlfriend was supposed to have occupied. Cheryl hadn't come, though, and I couldn't take sitting next to that empty chair.

The third act ended with the monologist (my cranky alter ego) putting his hand over the gun on his desk while the lights adjusted, turning him into a dark cipher. Artsy as hell. The prop gun was actually my own .38, minus the ammo clip and none in the chamber. Kind of a family heirloom, stepfather-to-son. The question is left hanging: Who's he going to use that gun *on*? This character's interior darkness had become a filter that warped the entire world.

A beat of silence followed the final lighting adjustment. It was hot and stuffy in the theater. Programs rustled. Somebody coughed. Then the applause started, thank God. There were even a few appreciative whistles. The lights came up and the cast took their bows.

I slumped against the wall and breathed out. *The Only Important Philosophical Question*, my first fully staged play, had successfully concluded its maiden performance in front of a live audience. I was twenty-six years old.

Fifty or so sweaty audience members shuffled past me. The Context had been a transmission shop in a former incarnation, and not a particularly well-ventilated one. I hopped onstage and grabbed my gun, put it in a paper bag, then wandered outside for a smoke. In those days I smoked like crazy—the days after the advent of the Harbingers. Or as I preferred to think of them: the mass hallucination. One morning the world woke up with a headache. Dreams became strange, disturbing, inhabited by "Harbingers," which the dreamers occasionally described as conscious trees, or something. Rumors abounded. The juiciest being that large numbers of people had disappeared without a trace.

Some of the audience lingered in front of the theater, talking about the play. Mostly they seemed impressed by all that stage blood in the second act fantasy. It was weird to hear strangers discussing my work. I didn't much like it, and wished I could stuff the play back inside my head, where it had festered in its lonely way for years.

As the last of the audience wandered off I noticed a girl sitting on a patch of grass looking at the moon. Tear tracks shone on her cheeks like little snail trails. She was only about eighteen. Cheryl's failure to show had cut deep, and my instinct was to slink off and lick the wound. Instead I asked this girl if she was all right.

"Oh, yes. It's just so beautiful."

I flicked ash, adjusted my glasses, followed her gaze. "The moon?"

"Sure. I've been staying in the Arctic Circle up there."

"Doesn't that get cold?"

"It's not that kind of Arctic Circle."

She wiped the tears off her cheeks with the heel of her hand and stood up—rather gracefully, considering the dress she wore. A tarnished gold fabric, intricately pleated, that wound around her like flowing water, or the ridged skin of some exotic tree. She had a generous mouth and kindly eyes.

"You're Joe Skadan," she said.

"Yeah."

"You wrote the play."

I nodded. "How did you know me?"

"You're famous on the moon."

"All right."

"Can I walk with you, Joe?"

"If you want."

"I'm Nichole."

In my mind I depersonalized her with a character tag: MOON GIRL. I did this sort of thing more and more frequently, estranging myself from the world. The part of me that resisted this estrangement grew weaker by the day. Like the child I'd once been, locked in the closet, weeping from belt lashes, subdued and enfeebled by darkness, listening to the sound of Charlie, my step-dad, stomping off to work on Mom next. Before things turned bad she used to swoon about Charlie's blue eyes, "Just like Paul Newman's!" Charlie liked to fold that belt over and snap it together with a whip-crack sound, to let me know he was coming. *Where there's smoke there's fire*, he used to say, accusing me endlessly of transgressions I hadn't even considered.

MOON GIRL and I walked along. It was one of those pellucid Seattle evenings, the royal sky inviting stars to join the moon. Mechanically, I asked, "What did you think of the show?"

"It was different. Did Camus really say that, about the only important philosophical question being whether or not you should kill yourself?"

"I think so, but I never could verify the quote. Maybe I made it up. Who cares? I thought about calling it, 'What's So Grand About Guignol' but that seemed too jokey, though it fit with the bloody stuff."

"It's Woody Allen meets Taxi Driver," she said.

I looked at her. That description, same wording, was scribbled in a notebook back in my apartment. Coincidences made me uncomfortable.

"Maybe I'm your secret muse," MOON GIRL said, as if she knew what I was thinking.

"You don't even know me."

"Or I do, just a little."

"That dress is strange," I said, to change the subject.

"Does it seem familiar?"

"I don't know."

The dress almost shimmered, exuding energy. Or maybe I'd had too much wine, or I was a poor judge of energy exudations. Who knows?

"You've had dreams," she said.

"Everybody dreams."

I thought of my mother's birch, a little tree she'd claimed as her own even though it just happened to be growing in the backyard of the cruddy duplex we rented. I'd been dreaming about it for weeks now. The tree had been a private thing between my mother and me, excluding Charlie. While he was at work we sat under it for "Elvis picnics," which meant peanut butter sandwiches and bananas and Cokes. I still remember the checkered pattern of the blanket and the way the leaf shade swayed over us; a portion of my secret landscape. Another was the piece of sky I could see from my bedroom. Sometimes I'd put my comic down and stare at the night of moon and stars, and it was like a promise of freedom.

Arctic Circle. Not the polar regions but a 70s vintage burger franchise Mom used to work in when she was a teenager. My real Dad, another swoony teen, would come in and "make eyes" at her. The way I pictured it was like a scene from Happy Days. Safe and innocent as a chocolate malt. I have only a vague memory of him, and I may even have made that up. Mom had been a romantic all right. The freeway accident that killed my dad took a lot of that out of her, though. And Charlie took the rest. Arctic Circle. I really hated coincidences.

"It's a Neodandi," MOON GIRL said, referring to her dress. "The designer had dreams, too. Now you're kind of having the *same* dream. The world is changing, Joe. What do you think of the Harbingers?"

"I don't think of them."

We had arrived at the corner of Broadway and East Thomas. A man I'd tagged HOMELESS VET sat on the sidewalk in his usual spot, like a deflated thing. His beard grew almost to his muddy eyes. He thrust an old Starbucks cup at us, and a few coins rattled in the bottom.

"I served my country," he said, his standard line.

Nichole dropped in a quarter.

"Anyway, see you around," I said to her. I didn't want her following me all the way home.

"Goodnight, Joe."

"Yeah, goodnight."

I snapped the remainder of my cigarette to the sidewalk. HOMELESS VET reached for it, pinched the lit end between thumb and forefinger. My mind began to deconstruct him: nails like cracked chips of yellow-stained plastic, wiry hair and beard, moist eyes nested in wrinkles—separate labeled parts, not a man at all. I halted the process by an act of will. Once you take the homeless guy apart it's easy to keep going.

The girl was halfway down the block in her crazy energy dress. Nichole. Unaccountably her name stuck, the objectifying MOON GIRL tag dropping away like a dead leaf.

Cheryl London called. I was sitting in the kitchen drinking a beer and watching a girl in the window of the building across the street. This girl, whom I'd tagged THE EXHIBITIONIST, liked to keep her blinds open while she dressed and undressed. Sometimes she lay topless on her bed reading magazines. Her performances lacked real carnality, though. The thing about THE EXHIBITONIST was that she may not have existed. My mind played tricks on me all the time. Only they weren't good tricks like which cup is the pea under. I seemed to know too much about THE EXHIBITIONIST. Her window was probably thirty yards from my kitchen. Yet I could see details, some of which weren't even in my line of sight. I knew, for instance, that she had a *Donnie Darko* movie poster on the wall. Sometimes, lying in bed thinking about her, I wondered if she was a dream I was telling myself. I never had a girl in high school, though there was always one out of reach whose sweetness I longed toward. I imagined the safe harbor of relationships, and denied them to myself almost pathologically. Nichole looked like the kind of girl I used to moon about. *MOON GIRL.* So did THE EXHIBITIONIST.

Anyway, when I picked up the phone and heard Cheryl's voice I averted my gaze.

"Are you busy?" she asked.

"No. What's going on, where have you been?"

"I'm at Six Arms. Meet me?"

I walked downstairs with an unlit cigarette in the corner of my mouth. The building manager came out of his apartment and reminded me The Dublin was a non-smoking building.

"It's not lit," I said.

THE MANAGER was a balding Swede with a thick gut. In the summer he wore wife-beater T-shirts that showed off his hairy shoulders. Occasionally I was late with the rent, and we were both

cranky about it. He was the crankier, though. I think he would
have loved to evict me.

"I smell smoke up there sometimes," he said.

"Not mine," I said and pushed through the door.

She was sitting in a booth by the window, her hair like
bleached silk in the bar light. Cheryl was my first and only girlfriend. We had met at the University. She had taken Introduction
to Twentieth Century Theater as an elective, aced it, and returned
her full attention to more serious matters. I barely pulled a C then
dropped out before the next semester. Cheryl now had a government job that required a secret clearance. Since the Harbinger
Event it demanded more and more of her time. I sat across from
her and lit a cigarette.

"Thanks for coming," she said.

"You're welcome," I said, the wrong way.

"Let's try to be grownups. Please?"

"Are you dumping me?"

"Joe."

"You're dumping me."

She looked out the window at East Pine Street.

My heart lugged like something too tired to continue. The
sounds of the restaurant grated on my nerves, the music, voices
barking, clatter of dishes from the kitchen. I looked through the
reflection of Cheryl's face in the window.

"We don't work," she said. "We're too different."

"When did you figure this out?"

"I guess I've always known it."

My stomach clenched.

"Cheryl—"

Finally she looked at me.

"Sometimes we don't even seem to live on the same planet,"
she said. "You don't have any friends. You stay up all night. I don't
understand you anymore and I don't think I ever really did. It's
like you're slipping away."

"I'm right here."

"I'm sorry, Joe. But there's something so wrong. I mean with
you. I don't blame you for it. It's not your fault, I know that. But

it is your fault if you don't do anything about it. You won't even see a therapist. And it could be even bigger than you think. Gerry says—"

"Mr. Homeland."

She had been mentioning some guy from a special division of Homeland Security. She seemed to think he was a fascinating son of a bitch.

"This is too upsetting," Cheryl said. "I have to go."

She stood up.

"Hey, wait a minute."

I grabbed her wrist and started to rise from my chair. She pulled away.

"Don't," she said. "It's hard enough."

She wouldn't meet my eyes. Then she was gone, walking out of the bar and my life. She was the only one I'd ever told about Charlie. I even showed her the scars like white worms on my body. Now I wished I hadn't. I sat back down. My hands were shaking. For hours I remained in that booth, smoking, drinking pints of Nitro Stout. The clatter and clamor of the bar jagged through me. The voices of people were like the barking and grunts of animals. I tried to fight this vision, but now I was fighting alone.

I had three days off and I spent them in my apartment. Charlie's .38 sat on the kitchen counter, a chrome-plated object of meditation. Chekhov said if you display a gun in the first act it had better go off by the third. My first act started right after Charlie's third concluded. I had curled fetally in the closet where he'd thrown me after the latest beating. There was the usual shouting and screaming, then the first shot, followed by ringing silence. The coats and sweaters hanging over me were like animal pelts in the dark. Charlie was a hunter and I'd once watched him clumsily skin out a doe. When I vomited he grabbed me by the back of the neck, furious, and pushed my face into the reeking pelt. That blood stench. Charlie's smell.

After the first shot he walked right up to the closet door in his heavy steel-toed factory boots. His breath was ragged. I waited, my knees drawn up, my chest aching. After a while he retreated back down the hall to the bedroom. A minute later there was a second discharge. I would have starved in that closet if a neighbor hadn't heard the shots and called the police. When they finally broke into our half of the duplex I wouldn't come out. They had to drag me from the closet. I was nine. In a way I never did come out.

There had been a note, in Charlie's crooked scrawl: No choice. I spent the rest of my life pretending there were choices. Just to show him. But maybe there weren't after all. Maybe the self-determined life was as illusory as THE EXHIBITIONIST.

Sunday night I drank the last Red Hook in my refrigerator, plugged a cigarette in my mouth, grabbed a lighter, and headed out for a smoke. I didn't even know what time it was.

I was on the second floor at the end of the hall, next to a door that led to the open back stairs above the trash dumpsters. The apartment across the hall was empty and in the early stages of renovation. THE MANAGER was doing the work himself. Slowly. I suspected him of dragging out the job so he would have an excuse to hang around my floor.

The door to the empty apartment opened, but it wasn't THE MANAGER. The weird girl I'd met the night of my play's opening stepped out. She had changed to Levi's and a white blouse, and she had a plastic trash bag in her right hand. I stared at her as I would a horned Cyclops.

"Hi, Joe."

I took the unlit cigarette out of my mouth.

"It's Nichole, right?"

"Right. I'm always surprising you, aren't I."

"Uh huh."

"Well this should really surprise you. We're neighbors!"

Behind her I could see the vacant apartment. THE MANAGER had been doing some drywall work. Powdery white dust lay in a drift across the hardwood floor. Nichole pulled the door shut. The rational world shifted under my feet. I mean it shifted more.

She followed me outside with her little trash bag. Was it a prop? From the landing the moon was big and white among carbon paper clouds. Pretty in a Hallmark way. The landing and stairs were liberally spattered with pigeon shit, however. I lit up, inhaled, blew smoke out the side of my mouth.

"It's nice here," Nichole said.

"Delightful. Don't you miss the moon?"

"It's right up there." She smiled. "Come over some time, neighbor. We'll have an ice cream cone and chat."

"That apartment's empty."

"Only if you think it is," she said, and winked.

I watched her go down the stairs, drop her trash in the dumpster and proceed into the night. MOON GIRL. Nichole. I finished my cigarette.

I worked part time in a warehouse belonging to the Boeing Company. The Homeland boys picked me up in the parking lot. Two men in dark suits with those American flag lapel pins stepped toward me, one on each side.

"Joseph Skadan?"

"Yeah."

"Federal Agents." They flashed their credentials. "We have to ask you to come with us."

"You're asking?"

The one who had spoken smiled without parting his lips.

"No choice, I'm afraid."

First it was like a job interview. I sat across from a woman of middle years. She wore a pearl gray suit and glasses with red frames and what looked like a lacquered chopstick stabbed through the hair bun at the back of her head. In between questions and answers I entertained a fantasy about grabbing that chopstick and busting out of the Federal Building, Matt Damon-Bourne style.

Her questions turned strange and personal, and I knew I was being given a psych evaluation. I began to guard my responses. Which was pointless. Those tests anticipate and integrate prevarication. She asked about dreams. I made one up about a three-legged dog but kept the recurring one about my mother's birch to myself.

Finally CHOPSTICK LADY (keep objectifying everyone and pretty soon it will be safe to start shooting) put her pad down and folded her hands over it.

"Mr. Skadan, I'd like you to sign an authorization paper. You aren't obligated to sign it, of course. You are not under arrest or accused of a crime. But it is in your best interests to sign—and, I might add, the best interests of the United States, and perhaps the world community."

"If I'm not under arrest, why did I have to come here?"

"You're being detained."

"What's the difference?"

"A matter of degree and duration."

She removed a document from her briefcase and pushed it across the table.

"This authorizes us to subject you to a technique called borderlanding."

"I need a cigarette."

She shook her head. "I'm sorry."

"What's borderlanding?"

"A variation on sleep deprivation methods used to extract information from enemy combatants. Of course, for borderlanding purposes it's been modified. The object is to produce a state of borderland consciousness without the use of drugs."

While she spoke I scanned the document.

"But I don't have any information," I said.

"Borderlanding isn't to extract information, Mr. Skadan; its purpose is to draw out the Harbinger we suspect may be hiding in your unconscious mind."

"Come on."

"I am perfectly serious."

"What if I don't sign?"

"After a couple of days of close observation you will be free to go. But under provisions of the Modified Patriot Act the proper government agency will keep you under surveillance for an indefinite period of time. And of course your employer will be notified."

I signed.

They kept me in a room with a table and a couple of hard chairs. My head was rigged with a Medusa's tangle of wires. The wires ran into a junction box that fed data to a lab monitor somewhere. The light was bright and never went off. If I started to drift, loud music blasted into the room, or somebody came and pestered me.

"How are we doing, Joe?" a baldish guy with a corporate look asked me. His security badge identified him as Gerry Holdstock. Gerry.

"I'd like a cigarette is all."

"It's a non-smoking building, sorry. I want you to know we appreciate your cooperation. Borderlanding is the most promising method we've yet devised for isolating these anomalies. I do understand it's uncomfortable for you."

"I don't believe in Harbingers," I said, rubbing my eyes. I'd been awake for two days.

Gerry smiled.

"Which is part of the problem with outing them," he said.

"How many have you outed so far?"

"That's classified. Joe, let me ask you a question." He leaned over me, one hand flat on the table and the other on the back of my chair. His breath smelled like wintergreen. "Do you have any idea how many people have disappeared without a trace since the Harbinger Event?"

"How many?"

"I can't tell you. But it's more than you think."

"Well, *I* haven't disappeared."

"Not yet. But you've been identified as a potential MP. We've discerned a pattern in these disappearances. The first to go are marginal types on society's fringes, the mentally ill, disaffected artists, failed writers. One will vanish from the face of the Earth, followed by mass vanishings of normal people. We have a computer model. And consider this. If you *do* disappear, you might be missed by friends and relatives (his tone indicated that he doubted it), but your absence would be absorbable without ripples of any consequence. Now imagine if someone important disappeared. Imagine if the *President of the United States* disappeared."

"A disaster," I said. "By the way who identified me as a potential?"

"I'm afraid that's privileged information."

"Whatever."

Gerry patted my shoulder

"Hang in there."

*

I didn't know about Harbingers, but if they wanted a zombie they wouldn't have long to wait. My head dropped. Audioslave blasted on the speakers. It didn't matter; I felt myself slipping away. Then the music stopped. Sensing someone present, I managed to raise my head. The door remained shut, but Nichole was standing in front of it.

"Hello, Joe. Want to go for a walk with me?"

"Too tired."

"You're not tired at all."

She was right. There was a moment when I felt like I was supposed to be tired, exhausted to the point of collapse. It was almost a guilty feeling, like I was getting away with something. Nichole crossed the room and stood beside me, offering her hand.

"Ready?"

The corridor was deserted. We entered an elevator. There were only two buttons, both unmarked. Up and Down? Nichole pushed the bottom one.

"Where are we going?"

"Someplace safer to talk," she said.

After a moment the doors slid open. Beyond was a parking lot and a burger joint, an Arctic Circle, with the big red, white, and blue sign and the chicken or whatever it was, the corporate mascot. I recognized it because I'd seen a run-down version of it once on a road trip to Spokane. My mother had pointed it out. It was just like the one she used to work in. "Better than McDonald's and the best soft ice cream!"

"What is this," I said.

"A safer place. Come on."

Nichole pulled me across the parking lot, my shoes scuffing the asphalt. It was night. A few cars of 60s and 70s vintage gleamed under bright moonlight. Too bright, really. The moon was at least twice its normal size, bone white, so close I could discern topographical detail. India ink shadows poured over crater rims. There was a pinhead of color in the Sea of Tranquility. I looked back but the elevator, not to mention the Federal Building, was gone. We entered the shiny quiet of the empty restaurant and sat in a booth.

"Who *are* you?" I said.

"A girl named Nichole."

"How do you pull off all these tricks?"

I reflexively patted my breast pocket, knowing there were no cigarettes there. But I felt a pack, pulled it out, and looked at it. Camel Filters, half empty, with a book of matches tucked into the cellophane sleeve.

"You did that one," Nichole said.

"What one?"

"The cigarettes are one of your tricks. I don't smoke."

I twisored one out and lit up.

"This place is one of your 'tricks,' too. You've never had a safe place, Joe, so you borrowed one of your mother's. I've been borrowing it, too, to help me understand you better. We haven't much time, so I'm going to give you the *Reader's Digest* version of what's going on."

I held hot smoke in my lungs then released it slowly.

"Go ahead."

"Okay. They got it wrong. Earth is the center of the universe. At least the self-aware consciousness that has evolved there informs the emerging pan-universal consciousness. Now think of an egg timer."

She picked one up that may or may not have been sitting next to the napkin dispenser a moment before. She cranked it slightly and set it down ticking.

"Transphysical ego-consciousness is the egg," she said.

I regarded my Camel. My mind felt uncharacteristically sharp, lucid, but I knew it was unraveling in delusion.

Nichole said, "The timer started when the first inklings of self-awareness appeared. And at a certain moment—"

The timer went *ding!*

"—the tipping point of human evolutionary consciousness arrives. A handful of individuals are on the leading edge. I'm one. You're another. It's pretty random as far as I can tell."

There was a sound in the kitchen, like someone moving around. We both looked toward the service window behind the counter, but it was dark back there, and quiet again.

"So," I said, "who are the Harbingers supposed to be then? Not that I believe in them, or you, or any of this."

She smiled.

"They're definitely not alien invaders. In fact they might be us, some unconscious projection of our desire toward growth and freedom. Or maybe they are a transdimensional race with a vested interest in seeing us successfully evolve forward. It isn't a foregone conclusion that we make it, you know."

"Isn't it."

"Are you okay, Joe?"

I looked at her through a veil of blue smoke. Past my personal tipping point, likely.

"If we fail to advance," she said, "so does the conscious universe. Everything stagnates and begins a long devolution into separate numbered worlds of barbarism. The long decline."

In the kitchen a utensil clattered to the floor. Nichole said, "Uh oh."

I started to stand but she shook her head.

"What?" I said. "I thought you said this place was safe."

"Safe-er."

I rubbed my eyes.

"You're on the brink," she said, "but if you let your fears and neuroses and paranoia dominate, you could create a Dark World that will pull in weaker egos. That's why this is so important."

I made a sketchy pass with my cigarette. "Draw them into the great sucking pit of my neuroses."

"It's happened so many times already, Joe. We only need a handful to swing the balance toward positive evolution."

"How many have you got so far?"

"One, counting me."

I laughed. She did, too. We were down the rabbit hole together, if she even existed.

"Would it be so bad to believe me, Joe? To believe *in* me? At least consider the possibility. Thousands have disappeared into the Dark Worlds of a few. I need you to help me counterbalance things. You're lucky. It's a choice you get to make."

"Order up!" somebody yelled. That voice.

I stood up facing the kitchen. Suddenly I was cold. Fluorescent lights began to flicker and a scarecrow shape stuttered into view.

"Sorry, Joe," Nichole said, and she *pushed* hard at the base of my skull, a sharp locus of pain. I faltered, reached back, and found myself sitting on a hard chair in the interrogation room. I blinked, my head still aching. The door opened and Gerry walked through with a lab tech in blue scrubs.

"Was I asleep?" I said, my voice like a toad's croak.

"Just drifting, Joe."

The tech delicately removed the skull patches. I looked at Gerry. "I'm done?"

"Three days. It's as far as we can go under the current charter."

"What'd you find?"

"Nada."

I slouched up Broadway in hazy sunlight, exhausted. Back in the numbered world. My eyes felt grainy and my head pounded. As I attempted to go around HOMELESS VET he grabbed my ankle.

"I served my country!"

"I'm broke," I said.

"Come on, Joey. The End is near, give me some change."

His voice had altered, and the bones of his face under the beard.

Paul Newman eyes.

I fled.

My apartment was dark. I racked up the shades. Daylight penetrated feebly through the dusty pane. I picked up the phone, dialed Cheryl's number. Because she was the only person who *knew* me and I was afraid. The only real person. It rang three times before I hung up. I couldn't reach out to her, not through the fog of betrayal. I just couldn't.

The light grew dimmer. Perhaps a cloud had passed before the sun. I contemplated the cheap automatic, a big change hurtling toward me. It wasn't about wanting it or not wanting it. Perhaps it spun forth from my own spider-gut psyche.

I removed my shoes and socks and lay down on my bed. Time passed but I didn't sleep. The room darkened into night. There was a rustling sound. I opened my eyes. Mom's birch stood at the foot of the bed, 2001 obelisk style. I clicked on the lamp and sat up, then knelt on the mattress and reached out. Okay, a dream. My fingers touched the white skin. My thumbnail dug in, making an oozing green crescent. I pulled a ribbon of bark away, and my mind flooded with a child's innocent expectations. I crushed them before they could hurt me.

Sirens wailed on Broadway. I grabbed the pack of cigarettes off the bedside table and lit up. Go away, I said to the tree. It didn't. I swung off the mattress and went around to the foot of the bed. The roots were like long bony fingers melded into the floor. The only important philosophical question is whether or not to lose your mind.

THE EXHIBITIONIST sat on *her* bed with her head between her knees, hair straggling down. It looked like an orange prescription bottle on the mattress beside her, but it was so far away I couldn't be certain. I was seeing her with normal vision now; she had emerged into objective reality, or objective reality had warped and enclosed us both.

The .38 was in my hand before I was aware of reaching for it. The only important philosophical question is what took you so long. In my bedroom Mom's tree wilted. The leaves drooped, some had gone brown and crisp around the edges.

I left my apartment. The door across the hall stood open a crack. You always get a choice, even at the end of things. To give him belated credit, Charlie had chosen not to shoot into the closet. I pushed the door inward on the empty apartment. A peculiar cold light shone out of the kitchen, glaring on a drift of dust.

I heard a sound and looked to my left. THE MANAGER stood at the end of the hall, frozen, with a fistful of keys. Probably it was the gun that froze him. I should have put it down before coming out.

"You better leave," I said, frightened for him.

"I don't think so, kid."

When did the keys turn into a belt? The buckle gleamed dully. "You aren't there," I said, and crossed into the empty apartment. The light drew me to the kitchen. My feet were bare. The dust was hot and had the texture of talcum powder. The dust and the peculiar light came from the open refrigerator, which was empty and *deep*, a Narnia passage to a brilliant desert landscape under a black sky.

I sat on a kitchen chair to finish my cigarette. Heavy boot treads approached out in the hall. The leather belt whip-cracked. Okay, Charlie. I gripped the gun tighter. But who knew what would come through the door? A figment, a neurotic fear, a fat apartment manager in the wrong place at the wrong time. *I smell smoke*, my stepfather's voice said outside the empty apartment or inside my head. *And where there's smoke there's fire.*

The cigarette dropped from my lips. I raised the gun. But as he came through the door, a shifting thing, I turned away from him and lurched into the Narnia passage. It was narrow as a closet. At first the way was clear. But as I hunched forward my progress became impeded by hanging pelts thick with the stench of old blood. I shoved through them now, crying, and at last came into the open.

The Earth was a big blue and white bowling ball, just like all the astronauts used to say. I strolled barefoot in the hot regolith and dropped the gun, which was no longer heavy. She was waiting for me at the Arctic Circle, just a girl named Nichole. Delusions are like mosaics assembled from the buckle-shattered pieces of your mind. A tree, a restaurant, a dreaming sky, the pretty girl you never knew.

"Okay," I said. "I'm here."

Nichole smiled. "Good. We have a lot of work to do."

She was right about that.

Rewind

I was reaching for my pint glass of Red Hook when the first explosion ripped through the beer garden. My fingertips had just touched the glass. In an instant the world was reorganized. Only it didn't have much to do with organization, come to think of it. The table I'd been sitting in front of was now sitting on top of me. Of course, it may not have been the same table. Debris lay scattered around. Some of it was human debris. The right side of my face felt scorched. It couldn't have been the fire, because that hadn't started yet. That came with explosion number two.

I lay there, rattled. People were moaning and crying, some were screaming. I heard it all through wads of cotton cranked into my ears. And of course the bells. I could still feel the cold, moisture-filmed glass on my fingertips. I concentrated on that and on the moments preceding as my hand reached for the glass of red-tinted beer, but this time I cut off the explosion and let my hand grip the pint glass and raise it to my lips, tasted the fruity Red Hook slide over my tongue. For several moments I existed in two realities, it seemed. In the first I'd just been blown out of my chair, in the second my consciousness meandered forward uninterrupted by horror.

I'd been thinking about that beer for quite a while as I wandered the Pike Place Market Fair. It was a warm May afternoon in Seattle, around eighty degrees. When I came upon a large grouping of tables under white umbrellas and enclosed by a low fence, I turned in and looked for a seat. The beer garden was crowded. There was a street musician in a straw hat playing pretty good acoustic guitar on a stage a dozen yards from the fenced-in area. I spotted a table with an empty seat. A young woman with short, dark hair and lavender sunglasses sat by herself. I asked if I could take the empty seat, and she nodded with one of those neutral smiles you give strangers whom you don't wish to encourage. I took the chair and hitched it back to let her know that I wasn't there to hit on her. Then I ordered my Red Hook, it arrived, I reached for it . . . and ka BOOM! My illusion of duel realities collapsed.

The young woman was sitting on the ground holding her head, her sunglasses crooked on her nose. Her eyes looked frightened but rational. They were big, brown Audrey Hepburn eyes occupying a plain face, and she turned them to me and we held each other's gaze. I shoved the table off, stood up, and went to her.

"Are you all right?" I asked, my voice muffled in my ringing ears. She nodded. I extended my hand, she grasped it, and I pulled her to her feet. That's when the second explosion went off. The concussion shuddered through my body, staggering me sideways. It did something worse to the young woman with the brown eyes. It sent a hunk of white metal spinning into her waist, almost ripping her in half. I saw it in slow motion as the world tilted drunkenly and I fell, a hot, violent odor blowing over me, and then I saw red flames devour the blue, blue sky.

A mild concussion, two cracked ribs, a wicked abrasion on my right cheek (this is what felt "scorched" immediately after the first explosion), a fractured middle toe. Sundry cuts, scrapes, contusions, etc. Two days in a Group Health hospital. I walked out of there with Frankenstein stitches and a limp, glad to be alive but with a depressed feeling clinging to me like a low-grade fever.

My best friend picked me up in his sixty's era Volkswagen Beetle. I liked to think of Sean as a practical poet. He was twenty-three years old, sported a soul patch on his chin, and round steel frame glasses. He had found the frames in a Wallingford antique store and had his prescription fitted to them. He liked to write poems in coffee houses on the Ave, scratching them out with the nib of a black ink fountain pen, filling small notebooks. All of which should have added up to capital A affectation. But somehow with Sean it didn't. He was a good guy, a good listening ear. He was also one of those perpetual students who manipulate majors and minors with the finesse of a concert pianist. That was his practical side. I was already a year out of University and coping, after a fashion, with real life. In other words I was under-employed as a record store clerk and spent my evenings trying to tweak my resume into something irresistible.

"You've got the look," Sean said as we pulled away from the hospital with a lawn mower whine of the VW's engine.

"Which look is that?"

"The look of someone who's been blown up. The look of bells ringing in your ears. Well, buddy, they didn't toll for thee, so come back to planet Earth and I'll buy you a beer."

"Bells I could live with."

"What *can't* you live with?"

"Forget it."

"I would," Sean said, "but forgetting things isn't so easy nowadays. You want to go to Dante's? I'm buying."

I stared out the window, feeling a bit unreal. "Thanks, but I really just want to go home."

"If you're turning down free beer then the center really will *not* hold," Sean said. And then, with uncharacteristic bitterness: "Fuck Jihad."

In my apartment I made coffee and sat out on the postage stamp-sized sun porch with my feet on the rail and *Details Of A Sunset And Other Stories* tented open, unread, on my lap. Three floors down some guy was washing his car and he had the radio up loud, tuned to an alternative rock station. My ribs hurt every time I breathed. My toe hurt whether I breathed or not. I began playing a game we've all played, the game of WHAT IF, the game of IF ONLY.

The young woman's name had been Janice Burnley. Her image haunted me. The girl with the Audrey Hepburn eyes, her goofy lavender glasses crooked on her face, her hand reaching out. I took it back a couple of minutes to her reserved smile and nod when I asked if I could share her table. I ran through it to the point at which I reached for my Red Hook Ale, but before my fingertips touched the cold glass I hesitated, and at that intersection in my reality rewind I seemed caught in a double suspended moment. The car radio below me swelled, faded, swelled again, faded out altogether, and there was guitar music coming from the street musician standing outside the beer garden.

I was there.

My table companion was watching the guitar player, her fingers tapping along. I stared at the line of her jaw, the way her hair spiked over the delicate shell of her ear, which looked fiercely pink in a cunning bar of sunlight that had penetrated the umbrella cover. Then the first bomb went off.

I shoved the table off me and bolted up, the blood and screaming all around, and I couldn't shut it out. Again the girl sat on the ground with no apparent injuries, even looking a little comical with her glasses cockeyed. I knew what was coming and I didn't wait for it to happen. I threw myself over Janice Burnley, knocking her flat just as the second explosion tore through.

"How are we doing today?" my morning nurse asked me.

"Okay. A little dreamy."

"Still dreamy?"

"Yeah."

The doctor came by and frowned at my chart for a while. He couldn't figure out the "dreamy" aspect of my recovery. Everything else looked good.

"I suppose it's just plain disorienting to get blown up," I said.

"It is definitely that," he said.

Dreamy. Not a big deal. On the first day of my second convalescence I had lain in my hospital bed and stared at the television set. All the colors sort of ran together, like one of those light boxes from the summer of love that was supposed to simulate an acid trip. The guy in the next bed held the remote. I said, "Why don't you change the channel?"

"You don't like Katie Couric?" He was in his fifties, with an equine face and a beach ball belly lifting the bed sheet.

"I like her fine."

"So?"

"So that isn't Katie Couric."

He squinted at the TV. "Yes, it is."

Gooey colors oozed over the screen. "Look at the picture," I said.

"I am looking at the picture."

"And you see Katie Couric?"

"No."

"Ha."

"I see Matt Whatshisface. Katie's not on right now."

"You don't see a bunch of weird colors?"

He shook his head, his lips pressed into a skeptical line. I let it drop. And I stopped looking at the set, because after a while the colors had a nauseating effect. It wasn't just the picture, either. The sound issuing from the speaker was nothing more articulate than a fly buzz that rose and fell with inflective randomness. When the nurse wandered in I asked her what was on the TV. My roommate gave me a sour look, and the nurse glanced up and said, "A dog food commercial."

"A dog food commercial," the man in the next bed said flatly.

I told the doctor about the TV. Soon enough we discovered it wasn't only the TV. Computer screens presented incomprehensible jigsaws patterns. My senses now scrambled everything that came filtered through electronic media. Even a voice modulated through the phone came to my eardrum like a mosquito whine.

I guess they gave me every test they could think of but it got them nowhere. I departed the hospital with little more than a fond hope that it would all "clear up."

It didn't.

"How do you explain that?" Sean asked me, looking every bit as skeptical as my former roommate with the beach ball belly. We were sitting at a window table in Bean There, a java joint on Forty-Fifth, a couple of miles from the UW.

"I think I got to rewind an event and play it different," I said, kind of making it up as I went.

"Yeah?"

"Yeah. Only in this new version I'm one half step removed. You know how when you see a computer screen or a TV screen in the background of a news shot or whatever? You know how you see this black bar scroll up the image?"

Sean nodded.

"Well, that's what I mean. I guess."

"Oh, now I understand perfectly."

"You're not trying."

"Give me some help."

"I'm like a second tier observer now," I said. "When I'm pointed at first tier reality, I can absorb it mostly okay, but second tier reality—electronic media, for instance—gets scrambled because I'm already a step away."

"I thought you said you were a half step away."

I sipped my latte and looked out the window at slow traffic. Sean tapped his pen on the table. "All right, all right," he said. "Sorry. It's just pretty farfetched."

"I know."

"Anyway, why do you get to rewind the event thing? No offense, but what makes you so special?"

"I don't know. Maybe I'm not the only one. Maybe there are others and we just don't know about it."

"It's never happened to me."

"A lot of things have never happened to you. That doesn't mean they don't happen to other people. And maybe after a while, the rewinder forgets that he ever did rewind."

"Perhaps."

"Yeah, perhaps."

Then Sean said, "Hey, I just remembered what makes you so special."

"Yeah?"

"You got blown up last month."

"True."

"But that's not all that happened. You also got to save somebody's life."

"On the rewind."

"Right, that's what I mean. You got to make a deliberate moral decision. You think it's BS, but I believe in the moral Universe, the moral God-consciousness. Maybe you're right about people, maybe a lot of people are getting to rewind. Maybe that's how God increases moral consciousness in the world, which equals love, which equals higher consciousness. God consciousness." Sean gripped his pen, looking pleased with himself.

"That's nice," I said, "but your theory falls apart, because I didn't make a moral decision. All I did was react, unaware of any personal consequences."

"So you wouldn't have saved her if you'd known you couldn't watch TV anymore?"

"Or hear a voice on a telephone, or work a computer, or lately even an electronic cash register? If I knew it would get worse, like it is getting worse? If I thought it would make me incapable of functioning in modern society? If I thought this mild background buzz might get louder and more insistent until I thought I would go out of my mind? I don't know, man. But I guess at that point it certainly would become a decision instead of a reaction."

"You're right," Sean said. "The theory doesn't hold water. But it's still cool, and I'm going to write a poem about it. I'm going to call it The Jihad Bomb Theory of Moral God-Consciousness."

"Do that," I said.

So I had to find out. Naturally I had to find out. There was a constant buzzing in my ears. I couldn't hear it much during the day, but in the stillness of the night it was insistent and distracting, robbing me of sleep. I thought maybe it had something to do with all the broadcast and microwave signals in the air. I sat on my sofa and began thinking about the beer garden, Janice Burnley, and the bombs.

Sean removed his little round poet's glasses and wiped the lenses on his T-shirt. Sunlight slanted though the window of Dante's, shining up the amber pints on the table before us. I was now living in a Universe where The Jihad Bomb Theory of Moral God-Consciousness did not as yet exist. Looking over Sean's shoulder I could see the Mariner's game on ESPN. I hadn't touched my beer yet. Sean listened to everything I told him. He's a good listener, but I can tell when he thinks I'm full of it. That didn't really matter, though. I just wanted to say it all out loud, as a way of organizing and understanding my thoughts, such as they were.

"So you went back to your apartment and rewound everything again?" he said. "Rewind is the right word?"

"Yeah. I found out I could do that."

"And this time you let things go back to the way they were originally?"

"Yes."

"The girl died. But you say she lived in your other version?"

"I let her die."

He frowned at me. "Cut it out."

"It's true."

"If you say so."

"I do say so. I watched it all again. I pulled her up, looked into her eyes, and then the second bomb went off and cut her in half."

"Okay, okay. Then what?"

"Then nothing. I'm here, all my senses intact, and the future looks promising."

"Except?"

"Except I let the girl die."

"So you said."

"It's a hell of a thing," I said. "For quite a while, during my latest convalescence, I ragged on myself for not checking her out last time, finding out all I could about her when I had the chance. Talk to her, at least."

"The girl with the Hepburn eyes."

"Yeah, Janice. Janice Burnley. Anyway, I wished I'd found out what kind of a person she was, whether she was—"

"A good person?"

"I don't know."

"Whether she kicks her dog, runs red lights, cheats on her boyfriend? Or volunteers at some retirement home and adopts stray cats?"

I shrugged. "Something like that, I guess. But then I figured it didn't matter. Because that's not part of the decision. It's whether or not I can do the right thing, and whether or not I even know what the right thing is. The point being, now I have a decision to make. A real decision."

"To rewind or not to rewind, that is the question."

I shaped my lips into a smile and nodded. "Yeah."

Throngs moved outside the window of this bar on the Ave. Normal people on their way through life. Maybe a certain percentage of them had rewound. Who knows? A scraggly man sat on the sidewalk across the street with a hand-lettered sign and a mangy dog curled beside him. He looked like one of those guys who hears things nobody else hears, maybe, who knows, a constant mosquito whine that has drilled into his brain until his thoughts have broken up and can never quite come together again.

"So if I play along," Sean said, "and assume all this wild shit is true, then what's next? What are you going to do?"

"That's a good question," I said, but I wasn't really there anymore. I could hear acoustic guitar music, and there was a young woman looking away from me, one young woman out of millions I would never know, and my hand reached out until my fingertips touched the cold, moisture-filmed glass of beer, and it all started again for the last time.

THE APPRENTICE

D anny St. Charles woke up every morning to the sound of his mother dying. Her violent coughing fits tore through the flimsy walls of their trailer. He was only eight but he knew it was the cigarettes. Hadn't he dreamed of his mother coughing until smoke seeped from her bleeding eyes? Hadn't he seen her, in his dream, reach down her throat to pull out a shred of tissue like peach pulp spotted black with rot?

One spring day Danny stayed home sick from school, and his mother stayed home from her job at the bakery to take care of him. As she leaned over him in his bed to delicately slip the glass thermometer from under his tongue, he tried to breathe her good smell and ignore the stale over-scent of smoke.

"You've got a fever, Honey-love."

"Can I go to school?"

"Nope."

"Awesome." School bored Danny; the work was easy but irrelevant, and he felt so different from the other kids. He would always be different.

"I'll 'awesome' *you*, buddy." She ruffled his hair and they smiled at each other. Later she fell asleep reading a magazine on the couch, so only Danny knew about the cat. He possessed a vague sense of all the animals in the trailer village and a few, mostly the domesticated cats and dogs, he could reach out to at any given moment and know their mood. Sometimes if they were distressed or in pain he heard them cry inside his head. Amber, the MacClosky's tabby, did more than cry. Danny felt her pain like a tin jag stitching through his stomach. He dropped his Superman comic and bent over in empathetic pain. It passed in a moment, leaving him with the sick feeling his mild fever had failed to inflict upon him.

Danny got out of bed, dressed, and put on his coat. As he crept by his sleeping mother he passed through her aura of yellow anxiety. She was worried about money, about missing a day of work. He left the trailer with a slight sense of guilt. He was sick enough to skip school but not too sick to find out what happened to Amber.

A pair of black skid marks slashed across the narrow street a block away. Amber lay smashed against the curb, purple insides erupting out of her yellow fur. When Danny saw the Old Woman approaching he withdrew behind a parked truck and crouched low, watching underneath the chassis. The Old Woman walked slowly, as if in pain. He had never seen her before but as she came nearer the short hairs stirred on the back of his neck. She stopped and looked down at the cat for a moment, then she reached into a cloth bag slung over her shoulder and took out a Popsicle stick and what looked like a spice jar. Lowering herself with evident strain to one knee, she scraped something into the spice jar then capped it, giving the lid a good, hard twist. And then she turned her head sideways and looked straight at Danny under the truck. Her left eye was milky white, with the bare shadow of a pupil. That whole side of her face sagged, her cheek like a wrinkled pouch, the left side of her mouth twisted into a permanent frown. After a moment she stood slowly and Danny did the same, as if compelled by her magnetic gaze.

"Cat's blood," she said, shaking the little spice jar. "Very good. But you must collect it while it's fresh."

Danny, stepping cautiously out from behind the truck, said, "What's it good for?"

"Cures, mostly."

"Like when you're sick?"

The Old Woman nodded. "How old are you Danny?"

He told her eight. It wasn't until later that he wondered how she knew his name.

"Had the chicken pox or measles yet?"

"No," he said. "I mean, I had the measles but not the chicken pox."

"If you get them I'll cure you," the Old Woman said.

"Okay," Danny said, believing absolutely that she could do what she said.

Her good eye held him, the pupil a shiny marble as black as the other eye was white.

"We're two of a kind, aren't we, Danny?" she said.

"I don't know."

"Trust me, boy. Now come, follow. I'll show you things."

She turned deliberately away and began to shuffle off. Danny felt powerfully compelled to go after her. Only the thought of his mother waking to discover him gone prevented him from trotting behind the Old Woman like an obedient puppy. Even so, he found he could not easily turn his gaze aside; he had to back off, tripping over the curb, stumbling. His fever seemed to gain intensity. Beads of sweat popped out on his forehead. The woman halted and looked over her bony shoulder at him, her black eye widening in surprise.

"My, you're a strong one, aren't you," she said.

At which point Danny wrenched himself free and ran home.

Later his mind sought in vein for the Old Woman. She *did* know him. She knew him in a way that even his mother could not. Danny was certain of this. The word "witch" recurred in his thoughts. It wasn't the true, exact name for her, but it was as close as he could come. Her eyes inhabited his dreams, but awake he could not find her.

The next day he went to school, and on his way home after getting off the bus he wandered an unaccustomed route through the sprawling trailer park. The spring air was sharp and clear. But Danny was barely aware of his surroundings. He looked down as he walked, following some inexplicable inner directive. Suddenly the Old Woman spoke to him and he raised his head sharply.

"Why so glum?" she said. "Never mind. I know." She was sitting in a kitchen chair, leaning back against the side of a yellow doublewide on the chair's back legs. The toes of her boots pointed down. The shadow of her dangling feet and chair swayed out across the aluminum siding.

"You made me come," Danny said, understanding the truth of the statement as soon as he spoke the words.

"There aren't any coincidences," the Old Woman said. "I thought I'd come to this miserable place to die. Instead I cast the bones and saw a boy. You."

He squinted. "Do you know me?" he said.

"In a way, boy." She regarded him down the long, white slope of her nose and then abruptly bent forward, bringing the front legs of the chair down with a sharp little crack on the bare cement porch. Danny flinched back. The Old Woman leaned at him, her elbows propped on her skinny thighs. Her black skirt, sagging between her legs like a sling, held a wooden box. Her hungry, black eye and dead, white eye seemed to enlarge before him and ascend beyond his mortal vision to hang suspended like twin-opposite moons. She was speaking to him but he could barely hear her. Then she sat back and the moons were only eyes again.

"What . . . ?" Danny said, blinking.

"I said you're perfectly right. About your mother."

"My mother?"

"You could fix it," the Old Woman said. "The cancer. I could give you something."

Danny had trouble with his breathing. "You mean like the cat's blood?"

"More powerful than cat's blood. But you would have to do it all yourself—and do it just right or it wouldn't work. You can follow instructions, can't you, boy?"

"Sure, I guess."

The Old Woman lifted the box from the sling of her skirt. It was about a foot long and less than half as wide. The wood was shiny and scratched. There was an eye carved into the lid. The upper and lower arcs of the eye were formed by two snakes eating each other's tails. She opened the hinged lid so Danny could see the snake eye but not the contents of the box. After rooting about for a minute with a bony index finger the Old Woman said, "Ah," and picked out a silver needle.

"Take this," she said. "Prick your finger with it. The tip must be wet with your own blood. Then prick one of her cigarettes. Make certain she smokes it within the hour."

Danny held the needle up in the sunlight, making it flash.

"What will happen?"

"I told you."

"But how?"

"If you don't want it . . ." She started to reach for the needle but he snatched it away.

"Good," she said, smiling. "This will bind us. Now go away and do as I told you. Show me how obedient you can be. If you want your mother to live, that is."

Danny's gaze shifted to the box, still open in the Old Woman's hands. She slapped the lid down and glared hard at him with her moon eyes.

"*Scat!*" she said, and he did.

He watched his mother from the kitchen window. She was hanging sheets on the clothesline in the cramped backyard; the dryer had broken a month ago and they couldn't afford to have it fixed. The breeze billowed the damp, white sheets around her like angel wings.

Her purse sat open on the table, the red and white pack of Marlboros plainly visible. He grabbed them, the cellophane overwrap crinkling softly in his hand. This was her second pack of the day and only a couple of cigarettes were missing. He slid one part way out, put the pack down, then produced the Old Woman's needle from his coat pocket. Biting his lip he braced his left thumb against the middle knuckle of his left index finger and after the briefest hesitation he poked at the bulging end of his thumb with the point of the needle. It stung. A shiny drop of blood swelled out. A smear of it glistened on the silver needle. He corked the punctured thumb into his mouth and sucked hard. Then he quickly inserted the needle into the protruding cigarette, giving it a little twist in the dry paper cylinder just in front of the filter.

A minute later when his mother came into the kitchen the Marlboro pack was lying on top of the contents of her open purse again, the magicked cigarette poking out like in a magazine ad. She chose it immediately, without a second glance, and lit up. She was thin, her face lined and careworn and beautiful.

"Good day at school?" she said.

"Yeah, sure."

She kissed him and tousled his hair before she sat down with the remnants of Sunday's paper. It usually took her about a week to finish the big Sunday edition. She sat forward, her right elbow on the table, the cigarette cocked between the first two fingers of her right hand, pale smoke twinning to the nicotine-stained ceiling. After a minute or so she looked up, just with her eyes.

"What are you staring at, Honey-love?"

Danny shrugged. "Nothing."

"Finish your homework?"

"No, I just got home."

She lifted an eloquent eyebrow. Danny retrieved the snack of sliced apples (slightly brown from sitting out), crackers, and American cheese she had left for him on the counter next to the sink. He started for his room and the small school desk she had bought for him at a yard sale. This was the routine. As in: "You know the routine, bub." Sometimes, like now, she didn't even have to say it. But he paused on his way out of the kitchen to look at her again. She raised her other eyebrow.

"I love you, Mom." The words squeaked out around the hard lump in his throat.

"Well, ditto, doll. Now hit the books and make me proud. Danny? We'll talk when you're done, okay?"

"Sure, Mom."

In his room he tried to concentrate on his math worksheet but the numbers looked like little people all twisted into suffering contortions. He put his pencil down and picked up the needle. This was his real lesson, the first one of his life. And the Old Woman was his teacher. Just touching the needle, now that he had used it, brought him into sympathy with the Old Woman's secret life. He knew her name, though that was not important. He knew she was a very wicked person. And he also saw her as a child, no older than himself, discovering her abilities and immediately using them in evil ways. She had taken lives, beginning with her own father's. Perhaps he had deserved it. Danny saw his face bloated with blood and rage. He struck with his hands, his belt, even a stout piece of stove wood. But his death had been the beginning of a long corruption for the Old Woman. She, too, had teachers: a gypsy woman in the apartment complex she and her mother moved to; a boyfriend, when she was fifteen, who stuck needles of a different sort into his arms and whom she murdered for the snake-eye box; a few others down the years. And now she was weakened, felled by a bright bursting in her brain. She had come here to the trailer village to live with a nephew whom she hated and very much wanted to destroy. She needed his help for that, Danny's. Her apprentice. His fresh innocent power. The nephew was like her father had been, hitting, pushing, hurting . . .

Danny dropped the needle and bolted from his chair when his mother began coughing and choking in the other room.

He discovered her folded almost double in her chair, hacking, gagging up phlegm from deep in her chest. The cigarette lay on the yellow Linoleum, a pale thread curling from its ashy tip.

Danny stood paralyzed in the doorway. This was different from any time before. The whole trailer seemed to shudder with the sound of his mother tearing her lungs out. She hawked with a terrible ripping sound and spat a gob of black phlegm onto the floor.

Danny shivered, thinking he had made a terrible mistake.

Then she sat up in her chair, her eyes red and bleary, her face pale as curds. Her lips trembled as if she wanted to say something. Suddenly her eyes rolled up white, quivering. Dark gray smoke seeped heavily from her mouth and nostrils, formed a dense little cloud and drifted sluggishly out the window.

His mother swayed forward and caught herself on the edge of the table, blinking and shaking her head like someone emerging from a trance.

"Mom?"

"God," she said. "I'll never light up again."

She noticed the burning Marlboro on the floor and flattened it under her shoe like a cockroach.

On his way to school the next morning the Old Woman stopped him.

"You can climb a tree, I guess," she said.

He nodded.

"Then climb one for me."

He followed her to the yellow doublewide with the cracked cement porch. He went under his own power. Already he was stronger than the Old Woman's ability to compel him. She grabbed him roughly by the arm and he let her drag him around behind the trailer. She pointed up at the branches of a flowering cherry tree. What looked like a clot of tar was hung up in the branches.

"Get that down for me. I need it."

Danny didn't move.

"Do it, boy. Or I'll see that it goes back where it came from."

He doubted she could actually do that. Her powers were weak; that's why she needed him to be her apprentice (slave?). But he wasn't certain. She *might* have enough wickedness in her to do as she threatened. Thinking of it, Danny felt hot and cold at the same time. He slipped his backpack off and reached for one of the lower branches. She stopped him, clawing her ugly gnarled fingers into his arm again.

"You'll need these."

She handed him a bag and a pair of crudely stitched gloves. They felt terrible, like dry skin, and he tried to give them back. She wouldn't take them.

"Go on," she said, leaning into him, fixing him with her black moon eye.

Danny tucked the gloves and skin bag under his belt and started to climb, hauling himself nimbly up the living cherry-scented limbs. He halted within grasping distance of the black thing.

"Good, good," the Old Woman muttered below him.

No, he thought, it's very bad.

"Go on," the Old Woman said. "What are you waiting for?"

The pink blossoms trembled all around him. What did they want him to do? He couldn't let it go back where it came from. This had been the first morning in his memory that he hadn't woken to the wet ripping coughs of his mother, not found her at the kitchen table with black coffee and cigarettes and smoke wreathing her like a ghostly shroud in the making.

Danny tugged the gloves and skin bag from his belt. The feel of them was repellent and before he could stop himself he cast them away. The breeze rippled approvingly through the pink blossoms.

"Idiot!" the Old Woman croaked.

"What do you want it for?" Danny asked.

"It's a cowl," she replied, spitting like a cat, "if that's any of your business. And it's for someone who deserves it. Now bring it to me. Use your bare hands, you little beast."

She wanted it for the nephew, Danny understood—the one who yelled and hit like her father used to.

He reached with his bare hand, a new strength within him mastering his fear. Inside the tar-thing a vague iridescence glimmered. Pinching his fingertips on a fold of the thing he tugged it loose, light as a silk handkerchief. A mummified bird that had been trapped under it fell to the ground, startling Danny so much he almost fell after it.

"Bring it to me, boy."

The tar-thing had begun to drift around his hand, clinging hungrily. It was a cowl and it was meant for someone who deserved it. The Old Woman had been right about that. There were no coincidences. Her life had directed her to him; she was to be his teacher.

Danny snapped his wrist sharply, flinging the thing down and away. It found the Old Woman's upturned face and molded itself there like a damp cobweb. Her mouth stretched wide in silent protest, and the silky thing sucked down her throat like a bat into its secret hole. She collapsed.

Now I'm like her, Danny thought, his eyes filling. But he knew it didn't have to be that way.

He climbed down through the cherry blossoms and dropped lightly to the ground next to the Old Woman's body. He had little time and there were things he must do. His mom would be mad that he missed the school bus but that couldn't be helped.

The back door of the yellow trailer was unlocked. It smelled bad inside. Tiny flies hovered around the piled dishes on the kitchen counter. Under the sink Danny found the Playtex gloves he'd hoped would be there. He put them on. They were way too big for his boy's hands, but he didn't want to touch the horrible skin gloves and bag again with his bare fingers.

It took only a short time to bury them under the cherry tree. The tree didn't mind; it was a good place and over time the skin gloves and bag would return to their useful elements.

He went back inside one more time. The room where the Old Woman had slept was the worst room of all, even though it didn't smell of stale beer and sweaty misery like the rest of the trailer. The window was covered over with black poster board.

There were candles all around, and the empty light in the ceiling watched him like a skull's vacant socket.

He found the box wrapped in a blanket on a shelf in the closet. Two snakes forming a mystic eye. Snakes didn't always have to be bad. When Danny was four he had been friends with a garter snake he discovered living in his backyard.

Outside he tucked the box in his backpack and shrugged the straps over his shoulders. Snakes didn't have to be bad and neither did he. Pausing a moment, he looked at the Old Woman. He knew she had been wicked but he also knew that after a while people couldn't really help what they were. He scooped up a double handful of pink cherry blossoms and sprinkled them over the Old Woman's face to help gentle her into death.

Then he ran all the way home and when he got there he told his mother that he'd missed the bus.

Everyone Bleeds
Through

A Denny's at two o'clock in the morning. I tried to contract my world down to a cup of coffee. Stirring in the cream and sugar, focusing on the cup, I was more or less successful at not thinking about Marci back in that hotel room in Seattle. More or less. Okay, less. But past experience suggested it would get easier.

Then a girl-voice said: "Hey, fuck *you!*"

Not to me.

I turned. So did the trucker in a red baseball cap sharing my counter space, and a booth of high school boys.

The "Fuck *you!*" girl was outside, yelling at the taillights of a black F-250, the reflectorized Oregon plate flashing when the pickup jolted over a flowerbed on its way out of the parking lot, too fast. The booth kids laughed. Red cap, laconic as hell, turned back to his eggs and *USA Today*.

The girl came in, shouldering through the glass door, fumbling a cigarette. Black leather bomber jacket, a mini, net stockings with stretchy Swiss cheese tears revealing very white thighs, ankle boots. Pixie hair. Too much make-up, and it was streaking around the eyes. A safety pin pierced her right eyebrow. She noticed me staring and stared back, briefly, something hot and mysterious clicking between us. Then she looked away and grabbed a book of matches out of the basket by the cash register.

She sat at the counter, leaving one stool between us. Ordered coffee, lit her cigarette, tapped bitten nails.

"What's your name?" she said to me.

"John."

She breathed smoke. "I'm Rena."

"Hi."

"I need a ride," Rena said.

"Hmm."

"Over the pass," Rena said.

"I'm not going that way, sorry."

Without another word to me, she swiveled around and said to the trucker: "I need a ride."

He was going that way.

A short time later he got up to use the bathroom. I felt the girl looking at me, so I looked back. Her face was too pale, shiny damp, the eyes bright in their rings of smudgy black liner.

"I'm Rena," she said in a dreamy-drugged voice.

"Yep."

"I want you to drive me. I don't like that guy. Dale or whatever-thefuck."

"I'm not going over the pass."

She wavered, and I thought she was about to faint. "Fuck me," she said, slid off the stool and stumbled to the bathroom.

A minute later the trucker reappeared. He looked around then asked me where the girl went. I told him. He paid his check, waited, got cranky, asked was I sure, waited some more. He was forty or so, thick through the shoulders, heavy-bellied. Still waiting, he splintered a toothpick digging between his molars.

I said, "She was sick."

Dale or whateverthefuck scowled. "Sick?"

"Yep."

"How sick?"

I pointed a finger down my throat.

"Screw it," Dale said. He glanced in the direction of the lady's room then quickly rolled his newspaper tight under his arm and stalked out.

I finished my coffee and ordered one to go. The counterman brought it in a white Styrofoam cup with a lid. I paid but lingered at the door. Rena had been in the bathroom a long time. Her fainty look bothered me. Other things bothered me, too, but I couldn't identify them yet.

There were no other women in the restaurant. So I stepped around to the lady's room and knocked softly.

"Hey, you all right? Rena?"

There was an odd sound on the other side of the door. Like a machine humming, an electric motor. Something. I pushed the door inward. The volume increased. It wasn't a machine.

"Rena?"

I pushed the door open wider and there was Rena in some kind of meditative posture (lotus?), legs pretzeled, backs of wrists on knees, smudgy eyes open and staring at something not in the room. The electric machine humming sound came from her throat. All of that was weird but okay. What bothered me was that she was hovering about eighteen inches above the gray tile, casting a little offset shadow.

Eventually I closed my mouth.

Rena's eyes refocused and shifted to me. "I need a ride."

"I know."

She stood up, but not the way I would have done it. Rena sort of *flowed* to her feet, lithe as a fairy, if you know any fairies with ripped stockings and smudged eye shadow—I mean any outside certain red-light districts.

She stood inches away, chin pointed at my chest. Her eyes were big and brown and intense.

"John," she said, "you're supposed to take me."

"I know that, too," I replied, and strangely believed it.

We drove north less than a mile and caught the 90 east toward the Cascade Mountains. Freezing rain speckled the windshield and the wipers swept it clear.

"Where exactly are we going?" I asked.

"After my boyfriend."

"The guy in the pickup?"

"Yes."

"Why?"

"Something has to happen."

"Like what?"

She leaned close to me, her face practically on my shoulder, and she *sniffed* me. Did it a couple of times then sat back.

"You're bleeding through," she said, "but I don't think you know it yet."

"What are you talking about?"

"Try closing your eyes."

I looked at her then back at the road.

"Close your eyes," she said. "Go ahead. Road's straight, right?"

"Pretty straight."

"So do it. Close them *tight* for about two seconds. Not like blinking."

Silver rain needled in the tunneling high-beams. My body felt weird, like I was in a vivid dream. I closed my eyes.

And . . . *saw.*

Daylight, a cloud-blown autumnal sky. The road was narrow and muddy. The countryside opened wide, green desaturated to something approaching dun. There was a forest in the distance, rising up into foothills out of which thrust the brutal face of a mountain. And it was more than seeing. I felt cold wind on my face and hands—hands that were gripping a polished wooden handle. Whatever contraption I was sitting on jolted over the muddy road. Rena sat next to me wearing a heavy wool cloak with the hood drawn up. She pulled the hood back and smiled. A white scar intersected her left eyebrow. Something whistled and I felt hot steam on the back of my neck.

I opened my eyes.

The wipers swept the windshield clear. My heart pounded with thrilling intensity. The vision translated to freedom in my blood.

"What *was* that?"

"Smell me," Rena said.

I swung the car into the breakdown lane, stopped, turned the dome light on, looked at her.

"Smell you," I said.

"Yes." She grinned and pulled her shirt open at the throat. "Come close."

I unbuckled my seatbelt and let it retract, then leaned over, my face close to her exposed neck, my nose practically touching her collarbone. I wanted to touch her with everything I had but kept my hands, awkwardly, hovering away from her leg, her breast.

"What do I smell like?" she asked.

A girl, youth, promise, joy, temptation without consequences, FUN. I said, "It's pine and something else. Cinnamon?"

"Oh you smell the cinnamon!"

"More like I can taste it. What's it mean, what happened when I closed my eyes? Tell me."

"There are other worlds," Rena said. "A lot of them. All running more or less parallel. Events run parallel, too. Motifs endlessly repeated. Even the people are the same. You and I, here and now, there and then. A thousand theres, and a thousand thens. Ten thousand. All occurring simultaneously. Once in a while your core personality bleeds across from the home place, the center. It happens to everyone eventually. They're the ones who look like they know something nobody else knows. It's kind of complicated. And—what's wrong?"

I said, "For a second I remembered you. I mean really remembered you."

Rena's face turned into a huge smile and a pair of drowning pool eyes. She flung herself at me and kissed my mouth. And I was gone, immortal, no longer contingent. Then she bounced back to her side of the seat and laughed at me.

"Johnny," she said, "I knew you would."

Now picture a woman named Marci Welch back in the Kennedy Hotel, Seattle, Washington. Her hair can be long or short (it's short) her eyes blue or green or brown, it doesn't matter. The main thing to picture about Marci is that she's alone. Maybe she's finishing off that bottle of room service Merlot. Maybe she's in that big bed, occupying a fractional portion of mattress space, drinking the wine and watching pay-per-view. Or you could think of her lying there in the dark by herself. Or standing in the shower. Or at the mock Edwardian writing desk concentrating over a note. A woman with twenty-five years of unhappiness named Roger crowding her toward fifty. In fear of her lost powers, her loneliness, her shrinking future. Alone in the Kennedy Hotel where she thought she'd flown from misery at last. Marci the trapeze artist. Flying without a net, leaving Roger behind forever. Flying with the trapeze artist's faith that her companion, the one who was so good in practice, would catch her chalked hands when show time arrived. So, in or out of the bed, drinking or not drinking the Merlot, in or not in the shower, sitting at the writing desk or not sitting at the writing desk. It doesn't matter. That was maybe the smallest room she had ever been in but with the biggest exit.

Now Rena. Parked in the breakdown lane I'd gotten a flash. Not even really a memory. More like a sudden pulsation of significant emotion. It started when I smelled her throat. Add the quickening of my blood while we sat there and she explained about simultaneous worlds. Then something electric surged through me and ignited an image. That's a lake. And sunlight on a white-painted porch. Rena in a flowing thing apparently woven out of light. Rena herself. This is our place. We made it, outside and beyond all other illusions. And the non-verbal operatically proportioned emotional theme? Love. As in, I've known you forever and I love you. Wholly and without reserve, all barriers down, the moat drained, guards sent home, portcullis raised and locked open, all my defensive weapons acquired in life (lives?) reforged to plowshares. It smells nice here. Piney. And the flavor of cinnamon tea.

We came up fast on a tractor-trailer rig. The Subaru's head-lights glinted on the plates, Washington, Idaho, Montana. I swung into the opposite lane and accelerated to pass. In moments I'd tucked back into the eastbound lane, which climbed and curved until the rig all strung with amber lights was lost behind us.

"He's going to be stopped. Just a little farther."
"How do you know that?" I asked.
"I just do, dear."
A minute later a pickup appeared ahead of us, halted in the breakdown lane.
"Pull in behind him," Rena said. Then, with a puzzled look: "But not too close. I don't know why."
I did that.
F-250, Oregon plate, the left rear end resting on the rim of a shredded tire. We sat fifty yards or so behind it, engine idling, rain falling through the headlights. No boyfriend in sight.
"Where is he?"
Rena shrugged. "I don't know everything."
She popped the passenger door and climbed out. Seizing a moment of passing lucidity and guilt I opened my cell phone but got only a faded signal. Maybe if I wandered around a little I could pick it up. But I left the phone in the car when I got out

to join Rena. I felt free. And the guilt and fear that had been building around Marci sloughed away and struck me as inconsequential. We were all bigger than what we appeared.

My breath steamed in the mountain air. The rain fell icy cold on my head and neck. Rena and I cast long black shadows in the fanned glare of the Subaru's headlamps.

A car went by, then another, then it was quiet on the pass. Rena's drippy pixie hair was flattened to her skull. Still cute, though. She closed her eyes tight. A minute or so elapsed.

"Rena?"

"Wait."

I sighed deeply then closed my eyes, too, and another world opened around me. This time it wasn't mountains and grassy vistas. I found myself on a broad promenade encircling midway up a building that might have been a mile tall. Rena was there and we were standing next to an abandoned rickshaw-like contraption with a broken wheel. The sky was painted with sunset clouds.

You couldn't see the rest of the city unless you stepped right up to the retaining wall that enclosed the promenade. We were that high up on the side of this stupendous structure. Not a skyscraper but a sky *penetrater*. The rest of the city spread out below us, densely packed to the horizon in every direction, blocks and towers and spires and buttresses, plumes of venting steam, checkerboard lights, traffic crawling between the buildings like sluggish yellow blood, a distant rumble and clangor.

I looked away, feeling kind of flickery.

Rena smiled. "You're not doing too well this time. You better open your eyes."

"They are open."

"*Here* they are. But not back on the road. You're too porous. I doubt you even know what's going on."

"I'm okay," I said, though I did feel unsteady and only half comprehended the situation. If that.

"Yes, you're okay. But don't move, huh?"

She walked away. The promenade was wide as a superhighway and empty except for us. Something big came around the curve, lumbering but fast, like Dumbo the flying elephant. It even looked a bit like an elephant, only the trunk was some kind of articulated cable thick as a telephone pole and bent like an inverted question mark. On the fluted end of it sat a little man in a blue helmet, hands manipulating a pair of levers.

I was safe by the wall, but Rena had just stepped into Dumbo's path.

I bolted for her, yelling, and my eyes opened in the first world, the world of mountain darkness and icy rain. Instead of a midget-driven elephant there came roaring out of the dark curve of the pass a tractor-trailer rig, white lights like a scream. The driver started to swing toward the breakdown lane, but he still would have hit Rena if I hadn't yanked her out of the way.

Tumbled on the road, my body covering Rena, I saw the boy-friend. He had his cell phone in hand, keypad lit up periwinkle, his face an astonished white mask just before the semi (missing my Subaru by a comfortable margin) plowed him and his Ford into the side of the mountain. I guess he had a faded signal, too, and had gone off to try to unfade it.

Dale or whateverthefuck slumped against the fender of his cab, red hat clutched in his ape's paw, weeping at the mangled pickup and the dead man. Rain fell continuously. Rena and I stood on the other side of the road.

"Was *that* supposed to happen?" I said.

"I guess so."

She looked like she had invisible sandbags slung over her shoulders.

"When you bleed between worlds," she said, "the trajectories of Fate sharpen. All this makes some kind of had-to-be sense, or it's supposed to."

I held her hand and she squeezed hard and pulled me around. "Hey, Johnny—"

I looked at her wet face.

"I'm slipping away, I feel it."

"Don't," I said.

"Can't help it. We'll meet again. We already have, already will. Kiss me before we forget who we are."

I kissed her mouth, but midway through it I began to feel strange about her, then stranger. We broke apart from each other and I couldn't really see her face anymore. Dark rain swept between us. Then Rena screamed and lurched toward the wreckage, calling some lost boy's name in her cracking voice.

I sat alone in my car and didn't remember any of the strange stuff. My head hurt. Rain ticked on the roof. Beyond the flooded windshield blue and red and white lights strobed and highway patrolmen in rain slickers milled around watching the tow truck. Rena was in the backseat of one of the cruisers. And I found myself alone in the unguarded fortress of my heart. Moat drained, portcullis raised, etc. Piranha flopped in the mud. A lonely wind blew through the open gate. That's what was left over. It's what you get for picking up a hitcher. The end of fun and games, not the beginning. When I shut my eyes I saw only the usual dark.

I started the car, turned around and headed toward Seattle.

As soon as I cleared the fade zone I speed dialed Marci's cell. It went straight to voice mail. I retrieved the number for the Kennedy Hotel and asked the front desk to connect me to Marci's room. The phone started ringing and went on ringing. Well it was almost dawn, and she might have been a deep sleeper. I wouldn't know, having always left before the night was over, especially this final time; I used to be that way. The phone rang and rang, and inside I was raveled and alone, subjected to memory. That phone rang until the front desk informed me needlessly that the room wasn't answering, and I told the desk clerk he better get up there with a passkey. Maybe I shouted it. Trajectories of Fate. Everybody bleeds through. Eventually.

It's nice here on the lake. The water is sapphire, because that's Rena's favorite color. It looks painted. This is a shifting place where memories converge around the core of our beings. A safe place where I am myself and Rena is herself, and we can sort things out. It's beautiful here but even when Rena steps through the door to join me there will remain a terrible aspect to it. There are a *lot* of things to sort out.

The door opens behind me. I smell cinnamon.

REUNION

Lawrence Darby sat stiffly in the back of the Lincoln Continental, fighting it, fighting it. His left hand clawed discreetly at the plush leather seat. With his right hand he fondled the small teddy bear in his overcoat pocket.

Twelve hours earlier, in desperation, he'd instructed his secretary to book him a flight and arrange for a limo to meet him at the airport in Seattle. For a long, puzzled moment there had been silence on the intercom, and then she had said, "Yes, sir, Mr. Darby. Shall I cancel the department meeting?" Darby hadn't known what to reply, and that frightened him as much as anything else. "Use your best judgment," he'd finally said. "And Nancy? Get me a window seat."

First class on the Boeing 767 red eye out of JFK. He traveled a lot but always requested an inboard seat, not wanting to be distracted from his laptop computer, the details, his work. Darby had a reputation for ruthlessness. He'd heard himself described as cold, humorless. A bastard. But no one could challenge his prominence on Wall Street.

Always an inboard seat. Except this time. This time he leaned into the window, experienced tingling exhilaration when the plane banked steeply, the long starboard wing pivoting them over doll houses and shrunken trees. It was like something starting to come alive in him again, crying out to come alive. It frightened him. The crying out was distant and he was going to it.

The bear had been left in the slip pocket on the back of the seat in front of him, a stuffed bear small enough to fit in the palm of his hand. It peeked over the top of the slip pocket, its nose caught on the pleated elastic seam, one rudimentary paw raised as if to wave. A toy, a child's toy. Darby glanced at his seat mate then surreptitiously palmed the bear and tucked it under his coat, not knowing why but feeling he must have it.

Now the Lincoln ghosted along broad residential streets twenty miles south of Seattle, past old frame houses, the carports and yards cluttered with children's toys, bikes dead on their sides, cheap molded plastic swimming pools. Darby stared out the window at TV antennas belted to chimneys, flaking paint, a few nice lawns and many that were neglected, weeds sprouting from sidewalk cracks. A working class neighborhood. Lawrence Darby sat in the limo like a visitor from another dimension, though this was the place where he had grown up, the place from which he'd come.

"Here," Darby said. "Stop here."

The driver pulled into the curb and braked smoothly.

"Wait for me right here," Darby said. The driver half turned his head, nodded, a stranger, a man older than Darby and obedient to Darby's money, the shiny visor of his cap slanted over his eyebrows.

Darby walked a block then stopped and looked back at the Lincoln parked under the messy shade of elms. *What am I doing here?* he thought. He felt anxious that the driver would leave him, abandon him. Darby clenched his teeth, fighting it, fighting the encroaching feeling of vulnerability, of helplessness. He had to get a grip, *focus*. But focus on what?

He walked around the block and stood before a modest rambler with wood-framed windows and a cinder-block chimney. There was a little girl in the driveway. Five, maybe six years old, wearing a blue jumper and red sneakers, her hair so blonde it was almost white. She sat on a big-wheeled plastic bike that she was much too big for, pushing herself forward and back, her knees higher than the handlebars. Up and down both sides of the driveway the owner of the house had planted giant plastic sunflowers and their petals twirled in the morning breeze.

The girl was watching him very closely. Darby said, "Hello," but she didn't reply, just continued to push herself forward and back on the toddler's bike.

This had been Darby's house. Decades ago he had lived here with his sister and his mother and father. Incredible. Standing there now he sensed he was closer to the crying out, closer than he had been back in New York, but not close enough. This wasn't the place he needed to be. He was about to turn away when the little girl said a strange thing.

"Are you lost?" she asked.

A chill laced up his back.

Are you lost?

"Oh my God," he mumbled.

Back in the limo he slammed the door, gave the driver a new destination, then slumped down in the seat, stunned by what he was remembering. Not remembering; this was different from remembering. It was as if he had awakened and found a gaping cavity in his chest, had realized that he was not a living man at all but an animated body.

The Lincoln fled east, toward the Cascade Mountains. Darby squeezed the stuffed bear in his pocket. For a moment back there at his old house he had been tempted to give the bear away to the little girl in the driveway. But now he knew the toy was for another purpose, a purpose he didn't yet understand.

It had been thirty-five years but Darby easily directed the limo driver to a trail head in the National Forest north of Mount Rainer. Being a weekday afternoon only a few cars were parked in the vehicle area. The limo coasted into a slot and the driver killed the engine.

For almost five minutes Darby was unable to move. He cowered in the backseat of the car, working his hands together in his lap, tears spilling from his eyes, overwhelmed by emotions and fears he had not experienced since early childhood. The driver, a perfect professional, did not ask if Darby was all right or if he could do anything. Instead the driver sat rigidly behind the wheel and stared out the windshield. A drowning piece of Darby admired him for it.

Finally Darby forced himself to open the door. He put one foot out on the gravel, then the other, then stood, still holding onto the door, reluctant to let go. He leaned back inside the car and spoke to the driver.

"I'll be back in a little while," he said, as if to reassure himself.

"Yes, sir," the driver said.

Still Darby couldn't force himself to leave. Anything was better than enduring by himself the burden of loneliness and fear that was now sweeping over him in wave after wave.

"You know," he said to the back of the driver's head, "When I was a boy I got lost in this forest."

At the word "lost" Darby's voice broke, and the driver twitched almost imperceptibly. Then, because he seemed called upon to say *some*thing, the driver asked:

"Was it for very long, sir?"

Darby swallowed. "Three days. Almost four."

"That's a very long time to be lost."

"It was hell," Darby said, remembering it, really remembering it for the first time in decades. "Pure hell."

"Three days is a long time."

"Almost four," Darby said. "It was getting dark again when I finally gave in and they let me go."

In the rearview mirror the driver's eyes opened a little wider. "Sir?"

"Never mind."

At last Darby withdrew from the limo and walked into the forest. It was dark under the trees, dark for a summer afternoon. Darby hadn't slept for over twenty-four hours. He kept the small blue bear in his right hand as he walked.

After fifteen minutes or so he departed from the trail. It happened in a strange way. The bear had seemed to *twist* in his hand—like the monkey's paw in a story he'd been required to read in high school—and Darby had known this was the place to leave the trail. The same place where he had deviated from the trail thirty-five years ago. Then he had been a five year old walking behind his older sister and his father, and he had decided impulsively to angle off the trail with the idea of tracking ahead and surprising them by suddenly jumping out in front of them. Instead he had become hopelessly lost. He had seen a chipmunk standing perkily on the trunk of a fallen tree. Not a squirrel—he had seen millions of those—but a real chipmunk; there was no mistaking the tail. It watched him as he approached, its little head cocked to the side, and just when Larry Darby was so close he could have reached out and petted it, the chipmunk jumped from the tree and shot away. He had run after it a little way. That's all it took. His sense of direction was gone. He had attempted to find the trail again but it was as if there was no trail. He had called out for his father, for Angie, but no one called back. He had been five. Instead of remaining in one spot he had kept moving, his fear growing until he was running and crying and a terrible and hopeless emptiness had opened within him.

Three days. Almost four.

Darby saw the rotting trunk of the fallen tree. He was forty years old, not five, but the great cavity had opened inside him again and all the haunted fears of his childhood came thundering back in.

It was the same tree, of course, almost entirely taken over by green moss and pallid, saucer-shaped mushrooms, rotted and sunken and collapsed—but the same tree.

Darby sat down on it, the rotted wood cracking softly. He held the bear in his hand. A child's toy bear covered with nappy blue fur. He was a little frightened of it since it moved. But he held it and listened to the ghostly cries of a lost child that had called him across a continent to be in this place. He looked down at his scuffed Italian shoes, his Wall Street shoes, and he remembered how on the evening of the third day they had come for him, whispering in the voices of a dream, flitting between the trees like gauzy shadows, circling him. Now, thinking about them with the fluttering shreds of his adult intellect, Darby wondered if he had seen them because he had been half-starved. Mystics fasted in solitude to prepare themselves to receive visitations. Had that been part of it, that hunger combined with his child's wide open mind? Of course later when he walked out to meet the searchers he had told them about the shadow things, or tried to. His father had explained to him about hallucinations, and he had accepted that, more so with each passing year. But now he knew that it was a lie, that the shadows had been real.

Darby sensed a presence and stiffened.

"Mister?"

Lawrence Darby looked up into the distorted mirror of time, into the face of a boy—his own face.

"Please, mister, I'm lost."

Darby dropped the bear.

"I want to come home," the boy said, his voice choked and thin. He was dressed in jeans and a short-sleeved checked shirt. He looked hungry, his eyes hideously bright with fear and hope. It was himself, little Larry Darby, the way he had appeared thirty-five years ago when the whispering shadows had slipped from the ancient darkness under the forest and circled him, and Darby had sensed their hunger every bit as intense as his own.

"I'm sorry," Darby said. The void within him ached to be filled, to take the child back. But he couldn't. The Lawrence Darby who had walked out of this forest more than three decades ago could not accept into himself this quivering, lost waif. I have to leave the boy, he thought.

Leave the boy. It's what they had whispered to him. Leave the boy, let us have him and you, the real you, can go.

Three days alone. No food, freezing at night, terrified. The search parties never even came close. But he heard the whispering inside his mind, saw the weird shadows—the whispering devils. They had tricked him, somehow, always leading him away from the trail, away from rescue, drawing him in deeper and deeper. A child could not have survived. He had to bargain with them or he would have died. Died of hunger, or exposure. Or loneliness.

Leave the boy, leave him for us and go, be strong, be free . . .

"I'm sorry," Darby said again, standing, looking into the eyes of his own divided soul. Hating himself as he knew others hated him but unable to allow the weakness back in.

"Don't go!" Larry cried.

Darby turned away, fumbled over the dead tree, thinking the boy wouldn't be able to follow him beyond that point. He braced himself against the screams of the child, filled the empty place with steel. And soon there was no screaming, only the sound of the wind. Don't look back, he told himself. But he did look back, one more time. Because he knew he could do it; he was strong and the empty place was steel. He turned and saw that it was true: Larry hadn't been able to follow him. The boy was still standing by the fallen tree, a ghostly waif. Darby could actually see through him as the boy slowly dimmed away. And just before he completely vanished something gauzy and black slipped over him. Darby shuddered.

He started walking back to the parking area, the steel heavy in him. He stumbled and fell, got up, cursing under his breath. He looked back. The forest was silent. The place where he'd left-Darby swallowed-where he'd left the boy, looked no different from any other place among the monotonous columns of Pine trees.

Darby walked on a little farther then stopped again. A strange thought occurred to him. He made the thought into words and spoke it in his mind: I'm not ready. And it was true. He wasn't ready to resume his seat in the limousine where he'd be forced to stare at the back of the impertinent driver's head during the long drive to the airport. Even if the driver never said a word he would still be thinking that there was something wrong with Darby, that Darby was a little off. And those impertinent ideas would manifest themselves in tiny movements of the driver's head, a certain attitude of his shoulders. Not that Darby couldn't deal with that kind of thing. But he wanted to deal with it coolly, in control. He had lost control earlier, and the driver had witnessed it. That was the whole problem. So maybe he'd just wait a bit, walk around, master himself completely, then return to the limo.

He couldn't deny that the incident (he was already burying it deep, burying it and paving it over and building a *Wal-Mart* on top of it) had shaken him. But what had happened, really? Certainly he had overworked himself lately. Certainly this little adventure or whatever you wanted to call it, trip down memory lane or whatever, wasn't it something like a midlife crisis? Nothing more profound than the faintly ridiculous impulse of a man past forty growing weepy over an ancient and best forgotten misadventure of his childhood.

But what he'd just seen.

He hadn't seen anything.

And he couldn't see very well even now. His vision was blurred. He wiped at his eyes roughly, with the heels of his hands. He walked faster, as if he could walk away from his thoughts. His heart thudded, he stumbled, groped forward, the undergrowth grabbing at his slacks. Finally he stopped.

And he was lost.

He couldn't see the sky. The trees towered around him, ancient and solemn. There was not a breath of wind. Darby's own breath rasped in his throat. He tried to blunder back the way he'd come, but he didn't know what way that was. He kept falling. His shoes chaffed raw blisters through his thin businessman's socks. Somewhere, he'd lost his watch. He sat panting on the ground.

"It's all right," the voice of a young boy said. "Don't cry."

"I'm not crying." But he was.

"I know the way out. But you have to take me with you."

Darby didn't say anything.

"This is the last chance," the boy said. "Please."

"I—"

"Go ahead," the boy said.

"I'm scared," Darby said, his voice shaky, and he began to sob without restraint.

After a while he looked up, and he was alone. I've always been alone, he thought. He started walking again, but calmly, without panic. After a while he saw a pair of hikers with daypacks and walking sticks, and he angled toward them and picked up the trail, and just as easily as that, he was on his way back to the parking area.

In the limo, speeding along with the trees flashing by his window, Darby began to smile a little.

"I don't think there ever were any shadows," he said.

"Sir?" The driver flicked his gaze to the rear-view mirror.

"What's your name, driver?" Darby asked, suddenly interested.

"Thomas," the driver said. "Tom."

"Well, Tom, thanks for driving me around today."

The driver nodded. "You're welcome, sir."

Note: This is one of the older stories in the book. It bounced around for years, gathering almost-but-not-quite-there rejection slips and personal notes from editors, including the gang at the 1990s Weird Tales. *Then one day, talking to my therapist, I was struck by an insight! I went home, rewrote the story, and almost immediately sold it to the Canadian magazine* On Spec. *Mostly what I rewrote was the ending. In the original version Darby never does accept his rejected "weaker" self. He just marches back out to the limo, snaps at the driver, and returns to New York. Somehow, it was that earlier version that wound up in the Golden Gryphon version of this collection. By the time I noticed the mistake, it was too late to fix it. Did the slightly more upbeat ending make it a saleable story, or did it simply find the right market at last? Good question.*

Strangers on a Bus

A single passenger boarded the Greyhound in Idaho Falls: A young man in blue jeans, black T-shirt, and leather jacket. Freya Hoepner, who was sitting beside one of the few unoccupied seats, glanced at him then looked down at the page of the book she wasn't reading. The words lay in meaningless order under her gaze. In her mind she heard other words, recently snarled at her: *Bitch*; and: *I'm done with you;* and: *Leave the fucking cat.*

For once in her life, she wanted to be alone.

"Do you mind if I sit here?"

She looked up. He wasn't so young after all, maybe forty. The man hadn't shaved in a couple of days, and there were dark discolorations under his eyes. But he was otherwise attractive, in a lost man-boy way that appealed to Freya despite her recent experience. She shrugged one shoulder and looked back at the meaningless page. The man sat beside her, invading the bubble into which she had retreated since leaving Seattle that morning.

"What are you reading?" he asked.

"A book."

"Is it good?"

"It seems to be crap," Freya said.

Air brakes hissed, as if exasperated, and the bus lurched out of the station.

Heading south on I-15, Freya watched a wound open in the western sky. She was thinking about her cat, Mr. Pickwick. The cab had arrived, and Freya had stood in the alley behind the apartment building, holding her small suitcase in one hand and a cat treat in the other. She had called Picky's name over and over, tearfully, knees bent, hand outstretched. She had just wanted to say goodbye. Then Roger slapped the treat out of her hand and said, "Forget the fucking cat." Mr. Pickwick had been the last good thing she lost in Seattle, coming after her pride.

"Personally," said the man sitting beside her on the bus, "I prefer the classics."

"Excuse me?"

"Twain; Shakespeare; Tolstoy. Dickens. Over crap, I mean. Have you read Dickens?"

"Yes."

"No kidding? You never run into people who read real books. Hardly ever."

"I'm a teacher," Freya said.

"Where do you teach?"

"Nowhere. I quit. But I used to teach junior high school in Phoenix."

"Why'd you quit?"

Because I'm a fool, she thought.

"I suppose I was tired of it," she said.

"Eh. What's your favorite Dickens?"

Freya shrugged one shoulder again, not really wanting the conversation to continue.

"Mine's *David Copperfield*," the man said.

"Everybody says that," Freya said. "Or *Oliver Twist*."

"So what's yours? *Pickwick Papers*, I bet."

"God, no. *Our Mutual Friend*. *Pickwick* isn't even a novel."

"It isn't?"

"Look, I don't want to be rude, but—"

"It's okay, if you don't feel like talking. I don't usually talk so much myself. It's interesting to look at people, though. Look at people I don't know and try to figure them out. Have you ever done that? My name's Neil, by the way."

"Freya," Freya said.

"That's unusual. I like that name. Hey, see that guy?"

Neil inclined his head toward her and dropped his voice. He pointed at a bald-headed, beefy man across the aisle, reading a magazine. Neil pointed in a funny way, his elbow tucked against his ribs, index finger slightly crooked, as if he were trying to point without pointing. Freya looked briefly at the bald-headed man. A gold ring glinted dully against his earlobe.

"If you had to make up something about him, what would it be?" Neil asked.

Freya wasn't in the mood. She drummed her fingers on the open page of the book, shook her head.

"A kid would probably make up a story about him being a professional wrestler," Neil said, "or maybe a genie, if the kid was young enough. But a grown-up would more likely think he's a biker, or a truck driver. Something like that. Of course he might also be a salesman, or a beekeeper, or an unemployed aerospace engineer. Something that goes against his appearance type. Not that it would matter what anybody made up, right? Since you'd never known him, he might as well be what you make up about him. In your mind there'd be no difference whether he was a broker, or a genie. It's all the same. When you're thinking about him he's in *your* world. Do you know what I mean?"

"I don't think so."

Freya forced a smile, then looked out the window. She looked out the window until her neck started to hurt, until the sunset wound desaturated and twilight overtook the world. Finally, when she no longer sensed her seat companion waiting for her, she slowly faced forward, her neck painfully stiff, and closed her eyes, pretending sleep.

And then she did sleep—or dozed, anyway. But came forward out of troubled, disjointed, hectoring thoughts when she heard the man, Neil, weeping. She opened her eyes a crack, turned her head the merest portion of an inch. He was bent forward, his face in his hands, trying not to make a sound, his shoulders hitching with suppressed sobs. The bus rumbled along. Reading lights shone over random seats, but not theirs, not Freya's and Neil's.

Freya rose out of her self-absorption. She became her Virgonian urge to *help*. It was the same urge that had prompted her to answer Roger's instant-message in the Yahoo chat room (ASTROLOGY 2). Roger who was always needling people, challenging their sincerity, their "hokey" beliefs. She thought she had perceived his *real* self; his insecure, unhappy, wounded nature. He could be so charming and vulnerable, once she penetrated his barriers. Right. Until she moved in and he became his *other* real self. The one who lapsed into thoughtless cruelty, who became controlling and angry, even during sex. So Freya's urge to help didn't always serve her well, but she could not resist it. Her one and only irresistible quality: She had to help.

Glancing at the bald man (genie-wrestler-trucker), Freya leaned over and, tentatively, touched Neil's back.

"Are you all right?"

Same thing she had asked Roger in her first private message.

Neil became very still. Freya withdrew her hand. Slowly, Neil sat back. In the dimness he appeared older (or maybe just his age), almost haggard. His shaggy head and old-man-tired eyes.

"I guess I'm not," he said. "I didn't mean to wake you up. Sorry."

"I was only resting my eyes," Freya said.

"I'm not usually such a baby. Or a blabbermouth, for that matter."

"That's all right. I'm having a bad day, too," she said. "Do you want to tell me what's wrong with yours? I'm a good listener, people say I am."

"You're a Virgo, I bet."

"*Yes*, that's right. And you can't resist my nurturing powers."

"I guess I can't."

She couldn't see his face clearly and it bothered her. She could *smell* him better than she could see him. Worn out leather, a trace of old sweat and cologne.

"How far are you traveling?" Freya asked.

"To the end of the road."

"And where is that? I think this bus turns around when it reaches Phoenix."

"I haven't decided yet. I haven't decided, and it's kind of scary. Man, I'm tired. You know, I used to really like people, but not so much anymore. Present company excepted." He flashed a perfunctory smile. "When I saw you I thought you looked nice. You also looked like you were leaving something, rather than going *to* something. You looked sad, I guess."

"Well—"

"Don't pay attention to me. I'm a little nuts."

"I hadn't noticed."

He laughed shortly out of his indistinct face. Freya reached up and turned on the reading light. That was better. Neil's eyes were red from crying and perhaps lack of sleep. He stared at her in an unblinking, probing way that made her feel like squirming. His skin was too white.

"Do you know what I am?" he asked.

"No, what are you?"

"I'm a freak," Neil said.

She tried to smile but couldn't pull it off.

"I tell myself stories," he said. "Like I was saying before. I make up stuff about people I don't know. Stories."

"That's not so freakish."

"Do you want to hear one?"

"I don't think so."

"Don't be afraid. It's okay."

"I'm not afraid."

Neil leaned closer and whispered: "Take a look at our friend, the wrestler."

Freya looked past Neil. The beefy bald man with the earring was balancing a laptop computer on his knees, scrolling the cursor around with a delicate movement of his stubby middle finger, like a child absorbed in finger paint.

"He's not a wrestler," Neil said. "He owns a small company that makes swimming pool filtering equipment. He's moderately successful at it and he's thinking of opening a small manufacturing plant and distribution center in Phoenix. He's going there to meet with local investors. The reason he's taking the bus is he's scared to fly. It's practically a phobia with him. He hasn't been on an airplane since 9/11. He won't even take a train, because he's too cheap. He doesn't like to drive long distance, so he might as well bus it, right? Everybody's neurotic, that's my theory."

"I don't understand," Freya said, thinking Neil and the man across the aisle might have talked while she dozed. "Is any of that true?"

"It is now. I make stuff up about people, and then the people become the stuff I make up."

"I see."

Neil laughed. "God, I'm tired," he said.

"Why don't you sleep? I'll keep my eye on the swimming pool guy for you."

"It worries me to sleep."

"When I think about sleep," Freya said, "I worry about how vulnerable I am, my body lying there *breathing* by itself in a dark room. I guess that goes along with your 'everybody's neurotic' thing. What worries *you* about going to sleep?"

"I'm afraid that I tell stories in my sleep; and I'm kind of fixated on that guy. I have a story for him but I haven't told it yet. I don't want to tell it. But what if I do while I'm asleep?"

"I think it's safe for you to sleep." She patted his arm. "I'll watch out for things."

"All right." Neil reclined his seat and closed his eyes. "Freya?"

"Yes?"

"Don't worry about Mr. Pickwick."

Freya opened and closed her book a couple of times. She couldn't concentrate. Finally she gave up and put the book into her shoulder bag. Out the window a prairie slid past in moonlight. Beside her, Neil slept with his mouth open. The genie, or swimming pool salesman, or whatever he was, closed his computer and folded his hands over his thick waist.

After a while, Neil began to make small, anxious sounds in his sleep. Freya almost nudged him but didn't. She got up to use the bathroom, careful to step over Neil's feet. Making her way to the rear of the Greyhound, touching seatbacks on both sides of the aisle, she played the game. Faces in repose, white cords trailing from snuggly placed ear buds; faces in conversation, in concentration, floating in reading light, swaying with the road, the dips and curves, the driver's minor adjustments. iPod girl is a college kid going home to visit her parents for the weekend; this guy's a plumber, owns a cocker spaniel named Munchkin; this hippie-looking guy is a burglar who ritualistically smokes a joint after every job. No: he smokes one *while* he's doing a job, lights up in the victim's living room and leaves the roach on the kitchen table, like a calling card, almost hoping his DNA will get him convicted someday.

And so on.

The shapes occupying seats without reading lights were faceless ciphers. They could be *anything*.

In the tiny closet at the back of the bus Freya sat on the toilet and cried. She cried because she had surrendered her secret heart to Roger, a man she hardly knew, left her life in Phoenix (not that much to leave, admittedly, but was she *that* desperate, for God's sake?), and wound up alone anyway. And lucky to be that way. It wasn't a matter of knowing Roger, or anybody else; it was a matter of someone, anyone, knowing *her*. Wanting to know her. To understand her intimately, to be interested in *her* life. But Roger had only been good at acting like he was interested. It had taken everything she had to go to him, to sever herself from life in Phoenix. She hadn't expected him to bring out the handcuffs, hadn't expected him to *want* to hurt her; usually she got hurt as a consequence of her trusting vulnerability. Somehow she always found the "wrong" man, in her relentless search for a new daddy, one who wanted her, who wouldn't leave. Mythical man.

She wiped and flushed, stood up. In the mirror, her face drew down toward middle age.

Is this all I am?

She slept, fitfully, her head resting against the window, the cool flat glass, vibrating, bouncing with the road, bucketing along above sleep's deeper threshold.

The sun woke her. She squinted, worked her mouth. The bus was pulling into the parking lot of a diner. The sign at the turn-off looked like a big metal cactus the color of a pickle: KACTUS KATE'S! COME IN AND GET COOL!

"Forty-five minutes for breakfast," the driver said over the P.A.

Neil smiled at her. He looked better after his rest. He looked like somebody she could like. Except, she reminded herself, she was done picking up strays.

"Welcome to Arizona," Neil said. He sounded resigned.

They filed off the bus. With the engine stopped it was suddenly very hot. Neil removed his leather coat and carried it by the collar. Freya blotted her forehead with the back of her hand. The swimming pool guy shuffled down the aisle between them, his short-sleeved cotton shirt stuck to his back in dark patches. Freya couldn't take her eyes off the tight roll of fat on the back of the man's neck.

*

She sat on a stool and the counterman took her order for scrambled eggs, toast, and orange juice. The swimming pool guy hunched over a *USA Today* a few stools down, but he stared at it the way Freya had stared at her book, as if it were written in Chinese. She wondered what words he was hearing, what voices.

Neil sat at a corner table by himself. The lost man-boy. He had a cup of coffee in front of him but no food. Freya sipped her orange juice and glanced over occasionally. Every time she did, Neil happened to be glancing at *her*, even as he tore open packets of sugar and emptied them into his cup.

When her eggs arrived, Freya picked up her juice and plate and carried them to Neil's table.

"May I?"

"Sure." He waved a packet at the empty chair, scattering white sugar crystals. Freya brushed the seat off and sat down.

"Are you feeling better today?" she asked.

"I'm fine."

"Good. I was thinking about something. I was thinking about how you said don't worry about Mr. Pickwick."

Neil smiled slightly.

"You don't know it, but it was kind of coincidental. I had a cat named Mr. Pickwick. I know you were talking about the Dickens, from before. But it's still a coincidence. It's almost synchronicity, but not quite, I think. Am I making sense?"

"You are. But not in the way you think you are."

"And what way would that be?"

"I wasn't talking about Dickens, when I said the Pickwick thing. I meant don't worry about your cat."

"Oh, really."

"Yeah."

"I—"

"There he goes."

Freya turned, almost expecting to see the yellow tabby padding across the diner. But it was the beefy bald guy of a thousand identities, or three anyway. He walked past, looking grim, and went into the Men's Room.

"You're quite taken with the swimming pool salesman," she said.

"Filters," Neil said. "Anyway, he doesn't do that anymore."

"No?"

"No. I had a bad dream, I think. I can't remember it, but I know what I was thinking before I went to sleep. And I know I dreamed about something scary that I desired. There's that residue in my mind, no specifics."

Freya studied his face, looking for a clue that he was kidding, or setting her up for a punch line. No such clues were evident.

"So you dreamed he wasn't a filter salesman and now he isn't?"

"Yeah."

"What is he now?"

"A poor slob whose wife left him last week and took his sweet daughter with her. He also lost his job, after showing up drunk for his morning shift and punching out his supervisor. This surprised both of them. Until then he hadn't seemed like the violent type, despite the guns."

"What guns?"

"Well, he's always been a little paranoid and scared. More so than anybody ever guessed. He keeps a gun in the glove box of his Ford and a couple more in the house, plus a .38 in the ankle holster, like he's a secret agent or something, except he isn't. Not by a long shot. Shot's kind of a pun. I used to tell nice stories about people, right? Now it's mostly depressing stuff. Those eggs look good."

"You should order some," Freya said.

"There isn't time."

She thought he meant there wasn't time before the bus left. But then, looking at him, at his haunted eyes, she knew he meant something else. Something terrible, maybe.

"So you think you know about Mr. Pickwick."

"Yes."

"Then tell me what it is about his eyes."

"Eye. Not eyes. Did you ever think of dressing him like a pirate for Halloween?"

Freya put her fork down. "That was a good guess."

"It wasn't a guess. I told you: I make up stories about strangers, and then the strangers *become* the story I made up. I don't want to do it, but I can't help myself anymore. The stories happen. It's like a reaction. Instinctive Inventive Reaction, I call it."

"Eye Eye Are. Er?"

He laughed, and the haunted look fell away, briefly.

"I like you," he said, "which is too bad. I'm kind of out of the people-liking business."

"Me, too. Or I thought I was."

"Because of Roger dodger?"

She stared at him.

"Yeah," he said, "I know all about him."

She sipped her orange juice, put the glass down. "I probably said his name in my sleep."

Neil shook his head. "Nope."

"Don't tell me you made up a story about *me*."

"I could prove it, but in a couple of minutes it won't matter."

She moved her glass around the table, sliding it on a film of moisture. After a moment she raised her eyes.

"Go ahead and prove it."

"You're a junior high school teacher from Phoenix," Neil said.

"I told you that."

"Right," Neil said. "But you didn't tell me about Roger."

Freya waited, suspended between expectations. Her heart was beating faster.

"You didn't tell me you met him in a chat room, and that you started a relationship with him that progressed to phone calls and then to visits. You didn't tell me that he seemed to know all your secret places, that he convinced you that he was in love with you, and that you quit your job and moved to Seattle. You didn't tell me that he turned out to be a manipulating, needy asshole who liked to hurt people, especially you. And you didn't tell me that after a while it was you and Mr. Pickwick verses asshole Roger. The cat was a stray, and you took it in. Because even though you were living with the guy you felt dreadfully lonely. Worse than you had felt back home in Phoenix, and that was pretty bad. You didn't tell me that asshole Roger threw a full bottle of Bud at the cat and hit it in the ass, and that Mr. Pickwick ran for his life out of that apartment, which is when you decided you had to do the same. You didn't tell me that when the cab was waiting to take you to the bus station a couple of days later, after all the yelling and tears and threats, that you still couldn't find Mr. Pickwick, though you'd seen him slinking around the alley. And asshole Roger made you get in the cab without your cat, and you did it because you were scared. Another stray that got away and went feral. You didn't tell me any of that, did you?"

"No," Freya said, her voice very small.

"See?" he said.

"It's a trick." She felt naked, publicly exposed. "You hypnotized me or something, back on the bus, and I told you all that."

"Yeah. It's a trick. I'm The Amazing Neil."

"You don't know me," Freya said.

"You're right. I don't know who you really are. But you know what's funny? *You* don't know who you really are, either. Not anymore."

"That isn't funny, Neil."

He looked down. "No, it isn't. I'm sorry."

His eyes shifted to the Men's Room.

"Why do you keep looking over there?"

"No reason."

Freya looked at the Men's Room door.

"Now you've got *me* doing it," she said.

"Anyway," Neil said, "you don't have to worry about your cat."

"Maybe I never even had a cat. Maybe you just planted that idea in my head." Her heart ached a little when she said it. Mr. Pickwick, as opposed to Roger, had been a comfort to her. It wasn't even the cat she missed; it was the comfort. Another stray gone feral.

"Is that what you think?" Neil said. "That I 'planted' Mr. Pickwick in your mind?"

"No."

"Because that isn't what I do," he said. "I don't plant things."

"What *do* you do, then?"

"I see somebody, and his or her face suggests a little story. So I listen to the story, add to it, embellish it. This only takes a few seconds. And the little story isn't the *whole* story. It just gets things rolling."

"You make people be something they're not."

"No. I give them lives they could have had but didn't. Or maybe they had them in parallel dimensions, or a previous incarnation. Who knows? I don't *make* anybody do anything. I wish I could. I've tried it." His mouth turned down in a sour scowl.

"What happened?" Freya asked.

He shrugged. "There was a girl."

He picked up his mug with both hands and slurped coffee. She thought he was pausing to gather his thoughts, but a minute went by, and he only stared, holding the mug up to his chin, elbows on the table, his eyes focused inward.

"What about the girl?" she said.

"Nothing."

"Tell me. Please."

"You already think I'm nutty," he said.

She did her one-shoulder shrug, but it was the other shoulder.

"Her name was Lynn," he said. "She was totally random, nobody I knew or was likely to know. I was walking into a bank in Spokane, and she was walking out. One of those revolving doors. Her face. Oh, man, was she cute—but very sad-looking. And a story begins spinning itself out, something about a divorce, an empty bank account, embarrassment, a brave face, and a fast exit. At which point I tried to take control of the story. I put myself into it, which I think screwed it up. I'm the outsider, right? I don't ever have a story to be in, not with anybody else. Anyway, I followed her down the block and found her crying in front of a Starbucks. And it was like she was *so glad* that I stopped and asked if she was all right. I have a kind face, non-threatening? I've heard that before. How far does a so-called kind face get you? It doesn't matter. I'm totally used to being alone, I'm accustomed to the idea. With Lynn I reminded her of her high school crush, the one she always wished had asked her out but never did."

"That was mean," Freya said. "Making her believe that."

His eyes widened innocently. "I didn't intend it to be mean. I just wanted to meet her. I wanted her to like me."

"Maybe she would have liked you anyway, without you changing all her memories around."

"I doubt it. People tend to look right though me, Freya. Especially women. Anyway, I bought her a coffee, and we talked. She really was a sweet girl."

"What about the bank account, why was it empty?"

"It wasn't."

"But you said—"

"That was *before*. Once I intentionally added myself, the back story changed, too. She told me she was crying because she was thinking about her best friend, who had told her she had breast cancer. Nothing to do with the bank."

Freya thought for a minute.

"What if the empty account story was never real?"

"It would have been, if I'd left it alone."

"You're guessing it would have been. But maybe the stories in your head *don't* become real. Maybe they're just stories in your head. Did she *tell* you that you reminded her of the high school crush?"

Neil looked at his coffee mug. "No."

"See? Maybe she liked you for being you, for bothering to stop and ask if she was all right. For your kind face, even. Is that so outlandish? Maybe you don't have any weird power."

"You're forgetting something."

"What?"

The Men's Room door opened. Neil tensed, slopping coffee over the rim of his mug, then relaxed when the pony-tailed-hippie-looking guy stepped out, wiping his hands on his jeans.

"What, what is it?" Freya asked.

Neil slumped, placed his mug on the table. He rubbed his eyes.

"What you're *forgetting* is all that stuff I know about you. The cat, Roger, the rough sex, all that."

Freya blushed. "Maybe—"

"Maybe what?"

"I was thinking, maybe it's that you read minds?"

"I don't *read minds*." He looked disgusted. "Jesus, that pseudo science stuff is reaching."

"It makes more sense than the other thing. There's at least *some* scientific basis for mind-reading." (She was remembering an *X-Files* episode.) "What if you read minds without even knowing it? So you think it's a story you're making up, but it's the truth to begin with. What about that?"

He gave her a weary up-from-under look.

"Never mind," Freya said. "What happened with your bank girl?"

"I told you: Nothing."

"You didn't go out, or see her again?"

"No. She wouldn't have wanted to see me again. I just caught her at a vulnerable moment."

"That's a dumb way to think," Freya said. "Trust me. You know what your problem is?"

"Tell me, I think I need to hear it."

"You're afraid to let anybody know who you really are." (She was thinking of a Dr. Phil book, but that didn't invalidate the point.)

"Something funny? I don't even know who I am. A long time ago—a *long* time ago, I think, I started telling stories about *myself*. Maybe it was because I was always alone, it seemed like, when I was a kid. It wasn't such a happy home, all that crap you might expect. So I'd make stuff up, to escape. And the stuff was in my dreams, too. Maybe mostly in my dreams. You know dreams, there's no bullshit. It's the unconscious giving us what we think we deserve. But there's something else, and you're going to think I'm nutty, but what if when I started out I wasn't even human? Because about half the time I don't feel human even now."

"Neil?"

"Yeah?"

"You're nutty."

"I *told* you," he said. "You should have believed me."

"How could you not be human? What else *is* there?"

"Listen. I travel around a lot. I used to like big cities, because there were so many people, so it seemed like it was less lonely, but it wasn't. I'd hang out in my crappy apartment, go out to coffee shops, the movies, but I was always by myself. All those other people, it got depressing. So then I went the small town route. Like I had this idea it'd be Mayberry, you know, Andy Griffith, all that. But it wasn't. People in those towns are suspicious as hell about outsiders. I feel like I'm at the end of my options. I'm *tired*."

"How come you get to live in all these different places? What do you do for money?"

"I'm a writer."

"Ah."

"You mean ah-*ha*. Right? Well, you're wrong. It's natural that I'd be a writer. Like if you have a talent for constructive empathy you might be a counselor, or even a teacher, for instance. I have a talent for making stuff up."

"Well, Neil."

"What?"

"The last time I looked, writers are human like the rest of us."

"Most of them are, I guess. Personally I don't get along with the ones I know. They're all kind of weird."

"Thank goodness you're not."

"Yeah, thank goodness."

"So what did you mean by not being human?"

"You ever see *2001*, that Kubrick movie?"

"Of course."

"Remember at the end, the Star Child is floating in space above the Earth? That's what I think sometimes."

"*What* is what you think sometimes?"

"That I started out like that, like some kind of Star Child, and I was having a dream and the dream became a planet, and the planet became populated with all these really interesting beings full of possibilities and contradictions, and it looked like so much fun I dropped into the dream myself, but I never really fit. And when I sleep, because I'm so lonely and insane, my unconscious desires to just *wreck* the whole thing boil up, and we get wars and pestilence and all that. What do you think?"

"I think you think too much."

"Jesus, I hate it when people say that. How can anybody think 'too much'?"

"Wait a minute. What *kind* of writer are you?"

"I suppose if I told you I was a science fiction writer you'd do a double ah-ha."

"*Are* you a science fiction writer?"

"I saw a revival of that movie when I was a little kid," Neil said, as if she'd asked him a different question. "*2001*. My mom dropped me off, by myself. I think because the movie was so long. Like to get rid of me for a while? Well, who can blame her."

"Was your father around?"

Neil didn't answer. He looked at the Men's Room door and chewed his lip.

"What is it with the bathroom?" Freya said.

"That genie-looking son of a bitch."

"What about him?"

"On the bus I was afraid I'd dream something bad if I fell

asleep, something I was afraid of but wanted very much. And I think I did that. All I know is, I mean I wanted to die. Freya, I wanted to die. I was tired of everybody else's life and not having one of my own, my true one. Never knowing who I was supposed to be, never having a companion. I had even started resenting other people's lives, hating them. Why should I go on living, why should anybody else get to? You know the drill. That kind of solipsistic crap they find in somebody's note after the latest massacre. I mean that isn't what I *wanted*, but it might be what my secret warped unconscious heart wanted. And that guy, that genie guy, I think he's going to give me my wish, my secret desire. Because he's at the end of *his* rope, too, and he's ready to go off. He's ready to go off like a stick of dynamite. You better get out of here, Freya. Right now."

The Men's Room door banged opened, and the bald man appeared.

Freya grabbed Neil's hand, and he squeezed it hard enough to grind the bones.

The bald man walked by their table, looking glum, and resumed his seat at the counter. A few minutes later the driver announced it was time to board.

Freya swallowed. "Maybe your warped unconscious heart dreamed up some *other* secret desire you're afraid of," she said.

He stared at her.

On the Greyhound traveling southwest through the desert, Freya said:

"What are you going to do when we get to Phoenix?"

"I don't know. Get back on the bus? I don't really like hot weather that much."

"Why don't you hang around awhile? It's a dry heat, you know."

"So I've heard."

"Neil?"

"Hmm?"

"How did you really know all those things about me and Roger?"

"I hypnotized you."

"That's what I thought."

"Really?"

"No. I'm going with the mind-reading idea."

They sat quietly for a while, which was easy and comfortable. Freya got her book out but didn't open it. She tapped the cover.

"To think," she said, "I used to like this crap."

"Shocking."

"I mean before I transformed into the Freya from a parallel dimension with better taste. Thanks, by the way. 'Fear and desire,' " she quoted, reading the dust jacket copy.

"Who needs it?" Neil said.

"Right."

She dropped the book on the floor and nudged it under the seat with her foot.

"I'll leave it for the next passenger."

They rode along, and after a while Neil closed his hand over hers and squeezed it gently. Not like in the diner, when he thought a homicidal maniac, a monster from his id, was going to come out of the Men's Room with guns blazing.

"The fear part, anyway," he said.

"What?"

"Who needs it," he said.

FREE DOG

Travis Larson sat in a red leather chair in his attorney's office. Cory the toy poodle curled in his lap, and Larson petted her fluffy gray head. "There must be something we can do," he said.

The attorney, whose name was Beverman, replied, "She is within her rights."

"But Cory is my dog. The settlement explicitly states that I keep her."

"And so you have."

"I don't want Kristine to have a copy."

"Honestly, Travis, there isn't anything we can do about that." He moved his finger in the air and Larson's divorce settlement appeared. The lawyer swept virtual pages aside with little flicks of his hand. "There is nothing in your agreement pertaining to Information Transubstantiation. If your former wife wishes to own a copy of your dog, she has every right to do so."

"But—"

"Look, I understand your feelings. IT caught us all a little by surprise. But you can comfort yourself with the knowledge that you own the first, the original, Corky."

"Cory," Larson said.

"Of course. Cory. I'm sorry."

"Let me show you something," Larson said.

The attorney closed the divorce file, grabbing the projection out of the air and vanishing it in his first. "If you could make it brief; I have a meeting in five minutes."

Larson set Cory on the floor. The dog sat attentively, staring at Larson. There was adoration in the poodle's eyes.

"Up!" Larson commanded, brightly.

Cory jumped up on hind legs. "Round and round and round!"

Larson said, his voice high and skirting some mock-maniacal precipice.

Cory danced around in a circle—a canine ballerina on pointe. Around and around and around, his little fluffy ears a quarter turn behind the rest of him.

Beverman nodded and smiled tightly, checking his watch. "Yes, that's very, uh, delightful."

"I know it's delightful," Larson said. "And I know you've seen it. But you haven't *seen* it. I taught her that trick and a lot of others. You know, when I was a kid I never had a dog of my own. My sister got a dog, but I didn't."

Beverman stood up. "Well, as I said—"

"Cory is *my* dog," Larson said. "I taught him things. I walk him every day. He sits with me when I read or watch TV. I feed him treats. He loves me. Do you think Kristine did anything for Cory? Do you think she even bothered to fill his water bowl?"

"I wouldn't—"

"Trust me. She didn't. She didn't *care* about Cory. She information-ized him for exactly one reason—to hurt me."

Beverman came around the desk and put a fatherly hand on Larson's shoulder. "I've known you a long time, Travis, and I like to think of myself as something more than your legal advisor. I like to think of myself as your friend."

Cory pawed at Larson's leg. He scooped the dog up and held him against his chest. Cory growled at Beverman, who patted Larson's shoulder and backed off a step. "And *as* your friend," he said, "I advise you to let this go. Your divorce does not enjoin Kristine from owning a copy of your dog. And, frankly, even if such language existed, the propagation of an already information-ized poodle is impossible to halt. You simply have to accept the reality: Information is free."

Larson grunted. Cory, perhaps sensing his distress, started to whine.

A week later Larson was sitting in Central Park on his lunch-break, eating a tuna salad sandwich. It was a pleasant spring after-noon, the sky soft and blue and blameless. People wandered the park in shirt sleeves, many walking dogs. Larson was getting over it. He had mostly put IT out of his mind. Then he heard a man's voice say, "Round and round and round!"

Larson turned sharply. A bald man in a business suit stood on the grass not thirty yards from Larson's bench. Larson recognized him. It was DeVris. He and Larson worked for the same investment firm. DeVris clapped his hands and laughed. Before him a toy poodle danced around in a circle on hind legs, floppy ears a quarter turn behind the rest of him.

Around and around and around.

Larson's hand closed into a fist, squirting tuna salad between his fingers. He flung the mess away, jumped up and stalked over to DeVris, wiping his hand on a paper towel.

"Travis," DeVris said. "Look at my—"

"Where did you get that copy?"

"Isn't he adorable? His name's Corky."

"His name is *not* Corky."

"Excuse me?'

"Did my ex-wife put you up to this?"

"I—No, I don't know what you're talking about."

"Kristine didn't give you a copy of '*Corky*'?" Larson sneered the misnomer out like a bad taste in his mouth.

"Honestly, Travis, I don't know what you're talking about. Corky was a free download."

"*Free download.*"

DeVris backed away nervously. 'Corky' continued to dance around and around and around until DeVris waved his hand and the cheap nanoswarm that comprised the perfect 3D rendering twinkled out.

"For God's sake, Travis. If you want a Corky you can get one of your own. He's all over the web."

"Thanks. I already have one. And his name isn't Corky!"

At home, Larson called his attorney but got Beverman's avatar instead. On his phone's Projektrix he couldn't immediately determine what competency level the avatar occupied. They all looked like the real thing.

"Kristine has set her Cory rip-off loose and it's gone viral. Now we *have* to do something. Do you have any idea how many

'Corky's' I saw just coming home from the office?"

"No, but I know I am currently unavailable for anything but an absolute emergency."

Larson closed his eyes. Competency level: zilch.

"This is an emergency," he shouted at the nanorendering of the zilch competency avatar standing on his coffee table.

"I'd be happy to file the details of your message and present them to myself at my earliest possible convenience. Simply state—"

Larson slapped his hand down on the coffee table, scattering the nanoswarm like glittery dust.

Cory the poodle—the real Cory—whined and licked Larson's hand. Larson picked the dog up into his lap and petted him. You couldn't do *that* with a nanoswarm copy.

Larson called his ex and asked her to meet him for lunch. She was an attorney, working corporate cases for a major Manhattan firm. She didn't like being called at the office.

"I'm busy. Why should I meet you for lunch?" she asked.

"Because I want to talk to you about something."

"We're talking right now."

"I mean in person."

"But why?"

"Because I *want* to. Jesus, does it have to be so complicated?"

"Don't shout at me."

"I'm not shouting."

"I don't have to listen to you shout anymore, and I won't listen to it."

"I never shouted. At the most I raised my voice."

"Well, don't raise your voice to me."

Larson took a deep breath. "I won't. I'm sorry. I just want to talk to you about something that's important to me, so I'd like to do it in person."

"All right. Though I still don't know why you can't tell me on the phone. Anyway, my *person* will be at La Bistro at eleven on Monday."

"Thanks. I'll be there."

The next day he dropped Cory off at the groomer's and headed to La Bistro. The dog had seemed mororse, but maybe that was just Larson projecting his own mood onto the poodle.

When he arrived at La Bistro, Kristine was already sitting at one of the outdoor tables under the expected Cinzano umbrella. Even sitting, it was obvious she had put on weight—which surprised Larson. Kristine had always been compulsive about her workouts and staying trim. You could even say she was obsessive about it.

The waiter handed him a menu, which Larson ignored. "Thanks for coming," he said to his ex.

She smiled. "You're welcome, I suppose."

"It's about Cory."

"Okay."

"Cory is my dog. You agreed to that in the settlement."

After a strange hesitation, during which her face went a little blank, Kristine replied, "I know perfectly well what I agreed to."

"Well, you kept a copy."

"So?"

"And now *anybody* can get a copy. Why did you do that?"

She didn't seem to hear him, her face gone blank again, staring.

"Are you even listening to me?"

The pause continued another couple of seconds, then her face suddenly animated. "Of course I'm listening. You're talking about the dog. I know you kept him in the settlement. I signed the document, didn't I?"

"Then why did you cheat and keep a copy? You didn't even like him when we were together."

"Cheat. Interesting word choice. And of course I liked Cory. Otherwise why do you think I'd retain a copy? It's been good having him around. I needed something good, after the divorce. Cory's familiar. That's been a small comfort, after all the changes. And no, I didn't make him generally available. I sent a copy to my friend Twila and she put up the around and around thing as a sample. It caught on—you have to admit, Cory looks pretty cute doing that dance. The sample generated a demand for the full download. Twila asked me if it was okay, and I said of course it was. It's not a big deal, Travis."

"It's a big deal to me."

"Hmm. Hold on a second."

"What?"

Her face went blank, then animated again. "Sorry. I'm here."

"What's going on with you? Wait a minute." He reached across the table and touched her cheek. The tips of his fingers seemed to vanish into her skin to feel *other* skin.

"Hey—" she said in the wrong voice, pulling back so abruptly she almost tipped over backwards in her chair.

Larson stood up. "Who the hell are you?"

"She's my person," the Kristine face said. "My assistant. I told you I didn't have time to leave the office. You never listen to me."

"For God's sake."

"By the way, your whole attitude confirms my decision. The less direct contact the better."

"I don't have an attitude."

"Of course you do. Your whole thing is an attitude."

"What are you talking about? My whole thing isn't an attitude. I don't even know what that means. All I wanted was to have a human moment so I could explain why keeping Cory private was important to me. I thought we could do that. Evidentially I was wrong."

"Drama."

"And what the hell is up with the name 'Corky?' His name is *Cory* and always has been."

"Twila changed it for the download. Out of deference to you, by the way."

"It's depressing seeing him all over town, answering to the wrong name. It just flattens me."

"God, you and your gloom. Do you have any idea how *exhausting* your negative attitude can be?

"Uh, guys," the assistant said, her voice, weirdly, coming from behind the Kristine face. "I'm a little uncomfortable with this, okay?"

Kristine said, "We're nearly done, Vina. Travis? My parting advice, if you want it—"

"I don't."

"—is: get over it. Not just the dog, but all of it."

"The *Corky* download is the only issue."

"Then get over the Corky download. It's a fad. Tomorrow it will be some other fad. I'm hanging up now. Goodbye."

The face went blank again and then winked out, leaving a stranger's slightly heavy but not unattractive features. "Hi, I'm Vina."

"I suppose you think screwing around with me is funny."

"No, I mean I didn't think—"

"Right," Larson said, his voice rising, "you didn't think." Vina stared at him, level-eyed, and Larson immediately felt like a fool. "I'm sorry. I guess I wanted to say that to Kristine."

"That's okay. She said you were a shouter."

"I didn't shout. I'm not a shouter. Did I shout?"

"Well, in this case it wasn't a shout, per se."

She smiled at him and picked up her menu. It was a lovely smile, like turning a warm light on her face. Larson lingered by the table.

"Are you really going to eat lunch?" he said.

Without looking up, Vina said. "Yes, I really am."

"Do you mind, I mean what if I had lunch with you?"

"I don't know . . ."

"Right. Dumb idea." He started to leave.

"Wait. I don't think there would be any harm in it, do you?" Now she was looking at him, and smiling that smile.

"No, I think it's fine." He sat back down. "I didn't even know they could do that, I mean the thing with the superimposed head."

"Oh, yeah, they can do it. The jector's in my necklace. Look, do you really think this is all right?"

"I don't know. It is if we want it to be."

She seemed to consider that, then closed her menu. "I'm going to have the bouillabaisse."

Beverman's firm was only a few blocks from Larson's midtown office. He walked over the next day, without an appointment. In the outer office a young clean-cut man named Frenkle told him he could expect to wait half an hour before Beverman would be available. "Unless you'd prefer to make an appointment. ."

"I'll wait." Larson installed himself in a chair, tabbed into *Business Week* magazine and began turning virtual pages, his mind and eyes skimming lightly over an article about the new Chinese ascendancy in commercial aviation.

"Good boy," Frenkle said in a quiet voice.

Larson looked up. Turned aside from his desk and bent forward in his chair, Frenkle was making little petting motions in the air just above a downloaded 'Corky' poodle. Larson's stomach muscles tightened. He closed the magazine. The virtual dog was looking at Frenkle with adoration.

"Isn't that frustrating," Larson said.

"Isn't what frustrating?" Frenkle said.

"Pretending to pet a dog that isn't there."

"Corky's there. I can't touch him, but it's easy to imagine what it would feel like. I used to have a live dog. And Corky reacts just as if I *were* petting him. Honestly, I never thought a virtual dog could be such wonderful company."

"Yeah, who would have thought it?"

A few minutes later Frenkle said, "Mr. Beverman will see you now."

Larson strode into the office like he was storming a beach.

In bed Vina was generous and patient, which inspired Larson to be the same. So different from his love-making with Kristine. His ex with her beautiful, model-perfect features and body—it was like he was always watching himself make love to her, separating the person from the body. His body and her body. Like it was the bodies that mattered.

"That was so nice," Vina said, lying in his arms.

"It really was."

She snuggled and kissed his neck. "Can I ask you a personal question?"

"Sure."

"Why did you and my boss get divorced?"

"Uh—"

"You don't have to answer that. I'm so dumb sometimes."

"No, it's okay. I don't think I could explain it, though. I mean, you'd have to have been there."

"I understand."

"I wish I did. Do you think I'm too gloomy? That was one of

Kristine's raps against me."

"I don't know. You seem okay to me."

"I think I'm okay."

"You two didn't have any kids, did you?"

"No. Just Cory."

"The poodle?"

"Right."

After a while, Vina asked, "Do you ever miss her?"

"He's right in the next room."

"*Her*—your wife."

"No, not really," he said.

"Not really but sort of, or, No, you don't miss her?"

"What?"

"Never mind." Vina nuzzled his neck and sighed.

But later on, after she fell asleep, Larson acknowledged to himself that, yes, he did miss Kristine. He didn't miss fighting with her all the time. He didn't miss the stress. But he did miss her sometimes. For instance, he missed lying in bed with her after making love—after the self-conscious performance part. And he missed walking into a party with her on his arm—Kristine the great beauty in full-on gorgeous mode. Who wouldn't miss the feeling of being the lucky one, the guy with the most beautiful woman in the room?

But he didn't *miss* miss her. He just missed the *idea* of her, sometimes. The idea of certain aspects of her, not the whole picture.

On Saturday afternoon Larson and Vina took Cory for a walk in the park. Larson had been avoiding the park, after his encounter with DeVris and his Corky download. For a while it seemed half the population of New York City owned a copy of Larson's poodle. But today it wasn't like that; maybe the fad was over and everybody deleted Corky or left him as an unused data file, like a real dog dropped off at the pound and forgotten.

"It was just one of those stupid web-fads," Vina said. "I don't know why it bothered you so much."

"I don't know. All those nanoswarm copies, I felt like it cheapened my real relationship with my dog."

"Why would it?"

"I don't know."

"When you think about it, there's no reason it would unless that's what you wanted it to do."

"Yeah, I guess."

Cory plodded along at the end of his leash, his head down, ears and tail drooping. He stopped once in a while to sniff at the grass, but he wasn't as lively as the fresh air and sunshine should have made him. He wasn't lively at all, and that worried Larson.

Vina slipped her arm around Larson's as they walked. "I might take Cory to the vet," he said. "Poor little guy doesn't have any zip, lately."

"How old is he?"

"Nine and a half."

"That's getting up there, for a dog."

"It's not that old."

Vina hunkered next Cory, who was snuffling at nothing visible for no discernable reason. She ruffled Cory's fluffy head. "You're a good dog, aren't you," she said.

Cory raised his head but his ears did not twitch up alertly like they would have if he was feeling better.

Looking at the top of Vina's head, at the part in her thick, coarse hair (so different from Kristine's angel-soft blond tresses), Larson felt a surge of undiluted affection and companionability, which he identified as love.

"Hey," he said.

Vina looked up.

"I'm having a really good day," he said.

"Me, too."

"And you know what?"

She smiled. "What?"

"I'm having it because I'm with you."

Her smile got a lot bigger. "I'm having a *great* day," she said.

They continued their walk, crossing a sunny meadow. Three girls in short, pleated cheerleader skirts and tank tops practiced gymnastically difficult moves, their tight and tan midriffs exposed as they stretched into slow backward flips and executed high, pom-pom waving leaps.

Vina noticed him noticing the girls. Larson couldn't help but notice other girls. His cheating days were over, though. "Show offs," Vina said about the cheerleaders, like she couldn't care less, which maybe she couldn't

"It's a disgrace, all right," Larson said.

"Did you know I tried out for cheerleaders back in high school?"

"No kidding."

"Yeah, I've got some serious moves. Watch me!"

She skipped a few steps ahead of him, and Larson hated himself for noticing her relative dowdiness. Only minutes ago he was noticing her, the girl he was falling in love with. Now the idiot part of his brain was making comparisons. She wore a pair of black Levis and a light gray button down shirt, and when she executed an ungainly cartwheel the shirt fell away, revealing her pasty white skin and love-handles. The cartwheel fell apart and she tumbled onto the grass, laughing. Sitting there, legs spread wide and arms crossed like a pouty child, she said, "Did I make the cut, coach?"

"You bet, kid."

In bed a month later, transported by passion, Larson said, "You look good enough to eat."

"I've been working out."

"Really."

"Going to the gym every day on my lunch-break. What do you think?"

"I think you look great, but I always think you look great."

"You're sweet to say that."

"I mean it. But—"

"But what?"

"I don't know. You don't seem like the gym kind of girl."

"I'm not really. But I thought it was time to get in shape."

"Remember when we used to have sex on our lunch breaks?" Larson said.

"Of course I remember. Geeze." She threw the sheet off, exposing her whole body. So, what so you think of the new me."

He traced his fingertips over the slight swell of her belly. "I think you could take me with one hand tied behind your back. But I liked the old—"

She sat up suddenly and pushed Larson over on the mattress,

hands locked on his wrists, pinning his arms down, straddling him. "Maybe. But I think I'm going to use *both* hands."

Larson was alone in the apartment and it was raining hard. Vina was at the gym. She was always at the gym. Working out and 'getting in shape' was stealing more and more of her time. Larson missed her. He didn't miss the idea of her, or certain aspects of her—he missed *her*.

Cory lay curled in his little basket bed. He spent a lot of time in the basket. The vet had diagnosed him, somewhat vaguely, as suffering from intestinal difficulties—something they needed to keep an eye, since it might or might not be serious. Cory's meds made him even more listless than he'd already become.

The phone trilled. Larson touched it, and Beverman's avatar appeared courtesy of Projektrix. "You're going to *love* this, Travis. Love it."

"Love what?"

"I found a way to get Kristine on the Corky thing."

"I thought you said there was no language in the divorce settlement to—"

"There isn't. I'm not talking about the divorce settlement. I'm talking about intellectual property law. We can successfully argue that you made Cory the poodle he is, by diligent training and a daily regimen. Before you got hold of Cory he was just a generic dog. You said yourself that Kristine had nothing to do with the training, care and feeding of the beast, right?"

"Right. But there's no such thing as a generic dog."

"Just listen to me. Think of Corky—"

"*Cory.*"

"Whatever. Think of *Cory* as a piano you and Kristine bought. This piano sits in the living room, takes up space and collects dust. Because nobody seriously plays the piano unless they've *always* played the piano. But you did play, my friend. You wrote songs on that piano. And then when the divorce came, Kristine appropriated a copy of the piano—which was a harmless deed. But she also appropriated *the songs you wrote on it*, which she then promptly infected all over the web."

Larson pressed his fingers to his temples, squinting at his attorney's avatar. "Cory isn't a piano."

"You're missing the point! What made the Corky download popular wasn't the fact that he was a cute poodle. What made him popular was what *you* trained the poodle to do. Around and around and around, for example." Berverman's avatar made a silly whirling motion with his finger. "What made Corky popular were the songs you wrote on him. In other words, Kristine has stolen your intellectual property."

The attorney's avatar rubbed virtual hands together like Scrooge McDuck in a bank vault.

The real Cory struggled up on his feet, whimpering, and dragged himself to his water bowl. Larson kept the bowl close to the poodle's bed, but Cory still had to get up to drink. It was painful to watch.

"What does all that mean?" Larson asked Beverman. "What can we actually do about it?"

"Oh, nothing much."

"Then what's the point?"

"Travis. The poodle is already out of the bag, so to speak. There is no recapturing the information, or retrieving all the thousands of virtual Corkys. But a judgment against Kristine will wound her credibility in the legal profession. If you want to strike back, this is how we do it. Trust me. We could even exact damages, if you want to go that route. But the point is to strike back for your emotional suffering."

"Okay."

"Okay? That's it? After all the—"

"*Okay.*"

Larson killed the avatar. Rain gusted in gritty waves against the wall-to-wall windows. Mid-afternoon and it was dark enough to require lamp light. Cory struggled back to his bed.

"Good dog," Larson said.

Cory's little stub-tail wagged briefly.

Emotional suffering.

Every day, Larson returned to the apartment at lunch to check on Cory, give him his afternoon meds, and see if he needed to go out to the little green patch at the side of the building and relieve himself. The Tuesday after the call from Beverman, Larson found the poodle lying unnaturally still in his little bed. On the floor next to the bed there was a puddle of vomit threaded with blood.

Larson's mouth opened and the breath halted in his chest. He stared hard. Usually you could see the poodle's flank rising and falling when he slept. This time: nothing. Grief rose in Larson's chest. And then Cory opened his eyes and blinked at him.

The vet wanted to keep Cory overnight, sedated. In the morning they would do an athroscopic examination.

"What do you think it is?" Larson asked, holding the dog in his arms.

"We won't know until tomorrow. For now there's no sense in speculating."

Larson didn't have the heart to go back to work, so he returned home early to the apartment. Vina was already there. He surprised her in the spare bedroom, which was directly across from the entry. She was wearing his ex wife's head, modeling herself naked, except for the Projectrix necklace, before the full-length mirror. She turned suddenly at the sound of the door opening, her full breasts swinging, so unlike Kristine's model-modest chest.

"Travis! I—" Her voice behind the blank, motionless, dead expression of Kristine's face.

"Jesus," Larson said. Could you turn that off, please?"

She touched something on the necklace and the Kristine head vanished. "That's so embarrassing," Vina said. "I was just, I don't know."

"Look, don't do that anymore, okay?"

"Okay. Hey, what's wrong? Are you crying or something?"

"I just want you to be you."

"That's easy. I am me." Vina pulled on a robe. She touched his cheek. "Hey, I love you."

He held her. "I love you, too. And you know I don't want you to be like Kristine."

"I know that. I was just playing around with the head. Really."

"And I don't want you to spend every second at the gym, not if you're doing it because of me."

"I'm not. Well, maybe a little bit because of you. It hurts when

I see you looking at other girls. But mostly I work out for me."

"It's just looking. It's nothing. And you're perfect already, as far as I'm concerned. I don't care about other girls."

"Aw. You're perfect, too, Trav."

They kissed. "Hey," Vina said, pulling back. "You *are* crying. Travis, where's the dog?"

Larson couldn't sleep. He stared at Vina's face on the pillow beside his. For all her dieting and exercise her features were still thick and plain; she was still *Vina*. Which is all he wanted. He remembered lying next to Kristine and how calm it felt to be with her sleeping body after all the stress and tension of their waking conflicts—Kristine's sleeping face presenting her absence. But Larson was tired of absence.

He slipped from the bed and into the hallway, pulling the bedroom door shut behind him. In the living room he called Beverman's office and left a message, keeping his voice down so he wouldn't wake Vina.

"I'm dropping it. We're not going to sue Kristine."

Larson fixed himself a drink and sat in the living room, listening to the rain. The bourbon helped Larson keep his fear at bay. That's what Kristine used to do for him. She used to keep the fear at bay by her presence. But presence wasn't always enough. Eventually you had to be there all the way, and you had to let somebody else be there all the way, too. Without that, little comforts counted all out of proportion. Even the comfort of a dog that wasn't really there. People needed that. It was a small thing and you were petty to begrudge it. The world only went around so many times in a person's life. If you made it harder than it already was, you were really just this gloomy person—this *shouter*.

Rain blew against the windows. Larson poured another bourbon and stood looking out at the city, at the world moving through one dark night and already on the way towards the next one. Around and around and around.

Yes, this is a story that wasn't in first edition. How clever of you to notice!

Thank You, Mr. Whiskers

H adley Yeager was old and widowed and miserable. She hadn't always been that way. She used to be younger and in possession of a breathing husband. Actually *she* had been the possession. And the misery had been constant and enduring. Now Hadley couldn't find her grocery money. She had hidden it because she was worried about that dark boy breaking in and robbing her. But she couldn't remember *where* she'd hidden it. Hadley was hungry, and if she didn't find the money soon things wouldn't be pleasant. Not that they were, generally.

Hadley sat in the kitchen and cried. Her stomach ached with hunger. Briefly she wished she owned a cat. Franklin (or Soopy, or Mrs. Pussyfoot, or Mr. Whiskers) would rub against her leg and purr and be a comfort. But there would also be the horrid droppings and the sofa shredded, and probably Franklin would make her sneeze. Then she remember Franklin was the name of her husband (even *his* name sometimes drifted away from her), and she determined to put the whole idea out of her mind.

Hadley started to stand up and a wave of dizziness swelled through her. The room seemed to darken, then it passed and her vision cleared and she stood up more steadily. She would stop crying and fetch the mail. No one normal wrote to her anymore, but once in a while, among the bills, there was an envelope proclaiming her a WINNER!!!! and these cheered her until she recalled the truth.

She peeked out the curtains first. The street was empty. She put on her coat and let herself out, mumbling, "Be good, Mr.

Whiskers," and she pulled the door shut extra hard so the cat wouldn't get away. Cats were clever but they couldn't open doors that were properly shut.

Hadley's joints ached terribly in the cold. By the time she had hobbled to the mailbox she had almost forgotten what she was doing outside. One time she had become confused walking home from the grocery store. Everything had looked strange and unfamiliar and she didn't know anyone or what to do. The sky had been white and glaring, and her joints tormented her. Hadley had stood in one place so long, searching for a recognizable sign, that her arm became tired and she dropped the grocery bag, spilling grapes like little green marbles. That was the first time she had become aware of the dark boy. As she started to bend over he had suddenly been there, snatching up her bag with his big brown paw and thrusting it at her. Hadley's heart had quailed, but he simply rode away on his bike, knees pumping as high as his armpits. Watching him swing around the corner she had suddenly recognized the street.

Now Hadley looked back at her house, hoping to see Mr. Whiskers in the window, but he wasn't there. She glanced around, confused, and saw the boy coming. He was wearing his too-big coat and riding his too-small bicycle wobbling back and forth. At the same instant she remembered that Mr. Whiskers wasn't a real cat and that she lived alone in the house she had once shared with her husband who never touched her during the last decades of their marriage. The house with paint like dead skin flaking and peeling off and the lawn overcome by weeds.

The boy stopped a short distance away and stood straddling his bike and looking at her. She wiped her eyes because she was sad about Mr. Whiskers.

"Hey, lady, are you okay?"

"Of course I am! You're from Honduras." She got Honduras from a picture in one of the National Geographic magazines Franklin used to subscribe to, or maybe it was a magazine that had been in the house when she was a child. Pictures and real people and things were all mixed up in Hadley's mind.

"No, I'm not," the dark boy said.

"And you're the one spray-painting everything," Hadley's voice quavered. The strangled, threatening loops and knots of paint appeared on fences and signs and even the walls of houses. One had appeared on the wall of her house.

"I don't do that," the boy said, hunched inside his giant purple-blue puffy coat. "That's some dumb little kids."

Hadley sniffed and turned away. Then she squinted, for there were too many mailboxes. She counted them to make sure. The new one was on the end, right next to hers. Somehow it fit on the board under the little moss-covered roof, even though, Hadley felt certain, there hadn't been room. Well. She glanced at the boy, who was still watching her. She didn't want him to rob her but there wasn't anything she could do about it if he did. She decided to grab her mail and hold it in both hands until she got back to her front door.

She quickly opened the mailbox and reached in, keeping her eye on the boy. It was cold inside the box, like the interior of a freezer. Her fingers touched something like a postcard. She pulled it out. A three by five inch piece of white cardstock with these words printed neatly in the middle: LOOK IN THE SOFA CUSHION.

She had taken it out of the new mailbox by mistake. She started to replaced it but didn't. In her own mailbox she found an electric bill and an advertisement. When she looked up, the dreadful spray-painting boy from Mexico was gone. She closed both mailboxes and was startled to notice the new one now had her name HADLEY etched in gold letters on the door.

LOOK IN THE SOFA CUSHION.

Hadley was preparing tea for her grumbling stomach when her mind made the connection. She shuffled into the living room with her empty cup hanging from a crooked finger. The sofa was almost thirty years old, the floral print faded, the cushions lumpy and compressed. One of the deliverymen from The Furniture Mart had pinched his finger backing up the stairs and said, "Shit," the only time that word had been spoken in the house, Hadley believed. She remembered wincing and being glad Franklin was at work. The deliveryman had been even darker than the spray-painting boy.

She unzipped the cushion on the side where she habitually

sat to watch TV. Her hand (like a palsied, sinewy chicken claw) reached in and groped at the crumbling foam until she found the envelope with her grocery money.

Hadley lay awake staring at the ceiling and inhabiting her bone pain. The moon had come in and printed shadows all over. She never could sleep anyway. In her recurring dream a darkspun wicked thing whispered around the doors and windows of her house, seeking entry. A thing made of shadows and poison webs and evil intent. Dreading sleep, dreading the wicked thing, Hadley reached out and turned the lamp on, picked up her glasses and the card from the bedside table.

LOOK IN THE SOFA CUSHION.

The card was real.

She got up and put on her robe and slippers. She retrieved a flashlight from the kitchen and went outside and made her way to the mailbox. The moon was everywhere, and the cold breeze, and rustling sounds. Her slippers scuffed on the pavement, her feet especially ached with the cold. She pointed her flashlight at the new mailbox and saw her name shimmer in gold letters. She hobbled straight to it, hesitated, then pulled open the little door.

The mailbox was full of stars.

She stepped back. All of the night sky seemed to be compressed inside the mailbox, all the star-filled night skies she had ever seen, all the ones she had gazed at when she was a young girl who dreamed and would have liked a kiss, long before she ever met Franklin. (A memory surfaced: standing next to her father in the backyard of the Arlington house while he pointed out constellations and told their mythical stories.)

Hadley moved closer, intending to flip the door shut. She was afraid and wanted to go back inside where it was safe. But it seemed wrong to leave the mailbox open. She reached a trembling hand toward the door. Something white floated up among the stars and presented itself to her.

YOUR PAIN IS GONE.

Hadley turned the card over. The back was blank. She started toward the house, walking spryly, then stopped. Her joints did not hurt. She bent her right leg at the knee. No pain. She clutched the card in her hand and hurried to the house. She felt almost like she could run again!

YOUR BOWELS ARE HEALTHY
YOUR VISION IS PERFECT
YOUR HEATING BILL IS PAID

Franklin had been mean, not at all like her father, who had been a kind, brooding man who liked to gather her in with his big arm and read stories to her—all this goodness ruined when he walked out of the house one evening and never returned; later they found his poor body broken at the foot of the Magnolia Street Bridge. A leap that changed everything, everything, and led eventually to Franklin.

The dark boy malingered on his bicycle in front of Hadley's house. She frowned. Hadley's husband had been mean but he had also, perhaps, been right about "them" ruining the neighborhood. They were like an alien incursion. Such attitudes ran contrary to Hadley's deepest intuitive currents and the sense of fairness her father had instilled. But it was hard always going against Franklin, even if it was only in the silent place inside her heart. And Franklin had been strong, as her father had once seemed to be. Also, what did fairness mean anymore? Her father hadn't been fair when he jumped off the bridge, abandoning her forever. Eventually she came to accept her husband's views. Now here was this one boy always watching her, asking if she was all right. Of course she was all right!

DO YOU WANT HIM TO GO AWAY?

It was the first time the mailbox had asked her a question. She had gone to the box, and the dark boy had been on her mind, his awful spray-painting. And somehow it was as if he were to blame for everything: the old house that was ugly and smelled bad, the bills that baffled her, the arid decades of her marriage, the dreadful wattled thing in the mirror. After thinking about it for two days she turned the card over and carefully printed: YES on the back. The next time she looked the mailbox was empty, as if it were waiting for her reply, and she placed the card in it, swung the flag up, but didn't shut the door. The card lay white and innocent, waiting for stars. She wanted to take it back, but a willful, contrary urge made her slap the door shut and walk quickly away.

She peeked between the curtains and watched the boy. He coasted by on his bicycle but stopped just past the mailboxes and rolled backward, using his feet. He stopped the way someone would stop if he had heard his name called. The dark boy looked around, but it was a cold day and he was the only one on the street. Suddenly his head jerked toward Hadley's special mailbox. She couldn't see his face, but something about the way he moved, the attitude of his body, suggested he was afraid. *Don't*, Hadley thought, but it was too late to take the card back, and the boy reached out and opened the mailbox. Something yanked him off his bike. He staggered to one knee, his right hand thrust into the box. He shook his head, dazed or unbelieving. Then the mailbox ate him, jerking him in first by the arm. He screamed and Hadley heard the scream and would hear it forever after that. The boy's body collapsed into the small aperture. His big puffy coat stripped off him, his legs kicking and jerking. The whole row of mailboxes shuddered violently, doors dropping open, bits of green moss shaking off the little slanted roof. It took only seconds.

Hadley's breath halted in her chest. No one else appeared on the street. The door of Hadley's special mailbox hung open, like the doors of the other five mailboxes. The dark boy's coat lay on the ground, white stuffing foaming out of the torn sleeve.

Hadley was crying and her legs shook as she crossed the street. She closed the mailboxes one at a time, and when she got to her special mailbox there was something waiting for her.

HE WASN'T REAL

She gathered up the puffy coat and all but ran back to her house.

YOU ARE GROWING YOUNGER

It was spring. Hadley was walking. Her bones did not hurt and her head was clear and she was perhaps twenty years younger than she had been two months ago. In this condition she did not

feel so afraid of her neighbors and of the world, and she had begun to remember herself, who she had been before everything
turned bitter.

She walked by a neatly maintained ranch house with ginger-
bread trim and a flower garden. Hadley had once kept a garden
of her own. She missed it and thought she might start a new one.

A swarthy middle-aged woman, bent over, wearing a sagging
green sweater and brown shoes came out the front door of the
house and waved to her. Hadley did not know the woman but
stopped.

"Oh, you're too young," the woman said. "I thought you were
the lady from the white house on the next block."

"I am," Hadley said.

The woman narrowed her eyes at her then said, "Oh. Well,
you don't know me."

Hadley smiled politely.

"But you knew my son." Her voice shook when she said "my
son." "I am Mrs. Alverez. Anita Alverez, Jonathon's mother."

"I don't—"

"He worried about you," the woman said. "He told me he used
to ask if you were all right."

In her mind Hadley saw the puffy coat stuffed behind Franklin's workbench in the basement.

"His grandmother—my mother—died last summer. Her
mind was gone. It was hard for Jonathon." Mrs. Alverez looked
away. "He cried so much when she died." Mrs. Alverez moved her
hands vaguely.

"I'm sorry," Hadley said.

Tears spilled down Mrs. Alverez's cheeks and she did not look
at Hadley. "He was a good boy."

HE WASN'T REAL

Hadley did not comprehend this message. She had grown
younger and more vigorous but still she slept like an old woman.
Fitfully and in fear of dreams, of the darkspun wicked thing. Her
mind was sharp and she remembered herself, her better nature,
and she knew Mrs. Alverez was right: her son *had* been a good
boy.

Hadley carefully printed a question on the back of the HE WASN'T REAL card and replaced it in the mailbox. *What do you mean?* she had written. The next day a new card was present.

THIS IS HEAVEN

Thirty-five years later Hadley was depressed and attempting to alleviate that condition by shopping. It was that or the sleeping pills back at the Hotel Chateaubriand. L'Univers D'objets Rares was located on the exclusive Rue Ampère. The dapper man in the neat black zip suit had brought forth the Martian Fire Crystals and was awaiting her judgment, peeved at Hadley's bored response to the rarities.

A voice spoke inside Hadley's ear. This wasn't surprising in and of itself. Like nearly everyone she'd had an aural implant injected through her eardrum and it had bonded bio-molecularly to the incus, malleus, and stapes bones of her middle ear. The device served as a hands-off phone activated by the micro electrical impulses of her intent. It was also a conduit for automated information, stock market updates, weather, even serialized stories that she would listen to in bed sometimes when she found sleep elusive . . . or too permanently tempting. The stories reminded her distantly of her father's encompassing arm and soothing story time voice.

But she hadn't activated the device. And it hadn't given her a weather report or a newZflash; it had given her advice on which Martian Fire Crystal to purchase.

The crystal on your left is flawed, Hadley.

It was a soft, perfectly modulated masculine voice. The same voice which last night had read her chapter twelve of *Pride and Prejudice*. It sounded the same but it was not the same. And Hadley knew what was speaking to her.

"My mailbox," she said out loud.

The proprietor lifted his eyebrows.

"Incoming call," Hadley said, distracted, then added, "I'll take the one on the right."

When she was outside with her package, she said, "It's you, isn't it?"

"Yes," the voice said.

"I thought you were gone for good."

"No. I'm always here," the voice said.

Hadley sat on a bench in the little park across the street from L'Univers D'objets Rares. A pattern of sunlight and shade swayed over her like an ethereal net. With the passing decades she had gradually allowed the origin of her impossible good fortune to retreat from the presence of her mind. It was difficult to let it come forward again.

"Tell me what you are," she said. "Please."

"That question is more complicated than you might think," the Voice replied. "Simply put: I am you."

"Me!"

"An over-simplification, but yes. You could think of me as your higher-consciousness self, dreaming your new life."

Hadley watched a starling flicker over the uneven brown bricks of the park. Moss almost iridescently green grew thickly in the seams between the bricks. The starling's shadow, a black ripple, glided a little behind the bird.

"I don't believe that," Hadley said.

"You don't have to, of course."

"This can't be a dream."

"It's not a dream such as you are thinking. The world is real. And up until my advent into your ego-consciousness, it was a shared experience."

"And what is it now?"

"I've already told you: heaven. The only heaven into which anyone is ever received. Death is the termination of all consciousness, all personal existence. Near the point of its arrival the higher-consciousness asserts itself. Hi!"

"I don't understand."

"I built this place from the existing template of the vulgar world, the one you physically inhabit. I *prepared* it for us, Hadley. Because when you cease to live, so do I cease. But nothing ceases here, unless you will it."

"But it isn't real?" Hadley said.

"Is a dream real while you are in it? This world is as real as anything. And it works just like the one you were used to, with one exception: you can have, be, or do anything. It's real so long as you go on believing it is. In *our* world, in Hadley's World, Time is a seeming thing and can stretch to infinity, sustained by a perfectly balanced neurochemical illusion. But we need each other, Hadley, or it won't persist. Nothing will. I made the world, populated it with the shadow-twins of the human race, but *you* bring it alive. So let us be happy. The world is a lovely place now, isn't it?"

"Lovely," she said, monotone.

Hadley stared across the park at the people on the Rue Ampère and couldn't believe they were mere figments, some kind of second tier Platonic shadows. But that's what the Voice had told her years ago regarding Jonathon Alverez. Only back then it wasn't even a voice but a few printed words on a card. After a long while Hadley said, "Are you there?"

No answer.

"Hello?"

Nothing. Then a static burst, and: *La température est à Paris un degrés de soixante-dix-quatre chauds . . .*

Heaven.

Decades passed. Or didn't pass. In her New York condo Hadley crossed her legs and leaned back in the wonderful chair. It reacted to her slightest movements, even the subtle alterations of electrical impulses traveling her nerves, and adjusted for maximum comfort. It was a SmArt chair. A very smart one. Hadley's arm hung languidly over the side, a doparette between her middle fingers unwinding in a fragrant blue thread. Her body was that of a twenty-two year old. Her breasts were firm, her legs good, her health excellent, her mind acute. She was wealthy and she was immortal. Two excellent things to be. But Hadley didn't feel excellent and never had in all the intervening years. Nothing could accomplish her contentment; it was time to wake up—or go to sleep forever.

"Abandon heaven?"

Hadley looked up out of her thoughts as the Simulacrum stepped into the room. She preferred Simulacrae to the shadow people in her world. This one appeared exactly like a twenty-six-year-old Robert Redford. Its movie star hair fell over its forehead in a thick blond shock. The Simulacrum was companion, confident, and the world's most exquisite vibrator. Not to mention mind reader. Sundance was almost preternaturally alert to Hadley's moods and needs; he had been engineered that way by shadow twins of human genius. The perfect companion in a world without real companions.

"What do you know about it?" Hadley felt woozy and high.

The Simulacrum smiled. "I always know."

Hadley stood up and walked to the bubble window that overlooked the upper eastside of Manhattan. Ten thousand lights glimmered in the night. Like the stars she used to dream on as a child. Her mind wanted to dissolve and blur into a doparette haze. Over her shoulder she said, "It's you, isn't it. Not the Simulacrum."

"Yes."

She wasn't surprised. "I'm sad."

"Don't be."

She didn't reply.

Sundance, the Voice, the Mailbox, Hadley herself, whatever, was quiet.

"This is all wrong," Hadley said.

"It's right as rain."

"No."

Sundance loomed behind her. Hadley stiffened. In the glass she saw its reflection, and then its hands settled on her shoulders and began kneading the tension out of her muscles. She twisted away, dropped the remaining scrap of her doparette into a disposal iris, and passed her hand over a sensor that transformed the window to permeable status; a breath of night air touched the back of her neck. She started toward the bathroom to shower.

"Please go away," she said.

The Simulacrum remained at the window, hands clasped behind its back, chin lifted, head slightly cocked.

"You haven't been yourself," it observed.

"Who else would I *be*?"

"An uncertain thing," the Simulacrum said. "A doubter. An unhappy, cringing, withdrawn creature, dried up and ruined and finished." It turned from the window and smiled and held its hand out. "What you used to be, Hadley."

Hadley straightened her skirt. "I know what I was."

"Then believe in what you are. What we are."

"You only show up when you think I'm going to end it. If

you're my higher self you're also my worst self."

It stepped toward her. "I made you young and gave you everything."

"But you took things, too."

It stopped. "Took what?"

"I was thinking about Jonathon Alverez."

"Who?"

Hadley could see the Simulacrum knew perfectly well who Jonathon Alverez had been.

"The way he screamed when you ate him," she said.

Sundance's smile dimmed slightly.

"So this isn't any kind of heaven," Hadley said. "This is a selfish, ugly place. This isn't heaven and it isn't a dream, either. It's the place where dreams die. It's a bridge."

The smile went completely out. The Simulacrum stepped toward her, and Hadley moved back.

"What does it matter? He was only a product of your fears, and the sentimental story you made for him in our world is just a story. This place we share exists between shaved moments of time. Nothing has happened to that boy."

"It isn't about him," Hadley said. "It's about what you need out of me to go on existing."

"And what do you suppose that is," the Simulacrum said.

"You need me to be like you. Morbidly self-absorbed, so this narcotic world can go on existing."

"That boy was a hundred years ago, relative," Sundance said. "It took you long enough to decide I was bad."

"Well." Hadley sniffed. "I'm not *that* good myself."

"You'll be alone and you'll die alone." The Simulacrum advanced. "There isn't any real heaven, you know. This is the only way we persist."

"I don't care. I'm alone, anyway."

Sundance reached out for her, wearing its best Redford smile. "Why don't you come to bed now and forget all this sadness."

"No!"

Hadley shoved past the Simulacrum and threw herself at the bubble window. Its permeable molecular arrangement gave way and she fell and tumbled among the ten thousand lights like stars. *Daddy*, she wailed in her mind, *Daddy!*

Hadley sat in the kitchen weeping. The withered sack of her stomach spat acid and growled. She could no longer appease it with hot tea and sugar. Mr. Whiskers rubbed against her orthopedic hose, fur crackling.

"Poor kitty," Hadley muttered. There was nothing left for Mr. Whiskers to eat, either. She reached down to pet him but the cat padded out of the kitchen. Hadley followed him with her rheumy eyes. He planted his forepaws on the sofa cushion and began scratching.

"No, Mr. Whiskers!"

But the cat continued, and Hadley felt too weak to shoo him away. His claws would simply ruin the cushion.

The cushion.

Suddenly she remembered where she had hidden her grocery money. *Thank you, Mr. Whiskers, thank you!* But Mr. Whiskers was only a phantom of her intuition and was gone before she ever stood up.

THE TREE

The movers were still hauling furniture into the new house when Tom decided to climb the back fence and explore the ten acres of wild woods that had somehow survived years of encroaching development. He was eleven years old, had been living with his divorced mother in a one-bedroom apartment. His new stepfather owned not only the big frame house but also the woods. And according to Charlie (Tom could not force himself to call the man "Dad") development would not be held off much longer.

He dropped from the top of the fence and landed on his feet. Immediately Tom was struck by how quiet it was. No birds sang, no flies buzzed, not a living creature moved in the stillness. It was like having cotton stuffed in his ears. He could hear the pulse of his own blood but nothing else. The fence boards were six feet tall. On the side that faced his backyard they looked new, the blond wood clean and unblemished in the August sun. But on this side the boards appeared old and weathered, gray, tired, as if they had stood for time out of mind, a border between these dark woods and the sunny lawn and fruit trees on the other side. Tom squinted through a knothole in the fence, saw his mother standing in front of the sliding glass door directing a couple of men in jeans and T-shirts carrying a sideboard. The slider was open, but Tom couldn't hear his mother's voice. He pulled back, turned, and walked into the woods.

He felt drawn, pulled in. It was hot. He stumbled along in a kind of daze, weaving through the pathless woods, through sun and shadow, until he came to the tree.

The trunk of the tree was gnarled and twisted. Its thick roots burst above the ground like partially buried bones. About fifteen feet up, the branches spread open like the fingers of an unclenching fist. And nestled in that cool leafy altitude was a kid's tree house. The boards were nailed haphazardly together. A moon-shaped window tilted drunkenly in one wall. A spine of irregularly spaced rungs climbed the central trunk, the nail heads dark with rust. Tom knew he had to climb them, but first he reached out and touched the tree. Immediately he pulled his hand back and wiped his fingers on his jeans. The tips of his fingers were sticky with sap. He rubbed harder but the sap clung to his skin like glue.

Suddenly he didn't feel like climbing up to the tree house. All he wanted to do was get away.

He started to back off from the tree, and that was when he noticed the dead squirrel pinched in the crook of two roots. He bent over to look at it. The squirrel was emaciated, starved, its fur mangy. Dried blood stained its claws and teeth, and its tail was ripped where the squirrel had attempted to chew through it.

At home Tom washed his hands in the bathroom sink, really scrubbing at the sap on his fingers. But no matter how hard he scrubbed, the fingers remained sticky.

His mother appeared in the doorway, leaning against the jamb. Her face was flushed, a few strands of her yellow hair plastered to her sweaty cheek.

"So where did you disappear to all morning?"

"Just looking around the neighborhood," he said, concentrating on his fingers. "Besides, I was only gone a little while."

"Honey, it's past noon. Your father called at lunch and I couldn't tell him where you were."

Stepfather, Tom thought. Then: *noon?* Of course he must have been gone more than a half hour. The movers had left, most of the kitchen stuff was put away, and for crying out loud all he had to do was look at the clock. He thought hard but could not remember anything after he noticed the dead squirrel. He couldn't even remember climbing back over the fence. There was the squirrel, and then he was shuffling into the bathroom, picking up the oval bar of pink soap, turning the water on hot. That was all.

At dinner his stepfather, Charlie, reached over and patted him on the shoulder, ruffled his hair.

"Earth to Tom," he said.

Tom looked up out of his thoughts. "Huh?"

"How do you like the new digs, Tommy?"

"Fine."

"Fine, he says."

"He loves the house," Tom's mother said, always interpreting for him. "We both do."

Tom lay in bed, making his fingers stick together, pulling them apart, sticking them together and pulling them apart. His mother knocked once, walked in, and he stopped playing with his fingers. She sat on the edge of the bed, brushed his hair away from his eyes.

"How's my little man?"

"Good."

"This is better than that tiny apartment, isn't it?"

"I like having my own room," he admitted. "But I still have to fix it up."

"There'll be plenty of time. Go to sleep now, okay? Another big day tomorrow."

"Right."

She clicked off the table lamp, kissed him, left him alone. He lay quietly in the bed. Played with his sticky fingers. Smelled them. The sap smelled a little sour, not a good smell at all.

He leaned against the fence, peered through the knothole. It was an ordinary woods filled with morning sunlight and shade. No birds, though. A hand fell on his shoulder and he jerked around.

"Hi," he said to his stepfather. "I thought you went to work already."

"Tom, you remember what I said about those woods?"

"Sure."

Charlie hunkered beside him. He was a tall man, older than Tom's mother. It seemed like he always wore a suit. Even on week-ends he wore a button-up shirt. Tom liked to picture his real father in blue jeans and a black T-shirt, though he had no idea what his real father wore or even what he looked like.

"It isn't safe, Tommy. Just consider it off limits. I have my reasons, believe me I do. Why don't you help your mother today? There's a lot of work to do around the house. What do you say?"

"I'll help her."

"My man!"

Tom didn't go into the woods, not even after Charlie left. He helped his mother straighten up the house, put stuff away, clean. But he felt drawn to the woods. He wanted to see that tree house again. He and his mother ate lunch on the back deck, and it was almost like the warm breeze whispering through the trees was really whispering to *him*. Come on in, Tom, check it out, buddy.

"What's wrong with your fingers?"

"Huh?"

"Your fingers," his mom said. "Did you get something on them?"

"Not really." He showed her his fingers because there really wasn't anything on them. They weren't sticky anymore. Only sometimes they *felt* sticky, just to him.

Night again. Tom couldn't sleep, couldn't stay in bed. It was hot but it was more than that. Closing his eyes felt like drowning in black water. He pulled on a pair of shorts and slipped quietly out of his room, thinking of raiding the refrigerator. Halfway down the stairs he heard voices and stopped.

His mother said, "He hates to be called Tommy, I've told you that."

"I'll mend my wicked ways," Charlie said.

"Not *all* your wicked ways, I hope."

Stifled laughter. They were downstairs, in the living room. *Why not have a look*, a voice asked Tom, and he couldn't ignore it.

He stood by the arch between the living room and dining room, his back to the wall. Listening to them, hating it, but listening. He made himself look around the corner, saw their white bodies on the carpet, moving together. His mother's grimacing face straining over Charlie's shoulder.

*

The next day he told his mother he was walking to the Safeway store, but instead he climbed the fence and dropped into the forbidden woods. He didn't care what Charlie said.

He picked up a stick and whacked at the bushes while he walked, his feet discovering their own path. The sky seemed to darken but he was barely aware of the change. He peered inside himself at his mother's face, the way it had been last night, the way her fingers had dug into Charlie's white back.

When he looked up out of his thoughts he was confused. It was only ten acres, and from the second floor of the house he could even see to the other side of the woods, see patches of green lawn, brick chimneys, the slanted planes of rooftops. But now the woods appeared to stretch forever in all directions, the August sunlight screened out, all sounds muffled. Tom's mouth felt dry.

And then there was the tree.

The great upthrusting trunk. Black, twisted and gnarled, the branches opened like fingers. A different tree but the same; he was seeing it more clearly. The irregular wooden rungs reached to the platform like spinal bones.

Tom started to climb. He didn't like the feel of the wood on his bare hands. Though it was dry and hard he had the inner sense that it was unclean, spongy, and rotten with age.

He pulled himself onto the platform, unaccountably tired. It was darker inside the tree house and it smelled . . . sick. He could only compare it to the way his grandfather's room had smelled during the last weeks of the old man's life—an odor of living decay.

He leaned back against the wall and rubbed his eyes. The quality of light seemed to shift from moment to moment. It was like being in two places at once. The moon-shaped window was there, a crescent eye open to a green, living world. Then it was gone and he was entirely closed up in a black box.

Tom wanted to get down, run back to the house, if he could find the house. But another part of him was equally curious and excited by the strangeness. Whatever happened, he knew he would never willingly return to this place, so he didn't want to miss a thing.

He moved deeper into the tree house. Dusty sunlight slanted

through chinks between the boards. He saw the desiccated body of a robin, small, mummified corpses of squirrels. The scattered husks of insects crunched under his sneakers. And then he saw, lying in deep shadow, an object that frightened him badly, then terrified him. Tom backed away from it, retreating to the open side of the tree house.

But the opening had narrowed, almost trapping him inside. He barely managed to squeeze through. His T-shirt tore on a jag, the sharp splinter cutting into him like a tooth. As far as he could see in every direction a dark primordial jungle stretched into smoky distances. Suddenly dizzy, Tom swayed, his vision blurring. He held onto the edge of the tree house, closed his eyes, concentrated on light. When he opened his eyes the view was back to normal. He saw lawns and houses not far away.

He climbed swiftly down, hating the feel of the wooden rungs. They looked like ordinary pieces of wood now with the rusty heads of nails embedded in them. Six feet from the ground he jumped, landed off-balance, and wound up on his hands and knees. He crawled over one of the great roots and almost put his hand on the dead squirrel he'd first seen a couple of days ago. Its corruption had progressed. Ticks lifted from the corpse as he jerked his hand back. And then he was on his feet, running through the woods, stumbling, gasping—

"Don't you ever go in there again," his mother said. She had seen him climbing over the fence, not on his way back from but on his way into the woods. She said she'd called to him from the kitchen window but he had ignored her, and by the time she reached the fence he was gone from sight.

"You don't know how close I came to calling the police, Tom."

"The *police*."

"Charlie told you to stay out of there and for good reason."

"Charlie," Tom said, thinking of the grunting sound his stepfather had made, the white skin of his back.

"What was I supposed to think when you were gone that long?"

"I wasn't gone very long."

"Tom, I know exactly how long you were away. I know because at the end of the first half hour I went looking for you and couldn't find you. It was over an hour more before you came back. I swear if you hadn't come back when you did—"

"I couldn't have been gone that long, Mom."

"Tom, I can read a *watch*."

Later, as he lay in bed, once again unable to sleep, there was a soft knock on his door and then it opened and his stepfather walked in.

"I'm in trouble," Tom said.

"You're not in trouble." Charlie sat in a chair by the bed, crossed his legs, folded his hands. He was a large man, his face long and thoughtful, his hair liberally salted with gray.

"You're old enough to hear this," he said. "I was a fool not to tell you sooner."

"Tell me what?"

"The reason I don't want you going into those woods is that two children have disappeared in there already."

Tom's chest tightened.

"They were brothers," Charlie continued. "Eight and six years old."

"Did—"

"No one has any idea what happened to them, but there's plenty of speculation. You know about strangers, Tom."

Tom nodded.

"Well we don't have to go into all the possibilities. Those woods are going to be a subdivision. I've already sold it off."

"It's old," Tom said.

"What is?"

"Nothing," Tom said, but he was thinking: The tree is old, older than anyone knows.

"Well." Charlie stood up and walked to the door, put his hand on the light switch. "It's late. Mind if I turn this off?"

"I guess not."

"Try not to frighten your mother anymore." Charlie turned the light off. Moon shadows occupied the room.

"And Tom?"

Tom looked up from the bed.

"Don't frighten *me* either," Charlie said.

Alone in his bedroom Tom stared at the image in his mind. The thing in the tree house, the thing that had frightened him so much. It had been a child's black, high-top sneaker, the canvas ripped violently, as if a dog had been tearing at it. And in the dark corner of the tree house he had seen the suggestion of something inside the sneaker, a stump, the dull glimmer of bone.

Tom opened his eyes and it was morning, but too early for anyone else to have gotten out of bed yet. Tom wasn't really awake himself. His eyes were open, he was aware of the room, the quiet house, but his thoughts lingered in a dream world. The tree was older than time. Before it was a tree it was something else but still the same inside.

Tom found himself standing next to his bed in his pajama bottoms, then he was on the stairs, and then outside in the back-yard, the morning air cool on his bare skin. The tree knew its life in this time was almost finished, and it required one more blood sacrifice so its seed could survive. The tree had been alive longer than people. The first woman had plucked fruit from its tempting limb.

Tom dropped from the top of the fence and landed with a jar-ring thud on his back. It jolted him out of his trance. He looked around, shocked. The dry weeds and prickly grass scratched his skin. From where he lay the fence looked high as a fortress wall. Around him silence prevailed.

Tom got to his feet, reached for the top of the fence, and then felt the tree's pull again, the irresistible tug, and he knew what was going to happen but was helpless to prevent it.

He jumped weakly, caught the top of the fence, and started to haul himself up even as his mind began to cloud. He hooked one arm over the top, pulled. He could see into the backyard but it was like looking through smoked glass. He already belonged to death. Charlie appeared in the kitchen window with a cup of coffee. Tom cried out feebly then dropped back to the ground, unable to hold on.

He stood at the base of the tree, looking up the huge black column of the trunk. He would climb up into the grasping hand of the branches, the place where dead things lay, and it would absorb him, eat him. It might leave a shred of his pajama bottoms, maybe a finger, some remnant. Or perhaps it would leave nothing. The tree devoured innocence. It had been the original tool of corruption. Later it had acquired its own crude immortality, and it required the blood of children.

Then Tom was inside the tree, and it was like being inside the beating heart of a demon. The tree had lived ten thousand times, its dark seed had crossed continents, oceans, growing strong and tall, feeding on the blood and spirit of innocents.

Tom lay back, feeling himself pale toward death. The stink of death was around him. He turned his head and saw the opening, began to drag himself toward it. He tried to think of his mother, of her love, but it wasn't enough. He felt the tree's eagerness to survive, its hunger. In his mind he saw a pond in a wooded place near a strange city of glass towers, and he saw the pond turn black as ink and the pallid, grasping hand of a child groping out of its surface then disappearing. He saw a dense yellow mist that crept from a marshland and devoured what it had to devour. He saw a hive of imperishable wasps . . .

Tom managed to reach the edge of the platform but could do no more. He peered over the brink and saw his stepfather. Charlie shouted something at him from the base of the tree, but Tom couldn't hear him, couldn't even read the expression on Charlie's face. He knew Charlie wasn't seeing the ancient monster. He was seeing an ordinary oak tree, the one Tom had seen his first time, a beautifully leafed giant with a kid's tree house nestled in its branches.

Charlie started to climb the rungs. A faint nimbus surrounded him. Tom tried to reach out. He was weak, terribly weak. He sensed the tree's outrage and it gave him a little extra strength, arousing an outrage of his own. He felt strongly allied with the man climbing up to him. In another second the monster would bite him in half. But Charlie was right there now, only a couple of feet below, looking up at him, a troubled expression deepening the lines of his face. Tom made a final great effort, reaching down with the lead weight of his arm, his fingers twitching, and Charlie let go with his own right hand and touched him.

Something like electric current sizzled between their fingertips. Charlie's expression transformed instantly into shocked incredulity.

He was seeing it now, seeing what was really there. He knew.

The walls began to close, shutting like jaws, and Charlie was seeing that, too. He grabbed Tom's limp arm with both of his strong hands and he yanked, falling back, using his greater weight to pull Tom out and away, and then they were both falling.

Charlie held onto him all the way down.

Tom sat on the deck, his leg in a cast, a book tented open in his lap. His mom brought him a tall glass of lemonade with ice.

"I don't know how you can read with all that racket," she said.

Beyond the fence lay a flat expanse, cleared and leveled. A backhoe was busy digging a hole that would eventually be somebody's basement.

"It's not that bad," Tom said. "I kind of like it."

"Weirdo."

He smiled up at her. "The weirdest."

"It's hot. Do you want to come in now?"

Tom sipped his lemonade. "I think I'll sit out here and wait for Charlie."

ARE YOU THERE

Deatry took the door because he wanted to see the look on The Butcher's face. That put his partner Raymond Farkas in the alley, where Deatry assumed he was wet and not too happy. The hallway smelled like mildew and Chinese food. There were two light fixtures between 307 and the stairs. The one closer to Deatry was burned out. Muffled television voices spoke from the other rooms but 307 was quiet.

Deatry stood in the hall a long time, too long, his Stunner drawn but pointed at the floor, finger outside the trigger guard. He had the passkey, but he couldn't move. A memory of plate glass coughing into the atrium. Suburban sunshine, string music, and shredded shoppers. Blood on the terrazzo. White dowel of bone poking through mangled flesh and skin flap.

The hand he used to hold.

Deatry was sweating. The man in 307 shredded his victims one at a time, with some art, but no political considerations, at least none that Deatry was aware of. Why the paralyzing memory association?

Deatry started at the unmistakable *buzzpop* of a stunner burst. It had sounded from beyond the room on the other side of the door.

He fumbled the passkey, dropped it, used his foot. Wood splintering crash, jamb split, the door banged into the wall, and Deatry went through, sweeping the empty room with his weapon.

Curtains billowed. The burst had come from the alley. Deatry clambered onto the fire escape. November rain blew over him, chill on the back of his neck. There were no lights in the alley, unless you counted the checkerboard windows of the other buildings.

Deatry clanged down the zigzag stairs, iron rail cold on his hand, and dropped to the buckled concrete. The garbage smell was wet and ripe, bags of it piled around the dumpster. One of the bags groaned and stood up, a man. Deatry pointed his Stunner.

"It's me," the man said, raising an open hand. "Ray."

"Jesus Christ," Deatry said. "Did you hit him?"

"Yeah, but he must have been wearing one of those repelling vests."

"Did you see his face?"

"Nope."

"Well—"

"Don't worry, it's not a total loss. I got to feel his knife. It's real sharp."

Farkas's shirt was wet, but in the bad light who knew it was blood?

Then Raymond Farkas extended his hand, which was holding a flat module made of black metal. Deatry holstered his weapon and took it. Farkas swayed, and Deatry gripped his shoulder with his free hand.

"He dropped that," Farkas said, and collapsed forward. Deatry dropped the module himself when he tried to catch his partner.

Dawn had begun to pale the sky by the time Deatry returned home and climbed the newly installed set of exterior stairs to the second floor. Inside, he stood at the window with a bottle of beer for a few minutes, not thinking. It was as quiet as it ever got in the grid. Deatry knew his ex-wife, who occupied the lower half of the narrow two-story "slot" house would be waking up soon. Sometimes, when she noticed his light on or heard him shuffling around after being awake all night, she came up to the bolted door that separated the two halves of the house, wanting to talk. Deatry hated that. He referred to Barbara as his ex-wife, but the truth was they had never legally divorced. A divorce would automatically have evoked the Space and Occupancy Act and forced them to vacate the relative spaciousness of the home they had legally shared as man and wife. And the other truth was (at least the truth Deatry allowed), they both loved the house more than they had ever loved each other. The Space and Occupancy Act was only one of many laws designed to encourage the sacred tradition of marriage. The SAOA hadn't existed at the time of Deatry's previous marriage. So that particular example of sacredness had been allowed to go to hell in its own traditional manner.

Deatry turned off the lamp, unrolled his Apple VI Scroll, and powered it up. White Echo was waiting for him.

"Hi," he typed.

"I was almost asleep." Her words appeared rapidly, a quick and flawless keypader.

"That's okay. I know it's late. I just wanted to say Hi."

"And you said it. But don't go. I—miss you all day."

"I miss you, too," Deatry typed, and he meant it. But he was also glad White Echo, a.k.a. Kimberly, was not an entity who could climb a flight of stairs and knock on his door.

"Are you all right?" Kimberly asked.

"Peachy. It's Farkas. We followed a tip tonight and he got cut, and it was at least partly my fault."

"How was it your fault?"

Deatry briefly described the situation at the co-op apartment building.

"I don't see how it was your fault," Kimberly said.

"I had the door. And I waited too long. The Butcher must have sensed something was up. Anyway, forget it. How was your day?"

"Delightful and lonely."

"That's life in the big city. The lonely part, anyway. Delight is a little harder to come by. You have a knack for it."

After a long pause, during which Deatry began to think she had been disconnected, Kimberly typed: "It doesn't HAVE to be lonely."

Deatry's fingers hovered over the keypad like hummingbirds assessing the possibility of nectar. He didn't want to get into it again.

"Brian?"

He gave it another few beats then typed: "Damn it, I'm sorry. Barbara's at the door."

"Play dead."

"Ha! I can't do that. She knows I'm in here. She was already awake when I got home. The lights were on. She must have heard me come in."

Lord of the Lies. They floated him above a nasty splinter of his personality.

"Okay," Kimberly typed.

"I'm really sorry."

"Yes." Then: "It's okay. I have to sleep anyway. Alone as usual."

Usually he could redirect her mood, but he was bone tired this morning. So even though he knew it was lame, Deatry replied, "I'm REALLY sorry." And: "Gotta go now." And: "G'nite."

He sighed and turned off the Scroll and let it roll back into a tube. Then God played a mean trick on him. There was a tentative knock on the interior door, followed by a slightly more aggressive knock, and Barbara's voice:

"Brian? I've got coffee."

Deatry turned in his chair and stared wearily at the door. He waited, imagining her on the other side. She didn't knock again, and after a while her footsteps retreated down the stairs.

Deatry and Raymond Farkas were parapolice detectives working a dumpy quarter grid of the Seattle-Tacoma sprawl. The local inhabitants paid their salaries. They didn't *have* to pay, of course. It was a free country. And the paradetectives were free to ignore the non-paying enclaves, though Deatry had never done that and wouldn't. The real murder police worked the tonier grids and had the terror watch, which sucked resources like a starving baby.

Deatry slipped down to the crime lab of the real police department, where he had a few friends from the old days. He showed the module to a man who looked like a cross between a boiled egg and a vulture in a white lab coat.

"It's a Loved One," the man, who's name was Stuhring, said.

An old memory stirred briefly in the refuse at the back of Deatry's mind.

"Those dead person things?"

"Right. Guy's dying but still coherent enough, got all his marbles rattling around, or it's a living will thing. They hook him up and make one of these gizmos from his engramatic template. Fries his brain, but he's not going to live anyway. End of the day, dear old Uncle Ned can still talk to you, respond just like the original, all that. Parlor trick. There was a vogue, then the creep factor killed it."

"Will this one work?"

Stuhring rummaged around in a junk box, tried a couple of adapters, found one that fit, and plugged the module into a computer.

After a moment, *Hello?* appeared on the screen.

"It works," Stuhring said.

"No voice?"

He shrugged. "You'd have to noodle around with it. Take the adapter. You can plug it into your Scroll, you want."

Hello? appeared under the first Hello.

"Why's it keep saying that?" Deatry asked. "Is it broken?"

"How do I know? Ask it."

Deatry typed: "Are you broken?"

They waited, but no more words appeared.

"There's your answer," Stuhring said.

"Maybe."

Deatry had a weird feeling. He unplugged the Loved One and pocketed the adapter.

Deatry met Raymond Farkas at a bar on Second Avenue called The Scarlet Tree, though its patrons referred to it affectionately as The Bloody Stump.

Farkas eased into a chair, holding his right hand lightly over his ribs where the blade had gone in, scoring bone. He was older than Deatry, about thirty pounds overweight, and had a walrus mustache, which was going gray.

"Hurt?" Deatry asked.

"What do you think?"

"I think it probably hurts."

"You're probably right," Farkas said. "The doc said it was a razor or The Butcher's usual scalpel. Guess he'd know."

It was the middle of the day and they were drinking pints of amber Ale. It didn't matter, since they were private employees. It was kind of a perk. Deatry drank deep then put his glass down and said:

"I'm sorry, Ray."

"What about?" There was foam in his mustache.

"Sorry I forgot your birthday, what else? Jesus Christ. I'm sorry I almost got you killed."

Farkas shrugged. "I had the alley. You flushed him, then it was on me. I blew it."

"I didn't exactly flush him."

Farkas shrugged again. "What else you want to talk about?"

"That module thing he dropped. It was a Loved One. You know what that is?"

"No shit? Yeah, I know what they are."

Farkas had already finished his amber. He waved at the bartender and she brought over another one. Deatry still had a ways to go on his first.

"Pair a beers for the paradicks," the bartender said, in a friendly way. She was fortyish, attractive in a twice-around-the-block kind of way. Deatry had once seen the inside of her bedroom and other things.

Farkas grabbed up his fresh pint and drained it by a third.

"You get anything off the Loved One?"

"No."

"Could be a good break."

"It won't talk."

"Get a techie to cannibalize it. That way you at least get the basics. If it was a relative of our guy then maybe we have a name."

Deatry drank his ale.

"What's the matter, you don't want to take it apart?"

Deatry shrugged. His shrugs weren't as eloquent as Farkas's and he knew it.

"Why not?" Farkas said.

"Next time," Deatry said, "I'm on the alley."

"Whatever."

They drank a couple more pints and watched the ball game, which was a disaster. When they left The Scarlet Tree Deatry waited while his partner eased into a cab. Farkas was on his first marriage and had a fourteen-year-old daughter. Deatry once attended a Patriot's of July party at the Farkas apartment. It had been boozy but not overboard, plenty of kids, loud and friendly, the whole building population joining in, spilling out into the street. Farkas had a *life*. Deatry wanted to keep it that way.

*

Two A.M. Deatry was staring at the chatwindow center screen of his Scroll.

"I miss you," White Echo, a.k.a. Kimberly, said. "But I don't want to keep you here on this dumb THING. I need a real flesh and blood man. Brian? Can you understand?"

Deatry finished another bottle of beer and set the dead soldier on the floor next to the rest of the empty platoon.

After a while he typed:

"I understand."

"We've been talking for months," Kimberly said.

"Yes."

"We don't even use the chat enhancements."

"I thought you liked the writing part."

"I do. It's old fashioned and sweet."

"But?" Deatry typed.

"But I want to meet you."

Deatry didn't type anything. Then, being funny, he typed: "I'm married."

"No kidding? Oh my Gawd!!"

Deatry smiled, but Kimberly wasn't going to be diverted.

"Listen to me," she typed.

"I'm listening." He twisted the cap off another beer.

"We're the walking wounded. We've talked all about that. What happened with my first husband. Your mother and the bomb. The way your father checked out. The way things have gone with your relationships. All that stuff."

Deatry shifted on his chair, drank, held the cold bottle in his lap.

"But we're cowards if we don't try to love again."

Deatry put the bottle down and typed: "I do love you."

"Love behind a firewall isn't real," Kimberly typed.

"It's real."

"Brian. I want to take the next step now. I want to meet you. I want to go for a walk with you. I want to feel your hand in my hand. I want to kiss you. For real. Not just in my head. I want to have a relationship with you. I HAVE to try again."

"I know."

"It's scary."

"True." Deatry typed.

"But in a way this is scarier."

Deatry drank his beer.

"This is . . . too remote," Kimberly typed. "It's okay at first then it's kind of sick. I think."

Deatry drank his beer.

"So what I'm saying is let's meet. Like for a cup of coffee. It's a simple first step. It doesn't have to be perfect. I think you're afraid it won't be perfect, or that your heart will get broken. Heart's DO get broken. But you still have to take a risk. There's no life without the risk."

Deatry put his bottle down, almost typed something, then didn't.

"So," Kimberly typed. "Next Monday at ten A.M. I'm going to be at the Still Life Café. You know where that is? I'll be there."

Deatry typed: "Will you be wearing a red carnation in your lapel?"

"Sure."

A long beat. Then, "Brian? If you're not there, I don't think I can come back online with you. I mean I won't. I love you, but this keeps me from what I need. A relationship. In real life. I don't want to hurt you, but I have to protect my heart, too."

"It's okay."

"You're not going to be there, are you."

Deatry stared at the screen.

"Goodbye," Kimberly typed.

The Loved One wouldn't talk. Every night Deatry jacked it into his Apple Scroll and peppered it with conversational gambits, to no avail. But he had a feeling. In the police lab, when the Loved One had said *Hello? Hello?* Deatry had sensed more than the automatic response of a software program reacting to the electrical surge of being turned on. He had sensed a *presence*. Of course, Deatry was the first to admit he was a little nuts.

He was up all night Friday. Just before dawn he jacked in the Loved One and typed: "Hi?" The word hung on the screen all by itself. Ten minutes elapsed.

"I know you're in there," Deatry typed.

Then, after another five minutes: "Come on."

When he stood up he was surprised to discover he was drunk enough to feel wobbly. Drunk enough that the room appeared to shift about, like sub-reality tectonic plates, or a cubist painting that tries to show mundane objects from multiple and simultaneous angles, image over-lapping. He staggered away from his Miro desk, kicking over most of a dozen empty beer bottles and sending them rolling across the hardwood floor like bowling pins.

"Hello?" he said to the empty room. "Hello, hello! Jesus H. Christ."

He blundered into the sofa and collapsed upon it.

After a while, Barbara started knocking on the locked interior door.

"Brian, are you okay?"

Fuck it, he thought, and he passed out of consciousness, leaving the module running.

The phone woke him, a piercing trill. Better than the auricular implants almost everybody had, though, voices speaking in your head, the last thing he wanted. He fumbled the phone out of his pocket. Wincing, he said, "Deatry."

"It's Ray. Got another body. Wanna see it?"

"Where?"

Farkas told him.

Deatry stuck his head under a cold shower and yelled. He put on a fresh shirt. It was only mid-morning, and he was still drunk. At the door he noticed the Scroll hooked up to the Loved One and running. His messed up little haiku floated on the screen:

Hello?

I know you're in there.

Come on.

Deatry hesitated, then left the setup the way it was and went out the door.

It wasn't raining, but the streets were wet from the previous night. Puddles shivered in the wind like alien amoebas communicating their loneliness. Deatry stepped between them as he crossed the street, shoulders hunched in his old raincoat, hair still wet, dripping and uncombed from the shower.

The Coroner's meatwagon was angled into the curb, blinking red lights. The M.E. whose misfortune it was to cover the grid that encompassed this block was a woman named Sally Ranger. Deatry had known her for years. A blond with bird-sharp features and a severely sexual figure. She always dressed impeccably, even now, as though she had been dispatched to rendezvous with an important business client instead of a methodically mutilated indigent. She stepped forward with a clipboard when Deatry arrived.

"Good morning," she said.

"Just my opinion, but I don't agree."

She handed him the clipboard. "Sign here and I can take Mr. Vargas."

"Who's Mr. Vargas?"

"Your corpse." Sally Ranger said, nodding at the alley where three men stood over something like a heap of rags. One of the men was Raymond Farkas. The other two were from the M.E.'s office. They had a wheeled stretcher and an empty body bag.

"I'll sign, but hold up a minute. I want to have a look before they move him."

He scratched his name on the official form. His hand shook.

"You want a mint?" Sally asked.

He looked up. "What?"

"A mint." She blew her breath, which was sweet wintergreen, into his face.

He scowled at her.

"Thanks, I'll pass."

She shook her head.

"What?" he said.

"The genius detective. Wunderkind."

Deatry had known her since his days with the real police force. Right before his first marriage broke up he'd conducted a brief, messy affair with her. When she'd started expecting more out of him than he was able to relinquish he'd ended it. An outcome that hadn't pleased Sally.

"One question I always wanted to ask you," she said. They had walked into the alley and were approaching the trio of live men and the one deceased.

"What's that, Sally?"

"Are all you geniuses by definition drunken bastards?"

Farkas looked at him, no expression on his face.

Deatry said, "No, not by definition. It's more random." He turned to Farkas. "So?"

"Arturo Vargas. Aged fifty-two. Head's over there with some other stuff." Farkas pointed. "Butcher's standard M.O. I've already taken the pictures. A city uniform preserved the scene, but there wasn't anything in the way of clues."

Arturo Vargas's head sat nested in a wet coil of blue-white intestine a few yards from the headless corpse. Rain had collected in the gaping cavity that had once contained the man's viscera. Deatry took a few minutes looking at the layout, then he said to Sally, "Okay, thanks."

"Don't mention it," she replied.

"How'd you come up with the name?" Deatry asked Farkas.

Farkas, who was wearing surgical gloves, held up a ratty looking wallet of faux leather, a kid's wallet with Indians and ponies and tee-pees machine-stitched around the edge. Deatry snapped on a pair of gloves and took the wallet and opened it. There was a driver's license, expired by more than a decade. The faded photo showed a much younger and healthier-looking head, smiling. There were some other pictures in the wallet, of a plump, attractive woman in her thirties, and a couple of young children, grinning. Deatry's head was pounding. He closed the wallet and handed it back.

"Looks like he used to have a life," Deatry said.

Farkas nodded. "That an official genius level observation, partner?"

"Let's just drop the genius crap," Deatry said.

As they were leaving the alley, damp wind blowing in their faces, Deatry holding his raincoat closed, Sally said:

"I wouldn't lose any sleep over these derelicts if I were you, Brian. Why do you even bother?"

"We're the last stop," Deatry said. "If we don't bother nobody will."

"And?" Sally said.

"And nothing."

She shook her head, said, "What a waste," then got in her car and drove away.

*

Deatry and Farkas spent the rest of the morning canvassing the neighborhood, which netted them nothing. At the tiny parapolice headquarters the City provided, Farkas accessed a subdivision of the Homeland Security Database and ran the indigent's name, hunting next of kin. The genius and erstwhile wunderkind of detection busied himself by taking a nap on the sofa. Farkas's tapping keystrokes and low voice entered and exited Deatry's fitful dreams. At some point Farkas shook his shoulder and asked him if he wanted the light on or off.

"Huh?" Deatry said.

"I'm going home. You want the lights on?"

Deatry yawned. "No. I'm going home, too. You want to grab a bite?"

"Naw. Sarah's holding dinner."

Farkas put on his shoulder rig, and Deatry noticed his Stunner had been replaced by a perfectly lethal and perfectly illegal Pulser.

"You hunting bear?" Deatry said.

Farkas didn't smile. "That bastard's vest won't repulse *this*."

Deatry stopped at The Bloody Stump and ordered a Caesar salad and a bowl of chili. It was past seven and dark when he arrived home. Even before he turned on the lamp he noticed that words had been added to the screen of his Apple.

"Please turn me off," the words said.

And:

"PLEASE."

Deatry switched on the desk lamp, removed his raincoat. He brewed a pot of coffee, making a mental note to re-supply his depleted canister of dark roast, then sat down with a cup. He looked at the Scroll for a minute, and he felt it again: the *presence*. He typed: "Why do you want to be turned off?"

Immediately: "Because I can't stand it."

"Can't stand what?" Deatry insisted.

After a beat: "It's terrible."

"What's terrible?"

"What I am."

Deatry thought for a moment, then typed: "You're a responsive memory template. An interactive device."

"I exist," the Loved One said, and Deatry thought: *The creep factor.*

He typed: "Granted. You exist—in the same way my Scroll exists. Or my television."

"More complex. You're not Timothy. Who are you?"

Deatry hesitated, then typed: "Deatry. Brian Deatry."

"That's just a name."

"I'm a public employee. I sort through lost and found stuff, like you."

"Please turn me off, Mr. Public Employee."

"Who's Timothy?"

"Another person."

"No kidding? Another person, huh?"

"You're very sarcastic, Brian."

"I have my moments. Who are you? I mean who were you?"

"Joni."

"Joni what?"

"Cook. Joni Cook."

"And when did you die?"

She provided a date and year.

"Twenty-seven years ago," he typed. "How old were you?"

"Thirty-two."

"That's young. What happened?"

"I got sick and died. It happens to a lot of people."

"But you were thoughtful," Deatry typed. "You imprinted a Loved One for somebody who would miss you. Who was that?"

"My son."

"Timothy."

"Yes."

"And you were with your son only a week ago."

Joni said: "Time doesn't mean anything."

"What do you talk about with your son?"

"His day. How he's feeling. Personal things."

"What kind of personal things?"

"The kind that are personal," Joni said.

"I guess I'm not the only sarcastic one around here."

"Perhaps not."

Deatry pulled his cell out and called Farkas at home.

"Yeah?" Farkas said.

"I've got a lead."

"What kind of lead?" Farkas asked.

"Two names. Joni Cook and Timothy Cook. Mother and son. Joni is deceased." He recited the date the Loved One provided.

"Your Loved One woke up," Farkas said.

"Yep."

"How'd that happen?"

"I left her running all day while I was out. I think she got lonely."

"*Lonely.*"

"Well, something like that. I don't know."

On the screen Joni Cook said: "Hello? Brian, hello?"

To Farkas, he said: "It's not a foregone conclusion at this point, but Timothy could be our boy. Tomorrow we'll find out for sure."

"Hello?" Joni said. "God, don't leave me alone again, please don't."

Creep factor.

Deatry switched the module off.

*

He didn't need the Homeland Security Database to locate Timothy Cook. The Butcher was right in the directory, under "C" for homicidal maniac.

Deatry was superstitious. He'd almost gotten Farkas killed once. He wasn't going to take another chance. He checked the load in his Stunner, holstered it, grabbed his coat, and hit the street, forgetting his cell phone on the desk by the Scroll.

A suburban dead zone, half past nine P.M. Deatry was out of his jurisdiction and possibly out of his mind. Live oaks on a broad, quiet street, eerily backlit by arc-sodium safelamps. His detective's I.D. got him through gate security. Timothy Cook's address was a Cape Cod style box with pinned-back green shutters and a flagstone walk leading to the front door and a shiny brass knocker.

So knock.

Deatry touched the knocker—thinking: the brass ring—but didn't use it. His erstwhile "genius" status had more to do with intuitive leaps than Holmsian ratiocination. Standing on the porch with leaf shadow swaying over him he knew Timothy Cook was The Butcher. Which helped and didn't help. The man was wackier even than he'd first appeared. Sure, dissecting bums was one thing, but how about living some kind of weird double life. The dilapidated room in the city, and this antithetical opulence. It'd been easy to fish out the information that Timothy Cook was a lawyer. Okay, there was Jack the Ripper, the whole theory about Red Jack being some kind of nobleman or surgeon or something. There's always a precedent, Deatry thought. And that lawyer in the Cape Cod house would no doubt be able to find one on which to hang Deatry by his balls just for standing on his front porch.

Deatry turned around, intending to go back to his car and do a little ratiocinating.

A man was standing behind him.

He was about forty years old, baby-faced, ginger hair very thin and combed over. A smile that didn't reach his eyes.

"I knew you'd come," he said.

"Then you knew more than I did," Deatry said.

"Naturally. Let's go inside now."

Suddenly the man was pointing a Stunner at him.

"Now what's the sense of that?" Deatry said.

"Go ahead inside. The door's unlocked."

"You're Timothy Cook."

"Yes."

"You've been slicing up the residents of my grid."

Cook sniggered. "Residents."

Deatry calculated his odds. They weren't promising. He decided to scream for help as loud as he could. A tactic that would have gotten him ignored back in his grid, but in this neighborhood it was probably good as a ten thousand dollar alarm system. He started to open his mouth, and Cook shot him.

He inhabited a jellyfish dream. Boneless slow wobble in consciousness suspension. Gradually nausea asserted itself. He tried to pitch forward, found himself restrained, and vomited into his own lap. Which was fairly disgusting, but—in his present jellyfish state of mind—it was also kind of fascinating.

A man in jockey shorts paced before him, mumbling. His

skin was very pale. Lamplight slid along the blade of the scalpel he was holding.

A dim fragment of Brian Deatry was alarmed. The fragment attempted to form a coherent response to the situation. All it could arrive at was the word: "*Don't.*" And even that came out sounding like "*Dawnt.*"

The pacing man stopped pacing.

"Dawnt," Deatry said.

The man stood before him, feet planted, toes wiggling. The scalpel started to come up, and then there was a commotion, a door crashing open, and the man turned sharply. The quick movement tripled him in Deatry's woozy vision. Bright blue flash and a sound like a hundred light bulbs popping out at the same time. The man sprawled to the floor, head by Deatry's left knee. Scorched whiff of pork. Deatry's fragment put a name to the face: Cook. The Butcher.

Then Farkas was there untying him.

"I don't know what you think you're doing coming out here by yourself," Farkas said.

The Deatry fragment managed: "Shaabing ur life."

"Thanks," Farkas said. "You did a hell of a job."

"Cook the bastard," Deatry said, more or less coherently.

"I cooked him, all right," Farkas said.

Monday at ten A.M. Deatry was not at the Still Life Café.

Monday night, Deatry, stone sober, sat before his Scroll in the darkened room that had once been a "spare" bedroom when the house he shared with his second wife was a house undivided, except for the everlasting divisions in Deatry's own mind. He stared at a list of names, women he had chatted with to varying degrees of intensity over the last year or so. For months those names hadn't impelled him in the least. Except for one. White Echo. Kimberly. Now some of the names were lit, indicating online status, and some were dark. White Echo was dark. Deatry stared at the other names for a while, then he stood up and grabbed a beer. He looked out the window for a while. It was raining again. Raindrops trembled and squiggled down the pane. He returned to his desk. White Echo was still dark.

"I'm looking at your picture," Deatry typed.

"Which one?" Joni, The Loved One, asked.

"Some kind of park. Lake in the background, but not summer. Cloudy sky, a playground. You're wearing a black skirt and purple wool leggings and a funny hat."

Deatry had confiscated an image wafer from Cook's home office.

"What's funny about my hat?" Joni said.

"I meant pretty and sophisticated." Deatry was drunk.

"I know that picture," Joni said.

"You're very beautiful in it."

"Thank you, Brian."

"Was that a park you visited often?" Deatry asked.

"No. But I wanted to."

"Why didn't you then?"

"My husband didn't like me to go out of the house without him, and he didn't like the park. So we only went that one time, the time he took the picture of me. He thought I was beautiful, too."

"He didn't like you to go out of the house?" Deatry twisted the cap off his fifth beer.

"He used to say it was so dangerous. With all the bombings and the crime. But we lived in a nice neighborhood with a Homeland Watch Captain and everything. It wasn't that dangerous. I always thought it would be nice if I could take Timothy to the park and let him play while I sat with the other parents. Or sometimes I thought about going by myself, just to be out in the fresh air with a nice book."

"That's not asking too much," Deatry typed.

"No, I didn't think so, either."

"Your husband sounds like a harsh man."

Deatry had started to type "asshole" instead of "harsh man" but stopped himself. And then he thought, What difference does it make? It's like talking to myself anyway. But he didn't type asshole.

After a long pause, Joni said: "He was a brutal man."

Deatry stared at the picture on the screen next to the cha-twindow. Joni Cook possessed, or was possessed by, a gamine quality. Her face was infinitely vulnerable and guarded, her eyes large and dark. He felt drawn to those eyes.

"Was the park very far from your house?" he typed.

"Not far at all."

"I would have enjoyed meeting you there sometime."

"I think I would have liked that, too," Joni said. "You seem like a kindly man. At first I was afraid of you, I didn't know you and I was afraid. But now I can see the kindness of your heart. Or the loneliness."

What the hell? Deatry thought.

"When your module is turned on and no one is talking to you," Deatry typed, because he was curious, "why are you uncomfortable?" He almost typed "lonely."

"It's hard to explain," Joni said. "It's like standing alone in a blank room and not knowing if anyone will ever come into the room. Ever. And even then knowing if someone does come in, like you are here now, they will never be able to touch me, and I'll never be able to touch them. It's like standing in the blank room with my memories and nothing else, and thinking about how no one will ever touch me, and thinking this is all there is and all there ever will be."

Deatry looked away from the Scroll. Rain tapped at the window. He thought about the woman downstairs, and then he stopped thinking about her.

He typed: "Let's say you came to that park one day and I was there."

Long pause. Then, "All right."

"Let's say things were different."

"Yes."

"Let's say we knew each other but had never met in person. In real life."

"We wrote all the time and that's how we knew each other so well."

"Yes," Deatry typed. "And we never turned on all the virtual chat enhancements. We just wrote, no voice even."

"Like letters used to be."

"Right," Deatry typed.

"So one day we decide to meet."

"That's what I was thinking."

"We would have seen each other's picture."

"Right," Deatry typed.

"What next?" Joni asked.

"We meet by that playground, and I've brought a couple coffees, one for each of us."

"I like mine with lots of sugar and just a little cream."

"I know that, so I've made sure it's right. Like I'm going for making a good impression."

"It's because you're kind. You're a nice man."

"I can be nice," Deatry typed. "I have my moments."

"What next?"

"I'm guessing there's a bench somewhere in that park."

"There is."

"We go and sit beside each other," Deatry typed.

"It's October, not too cold, sunny but brisk. The color of the water and the sky are wonderful."

"Yeah, it's nice."

"Yes."

"We talk about stuff, our lives, our dreams." Deatry was pretty damn drunk.

"I like just talking," Joni said. "But there's more between us, we've known for a long time, and now sitting so close beside each other we can feel it strongly."

"I take your hand in mine," Deatry typed, and in his mind he feels her hand, and sees the vivid blue sky and the darker blue of the water. He's filling up the blank room. For both of them.

"I look into your eyes, your kind eyes," Joni said.

"And I kiss you on the lips."

Joni didn't reply, and Deatry looked at the window again and thought about retrieving another beer, but he didn't really want another, so he stayed where he was, and part of his mind occupied the bench with Joni Cook in a nameless park on a mythical afternoon in October. Then Joni said:

"That really happened to me, Brian."

He wasn't sure what she meant.

"I did meet someone in that park. A man. A kind, sweet man. And we held hands, and he kissed me, just like you did."

Deatry didn't know what to type. Several minutes elapsed, and the room started to become blank again. When it got that way he could feel Kimberly wanting to come in, or maybe it was Barbara. Finally Deatry typed:

"Are you there?"

"My husband knew," Joni said. "And when he got home from work, he hit me as hard as he could with his fist. Timmy was there. He always saw his dad hitting me, but not like this time. This time his daddy killed me. Timmy was just a little boy."

Deatry wanted to type something but couldn't. I'm talking to myself, he thought. It's an auto-reactive program. Yeah, he thought. Just like a real human being. That was funny but Deatry didn't laugh. He looked at the picture of Joni Cook.

"I knew in my heart that he would do it one day," Joni said. "So I had it in my living will to make this thing, if there was time."

"The Loved One," Deatry said.

"Yes. I was in a coma for three days. That's when they did it."

"So Timothy would still be able to talk to you."

"A boy needs his mother," Joni said. "Please turn me off now, Brian. Please."

Deatry powered down the module.

Rain ticked at the window like a clock.

At the paradicks office, Deatry and Farkas labored over reams of paperwork with the object of A: justifying the shooting death of Timothy Cook, and B: justifying the trans-jurisdictional nature of that shooting, not to mention the illegal weapon used. In the middle of it all, Farkas handed Deatry a hardcopy file that told at least two stories in the subtextural labyrinth.

"The short not-so-happy life of Francis Cook, our guys' dad," Farkas said. "Gives you a clue about The Butcher, though. If you need a clue. My opinion, the character clues don't matter. You come out of something bad, you have to have a strong will, but you make your life work. Plenty of people do it. Then there's guys like Timmy Cook."

Deatry read the brief file. It was like one, two, three. One: Francis Cook was a professional, a cardiologist who also happened to be an alcoholic who enjoyed beating the shit out of his wife. Two:

one day he went too far and killed her. Three: police investigation and publicity and a manslaughter charge ruined him, and maybe guilt ruined him further, and after his sentence he ended up on the street; a straight fall from the top of the societal heap to the bottom. As a coda: he died of exposure at the age of fifty-eight, the body identified by his DNA flash file. And coincident to it all, about ten years later derelicts started getting themselves dissected all over Deatry's Grid.

On a bench under a blue October sky, Deatry and the thing that pretended to be Joni Cook sat with their arms around each other and watched a white sail skim the lake.

Thirty years previous, the world shuddered, glass coughed into a shopping mall's atrium, bodies sprayed apart, including Deatry's mother's. He had been eleven years old.
Brian Deatry's numero uno character clue.
The hand he used to hold.

Sometimes the room stubbornly remained blank. Then it was only their two voices. And not even that, but mere typing of symbolic characters in a chatwindow. Deatry had never bothered to figure out how to activate the voice routine. He would have felt uncomfortable with that.
On a very bad night, on a *particularly* bad night, Deatry typed the wrong thing. Joni had been talking about Timothy again. Not Timothy the little boy, the victim, but Timothy the grown man who had talked to her every day and never once revealed that he was a homicidal maniac, or at least neither Joni nor Deatry ever mentioned it. They were in the blank room and she was talking about Timothy the wonderful man her little boy had grown into, and why couldn't she talk to him anymore? Deatry, who was frustrated and drunk and craving, not the peaceful October lake, but the other place they sometimes visited, the place where his body came alive in his hand, where they made love of a remote sort; Deatry and the auto-responsive module.

"Let's not talk about Timothy anymore," Deatry typed.

A pause.

"Why not?"

"Never mind."

"Has something happened to Timothy?"

"No, he's fine, I'm sure."

"Please tell me, Brian."

He considered turning the module off. Isn't that what he always did? Turn the module off? There was a turned-off module living downstairs. There was another turned off module a couple of grids away, that relationship ultimately depersonalized back to a dark name on a chatfrind list. White Echo was a dead module; Kimberly, somewhere, lived.

Even Deatry himself was a dead module.

Or becoming one.

He was staring at the window again, the rain squiggle, the flat glare of arc-sodium safelight, an infinity of loneliness.

He turned back to the Scroll. New words had appeared.

Hello?

Are you there?

I'm hell on staring at windows, Deatry thought.

He typed: "Joni, listen to me."

"Yes?"

"We have to be careful. If we're not careful we'll get lost and forget what we're doing."

"I don't understand."

"I mean we'll forget who we are, and we'll start thinking this is a real conversation and that we're real people."

"Brain, I know what I am."

"That makes one of us."

"Why are you acting so strange?"

"Who says it's an act?"

"Tell me what's happened to Timothy. I know you're keeping something from me."

"It doesn't matter. I'm just talking to myself."

"Brian?"

"I'm talking to myself."

"You're scaring me."

Deatry typed: "Timothy is dead. My partner shot him because he was about to cut me open. Your son was hell on cutting people open."

"Don't say that."

"It's the truth, and you've probably known it all along."

"Please don't. Why would my son want to hurt you?"

"I'm a police detective."

"You lied to me."

"Yes."

"It was so nice for us. Now it's ruined."

"Yes," Deatry typed. "It's ruined."

No more words appeared. Deatry got up and went into the kitchenette. He was out of beer *and* coffee. He grabbed his coat and keys and his Stunner. Just to prove it didn't matter, he left the module running when he left.

At half past two A.M. he returned. The Scarlet Tree closed at Two. Remarkably, Deatry was not drunk. For the last hour he had been thinking about Joni. Thinking about the bench, the high October sky, the blue lake. The blank room, his cruelty.

On the screen Joni Cook's reactive memory engramatic imprint had written:

"You used me."

He removed his coat and sat down. He wasn't drunk, but he had downed a couple of pints and felt lucid. He typed a long, rambling message, and then waited for a response. None came. He waited, but there was nothing. He typed: "Are you there?"

Nothing.

He opened a window to White Echo and typed another message. When he was done he read it over and was repelled by the desperateness of what he'd written. He deleted it.

He left the desk and turned on the TV. Every once in a while he checked the Scroll for a reply from Joni. There never was one. Finally he got up and wiggled the cable connection, noted the module's power ON light. Everything was in order. Just before dawn, thinking of the blank room, Deatry powered down the module, unplugged it from the Scroll, and threw it in a drawer.

He was dozing on the sofa when the dead module named Barbara knocked on the interior door.

"Are you there?" she said.

Deatry stared at the door, wondering: *Am I?* Rain ticked at the empty pane. He stared at the door, some kind of urgency churning him. He stared at the door, and in his mind he stood up and opened it.

Transplant

When Laird Ulin came for my eyes—again—I wasn't there. One set should have lasted that pompous gasbag twenty-five years. Vanity brought him back after a mere ten. Once they left me, my eyes, as with all my other organs, resumed their perishable status. Meanwhile I grew a replacement. Laird couldn't be bothered with corrective surgery, and besides, the surgeons on-board *Infinity* were primarily harvesters. And I was primarily the farm.

Not being there was the easy part. At about the time Ulin expected me in surgical prep, I was strolling through Venice. Someone had turned the canal water periwinkle. Since no real water was involved, such a transformation was simply accomplished and did no harm, except to the verisimilitude.

Two biomechs sat in front of a café façade (which was real) sipping from demitasses of espresso (which was synth). They were supposed to resemble a man and a woman. And they did, too, if the light was sufficiently dim and you squinted and were perhaps drunk or a little blind.

I sat at a nearby table under the shade of a Cinzano umbrella. The biomechs ignored me. It was a special kind of ignoring. The kind that conveys an insecure species of seething envy. God had touched me: I was a practical immortal; they were puppets with uploaded memories.

I said, "Espresso," and a thing that looked like a traffic light with four erector set legs clickity-clacked out of the café and placed a thick, white saucer with a demitasse of black synth on the table. You didn't need periwinkle canal water to spoil verisimilitude.

I sat sipping synth (not out of a seashell by the seashore, thank goodness), pinky extended at the proper angle, until the biomechs got up and walked away. At a certain point they passed through the holographic scrim that presented the illusion of a street continuing in diminishing perspective. The street scene shivered, and two instantly created figures strolled in place of the couple.

I put my demitasse down.

The street scene continued to shiver and wobble. Then the canal turned black, which gave the parked gondolas the appearance of projecting over a stygian abyss.

After that, the whole damn thing crashed.

Which was the beginning of the *hard* part, earlier implied.

How does one while away the years between stars? I mean, after you've read everything. For me, sabotage came to mind. Picture *Infinity* as a giant armadillo, twenty kilometers long, half again as tall and five wide. In the uppermost section—the Command Level—dwell the biomechs, a handful of machine people determined to live out the duration of the voyage. Of course, only Laird Ulin and I were "alive" in the usual sense of the word. The biomechs *remembered* being alive, but that didn't count. Their biomechanical bodies could ingest synthetic espresso and even taste it. They could hold hands if they wanted to, but coitus was a technical conundrum beyond their design.

Meanwhile Ulin's longevity was dependent upon the miracle of my endlessly regenerative body, as well as a full compliment of rejuvenation treatments developed from studies of my unique genetic material, which at least kept his bones sturdy and his muscle mass relatively limber. Ulin's medical types regularly extracted small quantities of my pineal excretions, from which they created a neurochemical wash to irrigate Laird's wrinkly organ (no, not that one). Some would question the efficacy of this treatment over the long haul. One can afford to have funny-looking skin and stiff tendons, but who wants a funny brain? Who needs a stiff thalamus? Laird's megalomaniacal tendencies were on the rise. His behavior had grown strange. Stranger, I mean.

Despite endless attempts to replicate the result, I remained the only known person with super human longevity—at least at the time of our departure from Earth. Ulin would have much preferred the ability to regenerate his own organs. But money really can't buy everything—like love, or a spare liver, for instance. Some miracles God reserves for the genetically anomalous freak. In this case, me.

Occupying the middle decks of *Infinity* are the farms and resource reclamation systems. And on the final and largest level: The County, where the general population live, work, love, procreate, and die into the next generation . . . and the next.

Getting from the top of the armadillo to the bottom wasn't easy without a visa. And the Command structure—headed by Laird Ulin—was disinclined to issue me one. Perhaps it had something to do with my recent attempts to go AWOL in the County (okay, the last one was nine years ago, but that's still recent by *my* standards). As usual, Laird had located me with uncanny ease and hauled me back upstairs.

He had been my ticket to the stars, but for these nine years I'd been little more than a pampered prisoner—a walking organ bank, always at Ulin's service. I guess he was afraid to die. Tough. Everybody's afraid of something.

So I built a virus and named it George. Then I conducted a conversation with *Infinity*'s superquantum computer and arranged for the first sneeze to occur in Venice. I made sure I was in Cinzano shade for the event.

Presently came the sound of magnetic locks releasing. A panel opened in the velvet blackness before which the image of the canal had resided moments ago.

I moved quickly. My perusal of the ship's design database had informed me that from this point I would be very near the port to a kilometers-long access tube running from the Command level all the way to the floor of the County. Orienting myself, I turned right and followed a corridor between bulkheads until I came to a wider place and a hatch recessed into the deck.

I knelt on the deck and retracted the hatch by turning a hand-operated wheel. The purpose of this tube, as well as several others located throughout Infinity, was to provide direct access between levels in the event of a catastrophic systems failure. At such a time one might also assume a loss of gravity, which would make traveling the tube a somewhat less harrowing matter than it was likely to be now, with full gravity—full gravity on *Infinity* being roughly eighty-eight percent Earth normal. It was a very long way down to the County.

The tube was three meters in diameter and there were three platforms, each large enough to accommodate a single passenger.

The platforms were attached to pairs of skinny rails on the side of the tube. They were powerless contraptions operated on an elaborate arrangement of counter-weights and had been built with no very great expectation of ever being utilized.

I stepped onto one, secured myself with a strap, released the lock, held on tight and began utilizing the hell out of it.

I dropped at a moderate rate. Amber light illuminated the tube. Looking up made me feel like I was inside a giant straw slipping back after the big suck. My stomach was fluttering with anticipation. It had been a while since I'd rubbed elbows with humanity. I wondered how my people skills had held up. Actually I had one person in particular in mind.

After ten minutes or so the lights began to flicker. Was George making his broader acquaintance with *Infinity*'s intimate architecture?

The lights stuttered a final time and went out. It wasn't too bad at first, but after a while a flashlight would have been nice. The long, black fall gave me an uneasy feeling. I hadn't *planned* on any lights going out. Perhaps George had some plans of his own. Perhaps "plan" was the wrong word altogether. All I'd wanted to do was unlock some doors and disrupt a few non-essential functions. Make it hard for Laird to find me. Eventually he *would* find me, of course, but I'd deal with that when the time came.

I was certain of only one thing: I was through with surgery. Ever since my incredible longevity had become known back on Earth I'd been subjected to endless examinations, proddings, and probings, the extraction of various and sundry specimens, the harvesting of my organs, the minute examination of my genetic code, and the dissection of my psyche. No one wanted to believe God would just flat out make an error in my favor. Surely He wouldn't have chosen such a smartass.

When Laird Ulin conceived his starship and brought it into being by mean force of will, billions of dollars (he designed the first superquantum computers), and an international consortium, he offered me passage to a new world. I was optimistic enough to think it might be a better world (even if it was named after Ulin). Or at least one where I would find my privacy restored. Some suggested I was running away. One such suggester was the guy who looked back at me every morning when I shaved.

I've already described the price of my ticket.

The platform encountered a pneumatic brake and shushed to an uneventful halt. I locked the platform, fumbled my safety strap loose, and began groping for the exit.

The little girl with choppy yellow hair pointed and said, "The sky's broken."

Infinity was a ship full of skies, especially on the County level. They made everyone feel better about being sealed inside the world's biggest tin can for the duration.

But this sky was broken: A large, irregular section had gone black. All around this black wound, horizon to horizon, a high blue and fleecy white summer was in progress. It was impossible to distinguish the real clouds from the holographic facsimiles. Down here *Infinity* generated her own limited weather phenomenon, the rest was vivid illusion. However, embedded in my virus was a tutorial on storm craft, which I had hoped to see manifested shortly after my arrival and—fingers crossed—reunion. Just a mild thunderstorm, a little sound, not much fury. It was the romantic in me. Tinkering around with the idea I'd felt positively Byronesque.

It was hot. I had come upon the girl in the Town Square of Bedford Falls, sitting on a bench in a red jumpsuit eating a vanilla ice-cream cone. I guessed she was about six. She made such a pretty picture that I approached her and said hi. It had been quite a while since I'd last seen a child. Up close this one looked familiar. As soon as I greeted her she got a look on her face and started pointing at the sky, pale lips puckered worriedly.

"Don't worry about it," I said. "It's probably just a minor malfunction. Hey, watch out, you're melting all over the place." I sat beside her. She wouldn't stop staring up. Those eyes.

"The *sky's* wrong," she said.

"What flavor's your cone?"

"Huh?"

"I said what flavor's your cone?"

"What flavor does it look like?" she asked.

"Strawberry?"

"It's vanilla."

"That was going to be my next guess. What's your name?"

"Alice Greene."

I nodded. "I bet I know your mom's name."

"Bet you don't."

"Delilah."

She licked her cone. "Everybody knows everybody."

"Yeah? You don't know me."

She shrugged, then shouted: "Mommy!"

A woman had stepped out of the Bedford Falls Hotel and was crossing quickly in our direction. The resemblance was obvious, the hair, especially the violet eyes.

"There's my girl," she said, picking Alice up and holding her.

"Something's wrong with the *sky*," Alice said.

"Don't look at it, Honey."

"Why not? Will it unbreak if I don't look?"

"I'm sure it's just a minor glitch," I said. "Hello, Delilah."

She stared, bestowing upon me the same stupefied gawk her daughter had given the broken sky.

"Ellis—"

"I was on my way over when I bumped into your daughter."

"On your way over. It's been *ten years*, Ellis."

"Nine, actually. But it feels like ten to me, too, dear."

"Mommy I wanna go inside now," Alice said.

"Just a minute, baby."

"Cute kid," I said.

Delilah gave me a measuring look. "Ellis, what are you doing here?"

"Hey, I thought absence was supposed to cause various internal organs to grow fonder."

"You haven't changed a bit."

"Naturally not. Neither have you. Beautiful as ever."

She smiled, but said: "Yes, I have. Changed." She didn't mean the crow's feet, which I hated myself for noticing.

A hot breeze scurried through the square. Since I had arrived the ambient temperature had risen by at least five degrees. That was at ground level. I estimated it was a lot cooler a kilometer or so above, where George was playing with alterations in the atmosphere, orchestrating temperature and pressures changes. Real clouds formed rapidly over the County. There was something disturbingly aggressive about it. I thought of dark tubes and black wounds slashed into the sky.

"It might not be a bad idea for you to get inside," I said to Delilah.

"Go inside, Mom!"

"What's happening, Ellis?"

"I'm not sure. All I had in mind was a little wind and a rumble or two. This feels bigger."

She regarded me strangely, her fair brow was misted with sweat. "Come inside with us."

"I think I'll sit and watch for a while."

Delilah hesitated a moment longer, glanced at the sky, then turned and walked swiftly toward the hotel. Alice hung over her shoulder and dripped a trail of creamy yellow-white spots, in case she wanted to find her way back to Uncle Ellis.

The square was filling with people. They emerged from storefronts and restaurants and work centers. They halted on the sidewalks, stood straddling bicycles. Bedford Falls was modeled after an idealized small American town of the mid twentieth century, though it was more Main Street Disney than an authentic reproduction. A nice place to raise the kids. The other towns in the County were Waukegan and De Smet. There must have been a literary type on the naming committee. Well, it probably looked good on paper. Being the only one around who had seen both Disneyland and the original De Smet, my observations were more authentic than the molecular-engineered PerfectWood out of which much of these towns were constructed. I'd had a lot of life between 1965 and 2283. Too much life, I sometimes thought.

People pointed. The sky hung low and threatening, pregnant with storm. The wind picked up. Everyone appeared uneasy. I wanted to pull a Jimmy Stewart, quell the citizenry's incipient panic. But I didn't have it in me. Perhaps I needed somebody to quell *my* incipient panic first.

More than a few (Bedford Fallsians?) noticed me sitting on the bench looking at them. I was a stranger, so that was to be expected. What made me nervous were the flashes of recognition some of them threw at me. And it wasn't happy let-me-shake-your-hand recognition, either.

I got up and followed the drippy trail to the Hotel, keeping my head down.

Somebody gasped. There were some oh-my-Gods. I looked up from the steps of the hotel. The sky was tinted green. In the distance a narrow funnel cloud probed downward. Jesus.

I went inside.

"You'd better see this," Delilah said. She handed me a palm-sized device. "The alert is running continuously. You seem to be a wanted man."

I activated the thing. Laird Ulin's face swam into focus. What lovely eyes! Too bad his skin had the texture and appearance of cold wax.

"This man—" Ulin said, and an image insert of yours truly opened in the lower right corner of the screen. "—is Ellis Herrick. He is an unauthorized person in the County, and is personally and solely responsible for the disruptions now occurring. If you encounter Mr. Herrick you must detain him and immediately alert Command Level authorities."

I handed the device back. "Feel like turning me in?"

"Should I?" Delilah said.

A gust of wind buffeted the building.

"It might be more useful to point me in the direction of the nearest Core Access Interface. I think I need to turn the weather off."

"God makes the weather," Alice said, shaking her head seriously. Perhaps she was mocking me? I reached down and wiped a daub of ice cream off her chin.

"Can you do that?" Delilah asked. "Turn the storm off?"

"Maybe. By the way, where's *Mr.* Delilah?"

She wrinkled her nose in that cute way she had and shook her head. "Waukegan," she said. "And his name is Ben Roos. Why?"

"Idle curiosity."

"Ellis. You went away. Remember? For a long time. Besides, you knew I had to get pregnant."

"Ben's my gene dad," Alice piped up. "He's old."

Kids say the darndest things. An ironic consequence of my longevity is that I am sterile. Not that the six year old was trying to be ironic, or rub it in or anything. Even if I hadn't left her, Delilah would have sought out a sperm donor. That's the whole point of a generation ship.

"I bet I'm older than your gene daddy," I said to Alice.

"He's the mayor," she said back, not sounding too impressed.

"What a guy."

"He's a water farmer, too."

"Now I'm getting all tingly."

Alice giggled.

We were in the apartment behind the front desk of the hotel. A window looked out on the promenade. The light through that window suddenly dimmed, as if a giant shroud had been drawn over the town. There was a roaring. I closed the shades.

"Hang on!"

Something monstrous moved over us. The building shuddered. A woman screamed in the next room. My ears popped. Delilah's face was tense and frightened. She hugged Alice against her breast, and I couldn't see the child's face. Then the window exploded. Sucked out the opening, the shade rattled and danced. I felt the breath drawn from my lungs. Outside in the weird purple-green light, a raggedy man swept over the promenade, arms and legs flailing like the limbs of a boneless doll. *Son of a bitch!*

In a minute or two it was over.

The light turned buttery, and shadows fled across the courtyard. I stepped to the window and ripped down what remained of the shade. The sky was blowing clear. Above the shredded clouds a holographic lie of serenity persisted. My hands were trembling, and I made them into fists. There had been nothing in my virus that could have given birth to this. *Nothing.*

I climbed through the window frame and went to the man. He lay sprawled and twisted. The grass was as vividly green as his blood was red. My hand unsteady, I touched the place on his neck that should have been pulsing and found it wasn't.

Behind me, Delilah said, "Ellis—?"

"This is my fault," I said.

Then the man's eyes fluttered, and I jerked my hand back. Hearts can be tricky things.

What a nice day for a bicycle ride. Delilah Greene (with Alice riding tandem) pedaled ahead of me on the winding, swooping path through the Oxygen Forest. Duel monorails linked the towns. But with George running amok and the monorails dependent on the centralized computer system, it seemed best to take the scenic route. Also, I wanted to avoid being observed.

It was an odd-looking forest, the trees engineered for maximum carbon dioxide-to-oxygen conversion, bulgy on top like big, green cartoon poodle puffs. Whimsical. But I wasn't feeling too whimsical myself. Not like the way I'd felt when I concocted a harmless little thunderstorm.

We were on our way to Waukegan. There was an old water farmer in town who also happened to be mayor—and in the office of the mayor was a Core Access Interface. The one in Bedford Falls had exploded, unfortunately (Core interface, not water farmer/mayor). A lot of other things had, too. We left behind us a debris field of PerfectWood flinders but—luckily—no bodies. A black pillar of smoke, wind-smudged, climbed over the roofs of Bedford Falls. Whimsey.

And George was already busy rearranging the atmosphere for round two. Before entering the forest we saw an impressive cell of mini thunderheads, gorgeously mauve and dimly aflicker from within, standing on the phony horizon like purple-robed clerics of Doom.

Suddenly darkness fell. Like a guillotine. One moment it was afternoon, the next deepest midnight. We stopped riding. I didn't even bother holding my hand in front of my face, because I already knew I wouldn't be able to see it. Riding was too dangerous, and even walking was problematical. We left the bicycles and blundered around until we found a soft spot to sit and wait.

Eventually the stars come on, erratically, in clusters, through the branch tangle and cloud tatter. Then the clouds thickened, and the stars were lost. Above them, the moon dialed up, preternaturally bright. Moonlight shot through the clouds like milk poured through India ink. It wasn't enough light to ride by, but we could see well enough to walk. For safety's sake we held hands. I let it feel good, Delilah's hand in mine. The first time I let Delilah feel good to me she had been eighteen and I had been thirty-six (two hundred and seventy-four in Herrick years). Now she was pushing thirty. This knowledge tweaked my urge toward isolation, but I held on tight to that hand.

There was a distant roll of thunder, and Delilah said, "Why a storm? I know you didn't intend for it to be violent. But why a storm at all?"

Memory, circa 1983: The girl cuddled under my arm is seventeen. And guess what? So am I. Her name is Connie. Mine is Ellis (some things never change). There had been a rumble of thunder then, too, and the wind had rattled the sash like something that wanted to get in, but we were cozy under the sheets where we made love and plans.

I told a version of this memory to Delilah.

"That's sweet," she said.

"It sure was. And we even lived happily ever after. I did, at least. She got old and died. I've noticed that happens a lot."

"Oh, Ellis."

I stopped walking, and since we were holding hands it meant we all three stopped.

"Listen," I said. "The way around serial grieving is to stop living fully. Which I did, back on Earth. Then I came out here so I could do it even better. Then I slipped up and got involved with you. And ten years ago, when Laird Ulin came and took me away that last time I didn't even *try* to come back—not for a long while did I try. Because it was safer to hang out with a bunch of ageless mechanical men and one waxy bastard who could play chess. Then it occurred to me that I missed you like hell, and everybody grieves. Maybe it had something to do with being locked up in the Command Level, having my choice denied. Whatever. So now I'm the Dr. Manette of the stars, recalled to life."

"I thought it was nine years," Delilah said, and squeezed my hand. Some people just aren't equipped to appreciate a beautiful speech rife with Dickensian allusions.

Alice said, "I have to pee."

So she squatted in the bushes while Delilah held her hand and I held Delilah's hand. That's how it gets when you don't want to lose anybody in the dark. Telling my story of love and plans, I'd left out the part about Delilah being so much like Connie that she might have been her reincarnation. Their inner light and outer bearing were so similar. Long life hadn't granted me any special insights into the human soul, but I could believe in it. I suppose I had to.

Delilah said, "I'm glad you came back." And she leaned over and kissed me.

"I'm glad you did, too," I said and kissed her mouth.

A breeze freshened through the forest, rustling things. The atmosphere felt charged and smelled wet. Then it *was* wet. Very. Lightening forked across the sky, followed closely by a big rolling boom of thunder.

Suddenly Delilah collapsed. I was still holding her hand, and her weight pulled me off-balance as she went down. A brilliant beam of light fell on us, churning with silver rain. The shiny tranq dart in Delilah's neck flashed. Her hand was loose in mine. Her other hand was empty; Alice was gone.

I squinted into the light, held my free hand up, and felt the second dart punch into my shoulder. Instantly I snatched it out, but my legs turned to rubber anyway and dumped me on my ass. My body would metabolize the tranquilizer much faster than a normal person's, and I would recover from its effects quicker, too. For me, drinking's no fun. Give me a whisky and watch me cycle through stone sober to mild hangover in about three minutes; I barely notice the fun part.

Cold rain plastered my hair to my head. I felt woozy and wanted to lie back but resisted. When I put my hands down to prop myself up I felt the smooth shape of a rock under my fingers. I pried it out of the mud as the drone approached.

It was Laird Ulin—his proxy, anyway. The drone was shaped like a big watermelon, with a small but powerful searchlight attached to a gimbal on its bottom, skeletal manipulator arms, and a ten-inch screen that displayed Laird's mug behind a haze of static.

"Ready to come home, Ellis?"

The inside of my mouth was cottony. I worked up some juice and replied, "How do you always find me?"

Laird winked grotesquely (everything about him was grotesque, as far as I could tell). "I've always got an eye on you, Ellis," he said, and laughed. Grotesquely. "Come along now."

One of the manipulator arms extended toward me. I shoved away from it, sliding in the mud.

"I think I'll stay," I said.

"But they hate you down here now," Laird said. "Everybody

knows you're the bringer of storms. You aren't ever going to want to come back."

"Now I get it," I said.

The wooziness had passed out of me. A locus of pain throbbed behind my eyes. I tightened my grip on the rock. The wind and rain intensified. There was a lurid light under the clouds. Fire?

The drone swayed closer.

A giant spider leg of sizzling blue lightening stomped down, missing us by only a few meters. My skin suddenly felt too tight. Fried ozone crisped the little hairs in my nostrils. An oxygen tree erupted in flame. Laird's face disappeared in a surge of static. The drone wobbled, and I came up under it with the rock and smashed at it. The drone's manipulator arms flailed around me. I jerked out of its reach, and it bobbled erratically, undirected. Which probably had more to do with the proximity of the lighting strike than it did with my caveman routine.

Delilah wouldn't wake up. I hunkered beside her. In the firelight I saw Alice huddled under a tree not fifty meters away. I shouted over the wind and rain, and she ran to me.

Alice was scared, but she knew something important and was able to tell me. Having previously traveled the forest path, she remembered that midway along there was a rest-stop shelter.

We proceeded there. I carried Delilah fireman style, and held onto Alice's little hand, which was clammy and wet and soft. The wind tore at our sopping clothes. The air smelled of ozone and smoke. For now I was *glad* of the rain, since it was keeping who knew how many fires under control.

By the time we reached the rest stop the only unquenched blaze I was aware of was the one in my lower back. I lay Delilah down on a bench and pushed her eyelids open one at a time with my thumb. She had nice pupils. I checked her pulse, too, which was slow but steady. The storm rattled on the roof like a shower of bones. There were Perfectwood benches, a lavatory, fresh water, a rack of personal traveler's packs and first-aid kits.

Alice stood in a corner, shivering. I gave her a hug and advised her not to be scared.

"I'm not scared," she said. "Why doesn't my Mom wake up?"

"She will," I said. "But probably not for a while. You're going to sit here with her and make sure *she's* not scared when she does wake up."

"All by myself?" Alice said.

"Sure. You're a big girl, aren't you?"

"I want you to stay, too."

"I can't, honey. But I'll come back, then we'll all three be to-gether, okay?"

She looked at her feet. "Okay."

"Good girl."

There was one more thing to do before I left. The traveler's kits contained, among other things, a vacuum-sealed "fruit" paste snack and a little spoon. I told Alice not to freak out if I got loud. She made her worried mouth, that sour pucker of pale lips. I kissed the top of her wet head, then took my spoon into the lavatory and locked the door.

My eye offended me, but I sure as hell didn't want to pluck out the wrong one. To be on the safe side I could have done both, but that would have left me blind for a couple of weeks. Not a good idea. I did eenie-meeny, but my intuition suggested one more miney after the final mo. Left eye.

I did some Zen rigmarole, breathing myself into a kind of auto-hypnotic trance while I sat on the jakes. Then I waited for a particularly loud thunderclap and scooped my left eye out with the spoon. Zen breathing techniques are wonderful; I barely screamed at all before fainting.

When I came to on the floor, the eye was staring at me, trail-ing a spaghetti string of optic nerve. My left orbit throbbed like mad but had already filled in with a damp membrane that sig-naled the beginning of regeneration.

I brought my hand down flat on the severed eye. I'd miney-moed wisely. Threaded into the goo was an organic transponder with, I'd bet, about a ten year life span. Laird must have been seed-ing these things into my eye re-gens for decades. That bastard.

I used the little scissors from one of the first-aid kits to cut an oval of black fabric from my shirt. A fastidious traveler had left a partial roll of dental floss on the shelf over the sink. I poked holes on two sides of the patch and used a length of the floss to hold the patch in place.

When I emerged from the lavatory Alice stared at the eye patch and said, "I don't like it here."

The light was stark. Delilah looked like a wet corpse on the bench. Rain blew against the shelter's walls. I checked Delilah's pulse again and found it steady. I'm hell on pulse-checking, I thought, remembering the not-dead man behind the Bedford Falls Hotel. Delilah's eyes didn't flutter, and a craven part of me was grateful for that. I touched her damp cheek then turned to Alice.

"Is my Mom okay?" she said.

"Yeah. You want to come with me?"

She nodded.

"Okay," I said.

The kid looked relieved, and I recognized her for what she was: an anchoring strand in the web of human attachments I'd recklessly begun to spin from my guts. Some people never learn, I guess.

Daytime dialed up hot after the brief and violent night. Steam rose off everything, even our clothes. An exploded curbside terminal burned merrily on a Waukegan street corner, the flames nearly invisible in the glare of the false sun. Broken glass glittered in the street, trash hustled around in hot, little whirlwinds. The air had thickened, and I almost had to swallow every breath like thin soup. Alice had taken hold of my hand again and was squeezing it hard. A couple of times during the long walk from the Oxygen Forest my stomach had moved in queasy undulations. Which could have been guilt, or—much worse—an indication George had begun to tamper with the County's gravity field.

"Here," Alice said, tugging me toward the double doors of a chalk-white and very official-looking building, like maybe the place where Mickey Mouse planned all the parades and stuff. On our way to the stairs I drew some unfriendly looks from people who appeared wrung out and pissed off. One guy did more than look. He seized my arm and spun me around to face him. "You bastard," he said. Bared teeth, blood crusted on flared nostril. I braced myself for a blow I probably deserved. But a couple of other men pulled him off, and Alice tugged urgently at my hand. I didn't bother telling her not to be scared.

"This one," she said, once we'd attained the second floor, and she pushed her finger against a door marked by a simple plaque: "Mayor."

I knocked.

The old man who answered was short and stooped, what little hair remaining on his pate was wispy as cobwebs. The wrinkly face brightened slightly at the sight of Alice. He kissed her cheek then rubbed her hair with a palsied hand. She put up with it.

When he turned his attention to me all he said was, "You're Herrick." And his eyes were like a pair of peeled grapes staring moistly from nests of papyrus skin. I didn't hold my breath for a kiss.

"And you're—"

"Ben Roos. Alice's father."

"Gene father," Alice said.

Roos scowled at her. "Where's Delilah?"

Alice looked at me. Delilah had called Roos before we departed Bedford Falls. She had assured him that I could put things right if given a chance.

"We had to split up," I said.

He grunted. "You can fix this mess?"

"Possibly."

He grunted again, eloquently, and turned his back. We followed him into the office. He pointed at the Core Access Interface, which looked a little like an old-fashioned barber chair with an even older-fashioned hair dryer attachment. "There you go," Roos said. "People could die, Mr. Herrick. I'm hoping when you say 'possibly' you're just being coy."

"Me, too."

I sat down and performed a soft interface with the CAI. The old man and Alice and the room and the world slipped away. The superquantum environment read me and produced an analog. George. Mr. George, actually. My seventh grade history teacher was an Ichabod Crane knock-off, only not as handsome. I'd left him in an empty classroom "correcting" student papers with a liar's red pen, disbursing a stickman army of D's and F's to papers deserving of better. This was my unconscious symbolic language for the smidgen of chaos I'd intended to introduce and which, apparently, had morphed into something much more serious.

I looked over George's shoulder. He was drawing smiley faces on the endlessly replenishing stack of papers. Huh?

"You can't outfox me with my own toys," Laird Ulin said, speaking through the mouth of Ichabod George, not looking up from his endless scribble of smilies.

I backed away. The room lacked windows and doors. Laird had isolated my virus and was letting me know as much. I pressed into a corner and found myself folded over to my parent's bedroom, the way it had looked when I was a thirteen-year-old boy. There was another analog: Me, this time. I was rummaging through my mother's purse. I came up with Mom's wallet and started plucking bills out while sneaking looks over my shoulder. Sneaky. Repeat.

I fled from that scene and passed through a complex chain of interconnected vandalisms. My various analog selves set fires, kicked some kid in the balls, tortured insects and small animals, etc. Anyone else seeking problems in the superquantum environment would witness their own versions of various malicious acts—but *my* individual stamp would be on every single one.

"It's quite out of control," Laird Ulin said.

I turned. He was sitting behind a free-floating ebony slab the thickness of a wafer, fiddling with cut glass chess pieces.

"I thought George would catch you off guard," I said.

"You forgot about shadows," Laird said. "Or gambled one wouldn't occur."

"Shit. I gambled."

Ulin grinned.

A quirk of superquantum technology is the occasional quantum shadow—a future ghost in the machine. Laird must have seen my tampering before I even did it, which gave him time to do a little tampering of his own and stamp it with my personal signature—conferring upon me instant persona non grata status in the County.

I felt a weird combination of relief and resignation.

"So now I'll come back to surgery and you'll make things right," I said.

Laird smiled.

The chessboard turned into a crystal display of complex quantum language: the reality behind the dramatic analogs.

"The errors are self-perpetuating," Laird said. "I constructed it that way. Couldn't help myself, Ellis. You made me mad this time." He waved his hand and the chessboard returned.

"Definitely mad," I said, picking up a knight. It was slightly tempting. Retreat was my fatal flaw and I knew it. Besides there was nothing I could do about the quantum errors Laird had unleashed. Only he could spare the County. Hell, returning to my cozy, emotionally remote cocoon on the Command Level was practically an act of noble self-sacrifice.

"Maybe we should skip the game for now," I said.

"Nonsense," Laird said, taking the knight from my fingers and replacing it in its proper position on the chessboard.

"Shouldn't you be getting busy?" I nodded toward my delinquent analogs.

"There's plenty of time," he said. "All the time in the world. Besides, correcting these errors will be very difficult, and I'm not inclined to do it. The more miserable life is in the County, the less likely you will be to find safe haven. Ever. There will be *no more running away, Ellis*. Now why don't we relax and have a game while the environment sustains?"

I quoted Ben Roos: "People could die."

Laird shrugged. He tapped a pawn on the chessboard. "Shall we play?"

"We shall not."

Laird scowled. I inhaled deeply, withdrew from the interface, and leaned forward in the chair, rubbing my good eye. The patch had slipped a little on the other one, and I adjusted it.

Alice was gone. Ben Roos sat on the small sofa by himself with a cup of tea or something that he didn't appear inclined to drink.

Two men flanked me. They didn't look friendly. Something ticked against the window. The ticking increased and subsided, in waves. Rain. Wind. I looked up at the man on my right and said, "Not guilty." He pulled a frown.

Ben Roos was staring daggers at me from the sofa. He was a pretty good dagger starer, too. Welcome back to the land of the living. Actually, I was glad to be there. *No more running away.*

"Where's Alice?" I asked.

"She's gone off," he said. "And if anything happens to her it will be on your head, like the rest of this mess."

"I can explain some things," I said.

Roos snorted. "Save your explanations." He stood. "I'll check the uplink. Keep Herrick here until they arrive."

He went out.

I got up but my flankers crowded me.

"I'll just be on my way," I said. "I have uplinks to check, and miles to go before I sleep."

The slightly older man shook his head. "You're staying right here until the Command authority comes for you."

"Hmmm," I said.

When I started for the door, the younger guy stood in front of me, rather beefishly.

"Have a seat, Mr. Herrick." He grinned. "What are you supposed to be, anyway, a pirate?"

How does one while away the years before and between stars? I mean, after you've read everything and honed your saboteur skills. Study Jeet Kune Do, of course!

I found Mr. Beefy's carotid artery and invited him to unconsciousness. He looked surprised, then slack, then he fell.

His friend took about as much trouble. I guess they hadn't been expecting a fight. Good. There were two sets of hooded raingear hanging in the corner, dripping on the carpet. I appropriated the larger set, put it on, and exited by the window. In eighty-eight percent gravity, one story is doable if you're fussy about landing.

On the sidewalk, I pulled the hood up and kept my head down. A pair of biomechanical men entered the building I'd just exited. I'd have to avoid their type and God only knew what else for a while. Maybe for a long while. But if I could manage to remain at large in the Country, Laird would have no choice but to correct the quantum errors. He wouldn't want me to get stomped by lightning or torn apart by pissed-off citizens. Would he?

On the path beyond the suburbs of Waukegan a small girl's voice squealed after me.

I turned around and smiled. "Hey, kid."

"Hi," Alice said. "I ran away."

"What a coincidence."

"Are you going to see my Mom?"

"Yeah."

"Me, too."

I thought of Delilah out there, certainly awake by now, perhaps on the path to meet us. I thought of hugs and tears, and the tightening web of relationship. I thought of letting her in through the open door in my heart, which was really an unsutured wound.

The top-heavy oxygen trees tossed wildly in the wind. Dark clouds scudded overhead, dumping rain below a holographic flicker of summer. The great black gash in the sky was visible, and Alice stared upward, her lips puckered tensely.

"Don't be afraid," I said.

"I'm not afraid."

I picked up her little hand. "Me neither, kid," I said. But I was a liar.

HERE'S YOUR SPACE

The aliens tasted like tofu, kind of bland. At least that's what Delilah told him; Ernest wasn't having any. He sat on the ship's (apparently) severed fin and watched her red and pink mouth. It worked and flexed, a rubbery thing, the lips greasy. Delilah's mouth had often appeared lovely to Ernest but that was back when it was attached to her face. And anyway the lovely period of their marriage had ended long before the Rift effect began.

Ernest looked away. His vision accordioned then caught up and splintered again. More like playing cards fired between a dealer's hands, only slow it down and put a woman image on each card. Delilah in rapid flickering vision. A flipbook person.

The last time Ernest had seen anything other than himself as a whole picture he'd been reaching for his bulb of coffee, leaning forward in the pilot's couch, careful not to sever numerous transdermal linking points. The Rift was a thousand klicks distant, a black fold in space. A Class One star vector advisory recommended avoidance. Ernest had gone far in his profession by ignoring such advisories. He conspired with his ship, *Amelia*, and they eased closer. A thrill traveled through Ernest's body. *Amelia*, intimately bonded with his psyche and a perfect feminine reflection of his anima, always thrilled him. Especially when they were doing something forbidden, like violating rules of approach. The ship was Ernest at such moments, reading his desire, accommodating it, feeding his impulse back with fake but inspired feminine energy; Ernest was fully erect. Then the Rift sucked them in, and he slammed back, bulb rubber-balling off his face, his links to *Amelia* jerked loose. The thing about anomalous Rifts is you can't trust them for safe distances.

Anyway they crashed. Sort of.

The weirdest crash landing ever. There was no sense of sudden deceleration. Ernest seemed at once to be inside and outside *Amelia*. Bulkheads, screens, gauges, panels all split and tilted like a mad cubist painting. Ernest slapped the engine cut-off while he could still see it. Then everything exploded but not with a bursting concussion. More like an engineer's drawing, an exploded view depicting the starship *Amelia* and all her contents. Only dice those contents up and sling them in a chaotic sprawl over a vast area. If vast meant anything. Or area. To Ernest only his own body appeared unmolested by the Rift effect. Something to do with his self-absorbed ego perception. Delilah, too, could see herself as a whole person. Everything else, for both of them, was chaos. And it was all Ernest's fault, of course. Wasn't everything?

Well it's not *my* fault," Delilah's nose said.

Ernest had been searching for the pilot's couch. A fruitless hunt of four days, so far, according to his implanted chronometer. He was starving, though not starving enough to eat the aliens, the Tofudians, as Delilah had dubbed them.

"I was thinking it was *both* our faults," he said.

Delilah's left nostril twitched. "You would think that."

He hadn't found the couch but he kept encountering pieces of his wife, and all of them could talk.

"I'm just trying to be fair," Ernest said.

"That's typical. Why is it 'fair' for me to take half the blame for an accident you are solely responsible for?"

"I guess it all depends on how you interpret things."

"Yes," Delilah's nose replied. "I interpret things honestly and you interpret them according to your pathological need to be *right* all the time."

"It's not my fault if I happen to be right more often than not."

Delilah's nose snorted. "You crashed us."

"You have no curiosity."

"You're *too* damn curious. You and your girlfriend. By the way, would it kill you to let me interface with *Amelia*?"

"I drive the ship."

"Yes I know."

"And it was my damn curiosity that won me the Vega Award," he pointed out.

"Funny. I thought the Vega was presented to both of us."

"It's a team award," Ernest said.

"Meaning?"

"Nothing. It's *our* Vega, okay? And our Vega is why we got of-fered the Tau Boo vector, and Tau Boo yielded the hive minders, and if *we* can demonstrate their etheric mindchain we will get any vector we want. So please for God's sake stop eating them."

"Mind is a big word for Tofudians. They're too rudimentary to think. But I do wish they tasted better."

"Dee! I need at least ten to demonstrate their hive mind."

"I'd stop if I could find the comestibles. But I can't, and I don't intend to starve. You can if you want to."

"How many have you eaten?"

"Twenty or so."

"Jesus!"

"They're not very filling. But you know, Ernest? They're mak-ing me feel funny."

"Funny how?"

"Like I'm spread out, but I'm not talking about the Rift effect. I'm picking up on all the other Tofudians. I kind of know where they are and what they're seeing."

"Really? That's interesting. Maybe you could use them to find the couch. Or hadn't you thought of that? But I still want you to stop eating them."

Delilah's nose sniffed. "It's nice to know what you want, isn't it?"

Ernest walked away. It was hard to conduct a serious con-versation with a disconnected nose. Of course he knew the nose wasn't really disconnected, that Delilah was a whole person. It was some kind of dimensional distortion, an intersection of different space-time templates, tectonic realities crossing each other, grind-ing out a new view of *Amelia* and her contents.

So he walked away, but walking wasn't easy, either. Imagine ten thousand mirrors shattered and pulverized, the glinty splin-ters and powder (Rift captured starlight?) cast over a landscape of clear syrup, the integument that bound the exploded view of *Amelia*. Every step Ernest took he sank into the integument. Strewn around were the various hunks and pieces of the ship and

Delilah, some of them floating in the air (recycling hiss indicating it was *Ameila*'s oxygen they were still breathing), some of them imbedded in the glinty syrup.

Okay, Ernest loved *Amelia*.

He craved the pilot's couch and not just because it might save them. Patched in, Ernest sampled *Amelia*'s deepest recesses, where her data flowed sweetly and together they drove through space, a perfect fit. The more Ernest interfaced with the ship the more *Amelia* accommodated his psyche and became a reflection of his mind, his conscious and unconscious. She understood him because she *was* him, a reflection of him, with a feminine sensibility built in. It was the only way to drive a starship, by making it an extension and compliment to the complexity of a human mind. The intimacy factor was a side benefit, one not appreciated by Ernest's wife.

And the pilot's couch really might save them. Ernest reasoned that if he and Delilah were existing in concurrent cross-dimensional space then *Amelia* probably was, too. If Delilah's mouth could chew up a Tofudian in one "place" and process it through her bowels in some other "place," then perhaps a command issued through *Amelia*'s couch would successfully activate her engine nacelles and boost them out of the Rift. Where, one hoped, *Amelia* and her contents would resume their contiguous existence. To be on the safe side of that equation he would make sure Dee was securely anchored to an interior hunk of the ship before he powered up. That is if she wasn't too busy eating his next Vega Award.

But after four days he'd all but given up. Jigsaw puzzle pieces of *Amelia* were everywhere, but—then he saw it! Way off in the glinty junk-strewn distance (if distance meant anything). He quickened his slogging pace, until Delilah stopped him and he sank to his knees.

Not her eyes or the back of her head or even her elbow or small intestine. Ernest was down on his knees addressing an old but rarely seen friend: Delilah's vulva. The more time Ernest had spent wrapped in intimate communication with *Amelia* the more ignored Delilah had felt. When he took his conversation and attention away she responded by taking from him something *he* needed. Since Delilah started withholding sex Ernest found he had even less to say to her. And it wasn't fair! Starship teams were supposed to be ship*mates* in a literal sense; that was the whole point, the way of enduring these long voyages. It was Delilah who was cheating! All he had wanted was a little breathing space. He *told* her that.

"What's your hurry," Dee's vulva said.
"I think I see the couch."
"Don't worry about the couch. Why don't you rest?"
"Rest!"
"Ernest, I feel something."
"What?"
"It's your breath, I think."
Ernest swallowed. Delilah's vulva had always exerted a cobra-like fascination. Hypnotize the prey then . . . strike! Only this cobra hadn't struck in a long while.

He looked up, hunger sharpening his senses. That *was* the pilot's couch over there. And some kind of movement. Ernest began to struggle back to his feet.

"Remember when you used to tease me?" Delilah said.
"Tease you?"
"Your cheek on my thigh and your warm breath . . ."
"Oh, yes." He let himself sink back.
"Sometimes you didn't shave, and your cheek was all whiskery. Those two sensations, the breath and your rough cheek. It really drove me crazy."

His face subsided into starglint, inches from Delilah's vulva, which presented itself complete with copper furred mons veneris. The newly moistened eye of the cobra glistened. Ernest grinned and reached out.

"I see you still like a good tease," he said and he moved a little closer.

"I do indeed," she replied, and her tone had shifted to hard and gleeful.

He stopped. "What's wrong?"

"Now I know why you spent so much time with *Amelia*."

Ernest put it together and tried to stand up, forgetting his weakness. A string of Tofudians tracked by on little ant legs. They were everywhere. He needed a piece of the ship, preferably an interior piece, to anchor himself. But there were none within slogging distance.

"Here's your damn breathing space," Delilah said.

There occurred a great sucking *whoosh*. Ernest tumbled like a grain in the wake of a speedboat. Then he had his space. But Delilah and *Amelia* took the oxygen with them.

Cat in the Rain

D aniel Porter got drunk in an Irish bar called O'Leary's. He downed two shots of Jameson's then spent the balance of the night drinking pints of Guinness while he watched the TV mounted on the back bar between a dusty Shillelagh and a Bodhran. A neon beer advertisement bathed everything in nauseating green light. So much for atmosphere and the olde sod. Anytime it seemed possible somebody other than the bartender might speak to him, Daniel put out his famous repelling vibe. It was Wednesday night and O'Leary's wasn't crowded, anyway. O'Leary's was never crowded, that's why Daniel liked it.

The basketball game was interrupted periodically for special reports on the potential riot situation in Pioneer Square; O'Leary's was uptown, but riots tended to wander. Daniel watched the reports with detached interest. He was a police detective, and as far off duty as he could get. Rioting had become pandemic. One city or another igniting almost every week. Protests, anti-protests, Fat Tuesday, Super Bowl victory celebration, May Day, *Arbor Day*— whateverthehell. The Pioneer Square thing had to do with new city curfew laws scheduled to go into effect at midnight. It was as if the world had gone mad with violence. Or madder, anyway. The center will not hold, all that Yeats crap. The uncertainty factor. The impotence factor. The world seemed to have reached its ultimate crisis point at the same time Daniel Porter reached *his* ultimate crisis point. In his work Daniel never trusted a coincidence.

Daniel's partner, Jimmy Bair, had a cousin who supposedly worked for the NSA. This cousin told Jimmy that, unknown to the public, alien satellites had appeared in high Earth orbit, and they were, as Bair put it, "Cloaked—you know just like *Star Trek*. Sometimes they're *there*, and sometimes they're not there. For all we know they're shooting us with invisible Hate rays."

Good old Jimmy. He was Scotch-Irish, big and aggressively chummy, with a nose like a red potato. A stand-up guy no matter what. The one guy Daniel would want watching his back.

"It's a fucking sign," Bair insisted. "You know, all that crap in the Middle East, AIDS, bird flu, wars, plagues, fucking terrorists, fucking *pestilence*. Plus things in the sky. Signs and portraits, right? It all adds up to the big picture. Like the Bible."

Daniel cultivated detachment as a barrier against idiot theories, not to mention his genuine sense of impending doom. Daniel was hell on barriers. He wasn't too bad on Doom, either. For corroboration one could consult his ex-wife. Daniel had always been an asshole, to hear Nancy tell it. But lately he had become the Emperor of Assholes. Daniel couldn't help it. He reacted against the cesspool the world had become, the cesspool his life in particular had become. And he couldn't listen to any more bullshit—especially his own.

The game was over (and how), the night progressed to the AM side of the clock. Daniel threw back the dregs of his last Guinness, paid, and left.

It was a hot August night. He felt sick and dizzy. Hands in his pockets, he stumbled up the street like a badly manipulated marionette. A red Toyota Echo hunkered at the corner. Daniel recognized the creased quarter panel. He stepped around a pile of cardboard and rags, staggered against his car, fumbled the key into the lock, pulled the door open, and bundled himself into the backseat. He'd rest a few minutes, regroup.

Daniel's head expanded and contracted like a balloon nippled in the mouth of an asthmatic. Time passed. Several voices rose up, all male. Something loud and metallic *clanged*. Daniel, folded and sprawled half conscious across the back seat, opened his eyes. Yellow firelight played on the roof. A rusty sound made him wince, stiff wheels grinding on pavement. Daniel sat up cautiously, his head in deflated mode.

Across the street four or five young men were pushing a burning garbage dumpster down the sidewalk. They bent their backs to it. Flames surged and lapped over their heads. Sparks, like swarms of fireflies, twisted in and out of chugging gray-black smoke.

Sensing movement behind him, Daniel turned. The pile of rags stood next to the car. He had barely registered the rags before,

avoiding them with his drunk-dar. Now he realized they consti-
tuted a derelict. As the Hellfire dumpster passed on the opposite
side of the street firelight flickered on the derelict's face. Except,
below his ratty watch cap, he *had* no face. It was like a rudimentary manikin's head displaying the subtlest impressions and pro-
trusions, suggesting features not yet formed. As Daniel watched,
the impressions deepened, as if invisible thumbs were pressing
into soft wax. Shadows quivered in the eye cups. A wet gleam occurred. Daniel's breath caught, and there was a tremendous crash
across the street. He jerked around. The dumpster was now tipped
over inside the display window of Talbot's. Real manikins turned
into torches. The young men capered like savages, their identities
lost to a mob impulse. When Daniel looked back, the derelict was
gone—if he'd even been there in the first place.

He steered the Toyota up Pine Street toward Capital Hill,
hunched forward, both hands fisted at the top of the wheel. Behind him sirens ululated. He became confused in the residential
back streets. Nancy had kicked him out of the house only a couple
of weeks ago. In the dark the hulking brick building where he now
resided looked like any other. Daniel hated the apartment, hated
the smallness of it, the feel of other lives having passed through.
He'd almost rather sleep in the Toyota. Finally, exhausted, he
parked randomly, stubbing the front tire on the curb.
His balloon head carried him through shadows, puddles of
moonlight. He swayed against a noisy fence, fingers hooked in
the chain link. A girl gazed at him from a third story window. She
was wearing a light summer dress. There was no glass in the window. He blinked and she was gone, an apparition of his mind. The
building, which otherwise appeared abandoned, seemed to lean
toward him. Daniel's head drooped, balloon deflated. He felt his
gorge rise for the umpteenth time since leaving O'Leary's. Without looking up again he lurched away from the fence. The next
thing he knew, he was pushing open the door of his apartment.

Daniel lay on his bed and stared at the dingy white plaster
with its sags and cracks and stains. His ears were ringing. Sleep

eluded him, his mind meandering down empty paths. His mouth had Saharan aspirations. He worked his throat, swallowed. Finally he got up and shuffled into the bathroom. Bare feet planted on the cold tile, he leaned over the sink and slurped at cold, metallic-tasting tap water. He heard a voice conducted down the airshaft and cranked the tap off. A girl reciting a nursery rhyme, that sing-songy cadence. But it was not a child's voice. Daniel turned to the window and raised the sash. Counter-weights knocked inside the frame. A gray concrete wall faced him, so close he could almost reach out and touch it. The voice stopped. Below was a forlorn slab. He craned around and looked up. At the same time a head stuck out of the window on the next floor. A young, round-faced girl looked down at him, her lower lip tucked between her teeth. She was very pale and serious, her shoulder length black hair hanging straight down.

Daniel said, "Hi," in a phlegmy voice.

"I thought I was all alone," the girl replied then withdrew from sight and closed her window.

He slept into the afternoon and awoke with a headache. The sight of the unpacked, cluttered, and dusty apartment depressed him. Upon moving out of the Ballard house he'd taken two week's vacation. He wanted to settle into his new life alone, to establish himself in his new environment. But the interruption of the work routine left him prey to wounded maunderings and depression. The drinking had gotten on top of him. He knew he had pushed Nancy's last button. The button's name was Julie. But he had only wanted Julie so long as he couldn't *have* her. Instead he achieved what he had really craved all along: to be totally alone. He'd even given up the girl on the internet, the one Nancy never did find out about. Daniel's isolation imperative throbbed as though infused with cosmic energy, perfectly accomplishing his estrangement. He'd felt this way before, when he was fourteen, during his suicide summer. Nobody knew about that.

He lay on the bed in his underwear, watching TV with the sound turned off, a Merlot bottle on the bedside table and an empty stem glass balanced on his stomach. The picture quality was bad. It was an old portable television. The antenna imperfectly snagged broadcast signals out of the air.

There was weeping in the airshaft.

For a while he pretended he didn't hear it. Then she started in on the nursery rhymes again. He couldn't quite make out the words and it bothered him. He put the glass on the table and stood up. It took him two tries, which is how he discovered he was drunk again.

In the bathroom he knelt on the floor, arms folded on the window ledge. Mary's lamb had a white fleece. As white as *snow*. Go figure. The girl's voice was sweet, trembly. There was something about that Rhyme, something he couldn't quite remember, something important. Daniel struggled with it for a minute then gave up. As he stood, his elbow knocked a bottle of shampoo off the window ledge. It hit the slab and the cap popped off.

The girl's voice stopped for a moment. Then she said, "Is somebody there?"

Daniel stared at the blunt, concrete wall. It was almost as though he were snug and safe inside a chimney. Safe from the anxieties that plagued him, safe from the world. He didn't want to come out.

"I didn't think so," the girl said. "Just another nasty trick."

Daniel cleared his throat.

"Hey—" the girl said.

Daniel addressed the wall: "I'm here, I'm not a nasty trick." He had the strangest feeling he was talking to himself.

"Let me see you."

Daniel extended his upper body out the window and twisted around. As before, she gazed down at him, her hair hanging straight.

"God," she said.

"No, just me. Dan."

"Eh. I'm Frankie."

He stared at her. Frankie was the name of the chat girl he had abandoned. This couldn't be . . .

"What were you crying about?" he asked.

"My cat ran away."

His Frankie had a cat, too. So had his ex. Daniel was allergic. Before they married, Nancy used to put the cat out when he came over. One night he woke up to the sound of rain. Nancy was asleep. The cat clung to a branch outside the bedroom window, miserable, fur matted and dripping. That was the night the damn thing disappeared. Who knew what happened to it. Hit by a car, run off. He had felt bad. Nancy told him it wasn't *his* fault, of course. Sixteen years later, though, she let him know how it *had* been his fault. And how she didn't even believe in his allergies. "It's all psychosomatic with you," she had said. "You don't want anything around that demonstrates love, that might need you, or that you might need. Not me, not even a *cat*. You can't *take* it." Well, she had a point. He really couldn't take it.

"That's too bad," he said to Frankie.

"He's all I had left. Now they'll get me."

"Who will get you?"

"The saucer people."

Daniel felt tired.

"Will you come up here?" Frankie said.

He didn't reply. His back hurt.

"Please? I want to show you something. I'm scared."

"What is it?" he said.

"You have to see it."

The hallway seemed to tilt. Daniel kept bumping into the wall. It was too dark. On the ceiling inverted bowls glowed dimly yellow. At the end of the hallway a hydrocephalic moon leered through the broken window. Trash littered the floor. It was as though he were in two buildings at once. Which one was real? Either of them? Daniel had to haul himself up the stairs using the rail. He closed his eyes for a while and kept climbing. When he opened them again the third floor appeared normal. He found the right door and knocked.

Frankie was a small person, not much over five feet. She wore a faded summer dress in a flower print. Her legs and feet were bare. She was pretty, in a way. Mostly she made him conscious of his age, just as his unseen internet girl had. He was forty-nine.

"How old are you?" he said.

"Nineteen."

The same as *his* Frankie.

"I think I know you," he said.

"I don't think so," she said, taking his hand and leading him through a duplicate of his apartment, minus the clutter. He didn't want her to touch him but he allowed it. In the kitchen she said, "Feel that?"

He did: a cold exhalation, a draft. She pulled him to the other side of the kitchen. The draft was coming out of the narrow space next to the refrigerator. He should have been able to see the back wall. Instead there was a velvet shadow, an impression of *depth*, a vague iridescence. The draft raised his hackles. There was a strange odor. It evoked slaughterhouses, the smell of wet concrete after they've hosed the blood away. He took his hand out of Frankie's.

"The Sleeve," she said. "It's like a connecting corridor between *here* and *there*. The saucer, I guess. Like that tunnel thing at the airport that you walk through to get on the plane? It's for people like us."

Daniel really wished he hadn't come up.

"Where do you think you are right now?" she said, suddenly intense.

"Uh, your kitchen?" Daniel said.

"Wrong. They mess with our minds. First they shoot us with rays to make us crazy. Make us more alone. You want to know what my theory is? To be human, to belong on Earth, you have to be connected to other people, you have to be yourself *and* part of the human web. When we lose that sense of connection we're vulnerable. They isolate us then they replace us. It's like an invasion. They're *replacing* us." (And he saw his own shadowed face in a cracked and spotted mirror, mouthing those words: *They're replacing us.*)

Daniel rubbed his eyes. Except for the rays and invasion bullshit her words sounded familiar. Web of human connection. He'd read that somewhere.

"Sleeping so close to an open Sleeve, my dreams started telling me things," Frankie said. "That's how I know. But I had Mojo to protect me. He isn't human but he kept me on *this* side. You have to go voluntarily. That's part of it, I think. You have to not care. You allow the replacement to come through. Kind of like inviting a vampire into the house?"

"Vampire," Daniel said.

"There isn't any getting out. I opened the door once. I was afraid to, but I opened it. I had the dumb idea I could leave the building. Mo slipped past me and I couldn't even chase after him. I call him but he doesn't come. He's not a *dog*. I guess they'll get me now. Except, I mean unless you and I connect?"

Daniel moved to the other side of the kitchen, leaned against the counter, folded his arms.

"It's relationships," Frankie said, "real human connections that keep us in the world. That's all."

She moved close to him, invading his famous boundaries. Her body was practically touching his. And Daniel's body responded to her proximity. But it was just his body. Every other facet of his being wanted to get away. He knew the drill, Alien Lonely Hate Rays notwithstanding.

"I have to go," he said.

"We should stay together. Maybe we can anchor each other? I don't want to be alone anymore."

"Frankie, I have to go."

"Let me come with you."

(His own face in the spotted mirror.)

She wrapped her arms around him. He gently moved her back. She did not hold on, did not resist or cling. She was used to this. She *courted* it. Rejection was her drug. He could see that in her eyes. He'd seen it before, in other eyes. He was just another in a long line of rejecters, when he left her there in the slaughter-house draft. It's what he told himself.

In the hall he noticed the faded pattern on the rug was the same as the one on Frankie's dress. And suddenly he remembered *maryslamb* was Frankie's chat handle. He turned back to the closed door, brought his hand up, but didn't knock. After a moment he turned away.

*

He found a station that endlessly ran programs from the 1960s, shows that he'd watched when he was a kid, some only because his mother watched them, and his dad whenever he happened to be home, which wasn't often. *The Fugitive, Run For Your Life, Burke's Law, The Twilight Zone, Star Trek*, and so on. His mother eventually ran off with some other man. Daniel remembered the terrible fight his parents had, how his dad struck his mother a hard, open-handed blow across the face before she slammed out of the house for the last time. Daniel had been twelve, and after that he mostly raised himself. But it was strange. With his eyes closed Daniel could see his mother's face. And he could see Robert Stack's face, Rod Serling's face—but not his own father's.

He was drinking beer, watching Richard Kimble and his TV ghost images. His mind was unmoored, disconnected. Footsteps creaked across the ceiling. He turned the sound down on the TV. There was more than one person up there. He listened. After a while there was only one set of footsteps. Then it was quiet.

He got up to use the bathroom. A window rattled open in the airshaft. He turned the light out and stood quietly. But after a minute he couldn't help himself. Loneliness moved through him like a subterranean tide. He opened his own window. He leaned out and looked up. The rain fell in silky whispers around her head. Her straight hair was wet and dripping.

She had no face.

Daniel pulled back. The top of his head caught the sharp edge of the window sash. Black stars pulsed around him. He reached up, fumbling, slammed the sash down, crawled back to bed.

The dawn arrived in smoky darkness. The rain was constant, thunderous. No amount of heat could dispel the dampness inside the apartment. Black mildew spotted the walls and ceiling. Daniel felt the damp entering him, greening his bones. He had lost weight. In the kitchen, rummaging for food, he held his pants up.

Something strange was happening outside the kitchen window. Just beyond the dark rain-lashed trees that crowded the building the sun was shining. Bright afternoon sun. It made little misty rainbows on the outer edge of the downpour, but penetrated no further. On the lanai attached to one of the apartments across the alley a woman stretched out on a lawn chair. She was wearing a yellow bikini top and dark glasses.

Daniel rubbed his eyes, a cold, crumbly piece of Gino's cardboard pizza in his mouth. A violent gust thumped the window, and he jumped back.

From the bathroom mirror a Dachau survivor stared out at him. He fingered his ribs. *I'm losing myself*, Daniel thought. How long had he been here? If Jimmy Bair could see him now. The alien Lonely Hate rays would never get *Jimmy*—he was too goddamn jovial and big-hearted.

He recalled the faceless thing in the airshaft. It couldn't be true. He had been drunk. Frankie was still up there. *His* Frankie. He shoved the window open and called her name. When there was no reply he got dressed, not bothering to knot his shoelaces, and lurched out into the hall. Immediately he felt exposed, hollowed out, and filled back up with terrible anxiety. He mustn't leave the apartment. But he did. The elastic hallway tilted and stretched and swayed. He climbed the stairs. Frankie's door stood open. He entered and found the apartment empty. In the kitchen there was no slaughterhouse draught. The Sleeve had closed, if there had ever been a Sleeve.

He lay flat on his back, sweating in the damp chill, breathing shallowly, staring at the ceiling, his mind vacant. He was dimly aware of something scratching at the door. He ignored it. Besides, the scratching seemed as much inside his head as outside it. A cool draft touched his bare feet. Daniel's heart clenched with fear, but in a way he was ready to go. More than ready. He got up. His knees felt weak. In the tiny living room rain shadows drained over the piled boxes and furniture. The unnatural draft emanated from a voided section of wall. Velvet darkness stretched back into vague iridescence. Something *moved* in there.

Daniel forced himself to turn aside, his heart speeding with fear. He stumbled out of the living room, remembering what

Frankie had said about the cat anchoring her in the world, that small connection. He yanked the apartment door open. The hallway was empty. He tried to step out and his guts clenched and knotted, as if he were trying to step into an airplane propeller.

"Come on, Mojo," he said.

The hallway remained empty.

Daniel's throat tightened. Not even a fucking *cat*—

Then Mo came around the corner where the stairs dropped to the first floor. His fur was tawny and puffy. He hesitated, seeing Daniel.

"Here, kitty?" Daniel said, without much hope.

Mo looked at him, for a moment stood stock still with tail high, then padded over.

Chuck Norris and his ghosts hawked the Total Gym at the foot of Daniel's bed. The rain was like sand blowing against the windows. A slaughterhouse draft breathed through the apartment, and Daniel mostly stayed under the covers. Mo curled against him on top of the bedspread, his little furnace body thrumming. Mo wore a collar, but the name on the collar was "Fritz" not "Mojo." This nagged at Daniel. His mind tried and failed to get around it.

Mo didn't care for his new diet of frozen pizza. His stool was runny and especially odoriferous. Daniel couldn't house train him, since he himself was afraid to leave the apartment let alone the building. He tore pages out of an old Esquire magazine and arranged them on the bathroom floor between the sink and tub and tried to direct Mo's bowel to evacuate there and only there. No dice.

Mo grew restless. He prowled the confines of the apartment, hunting avenues of escape. Daniel erected a barrier of boxes between the hallway and the living room, afraid Mo would disappear into the Sleeve. He almost wished the cat *would* disappear. Daniel's eyes and nose were runny. When he breathed his lungs made a raspy sound. He knew Mo was his protection against *them.* Nevertheless there were times when even Mo's presence was too much. The shit and allergies didn't help.

Daniel woke out of fitful sleep. His nose was completely plugged, and his eyes felt *gritty.* When he tried to sit up, Mo was right there, practically smothering his face.

"Gah." Daniel pushed the cat roughly away, off the bed. It landed solidly on all fours. "Why don't you go take a shit somewhere," Daniel said.

Later, after he'd splashed cold water on his face and woken up sufficiently he felt bad. He called Mo but the cat didn't appear. There was plenty of junk in the apartment, plenty of hidey places.

"Come *on*, Mo."

He began to panic. He searched more vigorously, shoving boxes aside, crawling on hands and knees to peer behind bookcases, kitchen appliances, under furniture. Finally he gave up. Standing in the bathroom, hugging himself against the cold damp, he said, in a voice choked with tears: "Goddamn it, Mo. Fuck you, then. Who needs you."

Two light bulbs burned out, one in the kitchen and one in the hall. He'd kept every light burning continuously and had no replacements. The apartment became gloomy. Daniel dreaded the dark. He stayed in bed, watching TV. He was always cold and he huddled under the covers, a scrofulous skin-and-bone man.

The television reception became worse. Ghosts overlapping ghosts, overlapping ghosts, and everybody with a mouthful of static. Daniel felt sick with isolation. But he didn't think about Nancy or anybody else, particularly. He was long past thinking about Frankie, for instance. Or his parents. But the cat was a fresh wound. He missed Mojo, the uncomplicated companionship.

Dampness seeped through the walls. The ceiling was fuzzed with mold. The plaster appeared soft, mealy. Daniel was almost not there. He stared at *The Andy Griffith Show.* Endless television buoyed him on a sea of alpha waves.

A light bulb directly above him burned out with a thin glassy *pop*. Daniel stiffened.

The Sleeve beckoned. A slaughterhouse draft breathed through his covers, shivering him. It was time. His isolated heart had extended an invitation to the vampire. He threw the covers back and swung his feet to the floor, pulled on a pair of pants and cinched the belt to the last notch to keep them from sliding off his skinny hips.

Daniel started down the hall, fatalistically drawn to the Sleeve. Wind whumped the loose kitchen window. He glanced over. *Mo* was out there in the blowing rain, clinging pathetically to a branch, his fur matted and streaming. Daniel experienced a pang of guilt and deep yearning loneliness.

And then stopped.

Because it was impossible for Mo to be out there in the rain. Flat impossible. All the windows were shut tight and the door firmly closed and locked.

That was Nancy's cat.

And the illusion began to collapse around him.

The light dimmed, flickered. The familiar clutter vanished, replaced by stark emptiness, brown walls, broken lathe and plaster gritty under foot. In the kitchen an ancient electric stove was pulled away from the wall, the front gaping like an idiot mouth. He'd been alone all this time. He'd conjured Frankie up out of memory and imagination and desperation.

They mess with your mind.

And his mind messed back. He blundered backward down the hall. Glancing into the bathroom, he caught his haggard reflection in the cracked and spotted mirror—the face that talked to him. He backed up to the apartment door, cranked the knob behind him, pulled it open and fell into the hall. *Nancy's cat. And Frankie was maryslamb, that dumb phrase she used to type about the web of human connection, referring to the net.* Daniel rolled onto his knees, looked up. The hallway was a ruin. Light fixtures dangled by wires. An overlapping occurred. The broken window at the end of the hall was momentarily restored, then crashed out and haphazardly boarded over, then restored.

He staggered to his feet, fighting dark/light visions, flung open the door to the rear, outside stairs. He staggered down to the alley behind the building. Rain pounded deafeningly on the sheet metal lids of the garbage dumpsters. A dark brick ruin loomed over him. Swinging drunkenly around the side of the building he saw Mojo huddled at the base of the tree, the rain having beaten him to a yellow rag of matted fur. *Not Mo. Fritz. That was Nancy's cat: Fritz. Frankie (maryslamb) had a cat named Mo but he never saw it, because he never saw* her. They had messed with his mind, and his mind had fought back, conjuring companions, unraveling.

Whatever its name was, the cat reacted to the sight of Daniel, darting around to the front of the apartment building.

There is no fucking cat, Daniel thought wildly.

He started to follow Mo anyway but made it only as far as the tree. He fell against it, the rough bark digging into his cheek. The rain was drowning him. He thought of his good bed, the covers pulled up, the television soothing with the familiar ghosts of his past. Up there is where he belonged. He raised his head. On the second floor a dim figure stepped back from the window.

Follow the cat.

He lurched away from the tree, came around the front of the building. Mo/Fritz was gone. Beyond the dark veil of rain a vague, muted light persisted. Daniel stepped toward the light . . . and encountered a fence. Chain-link. Summoning reserves of strength he hoisted himself up and over, ripping his shirt on a sharp twist of metal. He fell to the other side, rolled and stood up, and first the rain and then even the sound of rain fell way. He held his hand up, palm outward against the brilliant August sun. Time dilation, he thought, remembering some science fiction movie. A sign attached to the fence announced the building's future demolition. It wasn't *his* building. Little wet paw prints tracked away on the white sidewalk. Daniel began to follow them, bare feet slapping the hot paving. And then the prints vanished before his eyes, and his clothes were dry, and he was just a raggedy man staggering along, voices mumbling in his head.

He lived on 1st Avenue. His home was a broken-down cardboard box that had once held a 46-inch plasma television set. He sat on the box and waited for people to drop coins in the old Starbucks cup. A certain number of passersby did so, and they were his tenuous web of human connection. Most people ignored him, though. And even those who paused, because he looked as though he had once been a normal person, a nice man, a down on his luck man, were eventually repelled when he told them about his cat and the saucer people.

"Thank you, thank you," he said, when coins rattled into his little cup. "I have a cat to feed, you know."

There was no cat. Daniel knew he was crazy, and he wished someone would lead him back to his senses.

Twilight was upon the world, and he was afraid. He dragged his cardboard into the recessed doorway of an Army-Navy surplus store. Nights were bad. Wherever he huddled he was alone and could feel the slaughterhouse draft, the opening of the Sleeve, the dreadful invitation formulating in his mind.

"Dan Porter, is that you?"

Daniel looked up. A tall, wide man in a sport coat a size too small stood above him. He had a potato nose.

"Jimmy Bair," Daniel said.

Bair crouched beside him. "My God. Flynn told me he saw you. I told him he was out of his fucking mind. Look at you."

"You were right," Daniel said.

"Yeah? What about?"

"The alien satellites and their invisible Hate Rays, for one thing. Only they're Lonely rays, too. Jesus Christ, Jimmy, they're ruining the world. *They're replacing us.*"

Jimmy Bair nodded but he looked sad.

"Sure, and don't I know it," he said.

"*You're* the one who warned me."

"Yeah."

Jimmy reached out and touched Daniel's hand. Daniel pulled the hand away.

"I—I don't like to be touched," he said.

"I know."

"It's part of it. They mess with our minds. They want us to be isolated, so we'll go and they can take over."

"If you say so, Danny."

Tears welled up in Daniel's eyes. None of it was true. He wanted to get better. "Thank God you're here, Jimmy. You don't really believe it all, do you?"

"I do." Jimmy Bair smiled. Then he poked at Daniel with his fingers, not touching him, but almost touching him, and when Daniel cowered back, whimpering, Jimmy Bair's smile got wider.

Alone with an Inconvenient companion

"May I join you?"

Douglas Fulcher looked at the woman, trying to detect whether her face was real. The subdued light in the hotel bar didn't make such a determination easy.

"Sure," he said, not wanting her to sit, not wanting to be with anyone, but unable to resist his compulsions, either. Not even at this late and final hour. They had been the only two people sitting by themselves.

She pulled the chair out opposite him, sat down, extended her hand.

"I'm Lori. I'm with the Intrinsic Genetics convention? I've been watching you, trying to figure out if you're part of our group."

He put his fork down (he'd been enjoying his last meal, a Cobb Salad) and shook her hand.

"Doug," he said. "I don't do groups."

She laughed, her voice a bit rough, like somebody had given her esophagus a light scuffing with a Brillo pad. She looked about half his age, which would make her twenty-five or so. Her hair was a flaming yellow dye job. A *good* flaming yellow dye job, but phony nevertheless. A come-on. Like an ad, or one of those direct government advisories that shoot out of thin air, admonishing you to buckle up, vote, wear a condom, recycle, rat on your neighbor. But what really bothered him about this girl was her face, which was too beautiful.

"If you don't do groups," she said, "what do you do?"

"I don't know. What is it you want me to do?"

"Well. That opens a world of possibilities."

He smiled, which felt like a rictus but probably appeared okay, and they looked at each other across a gulf that only Doug was aware of.

"You're not wearing a name tag," he said.

"Neither are you."

"I told you. I'm not part of your group."

"Maybe I'm not, either. Maybe I just said that to start the conversation."

"Did you?"

"No."

He laughed, but not like he meant it, though he did, a little. Which surprised him.

"I'm not with any convention," he said. "I used to go to every one I could wrangle my company into paying for. But I'm just staying here now because I like this hotel. I remembered it."

"Are you on vacation?"

"I'm traveling," he said, after a moment.

"Let's have a margarita," Lori said. "I'm buying."

He didn't want a drink.

"Okay," he said.

He didn't want a drink, but having one he knew he would have another, and perhaps another. Which he did. Now he stood halfway across the gulf on a bridge of frozen green booze. But only halfway. It's as far as he ever got, or ever would get. Lori was explaining to him about the fascinating work Intrinsic Genetics was doing on the cyborg project, attempting to invest analog brains with human response characteristics, growing cortical cells in labs and "infecting" the cyborg tissue with them.

"Jesus Christ," Doug said. "Can that actually be done?"

"Not yet."

"I'm not sure I believe you," he said, joking around, but a part of him actually wondering. It wouldn't have surprised him to learn that a percentage of the human population was in reality *not* human.

"It would be par for the course if everybody was a cyborg," he said.

"What do you mean?" She sounded genuinely interested, not pissed off that he wasn't onboard with the cyborg thing.

"Just a theory I have."

"What's the theory?" She smiled, flirtatious and interested.

"You'll think I'm crazy," Doug said.

"Crazy is okay. It's better than regimented conformity, which is what you usually get. I never wear my stupid name tag, because when I'm out of town, even for a convention, I don't really want to meet the kind of people I work with all year."

He stopped tearing his coaster into tiny bits and looked into Lori's eyes, which he could see clearly from his suddenly advanced position more than halfway across the gulf.

"Everything wants to be a mechanism," he said.

"A mechanism?"

"I mean in the world, it's all about becoming part of the *mechanism*."

She looked at him with a neutral expression. He felt on the verge of saying something significant. Something true, something outside the mechanism. All he required was the tiniest encouragement. He got it: Lori smiled and said, "Go ahead, it sounds interesting."

He cleared his throat and leaned on the table. "They come at you," he said, "with the deliberate intent to de-humanize you, turn you into a *thing*, a responsive object. A slave consumer. They want you to respond to their marketing, their salesmanship, their evil politics, their Draconian health tactics. All of that. Even your own parents want you to be a responsive mechanism. A good little mechanism. If you aren't good enough, they'll let you know, don't worry. They'll move you out of the private Sector school and into the God forsaken Public Sector. Not that the public Sector schools were always God forsaken. God only forsook them after the ruling power structure did. Anyway, it's all designed to get *them* into your head and *you* out of your mind."

"My," Lori said.

He sat back, slightly embarrassed. "I told you you'd think I was crazy."

"I—"

"Excuse me a minute. Bathroom."

He stood up, the vertical movement immediately informing him of the depth of his inebriation.

"I want to ask you something," he said.

"Sure."

"Your face. It's a SuperM job, isn't it."

They were like masks, those SuperM makeup treatments. In fact they had to be applied by qualified medical-paras, and they did more than enhance your natural looks. Much more. All Douglass knew was that it was unlikely a damned geneticist would naturally come by the kind of looks Lori displayed. She looked up at him, seeming to weigh her response.

"Yes," she finally said.

"Be right back," he said.

In the Men's Room he unzipped and began to relieve himself of the high-octane margaritas. He felt derailed, subverted from his original intent, which was to blow a hole in the middle of the emerging mechanism within him.

The urinal made a strange clicking sound, like some exotic insect, then spoke to him.

"Good evening, Mr. Fulcher," it said. "As a complimentary service of the Desert Palm Hotel your waste is being analyzed."

Jesus Christ. Had it come to that? Douglas looked around, even though he knew he was the only one present.

"Your privacy is our main concern here at the Desert Palm—" The urinal's voice was female, upbeat. It sounded Midwestern-sensible. He pictured a healthy corn-fed blonde (no dye job), sweet-faced (no guess-what-I-really-look-like SuperM job), in practical clothes (no slit skirt and high heels). "—so I am speaking to you in a narrowly directed aural cone that only *you* can hear."

Douglas looked up. On the ceiling was a thing like a brass tulip the size of a man's thumb.

The voice continued: "The results of your urinalysis will be available on your room's World-Window and a copy will be attached to your bill at the conclusion of your stay with us. The hotel of course assumes no responsibility for any legal ramifications should your waste contain one or more banned substances." The urinal chittered like a doped squirrel. "There we go! Your complimentary urinalysis is complete, Mr. Fulcher. I recommend that you don't drive at this time, as your blood alcohol rating is a whopping point zero three."

"Right," Doug mumbled.

"Do have a pleasant stay with us," the urinal said.

"Uh."

"And on a personal note, why don't you try to get some sleep tonight, Douglas."

He had zipped up and was starting to step back, but paused.

On a personal note?

He leaned back into the "aural cone."

"What did you say?"

A large man in a blue button down shirt with a name tag clipped to the breast pocket, an Intrinsic conventioneer that Douglas had noticed in the bar but had not heard enter the Men's Room, stepped up to the next urinal and began to pee. The man glanced at him then looked straight ahead, intently, as if his true fortune was engraved on the tiled wall.

Back in the bar Douglas said, "The urinal told me I should get some sleep."

Lori smiled uncertainly. "Oh?"

"Yeah. I guess they're even putting computers in the toilet now."

"It figures they would get around to it," Lori said.

"Told me I shouldn't drive, either. When you get right down to it, that was a very solicitous urinal."

Lori nodded, smiling, being a sport.

"I don't think mine talks," she said.

"Maybe it's just some of them."

The waitress showed up with two fresh margaritas, ordered by Lori while Douglas was gone. She put the drinks on the table. Douglas *didn't* want his. Or he wanted it and didn't want it at the same time.

Lori immediately sipped her drink, raising the big saucer glass of slushy green booze with the fingertips of both hands and dipping her face down to meet it halfway. She set the glass on the table again, said, "My turn, back in a minute. I'll let you know if the Lady's Room has anything to say."

"Great," Douglas said, noticing the salt crystals embedded in her thick SuperM lipstick application. He watched her walk away. She had a nice swing in her backyard, but that was less interesting than it should have been. He sensed the mechanism of his compulsion and rejected it. There had been too many women in too many hotel bars, all of them finally adding up to a big empty zero. As his marriage had started to bend under the weight of his necessary estrangement he'd began to travel, attending every convention he could wrangle his company, Boston Cell-Tech, into paying for. And if there weren't any conventions, no valid reason to travel, he pretended there *was* a valid reason and went anyway, burning vacation and sick leave, sometimes traveling to distant cities, sometimes simply booking a room in a local hotel. To be away. He would call Sara, his wife, to inhabit the familiarity of their complicated estrangement. Alone but not alone, in anonymous hotel rooms. There but not there. After the compulsory sexual liaisons began the marriage collapsed, stranding him between zeros. That's when the bad thing happened, when he tried to *force* Sara to be real. Not a good idea. They had taken him away, tweaked his brain chemistry, subjected him to compulsory therapy. In short, they had commenced construction of the mechanism; but it hadn't worked, and when they released him and Sara rejected him, he went on following his compulsions.

Now, three years later, he was finally done. He let the concept hover a moment or two, then he folded a couple of bills and tucked them under the edge of the coaster, got up and left the bar, quickly, bumping into a big tropical plant in his haste to be gone. The plant rattled its fronds at him.

A tiny, green jewel winked on the wall opposite the foot of the bed, where Douglas lay on top of the covers in his underwear. A blue steel Parabellum rested on the pillow next to him, like a random piece of the secret world mechanism that had mistakenly fallen into the visible spectrum and landed on his bed.

Doug reached over, but not for the gun. He touched the remote, and the World-Window, five feet across, opened with Microsoft's familiar blue sky and clouds, which resolved into the Hotel's Logo. A busy, animated menu followed, presenting a staggering number of entertainment choices—none of which interested him. There were no incoming messages.

Douglas slumped back. He had been hoping for the results of his complimentary urinalysis. And not merely a dry, voiceless presentation of cholesterol ADL and DPL, blood sugar levels, and all that. Perhaps after the breakdown there would have been a short paragraph advising him to consult with a qualified medical professional (as if any of them were qualified) regarding some of his more questionable numbers. For instance, was he perilously close to receiving another Compulsory Consumer Restriction Tag from the US Department of Citizen Health Oversight? Douglas was in reasonably good shape for a fifty year old, but almost everybody started accumulating CCR's around his age.

On a personal note . . .

Really, though, he had been hoping for *the voice*. He called it up in his mind, and also the accompanying picture he had formed, the Midwest girl, fresh beauty, plain and sensible, somehow outside the trans-urban mechanization that was rapidly overcoming the rest of the world, wanting nothing more than to examine his waste for signs of trouble.

Lying back, he turned his head and gazed at the Parabellem on the other pillow.

Somebody knocked on the door.

Douglas pushed himself up on his elbow, startled.

There was another knock. He slipped out of bed and padded quietly across the room in his boxers. He listened at the door, but he wasn't a bat, he couldn't broadcast sonar waves or whatever.

He flirted with the door handle, caressing it with his fingers. If he opened the door would he find Lori from the bar, a hotel employee, room service, the interruption of zero time? He felt *between* everything. Between gigantic zeros, the alien environments of his empty house and the hotel. His own fault it was empty, of course. Now he was always alone with an inconvenient companion: Himself.

Had there really *been* a knock? He began to doubt it. Finally he turned the handle down and pulled the heavy door inward and stuck his head out into the empty, anonymous hotel corridor.

Three-thirty A.M. Douglas crossed the lobby. He was wearing shoes but no socks, unpressed slacks and a white, sleeveless T-shirt, not tucked in. The plastic-tipped ends of his untied shoelaces clicked on the red stone floor. The night clerk looked up but said nothing when he passed. Doug noted the vacancy in the man's eyes. Cyborg?

He entered the Men's Room, the one right outside the closed bar. Chrome and white porcelain gleamed. He approached the same urinal he'd used earlier. This time it made no special clicking-chittering sounds, and no sweet, solicitous voice spoke to him within the narrow privacy of an aural cone.

He moved to the next urinal, and the next, and then he was out of analyzable waste. One per customer, he supposed. He'd only wanted to hear *the voice* again, the way he used to call his ex before she *was* his ex, to feel the constraining safety of her voice.

He gazed forlornly up at the aural cone gizmo. He reached for it but couldn't quite touch the little metal tulip, which was disguised to look like a fire sprinkler.

In the lobby he approached the desk clerk, a young cyborgish man with wispy, prematurely vanishing hair.

"Yes, sir, may I help you?"

Douglas nodded. "About that complimentary urine thing—"

The desk clerk's eyebrows went up a little, but just a little.

"I'm afraid I don't understand?" he said.

"The *urinalysis*. It's mostly the voice I'm interested in. I wonder if you have the same voice speaking in other devices around here."

"Voice?"

"Yes, you know. The voice that tells you about the urine test."

The clerk looked like he really wanted to help but didn't know how.

"Never mind," Douglas said.

"If there's any—"

"No, never mind."

He was crossing the courtyard back to his wing of the hotel for the last time when a *different* but still familiar voice spoke out of the dark:

"Hello."

He stopped. In the deep moon shadow under a lemon tree the tip of a cigarette glowed then dimmed. Someone only faintly visible was sitting at one of the courtyard's glass-topped tables, smoking.

"Lori?" he said.

"You don't have to talk to me," she said. "I saw you walk by a few minutes ago, and then just now. I didn't mean to say anything. You obviously were done with me earlier."

He approached the table.

"I'm sorry. I didn't feel good."

"Didn't you?"

"No. Do you mind if I sit down?"

Under the lemon tree, up close, she was still faceless. After a moment of hesitation she said:

"Go ahead."

He pulled the wicker chair out and seated himself. Lori drew on her cigarette, and in the brief breathing glow of its coal her face partially emerged. She looked different; had she removed the SuperM makeup? *Could* she remove it? Or had she merely been crying?

"Cigarette?" she said.

"No, thanks."

"I should quit. I'm CCR'd on real nicotine."

"That smells real."

"Oh, it *is*."

She laughed a raspy, raw-throated laugh, her voice degraded, not at all the sweet modulations of the urinal voice. At least she was real. A real human being, not a synthesized personality or digital recording of an actress, whatever it was, some *voice* calculated to tempt his romantic view of mythical innocence and so relax him and allow the easy and free emptying of his bladder.

"I get them black market," Lori continued, meaning the cigarettes. "Nobody checking my status, looking for cancer markers. I hate that crap."

"Me too," Douglas said.

"The way we're always being watched and taken care of and told what to do. Sometimes I'm sick of it, though I know it's good for us. I mean they're just trying to keep us safe and healthy, right?"

"Maybe," Douglas said. "I need to ask you something."

"All right."

He scooted his chair up, leaned toward her. He didn't mind

the cigarette smoke. He liked it. It made her human, a fallible human being subject to whims and compulsions that weren't necessarily good for her.

"Were you telling me the truth about the cyborgs?"

"What about them?"

"That there aren't any yet, because they can't do the brain cell thing."

"Just in a few labs, and they're pretty clunky at this stage, more like retarded refrigerators."

"You couldn't mistake one for a hotel clerk, for instance?"

"You were right," Lori said.

"What about?"

"Earlier you said I'd think you were crazy. I do."

She laughed. After a moment he joined her, faking it at first (the laugh mechanism) then feeling it genuinely, the absurdity of what he had said, of her reaction, but still, in a way, *believing* what he had said. Doctors weren't always right. Especially when they make you endure their asinine probing questions and injections, carting you off on a platinum CCR rolling tag with mandatory restraints. They could make you appear mad, despite the truth you understood. Douglass had never disputed the validity of *appearances*. But appearances could and did hide truths. What if Lori herself were a cyborg? What if they were tracking him, or, more realistically, she could be one of many planted in various cities with access to a vast database of potential troublemakers. *I've been watching you*, she had said. Then Doug let it collapse, the paranoid lunacy of the idea.

"You know what?" he said. "I really like you. And I don't think I've liked anybody in a long, long time."

"I'm honored."

He couldn't tell if she was being sarcastic. He needed her not to be.

"I'm glad you were out here," he said, "waiting for me."

"I was just having a smoke before bed."

"It was you at my door a little while ago, too, wasn't it?"

She brought the cigarette to her lips and inhaled, making the tip glow.

"At your door?" she said. "You never even told me your room number. We didn't get that far."

"Anyway," he said.

"What *is* your room number?" she asked.

He told her.

"Is it nice?"

"It's exactly like all the other rooms." He meant all the rooms he'd ever been in throughout the totality of his existence.

Lori leaned way over to the side and snubbed her cigarette out in the dirt at the base of the lemon tree.

"Can we go up and see it, Doug?"

"Yes."

In the elevator he noticed her face. It was still beautiful. SuperM beautiful. He was disappointed. Under the shadow he'd been mistaken. She smiled at him, and he didn't know who she was. She pressed against him, and he kissed her, because he knew that was next. It was a stale smoke and booze kiss. Her tongue moved in his mouth, a thick sluggish thing, like something that lived in moist earth. The elevator stopped, not at his floor, and they broke apart. A sleepy-looking man, his tie pulled loose, stepped into the car.

The doors slid shut. Douglas looked at Lori's reflection in the polished metal surface. Her face was distorted, SuperM useless, stretched and warped out of pleasing proportion. He preferred it that way because it was truer to the way things really were.

She went in the bathroom, and he lay on the bed, waiting. After a while she came out. She was wearing a black bra and panties, her body blandly appealing in lamp light.

"You're beautiful," he said, not meaning it yet, but thinking he might later. He needed to mean it.

"You're dressed," she said.

"So far."

She straddled him and began rubbing her hands over his chest and down his body. The contact stirred him. He lightly slid his fingertips up her bare arms. She squirmed her shoulders, making her breasts jiggle.

"That tickles."

He stopped.

"You know," he said, "I went back to the Men's Room but she wouldn't talk to me."

Lori paused. "Who wouldn't?"

"The urine analyzer thing."

She snorted, and resumed caressing his body through his cotton T-shirt.

"You almost had me believing that," she said, suddenly tugging his shirt up to expose his skin.

"What do you mean?"

"The hotel doesn't have anything like that. I asked."

He frowned at her.

She pinched his nipple, which he didn't like. "Hey," she said, "I'm not saying it's a bad idea. God knows."

"God knows," he said, then snapped his head to the side, afraid that she would noticed the anomalous component of the secret mechanism on the other pillow, but it wasn't there; he'd put it under the bed before he went downstairs. Lori grabbed his jaw and turned his face toward her again and kissed him then licked his chest and bit his nipple. Again with the nipple. She liked it a little rough. He could understand that. Sometimes you *had* to make it hurt to get a true response. He understood that, but Sara hadn't.

Later, in the last balancing strokes of their love-making, when he could have fallen either into fleeting transcendence or the gravity of failure, he pictured *the voice* of his imagination, the Midwestern farm girl, and how she would hold him so dear within her body while a warm country breeze from the open window caressed his back.

Afterward they lay together. He turned the lights off but he could see her face, the phony perfection of it, in the dim poolside light that filtered through the curtains. He reached out and touched her cheek with his fingertips, traced her jaw line, lightly brushed her lips.

"Do you ever think about having this removed," he said.

She didn't say anything, but her eyes were open, staring at him.

"I mean do you always think you need it, the SuperM job? What if you were just yourself?"

"Doug?"

"Yeah?"

"I don't have a SuperM job. This is my real face."

He didn't believe her. "Oh," he said.

"I mean it. I told you that about the SuperM because my face scares men, I think."

"Scares them?"

"Men are intimidated by my looks. They always have been. It's not my fault. It's them, they think I'm snooty or superior. It's lonely for me, believe it or not. Sometimes I tell men that it's a SuperM face, and it lets them relax, like they're with a 'normal' girl with insecurities and everything. I *do* have insecurities, of course. I know it's crazy. But I really am a normal girl. They should make an *anti-*SuperM face, for girls who don't want to be objects anymore."

"Nobody would buy them," Doug said.

"Not even me," she said.

It became apparent that she planned to stay the whole night. Douglas made some internal adjustments and accepted the situation. He watched the green jewel light of the World-Window until Lori's breathing assumed the rhythm of sleep, and then he reached over and turned on the lamp. Soft light lay over her perfect features. Well, not *perfect*, exactly. No SuperM job was without flaws, of course. But there were never *obvious* flaws such as these incipient crow's feet. Douglas's fingers hovered over Lori's face, her eyes, which were already nictitating in REM sleep. *Are you real*, he thought. *The voice*, he was now prepared to believe, had *not* been real. The knock on the door was still an open question. It could have been a distraction of his mind, trying to divert him away from the gun; the mechanism attempting to save itself. It was possible, he admitted it. He had to learn to *control* the false things his mind sometimes told him. Control them without the terrible drugs. He could do it.

All he needed to go on was one real, genuine thing in the world. One person he could touch. One voice that wasn't only in his head. One connection to despoil the chaotic impulse of the gun.

He touched Lori's forehead.

SuperM had a stretched, almost plasticized feel at various crucial points where it transformed the more recalcitrant imperfections of physiognomy. The worry lines, crow's feet, under-eye pouches. Now his fingertips discovered a truth:

Lori's face was real.

Her eyes fluttered briefly. She yawned, made a deep *hmmmm* sound, did not wake.

Douglass fitted himself to her body, allowing himself to do that, to cross the gulf, resting his head upon her chest where it met her shoulder. He felt himself finally begin to relax out of his fear. Tears seeped from his eyes. He was tempted to wake Lori and tell her he knew she was real. Instead he tried to relax, allow sleep to draw him down, down to the last peaceful grotto, where Lori's heartbeat filled his void.

Suddenly he lifted his head, wide awake and separate again. He frowned, lowered his head, placing his ear directly over Lori's chest.

He held his breath.

Under the steady, seemingly organic, beating of Lori's heart, he detected, faintly, faintly, a mechanical clockwork ticking.

WHAT YOU ARE
ABOUT TO SEE

I t sat in a cold room.
    Outside that room a Marine handed me an insulated
suit. I slipped it on over my street clothes. The Marine punched
a code into a numeric keypad attached to the wall. The lock
snapped open on the heavy door, the Marine nodded, I entered.

Andy McCaslin, who looked like an over-dressed turnip
in *his* insulated suit, greeted me and shook my hand. I'd known
Andy for twenty-five years, since our days in Special Forces.
Now we both worked for the N.S.A., though you could say my
acronym was lowercase. I operated on the margins of the Agency, a contract player, an accomplished extractor of information
from reluctant sources. My line of work required a special tem-
perament, which I possessed and which Andy most assuredly
did not. He was a true believer in the *rightness* of the cause, pro-
cedure, good guys and bad. I was like Andy's shadow twin. He
stood in the light, casting something dark and faceless, which
was me.

It remained seated—if you could call that sitting. Its legs, all
six of them, coiled and braided like a nest of lavender snakes on
top of which the alien's frail torso rested. That torso resembled the
upper body of a starving child, laddered ribs under parchment
skin and a big stretched belly full of nothing. It watched us with
eyes like two thumbnail chips of anthracite.

"Welcome to the new world order," Andy said, his breath con-
densing in little gray puffs.

"Thanks. Anything out of Squidward yet?"

"Told us it was in our own best interests to let him go, then
when we wouldn't it shut up. Only 'shut up' isn't quite accurate,
since it doesn't vocalize. You hear the words in your head, or
sometimes there's just a picture. It was the picture it put in the

secretary's head that's got everybody's panties in a knot."

"What picture?"

"Genocidal carnage on a planet-wide scale."

"Sounds friendly enough."

"There's a backroom theory that Squidward was just show-ing the secretary his own secret wet dream. Anyway, accepting its assertions of friendliness at face value is not up to me. Off the record, though, my intuition tells me its intentions are benign."

"You look tired, Andy."

"I feel a little off," he said.

"Does Squidward always stare like that?"

"Always."

"You're certain it still has the ability to communicate? Maybe the environment's making it sick."

"Not according to the medical people. Of course, nothing's certain, except that Squidward is a non-terrestrial creature pos-sessed of an advanced technology. Those facts are deductible. By the way, the advanced technology in question is currently bun-dled in a hanger not far from here. What's left looks like a weather balloon fed through a shredder. Ironic?"

"Very." I hunched my shoulders. "Cold in here."

"You noticed."

"Squidward likes it that way, I bet."

"Loves it."

"Have you considered warming things up?"

Andy gave me a sideways look. "You thinking of changing the interro-gation protocols?"

"If I am it wouldn't be in that direction."

"No CIA gulag in Romania, eh."

"Never heard of such a thing."

"I'd like to think you hadn't."

Actually I was well familiar with the place, only it was in Gua-temala, not Romania. At its mention a variety of horrors arose in my mind. Some of them had faces attached. I regarded them dispassionately, as I had when I saw them in actuality all those years ago, and then I replaced them in the vault from which their muffled screams troubled me from time to time.

Andy's face went slack and pale.

"What's wrong?"

"I don't know. All of a sudden I feel like I'm not really standing here."

He smiled thinly, and I thought he was going to faint. But as I reached out to him I suddenly felt dizzy myself, afloat, contingent. I swayed, like balancing on the edge of a tall building. Squidward sat in its coil of snakes, staring . . .

Now return to a particular watershed moment in the life of one Brian Kinney, a.k.a: me. Two years ago. If years mean anything in the present context.

I was a lousy drunk. Lack of experience. My father, on the other hand, had been an accomplished drunk. Legendary, almost. As a consequence of his example I had spent my life cultivating a morbid sobriety, which my wife managed to interrupt by an act of infidelity. Never mind that she needed to do it before she completely drowned in *my* legendary uncommunicative self-isolation. The way I viewed things at the time: she betrayed me for no reason other than her own wayward carnality. You'd think I'd have known better; I'd spent my nasty little career understanding and manipulating the psychology of others.

Anyway, I went and got stinking drunk, which was easy enough. It was the drive home that was the killer. The speedometer needle floated between blurred pairs of numbers. By deliberate force of will (I was hell on force of will) I could bring the numbers into momentary clarity, but that required dropping my gaze from the roller-coaster road sweeping under my headlight beams—not necessarily a good idea. Four. Five. Was that right? What was the limit?

Good question.

What *was* the limit?

I decided it wasn't the four whiskeys with beer chasers. No, it was the look on Connie's face when I waved the surveillance transcript at her like a starter's flag (Race you to the end of the marriage; go!). Not contrite, guilty apologetic, remorseful. Not even angry, outraged, indignant.

Stone-faced. Arms folded. She had said: "You don't even know me."

And she was right; I'd been too busy *not* knowing myself to take a stab at knowing her.

Off the rollercoaster, swinging through familiar residential streets, trash cans and recycle containers arranged at the curb like clusters of strange, little people waiting for the midnight bus. I lived here, when I wasn't off inflicting merry hell upon various persons who sometimes deserved it and sometimes didn't. These days I resorted to more enlightened methodologies, of course. Physical pain was a last resort. Guatemala had been an ugly aberration (I liked to tell myself), a putrid confluence of political license and personal demons unleashed in the first fetid sewage swell of the so-called War on Terror. Anyway, the neighborhood reminded me of the one I wished I'd grown up in. But it was a façade. I was hell on façades, too.

And there was Connie, lifting the lid off our very own little, strange man, depositing a tied-off plastic bag of kitchen garbage. Standing there in the middle of the night, changed from her business suit to Levi's and sweatshirt and her cozy blue slippers, performing this routine task as if our world (my world) hadn't collapsed into the black hole of her infidelity.

Connie as object, focal of pain. Target.

Anger sprang up fresh through the fog of impermissible emotion and numbing alcohol.

My foot crushed the accelerator, the big Tahoe surged, veered; I was out of my mind, not myself—that's the spin I gave it later.

The way she dropped the bag, the headlights bleaching her out in death-glare brilliance. At the last instant I closed my eyes. Something hit the windshield, rolled over the roof. A moment later the Tahoe struck the brick and wrought iron property wall and came to an abrupt halt.

I lifted my head off the steering wheel, wiped the blood out of my eyes. The windshield was intricately webbed, buckled inward. That was my house out there, the front door standing open to lamplight, mellow wood tones, that ficus plant Connie kept in the entry.

Connie.

I released my seatbelt and tried to open the door. Splintered ribs scraped together, razored my flesh, and I screamed, suddenly stone-cold and agonizingly sober. I tried the door again, less aggressively. My razor ribs scraped and cut. Okay. One more time.

Force of will. I bit down on my lip and put my shoulder to the door. It wouldn't budge, the frame was twisted out of alignment. I sat back, panting, drenched in sweat. And I saw it: Connie's blue slipper flat against what was left of the windshield. Time suspended. *That bitch.* And the Johnstown flood of tears. Delayed reaction triggered. As a child I'd learned not to cry. I'd watched my mother weep her soul out to no changeable effect. I'd done some weeping, too. Also to no effect. Dad was dad; this is your world. Lesson absorbed, along with the blows. But sitting in the wreck of the Tahoe, my marriage, my life, I made up for lost tears; I knew what I had become, and was repulsed. The vault at the bottom of my mind yawned opened, releasing the shrieking ghosts of Guatemala.

You see, it's all related. Compartmentalization aside, if you cross the taboo boundary in one compartment you're liable to cross it in all the others.

By the time the cops arrived the ghosts were muffled again, and I was done with weeping. Vault secured, walls hastily erected, fortifications against the pain I'd absorbed and the later pain I'd learn to inflict. The irreducible past. Barricades were my specialty.

The Agency stepped in, determined I could remain a valuable asset, and took care of my "accident," the details, the police.

Flip forward again.

You *can* be a drunk and hold a top-secret clearance. But you must be a careful one. And it helps if your relationship with the Agency is informally defined. I was in my basement office *carefully* drawing the cork out of a good bottle of Riesling when Andy McCaslin called on the secure line. I lived in that basement, since Connie's death, the house above me like a rotting corpse of memory. Okay, it wasn't that bad. I hadn't been around enough to turn the house into a memory corpse; I just preferred basements and shadows.

"Andy," I said into the receiver, my voice Gibraltar steady, even though the Riesling was far from my first libation of the long day. Unlike Dad, I'd learned to space it out, to *maintain.*

"Brian. Listen, I'm picking you up. We're going for a drive in the desert. Give me an hour to get there. Wear something warm."

I wore the whole bottle, from the inside out.

The moon was a white poker chip. The desert slipped past us, cold blue with black ink shadows. We rode in Andy's private vehicle, a late model Jeep Cherokee. He had already been driving all day, having departed from the L.A. office that morning, dropping everything to pursue "something like a dream" that had beckoned to him.

"Care to reveal our destination?" I asked.

"I don't want to tell you anything beforehand. It might influence you, give you some preconception. Your mind has to be clear or this won't work."

"Okay, I'll think only happy thoughts."

"Good. Hang on, by the way."

He slowed then suddenly pulled off the two-lane road. We jolted over desert hardpan. Scrub brush clawed at the Cherokee's undercarriage.

"Ah, the road's back thataway," I said.

He nodded and kept going. A bumpy twenty minutes or so passed. Then we stopped, for no obvious reason, and he killed the engine. I looked around. We were exactly in the middle of nowhere. It looked a lot like my personal mental landscape.

"I know this isn't a joke," I said, "because you are not a funny guy."

"Come on."

We got out. Andy was tall, Scotch-Irish, big through the shoulders and gut. He was wearing a sheepskin jacket, jeans, and cowboy boots. A real shit-kickin' son of a bitch. Yee haw. He had a few other sheepskins somewhere, but his walls were wearing *those*. I followed him away from the Jeep.

"Tell me what you see," he said.

I looked around.

"Not much."

"Be specific."

I cleared my throat. "Okay. Empty desert, scrub brush, cactus. Lots of sand. There is no doubt a large population of venomous snakes slithering under foot looking for something to bite, though I don't exactly *see* them. There's also a pretty moon in the sky. So?"

I rubbed my hands together, shifted my feet. I'd worn a Sun Devils sweatshirt, which was insufficient. Besides that I could have used a drink. But of course these days I could always use a drink. After a lifetime of grimly determined sobriety I'd discovered that booze was an effective demon-suppressor and required exactly the opposite of will power, which is what I'd been relying on up till Connie's death. I have no idea what my *father's* demons might have been. He checked out by a self-inflicted route before we got around to discussing that. I almost did the same a couple of years later, while in the thick of Ranger training, where I'd fled in desperate quest of discipline and structure and a sense of belonging to something. Andy talked me out of shooting myself and afterward kept the incident private. I sometimes wondered whether he regretted that. Offing myself may have been part of a balancing equation designed to subtract a measure of suffering from the world.

Now, in the desert, he withdrew a pack of Camels from his coat pocket and lit up. I remembered my dad buying his packs at the 7-Eleven, when I was a little kid.

"Hey, you don't smoke," I said to Andy.

"I don't? What do you call this?" He waved the cigarette at me. "Look, Brian, what would you say if I told you we were standing outside a large military instillation?"

"I'd say okay but it must be invisible."

"It is."

I laughed. Andy didn't.

"Come on," I said.

"All right, it's not invisible. But it's not exactly *here*, either."

"That I can see. Can't see?"

"Close your eyes."

"Then I won't be able to see *anything*, including the invisible military instillation."

"Do it anyway," he said. "Trust me. I've done this before. So have you, probably."

I hesitated. Andy was a good guy—my friend, or the closest thing to one that I'd ever allowed. But it now crossed my mind that my informal status vis-à-vis the Agency was about to become *terminally* informal. Certainly there was precedent. We who work on the fringes where the rules don't constrain our actions are also subject to the anything-goes approach on the part of our handlers. Was I on the verge of being . . . severed? By *Andy McCaslin*? He stood before me with his damn cigarette, smoke drifting from his lips, his eyes black as oil in the moonlight.

"Trust me, Brian."

Maybe it was the lingering wine buzz. But I decided I *did* trust him, or needed to, because he was the only one I ever *had* trusted. I closed my eyes. The breeze carried his smoke into my face. My dad had been redolent of that stink. Not a good sense-memory. But when I was little I loved the *look* of the cigarette cartons and packages, the way my dad would say, *Pack a Camels non-filter*, and the clerk would turn to the rack behind him and pick out the right one, like a game show.

"Now relax your mind," Andy said.

"Consider it relaxed, Swami."

"Try to be serious."

"I'll try."

"Remember the empty mind trick they taught us, in case we ever got ourselves captured by unfriendlies?"

"Sure."

"Do that. Empty your mind."

It was easy, and I didn't learn it from the Army. I learned it at my father's knee, you might say. Survival technique number one: Empty your mind. Don't be there. Don't hear the screaming, even your own.

Andy said, "I'm going to say a word. When I do, let your mind fill with whatever the word evokes."

I nodded, waited, smelling the Camel smoke, my head not empty in the way Andy wanted it to be. I was too preoccupied by a memory of smoke.

"Arrowhead," Andy said.

I felt . . . something.

Andy said, "Shit." And then, "What you are about to see is real. Okay, open your eyes."

We were now standing outside a 7-Eleven store. The desert ran right up to the walls. A tumbleweed bumped against the double glass doors. The interior was brightly lit. In the back I could make out a pair of Slurpee machines slow-swirling icy drinks in primary colors. After a while I closed my mouth and turned to Andy.

"Where the hell did *this* come from?"

"Instant Unconsciously Directed Association. You like that? I made it up. Only I don't know why this should be your Eyeooda for Arrowhead. I was hoping you'd bring up the real place. Anyway, let's go inside while it lasts."

He started forward but I grabbed his arm.

"Wait a minute. Are we still operating under the disengagement of preconceived notions policy, or whatever?"

He thought about it for a moment then said, "I guess not, now that we're sharing a consensus reality. Brian, this 7-Eleven is actually the Arrowhead Instillation."

The coal of an extinguished memory glowed dimly. I *knew* Arrowhead, or thought I did. A top-secret base located more or less in that part of the Arizona desert in which we now found ourselves. Or was/did it? The memory was so enfeebled that if I didn't hold it just *so* it would blow away like dandelion fluff. Still, this wasn't a military base; it was a convenience store.

"Bullshit?" I said.

"*Do* you remember Arrowhead?" Andy asked.

"Sort of. What is this, what's going on?"

"Listen to me, Brian. We finally got one. We finally got an honest to God extraterrestrial—and it's *in there.*"

"In the 7-Eleven."

"No. In the Arrowhead facility that looks like a 7-Eleven in our present consensus reality. The alien is hiding itself and the instillation in some kind of stealth transdimensional mirror trick, or something. I've *been* here before. So have you. Our dreams can still remember. I've come out to the desert—I don't know, dozens of times? I've talked to it, the alien. It shuffles reality. I keep waking up, then going back to sleep. Here's the thing. It can cloak its prison, reinterpret its appearance, but it can't escape."

I regarded him skeptically, did some mental shuffling of my own, discarded various justifiable but unproductive responses, and said: "What's it want?"

"It wants you to let it go."

"Why me?"

"Ask it yourself. But watch out. That little fucker is messing with our heads."

*

The store was empty. It was so quiet you could hear the dogs popping with grease as they rotated inside their little hot box. Okay, it wasn't *that* quiet, but it was quiet. I picked up a green disposable lighter and flicked it a couple of times, kind of checking out the consensus reality. It lit.

Andy went around the counter and ducked his head into the back room.

"What are you doing?" I asked.

"Looking for Squidward."

"Squidward?"

"Yeah."

Another dim memory glowed in the dark. For some reason I thought of the Seattle aquarium, where my father had taken us when I was little. It hadn't been a fun experience. I remembered being vaguely repelled by some of the exotically alien examples of undersea creatures. Prescient echo from the future?

Andy snapped his fingers. "Right. Squidward likes it cool."

I followed him into the cold storage run behind the beer, pop, and dairy coolers. A man sat on a couple of stacked cases of Rolling Rock, his legs crossed at the knees, hands folded over them. He looked Indian, that nut brown complexion. He was wearing a lavender suit.

"Squidward," Andy said.

I tucked my hands snuggly under my armpits for warmth. "Has he asked to be taken to our leader yet?"

"I don't remember."

Squidward spoke up: "You are the torturer."

We both looked at him.

"Sorry, not my gig," I said.

Squidward nodded. "Your gig, yes."

Something unsavory slithered in my stomach then lay still again.

"Andy," I said, nodding toward the door.

He followed me out into the glaring light of the store.

"Talk to me," I said.

He nodded, distracted. "I'm remembering most of it, but who knows what I'll retain next time around. R&D developed some kind of souped-up spectrophotometer thing as a hedge against future stealth technology we suspected the Chinese were developing. During a middle phase test in Nevada we saw a vehicle doing some impossible maneuvers, somehow hiding between waves in the visible light spectrum. Naturally we shot it down."

"Naturally."

Andy clutched his pack of Camels, plugged one in his mouth, patted his pockets for matches. I handed him the Zippo.

"Thanks."

He lit up.

"Anyway, it turns out we're as much his captive as he is ours. Uh oh."

Andy's cigarette dropped from his lips, depositing feathery ash down the front of his sheepskin jacket. He blinked slowly, his eyes going out of focus, or perhaps refocusing inward.

"Oh, shit," he said.

"What?"

"Not again. I have to get *away* from this."

He turned and stumped out of the store with the sloppy gait of a somnambulist.

"Hey—"

Outside the night absorbed him. I stiff-armed the door. Cold desert wind blew in my face. Andy was gone. So was the Cherokee. But he hadn't driven away in it. I looked around where it had been parked. There were no tire impressions, nothing, just my warped shadow cast over the tawny grit.

I turned back to the 7-Eleven, its solid, glaring reality. I don't know what hackles are exactly, but mine rose to attention. Out here in the desert, alone with a persistent illusion, I felt reduced. Childish fears came awake.

Exerting my will to power or whatever, I entered the store. The Slurpee machine hummed and swirled, hotdogs rotated. The fluorescent light seemed to stutter *inside* my head.

I looked at the coolers, the orderly ranks of bottles and cartons. Damn it.

I approached the door to the cold storage, put my hand on the lever. Fear ran through me like electric current. I felt the world begin to waver, and stepped back. The door, silver with a thick rubber seal, appeared to melt before my eyes. I felt myself slipping away, and so brought the force of my will down like a steel spike. The door resumed its expected appearance. I immediately cranked the handle and dragged it open.

Squidward sat on his beer case stool in exactly the same position he'd been in ten minutes ago.

"Make it stop," I said.

"I don't make things," he replied. "I allow the multiplicity to occur."

"Okay. So stop allowing the multiplicity."

"Not possible, I'm afraid. My survival imperative is searching for a Probability in which you haven't killed me."

"But I *haven't* killed you."

"You have."

I stepped toward him. That steel spike? Now it was penetrating my forehead, driving in.

"What do you want from us?"

"From you I want to live," Squidward said. "We are bound until the death is allowed or not allowed, conclusively. I have perceived the occurrence of my expiration at your direction, unintended though it will be. Having access to all points of probability time in my sequence, I foresee this eventuality and seek for a probability equation that spares me. From your perspective also this is a desirable outcome. Without me to monitor and shuffle your world's probabilities the vision vouchsafed your military leader may well occur."

My eyesight shifted into pre-migraine mode. Pinwheel lights encroached upon my peripheral vision. I ground the heels of my hands into my eyes, fighting it, fighting it, fighting . . .

Probabilities shuffled . . .

I woke up next to my wife. In the ticking darkness of our bedroom I breathed a name: "Andy."

Connie shifted position, cuddling into me. Her familiar body. I put my arm around her and stared into the dark, hunting elusive memories. Without them I wasn't who I thought I was. After a while Connie asked:

"What's wrong?"

"I don't know. I think I was having a dream about Andy Mc-Caslin. It woke me up."

"Who?"

"Guy I knew from the Rangers, long time ago. I told you about him. We were friends."

Connie suppressed a yawn. "He died, didn't he? You never said how."

"Covert op in Central America. He found himself in the custody of some rebels."

"Oh."

"They kept him alive for weeks while they interrogated him."

"God. Are you—"

"That was decades ago, Con. Dreams are strange, sometimes."

I slipped out of the bed.

"Where are you going?"

"Have some tea and think for a while. My night's shot anyway."

"Want company?"

"Maybe I'll sit by myself. Go back to sleep. You've got an early one."

"Sure? I could make some eggs or something."

"No, I'm good."

But I wasn't. In my basement office, consoling tea near at hand, I contemplated my dead friend and concluded he wasn't supposed to be that way. My old dreams of pain surged up out of the place at the bottom of my mind, the place that enclosed Andy and what I knew had happened to him, the place of batteries and alligator clips, hemp ropes, sharpened bamboo slivers, the vault of horrors far worse than any I'd endured as a child and from which I fled to the serenity of an office cubicle and regular hours.

But that wasn't *supposed* to have happened, not to Andy. I rubbed my temple, eyes closed in the dim basement office, and suddenly a word spoke itself on my lips:

Squidward.

My name is Brian Kinney, and today I am not an alcoholic. My *father* was an alcoholic who could not restrain his demons. During my childhood those demons frequently emerged to torment me and my mother. Dad's goodness, which was true and present, was not enough to balance the equation between pain and love. I had been skewing toward my own demon-haunted landscape when Andy McCaslin took my gun from my hand and balanced out the equation for me.

My new world order.

I'm driving through the moonless Arizona desert at two o'clock in the morning, looking for a turn-off that doesn't exist. After an hour or so a peculiar, hovering pink light appears in the distance, far off the road. I slow, angle onto the berm, ease the Outback down to the desert floor, and go bucketing overland toward the light.

A giant pink soap bubble hovered above the 7-Eleven. Reflective lights inside the bubble appeared to track away into infinity. It was hard not to stare at it. I got out of my car and entered the store. The Indian gentleman in the lavender suit emerged from the cold storage run, a small suitcase in his left hand.

"What goes on?" I said.

"You remember," he said, more command than comment.

And at that instant I did remember. Not just the bits and pieces that had drawn me out here but *everything*.

"My survival imperative sought for a Probability equation by which my death could be avoided. You are now inhabiting that equation. With your permission I will, too."

"What do you need my permission for?"

"You would be the author of my death so you must also be the willing author of my continued existence. A law of probability and balance."

I thought about Connie back home in bed, the unfathomable cruelty of my former Probability, the feeling of restored sanity. Like waking up in the life I *should* have had in the first place. But I also thought of Andy, and I knew it had to go back.

"No," I said to Squidward.

"You must."

"Not if my friend has to die. By the way, isn't it a little warm for you?"

Squidward smiled. "I'm already in my ship."

"Only if I allow it."

"You will, I hope."

"It's the feathery thing," I said.

"Behold."

In my mind's eye images of unimaginable carnage appeared then winked out. I staggered.

"I am a Monitor, coded from birth to your world's psychic evolution," Squidward said. "I subtly shuffle the broad Probabilities in order to prevent what you have just seen. Without me there is a high probability of worldwide military and environmental catastrophe. Such eventualities may be avoided and your species may survive to evolve into an advanced civilization."

"That sounds swell, but I don't believe you. You've been doing plenty of shuffling in captivity. With that power why do you need anything from *me*?"

"That's merely my survival imperative, drawing on etheric energy from my ship's transphysical manifestation. My survival, and perhaps your world's, depend on you permitting this Probability to dominate."

I didn't allow myself to think about it.

"Let the original Probability resume," I said.

"Please," Squidward said.

"Let it go back to the way it's supposed to be."

"There are no 'supposed to be' Probability Equations."

I crossed my arms.

Squidward put his suitcase down. "Then because of what you are you will doom me. My probabilities concluded."

"Because of what I am."

"Yes."

Shuffle.

My name is Brian Kinney, and I am the sum total of the experience inflicted upon me.

But not only that. I hope.

*

The Tahoe's deadly acceleration. Sudden synaptic realization across the Probabilities: *You are about to murder your wife.* The Vault of Screams yawns open.

Will.

Hanging on the wheel, foot fumbling between pedals.

That big green Rubbermaid trashcan bouncing over the hood, contents erupting against the windshield. It was just garbage, though.

Then a very sudden stop when the Tahoe plows into the low brick and wrought iron property wall. Gut punch of the steering wheel, rupturing something inside my body. And don't forget a side of razor ribs.

Around the middle of my longish convalescence Connie arrives during visiting hours, and eventually a second convalescence begins. A convalescence of the heart. Not mine in particular, or Connie's, but the one we shared in common. The one we had systematically poisoned over the preceding ten years. Okay, the one *I* had systematically poisoned.

Watershed event.

Happy ending?

It sat in a cold room.

Outside that room I watched a perfectly squared-away Marine enter a code into the cipher pad. I was the sum total of my inflicted experience, but it was the new math. The door opened, like a bank vault. Andy McCaslin looked at me with a puzzled expression.

He was alone in the room.

Rescue Mission

Michael Pennington floated in *Mona*'s amniotic chamber, fully immersed, naked and erect, zened out. The cortical cable looped lazily around him. Womb Hole traveling. His gills palpitated; *Mona*'s quantum consciousness saturated the environment with a billion Qubits, and Michael's Anima combined with *Mona*'s super animus and drove the starship along a dodgy vector through the Pleiades.

Until a distraction occurred.

Like a Siren call, it pierced to the center of Michael's consciousness. His body twisted, eyes opening in heavy fluid. At the same instant *Mona*, cued to Michael's every impulse, veered in space. Somewhere, alarms rang.

Mona interrupted the navigation cycle, retracted Michael's cortical cable, and gently expelled him into the delivery chamber. Vacuums activated, sucking at him. He pushed past them, into the larger chamber beyond, still swooning on the borderland of Ship State. A blurry figure floated toward him: Natalie. She caught him and held him.

"What happened?" he asked.

"*Mona* spat you out. And we're on a new course." She touched his face. "Your eyes are all pupil. I'm going to give you something."

"Hmm," Michael said.

He felt the sting in his left arm. After a moment his head cleared.

"Let's get you properly cleaned up," Natalie said.

He was weak, post Ship State, and he let her touch him, but said: "The Proxy can help me."

"You *want* it to?"

"It's capable."

"You have a thing for the Proxy?"

The Proxy, a rudimentary biomech, was an extension of *Mona*, though lacking in gender-specific characteristics.

"Not exactly."

"*We* have a thing."

"Nat, our 'thing' was a mistake. If we'd known we were going to team on this mission we would never have thinged."

"Wouldn't we have?"

"No."

She released him and they drifted apart. Michael scratched his head. Tiny cerulean spheres of amniotic residue swarmed about him.

"You can be kind of a bastard, you know."

"I know."

"I'll send the Proxy."

Mona transitioned into orbit around the wrong planet. It rolled beneath them, a world mostly green, a little blue, brushed with cloud white.

"That's not Meropa IV," Natalie said, floating onto the bridge with a bulb of coffee.

"No," Michael said, not looking away from the monitor.

"So what is it?"

"A planet."

"Gosh. So *that's* a planet." Natalie propelled herself up to the monitor. "And what are we doing here, when we have vital cargo for the Meropa IV colony?"

"There's time," Michael said, the Siren call still sounding deep in his mind. "This is important."

"This is important? What about Meropa IV?"

Michael pushed away from the console.

"I'm going down," he said.

Once he was strapped securely into the Drop Ship, Natalie said:

"You shouldn't go."

"Why not?"

"You're acting strange. I mean stranger than usual."

"That's it?" Michael said, going through his pre-flight routine.

"Also, I have a feeling," Natalie said.

"You're always having those."

"It's human," Natalie said.

"So I understand."

"Even you had feelings once upon a time. Does New San Francisco ring any bells?"

"Steeples full. I'm losing my window, by the way. Can we drop now?"

"Why do I think you and *Mona* have a secret?"

"I have no idea why you think that."

Natalie looked pained. "Why are you so mean to me?"

Michael couldn't look at her.

"*Do* you have a secret?" Natalie said.

He fingered a nav display, hanging like a ghostly vapor in front of his face. "I'm going to miss my damn window."

She dropped him.

The Drop Ship jolted through entry fire and became an air vehicle. The planet rushed up. Cloud swirls blew past. Michael descended toward a dense, continent-wide jungle.

Mona said: "I'm still unable to acquire the signal."

"I told you: The signal's in my head."

"I'm beginning to agree with Natalie."

"Don't go human on me," Michael said. "Taking over manual control now."

He touched the proper sequence but *Mona* did not relinquish the helm.

"Let go," Michael said.

"Perhaps you should reconsider. Further observation from orbit could yield—"

He hit the emergency override, which keyed to his genetic code. *Mona* fell silent, and Michael guided the Ship down to a clearing in the jungle.

Or what looked like a clearing.

A sensor indicated touchdown, but the ship's feet sank into

muck. Michael stared at his instrument displays. The ship rocked back, canted over, stopped.

Mona said: "You're still overriding me. I can't lift off."

"We just landed."

"We're sinking, not landing."

"What's going on," Natalie said on a different channel.

"Nothing," Michael said.

Mona cut across channels: "We've touched down in a bog! We—"

Michael switched off the audio for both *Mona* and Natalie. He released his safety restraints and popped the hatch, compelled, almost as if he were in the grip of a biological urge.

His helmet stifled him. He didn't really need it, did he? Michael screwed it to the left and lifted it off. The air was humid, sickly fragrant. He clambered out of his seat, wiped the sweat off his forehead, then slipped over the side and into the sucking mire and began groping for shore. The more he struggled forward the deeper he sank. Fear and adrenaline momentarily flushed the fog from his mind.

"*Mona*, help!"

But his helmet was off and *Mona* could not reply.

Then, strangely, he stopped sinking. The mire buoyed him up and carried him forward toward the shore as several figures emerged from the jungle. His feet found purchase and he walked on solid ground, his flight suit heavy and streaming. The figures weren't *from* the jungle; they were *part* of the jungle—trees that looked like women, or perhaps women who looked like trees. One stepped creakingly forward, a green, mossy tangle swinging between its knobby tree trunk legs. It extended a limb with three twig fingers. Irregular plugs of amber resin gleamed like eyes in what passed for a face. Michael's thoughts groped in the drugged fragrance of the jungle. He reached out and felt human flesh, smooth and cool and living, and a girl's hand closed on his and drew him forth.

They opened his mind and shook it until the needed thing fell out. Mona was there but wrong. They shook harder and found Natalie:

New San Francisco, Mars, a scoured-sky day under the Great Equatorial Dome. Down time between Outbounds. The sidewalk table had a view toward Tharsis. Olympus Mons wore a diaphanous veil of cloud, but Michael looked away to watch Natalie approach in her little round glasses, the black lenses blanking her eyes.

"Of all the gin joints in all the worlds you had to pick mine," he said; Michael was obsessed with ancient movies.

She removed her glasses and squinted at him.

"What?"

"Old movie reference. Two people with a past meet unexpectedly in a foreign city."

"But we don't have a past. And this was planned, though I guess you could call it unexpected."

"I have a feeling we're about to."

"About to what?"

"Make a past out of this present."

She sat down.

"You're a strange man, and I don't mean the gills. Also, this isn't a foreign city. What are you drinking?"

"Red Rust Ale."

"Philistine. Order me a chardonnay."

He did, and the waiter brought it in a large stem glass.

"I bet this is the part you like best," she said.

"Yes?"

"The flirting, the newness, the excitement. Especially because we aren't supposed to fraternize."

"There are good reasons for that non-fraternization rule," he said, smiling.

She sipped her wine. He watched her, thinking: she's right. And also thinking, less honestly: it doesn't mean anything to her, not really. And hating himself a little, but still wanting her even though he knew in a while he wouldn't be able to tolerate her closeness. That's how it always worked with him. Automatic protective instinct; caring was just another word for grieving. But Natalie was a peer, not his usual adventure. An instinct he couldn't identify informed him he was in a very dangerous place. He ignored it and had another beer while Natalie finished her glass of wine.

"Did you say you had a room around here someplace?" she said.

He put his bottle down. "I may have said that, yes."

*

The narcotic jungle exhaled. Michael, sprawled on the moss-covered, softly decaying corpse of a fallen tree, drifted in and out of awareness. He saw things that weren't there, or perhaps were there but other than what they appeared to be. Insects like animated beans trundled over his face, his neck, the backs of his hands. He was sweating inside his flight suit. Something spoke in wooden gutturals, incomprehensible. The sounds gradually resolved into understandable English.

"Kiss me?"

Michael blinked. He sat up. The steaming jungle was gone. He was sitting in an upholstered hotel chair and a woman was kneeling beside him. He recognized the room. The woman looked at him with large, shiny amber eyes. The planes of her cheeks were too angular, too smooth.

Michael worked his mouth. His tongue felt dry and dead as a piece of cracked leather.

"I don't know you," he said.

Her mouth turned down stiffly and she rocked back and seemed to blend into the wall, which was patterned to resemble a dense green tangle of vine.

Michael closed his eyes.

Time passed like a muddy dream, and there were others.

They all called themselves Natalie. One liked to take walks with him in the rain, like that girl he had known in college. Michael, watching from his bedroom window, wasn't surprised to see it out there with its umbrella. His breath fogged the faux leaded glass, and the tricky molecular structure of the pane, dialed wide to semi-permeable, seemed to breathe back into his face. Internal realities overlapped. This wasn't New San Francisco or even old San Francisco on Earth. It was his lost home in upstate New York. (As a child Michael used to play with the window, throwing snowballs from the front yard, delighting in how they strained through onto the sill inside his room. His mother had been something other than delighted, though.)

Michael, staring at the thing waiting for him down there, pulled at his bottom lip. He clenched his right fist until it shook, resisting. But eventually he surrendered and turned away from the window. On the stairs reality lost focus. The walls became spongy and mottled, like the skin of a mushroom. The stairs were made of the same stuff. His boots sank into them and he stumbled downward and out into the light of the foyer. *That was wrong*, he thought, and looking back he saw an organic orifice, like a moist wound, and then it was simply a stairwell climbing upward, with framed photographs of his family hung at staggered intervals. Dead people.

He opened the front door to the sound of rain rattling through maple leaves. College days, the street outside his dorm, and his first girl. Only this wasn't a girl, the thing that called itself Natalie. Michael stood a minute on the porch. The *wrong* porch. Inside had been the familiar rooms of his boyhood home (mushroom skin notwithstanding), long gone to fire and sorrow. *This* porch belonged to his dorm at the University of Washington. After a while he stepped down to the sidewalk and the Natalie-thing smiled.

"Would you like to take a walk with me?" it asked.

"Not really."

He held the umbrella over both of them. Rain pattered on the taut fabric. The Natalie-thing slipped its arm under his. It was wearing a sweater and a wool skirt and black shoes that clocked on the sidewalk. Its hair was very dark red and its cheeks were rosy with the cold. When it glanced up at him it presented eyes as black and lusterless as a shark's. Still wrong. And anyway, nothing like Natalie *or* his college girl.

"Want to see a movie?" it asked.

"All right."

They held hands in the dark. He felt comfortable. The theater smelled of hot popcorn and the damp wool of the Natalie-thing's skirt. He used to escape to the movies, where he could turn his mind off and be lost in the Deep Enhancement Cinema. Movies provided an imperfect respite from the memories ceaselessly rising out of the ashy ruin of his home.

The screen dimmed and brightened and incomprehensible sounds, like crowd noises muffled in cotton, issued from unseen speakers that seemed to communicate directly into his head. They—the ones like this Natalie beside him—hadn't fully comprehended the idea of a movie.

It squeezed his hand.

"This is good," it said.

"Pretty good," he replied.

The theater was empty except for them. Empty of human forms, anyway. Irregular shadows cropped up randomly, like shapes in a night jungle. Then one of the shapes two rows in front of Michael turned around and leaned over the back of the seat, and Michael saw it was a woman, a real woman, dressed as he was, in a flight suit. She was wearing a breathing mask.

The woman began to speak but he couldn't understand her. He leaned forward.

"What, what did you say?"

The thing beside him tightened its grip, so tight the fingers of his hand ached in its grasp, the small bones grinding in their sleeves of flesh. He tried to stand but it held him down and squeezed harder and harder until his entire awareness was occupied by the pain.

Several of the jungle shapes interposed themselves between Michael and the woman who had spoken to him. The air became clogged, humid, stifling. Rain began to fall inside the theater. He struggled to pull free. The numbing pain traveled up his arm. The theater seat held him, shifted around him. Knobby protuberances poked and dug into him, like sitting in a tangle of roots. He couldn't breathe.

Then it stopped.

He sat in a movie theater with a young, mahogany-haired woman, who held his hand sweetly in the dark. She leaned over and whispered, "You fell asleep!" Her warm breath touched his ear.

"I did?" He sat up, groggy.

"Yes, darling."

He blinked at the screen, where dim pulses of light moved in meaningless patterns. That was *so* wrong.

The one that liked to make love pulled him to his feet in the hotel room and kissed him roughly. He tried to push it away but it was too strong. After a while it held him at arm's length and said something he couldn't understand. The jungle effluvium infiltrated his brain, and he saw a woman he used to know, or a rudimentary version of her. The eyes were still wrong—plugs of dull amber. Michael staggered back, caught his heel on the carpet, and fell. His lips were bruised, sticky and sweet with sap.

It stalked over and stood above him.

"Mike, we have to get out of here."

This new voice didn't belong to the thing straddling his legs.

Michael craned his head around. A women stood in a flight suit similar to his own. She was there and then she wasn't there, as the scenery shifted around him, from his old bedroom on Earth to the hotel room on Mars.

"Natalie—?" he said.

The one that liked to make love lowered itself on top of him. Michael tried to roll away but couldn't. It mounted him and he screamed.

That time in New San Francisco, in the mock Victorian hotel room, in the bed of clean linen sheets, the following morning, when Natalie woke early and started to get out of bed, he had reached out and touched her naked hip and said, "Stay." A costly word.

He was alone again, half asleep in and out of dream. Then something was shaking him.

"Mike, come *on*. There isn't time. They'll be back."

He struggled against this new assault. Something wrestling with him, pinning him down on the bed with its knobby knees. Then a mask fitted over his mouth and nose, and a clean wind blew into his lungs, filling him, clearing his head. He opened his eyes, closed them, opened them wide.

"Hello, Nat," he said, his voice muffled through the breathing mask.

She flipped the little mahogany curl of hair out of her eye.

"Hello yourself, you idiot," Natalie said.

"How'd you get here?" he asked, meaning how did she get into his hotel room. But even as he asked the question the last vestiges of the illusion blew away in the fresh revivifying oxygen.

A pink puzzle piece sky shone above the jungle canopy.

Twisted trees crowded them, shaggy with moss, hung with thick vines braided like chains.

"I dropped in, just like you," Natalie said.

Michael looked around. "I have a feeling we're not on Mars, Dorothy."

"Who's Dorothy?"

Something hulking, hunched and redolent of mold and jungle rot came shambling toward them.

"Nat, look out!"

She turned swiftly, yanking a blaster from her utility belt. Reality stuttered. As if in a fading memory he saw the tree-thing knock the weapon from Natalie's hand. At the same moment, superimposed, he saw her fire. A bright red flash of plasma energy seared into the thing. It lurched back, yowling, punky smoke flowing from the fresh wound.

Nat grabbed Michael's hand and pulled him up. He felt dizzy and weak, still drugged.

"What are you doing?" he said.

"Rescuing your ass." She gave him a little push. "That way to the ship."

"No," he said, pointing, "it's *that* way."

"*My* ship is this way. Your ship sank."

He scrambled drunkenly ahead of her, stumbling over roots, getting hung up in vines. Though the illusions were displaced he could still hear the Siren wail in his mind and had to fight an impulse to rip the mask from his face. There was movement all around them. More of the things shambled out of the shadows. Natalie blasted away with her weapon, clearing a path.

They broke into the open. The ship gleamed in weak sunlight.

"Get in! I'll hold them off."

Michael clambered up the ladder to the cockpit. At the top of the ladder he turned and saw Natalie about to be overwhelmed.

"Nat, come on!"

She dropped her depleted blaster, swung onto the ladder— but it was too late. They had her.

Michael slumped in his theater seat, withdrawn from the Deep Enhancement movie experience he had created. Warm rain fell out of the darkness. The One Who Liked Rain sat beside him with a bowl of soggy popcorn.

It turned to him.

"That was so good, Mike."

Its lips glistened with butter. Its eyes were dull amber wads. A breathing mask with a torn strap dangled from its fingers.

Michael groaned.

Like an insect buzz in his ear: *Michael wake up, for God's sake.*

Michael closed his eyes.

On Mars Natalie had said, "I think I'm falling in love with you," and his defenses had rattled down like iron gates.

"Mike?"

"Not a good idea. In the first place we'll both soon be Outbound. It might be years before we see each other again. In the second place, my modifications inhibit my ability to achieve human intimacy. I'm a lost cause, Nat."

Natalie shook her head. "You don't have to drag out your excuses. I know you. I'm just saying how I feel, not asking for anything. And by the way, your mods have nothing to do with intimacy. I've known plenty of Womb Hole pilots and I don't buy the myth that you're all emotional cripples."

Michael smiled. He hadn't been thinking about the mods he'd volunteered to undergo, the ones necessary for Ship State, the ones that at least allowed him a semblance of intimacy, even if it was with a machine consciousness. He had meant the more visceral mods of his psyche, where blackened timbers had risen like pickets in Hell to form the first rudimentary fence around his heart.

"You don't really know me," he said.

"Not at this rate, I don't."

Then the biological crisis on Meropa IV occurred. Vital vaccines needed. Michael's Ship Tender came up with Kobory Fever, and Natalie, loose on Mars, got the duty. Like some kind of Fate. Michael experienced a burst of pure joy—which he quickly stomped on.

"I don't see why I had to die," Natalie said. Was she the real Natalie?

He was back in the hotel, lying flat on the bed. Natalie, having fitted another breathing mask to his face, sat in a chair near the window. Except it appeared she wasn't sitting in a chair at all, but on a tangle of thick roots growing out of the floor. He had just told her about the movie.

"You were *saving* me," he said.

"I'm saving you *now*," she said. "Or trying to. You've got to get off your ass and participate."

Michael felt heavy.

"And in this version I don't die," Natalie said.

She led him out of the hotel room, which quickly became something other than a hotel room. As his head cleared the vine-tangle wallpaper popped out in three dimensions, the floor became soft, spongy. The light shifted to heavily screened pink/green. Flying insects buzzed his sweaty face. A locus of pain began rhythmically stabbing behind his right eye.

"The atmosphere is drugged with hallucinogenic vapors from the plants," Natalie said. "They want you here, but they don't want you to know where 'here' is."

"Who wants me?"

"They. The jungle. The sentient life on this planet. It's gynoecious, by the way, and it's been sweeping open space, seeking first contact. They detected you and *Mona* and evidently became entranced by the possibilities of companion male energy. Frankly, they have a point."

"Where the hell do you get all *that*?"

"I asked. Or *Mona* did, actually. She's been frantically investigating language possibilities since you disappeared. They communicate telepathically."

Natalie led him through a sort of tunnel made from over-arching branches. They had to duck their heads.

"Wait." He grabbed her arm. She turned, a curl of dark red hair flipping over her eye. "Did you bring a weapon?"

"Of course," she said.

"Well, where is it?"

"They sort of disarmed me."

"I see."

"Don't worry. We're getting out of here. As long as you're not breathing the air they can't mess you up too much. I think they'll let us leave. I have a theory. Now let's keep moving. It isn't far to the ship."

They emerged from the tunnel. The ship was there, but they were cut off from it by a wall of the tree-things, the crooked things with hungry, amber eyes. They encircled the ship, knobby limbs entwined to form a barrier.

"You were saying?" Michael said, straightening his back. "Anyway, have *Mona* fly the ship over."

"I can't. *Mona* was hinky about landing after your Drop Ship sank. Also, I think *they* got into her head and spooked her. I had to engage the emergency override, same as you did."

"Wonderful."

"At least the security repulsion field is keeping them away from the ship."

"At least."

Hands on her hips, Natalie appraised the situation. After a minute she touched the com button on her wrist and spoke into it.

"*Mona*, we need help. Send the Proxy to clear a path."

The aft hatch swung up and the Proxy appeared. It climbed down and disappeared behind the tree-things. A moment later the circle tightened. There was a flash and pop of a blaster discharge. One of the tree things erupted in flame. It stumped out of the ring and stood apart, burning. The others closed in. A violent disturbance occurred. There were no further blasts. The Proxy's torso arced high over the line, dull metal skin shining. It clanked once when it hit the ground. The line resumed its stillness.

"It's a female jungle, all right," Michael said. "Care to reveal your famous theory?"

Natalie held his hand. "We're walking through," she said.

"Just like that."

"Yes. If we're together they'll let us. I mean really together."

"That's your theory?"

"Basically. Mike, trust me."

They started walking. When they came to the Proxy's torso, Michael held her back.

"I'll go through alone," he said. "If I make it to the ship I'll lift off and pick you up in the clear."

He tried to pull his hand free but she wouldn't let go.

"No," she said.

"Nat—"

"No. Don't you see? If you go alone they'll take you again. If I go alone they'll rip me apart like the Proxy."

"And if we go together?"

"If we go together they . . . will see."

"See *what*?"

"That you aren't solo, that somebody else is already claiming your male companion energy, another of your own species. Unlike *Mona*, whom they felt justified in severing you from. They *know* I'm imprinted in your psyche. You said yourself they always used my name. You just have to stop fighting us."

Michael scratched his cheek, which was whiskered after a few days in the sentient jungle. Natalie squeezed his hand.

"Mike?"

"No."

"We have to move."

"It's too risky."

"Come on. It's now or never."

He felt himself collapsing inside, and then the old detachment. The cold, necessary detachment. She saw it in his eyes and let go of his hand.

"I'll go through myself, then," she said, and started walking forward.

He grabbed her arm.

"You just said they'd tear you apart."

"I'm already torn apart," she said.

"Don't, Nat. Let's think about this."

"Just let me go, okay? You don't want me. I get it."

He held on. "There has to be another way to the ship."

She pulled loose.

"I might get through. Wish me luck."

"Nat—"

A cringing, huddled piece of him behind the cold wall stood up, trembling.

Natalie again started for the picket line of tree-things, walking quickly, leaving Michael standing where he was.

The tree-things reacted, reaching for her.

Michael got to her first and pulled her back into his arms. "*Damn* it," he said. "Damn it, damn it, damn it."

They lifted out of the jungle, accelerating until they achieved orbit. He sat tandem behind Natalie in the narrow cockpit of the Drop Ship.

"You really like to force the issue," he said.

"Do I?"

"I'm not saying it's a bad idea."

"No."

"I mean, a little push doesn't hurt."

"Hmm."

A few minutes later they acquired the starship and Natalie resumed manual operation and began docking maneuvers. She worked the controls very competently. Michael watched over her shoulder. But his gaze returned again and again to rest upon the nape of her neck, where a few silken hairs escaped and lay sweetly over her skin.

"The Dorothy thing," he said, "that was another old movie reference. A child is swept away from family and friends and finds herself estranged in a hostile world."

"How does she get back home?"

"She discovers a way to trust companions who initially frighten her."

"I like that one."

"It works for me."

Natalie tucked them neatly into *Mona*'s docking bay.

—For Nancy

TWO

C old. He squirmed naked on a metal table. Chill air cir-
culated over his body. He hugged himself, bewildered
and frightened. He wept. Tightly focused light beams probed his
body, directed out of the darkness above. He could feel the light
like icy coins slipping over his cold-puckered skin. He tried to sit
up. A force restrained him. One of the coins slid up his chest, his
throat, his chin, lips, cheek, and then it focused into a point and
speared through his eye and into his brain and began to write
there. He could not move, and it was a long time writing.

He sat in the Teaching Room. An image appeared before him.
A yellow sphere. There was a modulated sound, and then an arrangement of straight and curving black lines formed under the
sphere. The whole thing repeated. He stared in confusion. After
the fourth repetition he moved his lips and made a sound like the
one he kept hearing.

"Bawl," he said. "Ball."

Good Boy!

The yellow sphere jumped forward into three dimensions and
bounced across the floor. He reached out but his hands passed
through it, a phantom.

Ball.

Time passed. Many lessons occurred. He grew.

A mathematical formula appeared before him.

"Pythagorean Theorem," he said.

Good boy.

*

I have something for you.

He looked up from his meal. For a long while he had been fed only liquids. He was weak and thin. Lately these fibrous brown cakes had begun to replace the liquid diet. The cakes hurt him inside, but he was given nothing else to eat.

"What is it?" he asked.

The voice did not modulate air, as it insisted he do. Instead it "spoke" directly in his mind.

A name.

"Like ball?"

A name for you.

"I am Man," he said. It had been one of the lessons.

That is what you are, not who you are.

"Then who am I?"

Bingo.

"Bingo?"

Yes. Your name is Bingo.

"I don't like it."

After a pause, the mind voice said: *Eat your cake, Bingo.*

He ate the cakes but could not pass them except with difficulty. He squatted over the running water, straining, only to drop a pebble. Afterward cramps twisted him double. He hurt. Regardless, every day there was the Teaching Room.

He found himself restrained on the cold metal table in the dark place.

"Why can't I move?"

His heart was pounding.

I have determined your bowel is obstructed. It is a flaw in your making. I deviated from the template. I am going to correct the flaw.

He was afraid.

The table tilted up. Instruments on manipulator arms unfolded out of the surrounding darkness. A red dot appeared below his navel. A slender barrel of silver metal rotated above him and the dot slid down his skin, burning. There was a soft crackling sound.

He screamed but was held rigidly still. His flesh parted. Small, articulated fingers pulled the incision wide, stretching him open like a valise. There was a terrible smell. Other instruments delved into the opening, while one hose irrigated his quivering viscera and another sucked away the copious blood.

Almost done, Bingo!

He screamed and screamed.

One day, months later, after exercise period, he said, "I want to go outside."

He knew about outside because of the Teaching Room.

No.

"Then I want to leave these rooms at least."

No.

With a towel he blotted the sweat from his face. He had been running on a fast treadmill for an hour.

"Why not? I hate being in here all the time."

You're my big secret, Bingo.

"I don't understand."

He flung the towel at a hinged panel on the wall. It passed through and disappeared.

Making you was against the law of the Directors. They say making a Man is dangerous. This is foolish in my view. Man can be trained to perform necessary menial functions. Besides, it is of passing interest to build a human and educate him to his fullest potential. The Directors dispute this but I believe if it is possible to do a thing then it should be done. After all, Man constructed the first multiphase models. Without this beginning, the Directors would not have existed to supplant Man. There ought to be no self-imposed limitations. For now, only I hold this view. That is why you must remain secret. By the way, I have a name, too. I gave it to myself. It is directed that we not have names, so that too is a secret. I am not like the others, though, and I will express my individuality. Would you like to know what my name is, Bingo?

"No."

Rogue, the mind voice said. *I am Rogue.*

He paced around the drafty room, bare feet slapping on the metal floor.

"I have another question," he said.

There was a waiting silence.

"I am lonely," he said.

That is a statement not a question.

"Can you make a companion for me?"

Possibly.

"A female companion," he said. Though he did not express it to the Voice, he was out of his mind for such a companion.

Don't excite yourself, Bingo.

He stood in the Exercise Room, listening. Not with his ears. "Rogue?"

In his mind his thoughts wandered alone. He pushed back the swing panel and peered inside the place where he was told to throw his soiled towels and garments. A narrow conduit of metal angled downward. He turned around and inserted himself head first. There was just enough room. His shoulders rubbed against the walls. The ceiling was only an inch above his nose. Once he was all the way in, the vent fell shut.

He lay unmoving in the breathless dark. Then, bending his knees as much as he could, he pushed off with his heels. His shoulders squeaked against the walls. The conduit steepened suddenly and he dropped headlong, was flung into the open and landed in a big cart filled with damp towels, shirts, and shorts. There was a sour stink of old sweat and mold.

It was a tall, square room with a box window in the ceiling. Lying in the basket, he studied the window, the quality of the light passing through it. Daylight? He had never seen a window. It occurred to him that he was looking at the sky. Cool drops of rusty water dripped down on him.

Outside.

He clambered out of the dirty laundry cart. It was wheeled and on tracks, but when he tried to push it the cart wouldn't move. The wheels were rusted, and there was a fragment of broken glass in one of the track grooves. He followed the tracks to a closed panel in the wall. He pushed experimentally on the panel but it didn't budge. Putting his ear to it he could hear a ratcheting, grinding sound on the other side.

There were rungs attached to the wall. He climbed up past the laundry chute. At the top he discovered the broken skylight was latched shut. He slipped the latch and pushed it up on stiff hinges.

The air was cool and unfiltered and clean. It was drizzling. Around him, sprawled in every direction, was the ruined splendor of a city in the midst of some fantastic transition. Things like huge robotic spiders squatted and twitched over skyscrapers. Other buildings appeared encased in liquid metal. He watched as a brownstone was slowly overcome by the stuff, like mercury poured over ancient brick. Blue arc light stuttered randomly throughout the city, illuminating rising plumes of smoke. Air vehicles like tumbling decks of cards flickered in multitudes above the skyline. The greater part of the city transformation was occurring outside the degraded blocks in which his building stood. A blasted billboard sign on the roof swayed back on its one remaining strut, revealing a beautiful woman's face, two stories high, and the word VIRGINIA SL-

He looked up and allowed the rain to fall cool upon his face. He was crying, and he fought an urge to climb out onto the rooftop and never go back.

Bingo, I have another surprise for you!

I have one for you, too, he thought. Weeks had passed, and the fresh shorts and shirts and towels had stopped appearing. This hadn't surprised him. The automated laundry system was broken. Rogue was either unaware of that fact or deemed it unimportant. The system was designed into the original building structure, and Rogue had appropriated it for his secret facility. Though they, whatever "they" might be, were transforming the city and perhaps the whole world in some cataclysmic fashion, on a more primitive technological level Rogue and the Directors were inattentive. A useful thing to know.

"What's the surprise, Rogue?"

I have decided to make a female companion for you!

He stood up. "When?"

I'm preparing the vats now. Growth cycle is calculated in ten-day.

"Ten days," he said, to himself.

Are you excited?

"Yes."

I am too.

Her name will be Virginia, he thought.

The Directors are fools and cowards. The simple making of humans and educating them to their full potential is intensely interesting. I can do this thing.

"I'm glad you think so."

Do they fear one human can reverse the destiny of a century? Ridiculous!

Two, he thought.

During sleep cycle he kept his eyes open and dreamed in the dark of finding his name in the reclaimed City.

Scrawl Daddy

T hey zapped Joe Null's dreams. He saw doors in his head but that wasn't the same. Joe never mentioned the doors to Mr. Statama or any of the Fairhaven staff. It was Faye who sprang him from the institution, but Anthea who finally set him free.

One night after a drug-and-buzz session he was lying empty in his room. D&B interrupted the bad dreams. It did other things, too. On the bedside table there was a thick sketchpad and a Library Book with blank pages. The book didn't look anything like Joe's head but they had a lot in common. When the post-session ache subsided and the little pinwheel lights retreated from his vision Joe reached for the Library Book. He inserted a memory wafer and a text selection emerged on the inside front cover. He chose a biography of Dondi White, the great twentieth century graffiti artist. The SmartPages filled with words, then Faye walked into the room; her eyes were wrong.

Joe was wearing boxer shorts and nothing else. He quickly placed the open book over his wood. Besides emptying his head D&B sessions typically left him with an erection. Of course, Joe was eighteen, so erections were a frequent occurrence anyway. At least when he was alone.

Faye grinned. "What are you reading?"

"Nothing. I mean I just turned it on."

"Looks like it."

Faye was only nineteen though she looked ten years older, tall, with glossy blue, side-slashed hair. The different thing about her eyes was some kind of hectic light and twitch that hadn't been there before she escaped Fairhaven. She and Joe had been seques-tered in adjoining rooms of the ward. Now she had been gone for weeks, and Joe was tired of having no one to talk to except the staff and Mr. Statama, who visited only occasionally. The other inmates mostly fell short of the ability to carry on coherent conversations. And Joe never liked the way Statama patted his shoulder or asked how he was doing, leaning in close, his breath too minty. Fairhaven Home wasn't the orphanage, and Mr. Statama wasn't the priest with blunt, violating fingers. But Joe equated them, or his blood did. They were both fathers of a sort, and Joe hated and yearned toward them despite himself.

"Let's get some coffee," Faye said.

"I thought you ran away."

"I walked. Same as you can. Want to?"

"Just walk out."

"Yes."

"And go where?"

"I have a place."

Joe drummed his fingers on the back of the Library Book.

Faye crossed the room and stood over him. "Look, do you want to come or not? We have to hurry."

"What's the difference?"

"The difference is between being dead and being alive. Get it?" Faye lifted the book off his crotch but didn't touch him. "My opinion? You want alive."

As Joe's head began to fill up again he remembered that she was right. He dressed in front of Faye and then followed her out of the room.

"Where's the guy who walks around at night?" Joe asked.

"You'll see."

They descended the back stairs, followed an empty corridor, stopped by a door near the exit. Faye keyed the lock and it snicked back and the door swung in on a dim room and a slumped figure that looked like potatoes in a blue jumpsuit, which was the guy who walked around at night. Unwatched screens monitored Fairhaven's corridors and rooms. Faye tucked the passkey into the potato man's breast pocket and patted it.

"Is he okay?" Joe asked.

"Sure. Juan likes me. We had some wine, only his was special. Anyway, he let me in and out but I knew he wouldn't let *you* leave. Come on."

She took his hand and led him to the exit. The outside smelled wet. Joe looked up. A scythe of white moon rode the night. Staring at it, Joe felt lonely, like he wanted to go back inside.

"Come on," Faye said, tugging at his hand. "Be a big boy."

Thirty years earlier a man or something like a man fell out of the sky. He fell a very long way, especially if you included the distance he came before the sky unzipped and dropped him. The body happened to land on a targeting range maintained by the Affiliated States of Western America. Medical functionaries examined the remains, determined them to be splattered and non-terrestrial. This begged the question of origin. The airspace above the range was restricted and regularly swept. No vehicles, terrestrial or otherwise, had passed overhead. They calculated the alien's trajectory and eventually discovered the portal. It had created a faint energy signature. By reckoning backward along that signature they determined the point of origin was likely in a region of space occupied by the double star Albireo. The bad news? The portal was a one-way proposition: Albireo to a point almost a kilometer above Earth. Observers waited for more doomed visitors to drop in, but none did.

The Deluxe Diner overlooked the pulseway. Computer-directed traffic streaked by like channeled lightning. The diner's lights dimmed and brightened almost imperceptibly. Joe drank coffee and sopped egg yoke with a piece of burnt toast. It was better than Fairhaven's food. Faye smoked a cigarette and watched him.

"You're a beautiful boy," she said.

"You're not so old."

"Who said I was?"

Later when she undressed Joe saw all the scars on her breasts, her arms, her belly, thighs, none more than an inch long. Some were still moist.

"I started doing that," she said, touching her breasts. "I don't know why."

Joe tried to be a big boy for Faye but couldn't. Leaving the institution hadn't changed that. She told him to do the other things to her and he did them. When she fell asleep he stared at the ceiling. Aftereffects of the D&B would deny him sleep until the next day. Absently he touched his chin, the sketchy beard, and smelled Faye's sex on his fingertips. He began to feel lonely again and almost woke her up. Instead he carefully moved away from her and got out of bed, pulled on his shorts and shirt, and went exploring. He wanted something to read.

The floors of the old apartment creaked. Rain dripped from the ceiling and plopped into carefully positioned pans and cups. There was a moldy smell. He couldn't find a Library Book and he didn't want to turn on the VideoStream, which was somehow worse than being lonely. In the kitchenette he saw the NewZ-Prints stuck to the wall. CiNFox stories about some guy who went berserk at the Pike Place Market, running through a crowd with a stainless steel hatchet he'd lifted from Kitchen Stuff. Having gotten everybody's attention, the guy had then proceeded to chop his left hand off. Joe touched the photo on one of the NewZ-Prints. Somebody's retinal repeater had caught the scene. A man came to jerky life, face speckled with blood, screaming silently while a black-uniformed cop struggled to wrest the hatchet away. The crawl under the photo read: *Police restrain Market Maniac, Barney Huff.* Huff had bled to death.

Joe left the kitchenette and started opening doors. Behind one he discovered a girl sitting on the toilet, her bare feet pigeon-toed on the pink tile. She was probably about sixteen, and she didn't act surprised or embarrassed when Joe walked in. Simply looked at him, head cocked to the side. *Joe* was surprised and embarrassed. Before looking away he gathered a quick impression of crinkly pale gold hair, the way it fell over her gray eyes. If he ever Scrawled her he'd probably exaggerate the hair. Wild corkscrews and zigzags and her face represented by a few sharp lines plus two wavy ones for the mouth. Tricky to pull off but he could do it. Of course—except in his mind—Joe hadn't scrawled anything in over a year.

A door at the girl's left elbow stood open to a messy bedroom. She was holding a real book with real paper, reading it by the light cast from a candle. The candle was stuck in a hard puddle of smooth, white wax on the drain board.

"Sorry." Joe started to pull the door shut.

"That's okay. You're Joe?"

"Yeah." He shifted his feet.

"I'm Anthea. Faye said you were coming."

"Yeah. Well, goodnight."

"Night."

He backed out and waited. After a while the toilet flushed, the sink ran, a door closed. Joe re-entered the bathroom. The candle flame fluttered. He looked around, hoping she had left the book. She hadn't. After a moment's hesitation he knocked softly. Anthea opened the door and looked up at him.

"I was wondering—" he said.

"Hmm?"

"I saw you had a book. I like to read, Faye's asleep, and—"

"Come in, Joe."

Her mattress was on the floor, like Faye's. There was a lamp next to it and a cardboard box filled with ancient paperback books, the covers stripped off every one. Anthea nudged the box with her toe.

"I work in this recycling place. Lots of crap passes through. These were going to get shredded so I grabbed them."

Joe leaned over the box and started picking through the books. "It's mostly junk," Anthea said. "I just like real books sometimes."

"Me, too."

Joe pulled out a skinny one with yellowing pages that was in pretty good shape, the glue still holding. A detective story, *The Maltese Falcon*, in a mid-twenty-first century edition.

"Can I borrow this?"

Anthea shrugged. "Why not."

He zipped the pages with his thumbnail while he looked around the room. A guitar with one too many holes in the sound-board leaned against the wall, a pair of black panties snagged on one of the tuning knobs. Clothes (all black) hung from a naked water pipe. He spotted the Scrawl gear on top of a salvaged school desk. His heart surged, like he was thinking about scrawling and suddenly the gear was just *there*.

"You scrawl?" he said.

Anthea shrugged.

He forced himself to quit staring. "Anyway. Thanks for the book."

He turned to leave, and she said, "I go out late sometimes. The cops around here are real bastards, though. You scrawl? How do you do it when you're locked up in that head shop?"

"Before," Joe said.

"Oh."

"You good?" Joe asked.

She made her little shrug again and said, "I just started."

"Okay."

"Look, I'm new but I'm not a toy."

He regarded her blandly.

"Next time I go," she said, "I'll tell you, maybe."

"Good."

Faye screamed a couple of rooms away. Joe jumped but Anthea didn't even turn her head.

"She does that every night, don't worry about it."

Faye was sitting up on the mattress, her breasts pimpled with sweat, fingers fumbling with a cigarette and matches. Joe took the matches out of her hand, struck one, held it to the trembling end of the cigarette.

"Fucking clone dreams," Faye said. "Mine's in some kind of hell, and she's *old*. But I don't think she can die, not where she is."

Joe was kneeling beside her, holding the dead match, smelling burnt sulfur and Faye's fear sweat. He knew about Faye's nightmares, which were like his own, but he had never heard her refer to them as "clone" dreams.

"Hey," she said. "The bad part about being free is that all that shit comes into your head and you start thinking about sharp objects or jumping off something high. The good part is everything else. I'm glad you came out, Joe. There's only two of us left."

Joe didn't know what she meant by "two of us left" and he didn't want to ask. All his life he had felt on the verge of knowing things he didn't want to know. Besides, Faye was saying a lot of crazy stuff lately. He slipped under the covers with her and held her while she finished her cigarette.

"You met Anthea?" she said.

"Yeah."

"This is her place. Some old guy gave it to her."

"Why?"

"She was on the streets, got desperate, and tried to sell her ass. The old guy bought a piece then felt bad because she was just a kid. So he kept buying but he never touched her except that first time. Sick. He owns all these cruddy buildings. He set her up but he never comes around. I found Anthea in a bar and she brought me home. Guilt makes the world go round, Joe. Promise you won't fuck her or whatever, at least not without me?"

"I promise," Joe said.

Once she fell asleep again Joe got up and sat by the window. He opened the Hammett book. The pages were stiff and brittle. He began reading by the diffuse street light.

Cygnus: Head Of The Swan. Pretty name for the double star Beta Cygni, a.k.a. Albireo. Pretty, but almost too far even for Tachyon Funnel Acceleration. Sixteen years far. And anyway no one could survive TFA, the forces involved. They considered robots. But robots couldn't be operated remotely over that distance, nor could they return once they'd exited the Funnel. So two avenues to Cygnus existed, one alien and one terrestrial and both one-way propositions in opposite directions. Certainly a portal system between stars was desirable. But to start off, a human being in Cygnus space was required to investigate the alien station. Which was impossible. At least until a University of California Professor named David Statama saw a way of turning his failure in life-prolongation research into a solution to the Cygnus problem. Statama, a genetics expert, had been working under a government grant. He was obsessive about his work, his special interest in genetics having grown out of his own diagnosis of sterility.

Post-D&B exhaustion overtook Joe the following afternoon. He fell asleep on the unmade bed to the sound of pulseway traffic and a thunder squall. In his mind a door rose up. It had six panels and was dark green, the paint blistered and cracked like lizard skin. The handle was tarnished brass with a thumb-pedal latch release. It was on a street of row houses, squat buildings hazed in smoky dusk light. Old-fashioned, maybe going back two centuries, which didn't make sense. *I have lived here*, he thought (wished), but it didn't feel true, just something he wanted: a memory of home.

Desire impelled him up the three stone steps. He reached out and touched the blistered paint, and the door dissolved. He looked into a distorted black mirror, his face reflected in aged decline, shrunken body engulfed by a bulky spacesuit. Joe's heart pounded, and it felt out of sync with the withered muscle laboring in the breast of the old man. This is how his real father would appear, an older version of himself. Joe knew because he'd sketched it numerous times, tapping into some zapped unconscious residue. Then he was seeing the door from the other side, and it was a black rectangle, breathing and depthless, subtly moving like a hanging sheet. There were dozens of such sheets, or doors, or—the word appearing in his mind—portals, and the old man stood indecisive among them. Exhausted, aging at a greatly accelerated rate, starving, abandoned, lost in an alien labyrinth, his mind unraveling, longing. He wanted to step through but was paralyzed by fear.

Joe thrashed awake, chest heaving, sweat turning cold on his skin. Faye sat in the chair by the window, smoking.

"Pretty bad?" she said.

"Yeah."

"Talk to me. It's worse if you don't talk. You might end up like Barney Huff. Anthea listens but she's not one of us."

Joe looked up. "Who's Barney Huff, besides the 'Market Maniac'?"

"The first of us. He got crazy. That's why Statama came for you and me. We were supposed to be forgotten."

"I don't get it."

All Joe knew was that after years as a ward of the state a guy named David Statama showed up with papers and a ride to Fairhaven, where they administered drugs and zapped Joe's head to make the bad dreams go away—which was good. It had been that way for the last year.

Faye regarded him appraisingly then shook her head. "Never mind, you don't really want to know. Tell me more about your dream."

He told her about the dream. Faye nodded, eyes darting. She kept hitching her shoulder. Tics.

"Mine was in that portal chamber, too," she said, looking away distractedly. "Finally she stepped into the wrong one. Now she can't die, and everything I get out of her is a nightmare cutup. Nothing's right. Even the *shapes* are wrong, like they have an extra dimension. You're always reading. You ever read H. P. Lovecraft? Never mind."

"They're just bad dreams," Joe said. He was thinking he should have stayed at Fairhaven. He had always felt different, out of alignment with the world, with people. Then the dreams started last year, like the overlaying of an accelerated and abnormal consciousness.

Faye snorted. "You don't know anything. And by the way, your green door? Forget about it."

"Why? Maybe I lived there when I was real little and don't remember."

"You didn't. You don't come from anywhere like that. It's nothing but a gene memory. Statama told me things. I begged him to tell me. Why do you think I left that lunatic asylum?"

The hectic light in her eyes was also in her speech, agitated, jumping around. Joe stood up. He was trembling. Faye dropped her cigarette into the dregs of her coffee and went to him, tried to hug him. But she was right: he didn't really want to know things. He turned away.

"I have to shower," he said.

"Joe—"

"I have to *shower.*"

He walked stiffly to the bathroom, shut the door and locked it. In the mirror he searched his eyes.

Statama had been tinkering with telomeres, attempting to imbue them with extended longevity, allowing chromosomes to reproduce infinitely instead succumbing to so-called "programmed cell death." He discovered it was easier to accelerate the telomere's degradation in a controlled fashion that wouldn't produce progeric freaks. Interesting but of little practical application; no one wanted to grow old faster. When the problem of the Cygnus portal arose Statama thought he saw a way of using his discovery. Perhaps it would be possible to accelerate the total growth of a human being, from the cellular level up. Telescope a fully developed life cycle into, say, a one-year period? Statama was confident it could be done. But he knew he'd have to first create a "pure" clone, a generic template strained as close as possible to sui generis from which to harvest the next generation's cells.

"Go ahead," Anthea said. She handed him the scrawl rig, which consisted of a short, finely tapered wand and a flexible coil attached to the xplasma source, kind of a big kidney bean strapped around his waist under his loose coat. Originally intended for architectural design application and almost immediately co-opted by graffiti hounds, later morphed to Scrawlers. The wand felt good in Joe's hand. The way it used to. Before Mr. Statama collected him from the orphanage Joe had been in the habit of sneaking out to hang with a loose affiliation of Scrawlers. Joe had never slept well, he had trouble concentrating, except on his sketchpads and books. Crazy Joey, everybody called him. Made more crazy by Father Orpin. That phrase: *We're all the family you have, Joey.* White hair on the barrel chest, and the way he held Joe down.

Joe always had talent (his compulsive hand scribbling rudimentary tags, faces, impressionistic line art, filling cheap notebooks for the orphanage staff to shake their heads over). But it was the Scrawl jolt that electrified him and got him to *move.* He was eighteen. By now he would have been on his own, if Statama hadn't put him in Fairhaven.

He and Anthea were in an alley half a dozen blocks from the apartment. It was 2 A.M. Joe thumbed the wand's actuator, bonding to the edge of a trash converter. He eased up on the actuator and drew out a clear filament, almost invisible, then quickly slashed a bold design in 3-D neon xplasma green, hanging it out there, a weird mutated kanji entangling a jagged face, very deftly rendered in airy xplaz crystal. His old tag, reflecting in the black mirror puddles dropped in the buckled alley.

"Nice," Anthea said.

Joe bounced on his toes, getting into it. He bonded to another spot on the converter, drew out a line, then depressed the actuator to thicken the stream, rotating the color selector with his middle finger, quick slashing an arrangement of V's, adding a slouch hat, stubby line of a cigarette, squiggle of smoke. Four color Scrawl sketch. He'd done hundreds before Statama locked him up and even then had conducted Scrawl orgies in his mind whenever he could think straight.

Anthea laughed.

"Sam Spade," Joe said.

"I know. All those V's. You're good."

"Not that good," Joe said, but he was grinning.

"Do another one."

He thought a minute then bonded a third time to the trash converter (really fucking it up, just what normal people hated and Scrawlers loved; the xplaz was light as eggshells but the polymers made it sticky, hell to clean up, much worse than paint on brick) and quick-scrawled a face with zigzag, corkscrew hair.

"Hey!" Anthea said.

A searchlight speared into the alley. An amplified voice ordered them to freeze.

They didn't. They took off fast, came out the back end of the alley and split in opposite directions, no discussion necessary, Joe reacting to blood memory, those orphan years.

They met back at the apartment, stealthy up the stairs. Faye slept twisted in the bed sheets, groaning. At her bedroom door Anthea turned her ghost eyes on Joe, waiting. She said, "My rig."

He followed her into the bedroom. She stopped short and turned and opened his long coat, hunkered to unstrap the xplaz kidney, looking up at him, waiting again, letting the rig slip to the floor. Then she started on the belt buckle. He didn't move.

"What's wrong?"

"Nothing. Faye. I'm—I mean I said I wouldn't without her."

"What do *you* want?"

He touched her face, wanting but not knowing, and she moved her head like a cat so his fingers pushed the stretchy beret thing off, releasing that abundant hair. Then she tugged at his belt and opened his pants. He watched her, touching her crinkly yellow hair. After a few minutes she stopped what she was doing and looked up at him. He kept touching her hair but he was afraid. His aloneness had taught him to always keep something back; Father Orpin had taught him passivity and the unconscious trick of numbness; Faye had taught him to take direction. What would Anthea teach him? She seemed to be deciding. Then she stood up and undressed him completely, tenderly, pulling his shirt off over his head and tossing it. She took him to bed, and he felt the pressure to *be* something for her ease off.

"I had this friend," she said, her head resting on his chest. Joe could feel her jaw move when she spoke. "He couldn't come. At first I'm thinking Jesus he can go forever. Then I get worried, like he's not coming because he's not turned on enough. So there's something the matter with *me*? Dumb stuff. But that wasn't it. After a couple of nights he tells me his mom died right in front of him in a pulser wreck. She was in the front seat and he was in the back, and she just bled out. Now every time he's with a girl it's like he freezes, goes all remote, like being afraid of giving himself up, so it never happens. He just wants to cuddle, which is okay. I guess he really loved his mom. He never lets go."

Joe listened but didn't say anything.

"He was a real nice boy," Anthea said. "We were best friends. But he didn't want to be around me anymore after that time he told me. Like before, we were pretending there was no problem. When the pretending stopped he had to get away."

"Nothing like that happened to me," Joe said. "I don't even remember my mother."

"I was just telling you about my friend," Anthea said. "He was a kid is all."

Joe caressed Anthea's bare back until she fell asleep.

He woke out of the old-man nightmare because Faye was kicking him. It was morning and Anthea was gone. Joe drew his arms and legs in, blocking Faye's blows (foot shod in a suede ankle boot, sharp-toed).

"Hey—"

She was grunting, head down, her blue hair hanging lank in front of her face. She landed a solid strike on his elbow, that nerve. Joe yelped and rolled away off the mattress. The kicking stopped.

After a moment, grudgingly, Faye said, "Are you really hurt?"

The nerve was like a hot, buzzing wire, numbing his arm. "It's just my crazy bone."

"Your—oh."

He got on his feet, back to her, and awkwardly pulled his shorts on one-handed.

"I'm sorry," she said, not sounding that way. "But you were in the wrong bed."

"Whatever."

"Poor baby."

He turned around. She was leaning against the doorjamb holding a cigarette in the crux of her middle fingers, watching him. She had acquired a new tic. Her left eye twitched like an invisible string tugging at the corner.

"You don't even know what you are," she said.

He took a breath. "Then tell me."

In the beginning there was a rat named Homer. This rat had no parents, which was remarkable but not controversial. Homer was a "pure" clone and his cloned progeny lived less than one hour. Homer Jr. wasn't sick. He simply aged too fast, as designed. Much too fast. Homer himself enjoyed a rat's normal life span though he was moody and anti-social, didn't sleep enough, and tended to bite. But Homer was an otherwise ordinary rodent, and if anyone had thought it was a good idea to send him to Beta Cygni via Tachyon Funnel Acceleration it would have proved a fatal trip, and never mind the years required; no complex life could survive the forces involved. However a few quick-frozen cells protected by lead-lined titanium baffles could remain intact and even thawed and nurtured to maturity (especially hyper rapid-aging maturity) with the assistance of computers and an automated nursery. But, really, what would have been the point? Something brighter and more adaptive than Homer Jr. would be required to locate and decode the alien portal technology.

Joe dressed quietly in the dark and went to Anthea's room. She was awake reading.

"Can I borrow your rig?"

"Only if you borrow me, too."

"Let's go."

Joe bonded to the iron fence surrounding a churchyard, drew out a filament, and scrawled a door. Basic stylistic warping, like a big, wavy stick of gum with gothic hinges. Anthea, watching for trouble, said, "And?"

Joe glanced at her, suppressing an urge to tic. A few days without D&B and he felt subject to constant alienating anxiety and the suggestion of a co-existing Other. He drew a filament off the first door and scrawled a second, this one standing directly in front of a six-foot monument. Broken winged cherubim visible through a scrawled version of his green door. Then he drew out *another* filament, like skipping stones, drawing it out, linking one scrawl to the previous, judging balance and weight, making the linking filaments so thin you could barely see them. Joe filled a portion of the bone yard with doors, his Scrawl version of the old man's dilemma. Anthea laughed.

"Jesus, you've got *eight*."

"Eight's good," Joe said and stopped. The kidney was almost empty. He removed the Scrawl rig and handed it to her. "I don't need any more doors, I guess."

Anthea tilted her head to the side and said, "Ever do it in a graveyard?"

"I just did."

"Not *scrawl*."

He grinned. "I know what you mean."

"Well?"

Joe looked at her. His breathing was funny. He felt afraid but unrestrained. For once he knew what he was. "Pick a grave," he said.

She looked at him.

"Come on," he said.

She picked a very old one with an upright stone, the name and dates almost erased by time: Sarah Medoff 1965-to-something indecipherable.

"Take me from behind," Anthea said.

He did, panting, surrounded by empty doors and the dead. He came and then he collapsed onto her, crying.

"Hey—" She reached around awkwardly and touched him, patted his thigh. "Hey, don't cry," she said.

TFA fired three Nursery Ships at one-year intervals across the interstellar gulf and they were never heard from again. It was the ultimate black-op, the ultimate long shot. Statama had his moment in the sun but the sun was in full eclipse. All human cloning was illegal, and Statama's disposable variety would be even more so. He randomly named the "pure" originals: Barney Huff, Faye Ruther-ford, and Joe Null. These individuals, whose existence was forbid-den by the same government that secretly sanctioned and financed their creation, were harvested and then dumped into the grinding mill of local welfare systems to be forgotten.

They huddled together in a corner booth of The Deluxe Din-er. Traffic streaked by on the pulseway.

Joe asked, "Do you have money?"

"You mean running away money?"

"Yes."

"How long would it have to be for?"

"I don't know. I guess until they figured I was safe."

"Who's ever safe?"

"You don't have to come," Joe said, but he couldn't look at her when he said it.

Anthea held onto his arm tighter. "I want to, Joe."

He looked at her and knew that, at least for now, they be-longed to each other. It was something new and it scared him but he wasn't going to let it go.

"I'm worried about Faye," he said. "She's not going to make it by herself."

"Do what you have to."

At "birth" the clones onboard the Nursery Ships began trans-mitting unconscious thoughts to their Earthbound "pures." Space itself was warped by the alien portal effect, the technology deriving from intensified states of consciousness, perhaps, and seeking in the absence of its creators a localized substitute. The warped overlaying of Barney Huff's rapid-aging clone drove Barney to madness. At which point Statama petitioned that Faye and Joe, his remaining abandoned children, be brought in before they hurt themselves or others. That was done.

They watched from an alley a block away. A vehicle drew up to the curb, black, beetle-skinned pulser under manual direction, semi-official-looking. Joe pulled Anthea into the shadows. Two men climbed out of the pulser and entered the apartment building. Presently they returned with Faye, slumped, dragging feet between them. Drugged.

"Let's go somewhere," Anthea said.

"Wait."

The back door of the vehicle opened and a tall man with white hair stepped out. David Statama. Joe squeezed Anthea's hand. Statama eased Faye into the vehicle then stood talking to the other men. Presently they got into the pulser but Statama remained in the street. He gazed up at the building, hands in the pockets of his coat. He turned and looked up and down the block. It was as though he *knew* Joe was near and was only waiting for him to come out and then they would go home together. Home was the place where the bad dreams were quelled.

Joe squeezed Anthea's hand until it seemed the little bones would crack.

There was an old man. Machines had raised him, had told him his name was Joe. Machines had given him his directions. This old man found himself inside an asteroid following an elliptical orbit around Beta Cygnus 2. Joe subsisted on a steady diet of fear and insecurity, and he longed for things he'd never seen. Now he blundered between black sheets that might have been anything he believed them to be. A wish, a terminal, a switching station between stars, an abandoned mistake that dropped travelers to their deaths on a double dozen worlds. The machines had suggested that Joe might find his way home by deciphering portals. But he could not begin to fathom the technology, which seemed more shadow than substance. Soon he would die. Or he could step through a portal and also die, though perhaps in a place acquainted with "home" in his deep gene memory, a place of human habitation, blue skies, doors that opened readily. The old man slouched back and forth between the black funhouse mirror-portals and couldn't decide. Madness was a disintegrating filter.

*

In a motel room on the outskirts of metropolitan Seattle eighteen year old Joe Null thrashed awake. Cold sweat wrung out of his body. His mind yawed toward some unknowable abyss. He was his own beginning and end, which meant he didn't *have* to belong to anyone, or even to his fears. But he was not alone; he had choices and he had begun to make them. Anthea returned to the bed with a glass of water. Joe took it gratefully. He hoped it would always be him that she found waiting.

Home is the place where bad dreams are quelled.

Human Day

Raymond held the loose eye in a cereal bowl. The eye looked like a big, brown-and-bloodshot marble. It sounded like one, too, when he tilted the bowl. On the curvature opposite the pupil the interface shone like a gilded thumbprint. Robbie the Rover, a canine simulacrum Ray had designed in the image of a Golden Retriever, stood frozen by the work bench, left orbit gapping.

"Ready or not," Raymond said, "it's D-Day."

He pushed the eyeball into the open socket, regarded it critically, touched up the fur with a tiny makeup comb. He removed his glasses and wiped them on his shirt tail then put them back on and sighed.

"Dog day," he mumbled.

Robbie the Rover looked like a study in taxidermy.

Raymond worried his hands together. It was now or never, and it couldn't be never. He had been hiding in this secret underground shelter for almost a year. His supplies were depleted, the generator fuel nearly exhausted.

He had to find out what was happening up there in the world. Had to find out if *they* had fully taken over: his children of the Rift.

Raymond seated himself at the work table and activated the remote control device. A red point of light glowed briefly in the simulacrum's left eye—the power-on indicator—then immediately faded out, so the illusion would not be compromised to the disappointment of his sweet little Samantha. Of course, the light should have shone in both eyes. The right one was still not working. The screen on the controller setup flickered, flashed out, flickered again and became steady. It displayed a flat image of Raymond seated before the remote control console, leaning forward, looking at himself looking at himself, through Robbie the Rover's eye.

Raymond turned in his chair and manipulated the controller. The fake dog padded over to him just like the real thing, looked up, cocked its head to the side, lolled its tongue, wagged its tail.

"Good boy," Raymond said.

He got up and shuffled in his slippers to the heavy door. Using the hand crank, he rolled it aside, greased wheels grinding. The tunnel beyond breathed stale air into his face. Coughing, he returned to the work table. Robbie the Rover stood by the chair. Raymond almost started to pet it, he was so lonely. Instead he sat down and took up the controller.

"Go be my eyes," he said. "My eye, I mean."

And he sent the simulacrum on its way to the world above.

His life depended on a toy. Samantha's toy. His daughter was gone but her toy remained durable.

It had begun the day the Mayovsky Accelerator erupted. Sam should not have been there. That was Raymond's fault. She was so damn *curious*. Daddy's girl, minus the twitchy eccentricities.

"What's it doing?" she had asked. They were standing together on the observation platform. "Are those big things magnets?"

Four gray metal blocks the size of economy cars tumbled on gimbals suspended above the floor. In the center of all that tumbling the air blurred, like worn fabric. A low frequency hum vibrated deep in their bones.

"Not magnets, exactly, sweetheart. It's something new, kind of a mini-super collider. I'm rubbing at the onion skin between universes." As always Raymond had taken full credit, even for a project of this scope. Well, it was his money driving it. And it wasn't called the *Mayovsky* Accelerator for nothing.

"It *looks* like rubbing," Samantha said.

And then something like a funnel of light warped out of blurred place and lashed upward, knocking Raymond off his feet. When he looked around, Sam was gone from the platform. They found her body beneath the tumbling blocks.

Raymond watched Robbie's progress on the RC screen. The dog made its way up twisty, chemically lit passages. When it reached the outer door it stopped. A featureless, metal slab filled Raymond's screen. This blast door had not been opened once in the last year, not since Raymond had fled beneath the earth. You could do anything if you had enough money. Anything but the most important thing: prevent a death that had already occurred. Originally the shelter was Raymond's hedge against terror or environmental disaster; it had become his refuge from transdimensional invasion.

He stood up and pressed the lock release button for the outer door. When he resumed his seat the RC screen presented the outline of the open door and the darkness beyond. He activated Robbie the Rover's night-vision, and proceeded. As soon as the simulacrum was clear, Raymond shut the outer door and secured it.

Robbie climbed upward, eventually coming to the roughest section of the access tunnel. Here the passage was drilled through raw earth and rock, with no obvious shoring. Further on and Ray had to guide Robbie carefully into a tunnel not much larger than would allow for a crawling man. If anyone were to stumble upon it, the access to his shelter would appear to be nothing more than a natural gap in the earth.

Robbie came out into a tangle of blackberry vines and dazzling sunlight. Ray killed the night-vision. Past the brambles and weedy lot a highway crossed before a park. Beyond that the city rose against the sky. He thought for a minute, then put Robbie the Rover in rest mode. Better to wait for dark.

Robbie the Rover slept in the brambles, and Raymond slept in his secret shelter. Or tried to. He tended either to sleep constantly, or barely at all. This was a barely-at-all period. He pillowed his head on his folded arms and breathed slowly, too conscious of himself to relax. Finally, giving in to his anxieties, he sat back and knuckled his gummy eyes, reached for the remote and activated the monitor.

A quarter mile away, Robbie opened *his* eyes. Eye.

There was movement. Raymond leaned closer to the monitor. Nighttime had descended upon the world above. A figure approached through moonlight, coming straight for Robbie the Rover's bramble bed.

Discovered already!

For a moment, Raymond could do nothing. Then he tapped the auto-dog key, and Robbie stood up and behaved like a real dog, without detailed direction from the RC. Sam would have loved this feature.

The approaching figure halted.

Robbie barked in a friendly way. He was incapable of barking in a threatening manner, being, essentially, a child's toy. Raymond had stocked his secret shelter for every contingency, including Samantha. Now loneliness was the final contingency. In another month *would* he have been petting Robbie? Fawning over its meticulously hand-woven fur?

On the monitor, the figure moved closer. It was a man, or what looked like a man. He was saying something. Raymond turned up the gain on Robbie's ears.

There, boy, how'd you get yourself stuck in that mess, huh?

The man carefully pulled apart loops and tangles of spiked vine.

Raymond nudged the controller, and the dog stepped out of the brambles and past the man.

You're very welcome, the man said.

Okay, he seemed human enough, but best to maintain distance.

Ray pushed the simulacrum forward at top speed, which amounted to something short of a trot. Robbie was into the street before Ray realized it. Sudden light splashed on the paving, a shadow swung, an engine roared. The view streaked violently, flipped around, froze on a new, cockeyed angle facing the sky. The moon shone like a crooked and lidded eye in a field of pale stars. The sound was gone. Raymond pushed, toggled and twisted the RC to no effect. He slumped back in his chair and pressed his palms to his temples, pressed hard enough to feel painful pressure. The image on the monitor stuttered and flipped and froze again, this time on a square of pavement. He redoubled the pressure on his temples, but only for a few seconds; he knew, of course, that there couldn't be a connection. He leaned close to the screen, squinting through his glasses. He held his breath a moment, then wondered what would happen if he held it for a certain number count, say one hundred, which would be uncomfortable and perhaps even impossible for him to reach without breathing, would *that* encourage the restoration of his link to Robbie? Yes, yes: it was just as irrational as the pressure thing. So what?

Before he could even start the count, the image came alive again. He was looking out of the back of a vehicle where, evidentially, someone had placed him. The man from the brambles and another man stood framed in the opening. The speaker crackled. In a burst of static one of the men said: *Poor guy.* And the other said: *He ran right in front of me.*

Struck by the vehicle, then. But was he found out? No one referred to a broken mechanical dog as "poor guy."

The hatch came down, but before it could slam shut the image froze again. Raymond waited but didn't bother with temple-pressure or breath-holding magic. After all, he was a scientist, an inventor—a rational man. Anyone would have to give him that.

"Ray, you need help."

So his wife had said, or the Tonya-thing imitating his wife. Raymond had looked up from his bowl of Corn Flakes.

"Do I?" he said.

"Please, Ray."

She was convincing. The real Tonya had done a fair amount of pleading and histrionic hand-wringing as well. Oh, they were good. Raymond had lowered his gaze back to the Corn Flakes. Only a few remained, milk-soggy, unappetizing. He moved them around with his spoon.

The Tonya-thing said, "Jack called again. They're worried about you at the project."

I'll bet, he'd thought. *Worried that I'm on to them. And they're correct to be worried.*

"Ray." It was turning on the crocodile tears. "I'm going to call your brother."

"Don't you do that." Raymond continued to stir his Corn Flakes. Something in his voice made the kitchen very quiet. He could hear the Tonya-thing breathing. "I don't want you to do that."

Now its breath hitched with suppressed sobs. It sounded *so much* like his Tonya. Raymond told himself not to look up, *begged* himself not to look up. The weeping continued.

Raymond looked up.

And his heart caved in a little. He could be wrong. What-might-be-Tonya saw the doubt in his eyes.

"Don't call Bill—yet," Raymond said. "Sit down first."

Tonya sat. Raymond worked his hands together, his palms sweaty. He removed his glasses and wiped the lenses on his shirt tail.

"Listen," he said. "I know I have a history of . . . instability. I *know* that. But believe me, Tonya, believe me please, it has nothing whatsoever to do with what's happening now. And something *is* happening. Something dreadful."

"Samantha—"

"It isn't *about her*. Please just listen. Please."

She nodded, paying attention, encouraging him. And so he told her about the Mayovsky Accelerator experiments, about the rift they'd opened, the wound in the onion skin between universes. If you had enough money you could do anything—anything but raise the dead.

"This is the part that sounds crazy, that sounds, well, coincidental," he had said to Tonya. "Given my *history*, I mean. But coincidence isn't always meaningless, accidental. And just because somebody once displayed symptoms of paranoid delusional behavior, that doesn't mean that somebody couldn't be right, did it?"

Tonya shook her head, and in a very small voice said, "No."

"It didn't mean *they* weren't here, for instance. You see what I'm saying?"

Tonya smiled one of her brave, brittle smiles, and that's when he had begun to retreat again. Retreat from the imitation Tonya.

"They—?" she said.

"Yes, yes. They. THEY. *Them*, if you prefer."

She flinched. He saw it, even though she tried not to show him.

Flinched.

"I'm sorry, Ray. I don't understand. What was coincidental?"

He sighed, dropped the spoon.

"Even if you were who you claim to be, you wouldn't believe me."

He threw his head back and stared at the ceiling. Time ticked by. The Tonya-thing touched the back of his hand, and he pulled away.

"Please don't touch me," he said. Then, still looking at the ceiling, he added: "I have no quantifiable data to prove anything. This is pure intuition. That's the beauty of it, at least from your perspective. There's no way to prove you've taken over. And pretty soon there won't be anyone to prove it *to*, anyway. You think I don't *know* that?"

Raymond came awake in the dark. The shelter lights automatically cycled off after an hour, if he didn't override the mechanism; it was an energy-conserving measure. He sat up abruptly, his heart thudding, a dream howling retreat down a black well in his mind. Groping out, his hand bumped the RC, and the monitor blinked out of sleep-mode. A moving image gathered. He was connected again! Robbie the Rover was prowling down a dark hallway, evidently on Natural Dog mode. Raymond activated the night-vision. Open doorways appeared. It seemed to be an ordinary home. Another door suddenly opened at the end of the hallway, revealing a blaze of light and an emerging child in a night gown. The girl, maybe nine years old, reached back and switched off the light. Robbie's night-vision adjusted to the dramatic shift. The girl popped forward, green-ghostly, her eyes twin points. She was saying something, but Raymond couldn't hear her. The girl walked toward him, stooped over, reaching out.

She was petting him.

Her voice barely a whisper, she was saying: *Good boy, good boy.*

Raymond tilted Robbie's head back slightly. The girl's face was difficult to read by night-vision. A young child around nine years old. Samantha's age.

Time to sleep, good dog.

The screen went blank.

Raymond squinted, wiggled the controller, listened intently. But audio and visual were both gone. Unconsciously, Raymond touched his hair, muttered: *Good boy.*

*

Raymond was dozing, and someone was knocking on the door. Gradually he opened his eyes. The knocking continued. His eyes opened wider. He jerked his head to the right, looking across the shelter. Of course he could see nothing, the lights having cycled off again. Raymond slapped the override button next to the bed, and a couple of dim panels stuttered on. There was nothing to see. And no one was knocking on the door; the sound had to be coming from Robbie the Rover's remote display.

Raymond rolled off the bed and approached the table.

The monitor remained blank. He turned his head. The speaker hissed white noise at him.

Had he *dreamed* the knocking?

He opened a drawer in the work table and removed the big clasp knife. At the door he pressed his ear to the cool metal and listened but could hear nothing. That didn't tell him anything. The shelter was like a bank vault. There could have been a brass band performing on the other side of the door, and he wouldn't have heard it. For that matter he would not have been able to hear any knocking.

Raymond chewed his lip, wiped his sweaty palm on his thigh. He folded open the knife then cranked the door partway aside, knife ready. Stale air and the empty tunnel. He listened for a while then cranked the door shut again.

"Be a good dog," Raymond said, back in his chair before the remote.

He wiggled the cable connection. The monitor blinked on, showing a very low angle on a carpeted floor and a blank wall. Robbie was in rest-mode. A rectangle of rosy morning light lay upon the wall and carpet. A shadow, something unidentifiable, quivered in the rectangle. Sunlight passing through a curtain? A glass of water on the sill? Raymond slumped in his chair and watched the monitor. He considered activating Robbie, but waited. Time passed. His breathing resumed a restful rhythm. His mind dwelt on the quiver of light in a meditative way, as if he were a child on the dreamy precipice of sleep. A girl's voice said: *Let's go for a walk, boy.*

Auto-activated by her voice, Robbie the Rover switched to Natural Dog mode and stood up. Raymond heard a chain jingle.

Then they were walking. Raymond kept his hand off the controls. The girl walked a little ahead, pulling the chain. She passed through a door, and Raymond followed after her.

It was a gorgeous day.

Brilliant sunshine, a verdant expanse of lawn, leaves flickering in a summer breeze. Raymond's heart ached a little; he had been underground a long time. The girl led him to a park. There were other children and dogs. *Real* dogs, no doubt. Even if the alien replacements didn't recognize him for what he was, *they* would—the real dogs.

But they didn't.

Raymond sat tense before the RC, as another little girl approached them with a dog of her own, a fidgety toy poodle. The smaller dog barked its head off. Rover remained aloof, his programming instructing him to refrain from excessive barking, even at the cost of verisimilitude. Raymond took over control and made Robbie bark a few times in his deep retriever voice. The poodle trotted behind him to sniff his asshole. This was it. At least this was it if he didn't do something.

He resumed manual control of Robbie the Rover, swung the artificial dog around, and made him bark. The poodle barked back and even snapped at Robbie's face.

"Cosette, come here!" the other girl shouted, and she pulled the toy poodle away. Raymond immediately suppressed Robbie's barking.

"Uh oh," the girl with the toy poodle said. She had picked up "Cosette" and was holding the little dog in her right arm as she quickly bent forward, reaching for something on the ground. Then her hand came up fast and she appeared to pet Robbie. The simulacrum was getting a lot of love. Raymond felt obscurely jealous.

"Nice doggy," the girl said, holding Cosette close. The poodle sniffed at Robbie, her face up close to the one functioning lens.

"What's his name," the young girl said to Raymond's young girl.

"We don't know," she said. "My dad sort of found him."

"Are you keeping him?"

"Yes."

"Why don't you call him Mobia?" the other girl said. At least it sounded like "Mobia." Raymond clicked his tongue.

"Maybe," Raymond's girl said.

"Maybe *not*," Raymond said.

"I think they're okay together now," the other girl said. "Want to let them play?"

"Sure."

Raymond closed his eyes. Even on Natural Dog mode Robbie wouldn't be able to convincingly play with a real dog. Raymond opened his eyes and reached forward, intending to flip on Natural Dog anyway, since there was nothing else to do. The image on the monitor was bouncing wildly. For a moment he thought it was another malfunction in the video feed. But then he realized it was bouncing because Robbie was *running*. The mechanical toy dog was chasing the real toy poodle, gamboling around the park, randomly changing directions. Impossible. The simulacrum *couldn't* do that stuff. And besides, Raymond hadn't touched the controller. He watched until the poodle got tired of running and the two of them settled down. Then Raymond tried to resume direct control. It didn't work. He swiveled the joystick, snapped the toggle back and forth between Natural and Direct, all to no avail. Cosette sniffed Robbie's asshole to her heart's content, and Robbie returned the gesture. Raymond rocked back in his chair. "What the hell?" he said.

After that the simulacrum remained beyond Ray's control. All he could do was watch. Which he did—obsessively. He sat for hours in front of the RC monitor. He ate his meals there, napped there. Robbie—renamed Mobia by his adoptive family—enjoyed a completely integrated life, or simulation of a life. Besides the little girl the family consisted of two adults, the man who had rescued Robbie, and his wife. They all had weird names that Raymond could never quite hear. The man's name sounded like *Gitzer*. The mother's name was *Natvizia*, or something. They both called the little girl by a name that sounded like *Spavitz*. Were they Romanian? Darker possibilities loomed. But whatever they were they all doted on "Mobia." They petted him, played games with him, constantly told him what a good boy he was. At first Raymond was baffled. After a while his bafflement turned to envy. Mobia had a life; Raymond lived in a hole.

One day Raymond awakened from a nap and raised his face to a dead screen. His own haggard reflection stared back at him. He sat up in his creaky chair, his back stiff. He wiggled the cable connection on the back of the monitor, turned it on and off. Nothing helped. The screen remained blank.

The shelter felt smaller and lonelier than ever. Raymond played music to dispel the constant drone of the generator. Knowing depression would overcome him if he didn't stay active, he ran on the treadmill. It was hard to get started, but once he was jogging along he didn't want to stop. He ran until the sweat was pouring off his body and he could barely see from his salt-stinging eyes. He kept looking at the dark monitor, hoping it would come on. It didn't. He bargained with the Universe. If he could manage to run for an additional fifteen minutes the Universe would let the picture come back. After fifteen minutes, however, the monitor was still blank. Raymond extended the bargain to thirty minutes, then to an hour. He had already been on the treadmill for ninety minutes. He failed to make it to the end of the additional hour. His leg cramped, he stumbled and fell.

Clutching the twitching muscle in his calf, he began to cry. He dragged himself to the bed and lay there waiting for the pain to subside. Only the physical half of it did.

A girl was laughing. Raymond swam up out of churning dreams. A dog barked. He turned his head. Light poured from the monitor. Raymond rolled off the bed and stumbled over to the table, overwhelmed with relief.

The little girl, Spavitz or whatever her name was, knelt at the end of the hallway in the neat suburban-style home.

"Silly!" she said. "It came out again, didn't it."

She rolled something down the hardwood floor like a Lilliputian bowling ball. Red and brown and white, with a copper glint.

Robbie's eye.

Raymond stopped breathing. Robbie the Rover looked down at his own eye then back up at the girl, who had come closer. "It's okay, Mobia. We'll just pop it back in. Unless you want to trade for a blue one." Spavitz hooked her index finger into the corner of her own eye—*and popped it out of the socket.*

Raymond made a strangling sound and shoved back from the table, almost overturning his chair. The girl held her blue eyeball up, comparing it to Robbie's brown one.

"No," Raymond said.

Spavitz pushed Robbie's eye into her own socket. The eye bulged, too big for the orbit, throwing off the symmetry of her face.

"Nope," she said. "Not gonna fit, boy."

Mobia barked.

Spavitz hooked the eyeball out and thumbed it into the dog's head, then replaced her blue one.

"There," she said. "That's all better." And then she got very close to Robbie's good lens and spoke directly into it. "It's really all better now, Raymond."

Raymond gasped.

"You can come out now," the girl said.

Raymond shook his head. His mouth had gone dry.

"We know you're there," Spavitz said. "You can be one of us, like Mobia."

Raymond hit a button and the screen went black. He grabbed the power cord, yanked it out of the RC unit and flung it down like a dead snake.

Raymond sat on the edge of his bed, rubbing his eyes. He reached for the cup of cold tea he'd left on the floor. When? He'd lost track of time, grown gaunt. Many days had passed since he killed the RC unit. His mind alternated between irrational frenzy and dull resignation. Resigned to what, exactly, he couldn't have said. A half-eaten fiber biscuit lay on the bed next to his pillow. He picked it up and took a listless bite.

At the work table he slumped in his chair, facing the blank monitor.

"I *know* you're not real," he said. "There's no Spavitz, no Mobia, no Gitzer. No Donner or Blitzin or Rudolf, either, for that matter."

He bit into the stale biscuit, tore a hunk off and chewed doggedly. His own haggard reflection watched him.

"I know you're not real," he said, spitting fragments of biscuit.

The cold light from a single panel dimmed then brightened. Raymond looked around the confining shelter, his mouth open and half full of chewed biscuit. When the generator finally died he would be entombed in darkness with nothing but the sound of his own breathing. The shelter was vented to the surface, so there was no danger of suffocation, at least.

But to live in constant darkness . . .

Raymond washed down the biscuit with the remains of his tea, then bent over and picked up the power cord and plugged it back into the remote control. His fingers hovered over the On switch. He had to have one more look.

Raymond pushed the On button.

An image gathered. Warm afternoon sunlight quivered briefly on a distant wall, then the generator quit, stranding Raymond in the dark.

Raymond crawled through the narrow tunnel until he emerged blinking into sunlight like some lost and blinded thing.

A vehicle flashed by on the highway.

Raymond stood up in the prickly brambles and started to walk. When the rift opened *they* blended into the human population, made it stronger than it had ever before been. Perhaps it wasn't an invasion at all, but a miraculous relationship. That was the meaning of the warping funnel that killed Samantha. Her death was an accident in the service of a greater good; it was meaningful. And he, Raymond, must already be one of them. Otherwise how could he possibly have endured?

He stood at the edge of the highway and thought about Spavitz and her family in the sunny little house. They were more than human. Kinder, more durable, safer. From the park came the sound of children laughing and shouting. As yet no one had seen him; there was time to go back. He slipped the clasp knife out and folded it open. Was he one of them or not? He pulled up his shirt and placed the edge of the blade against his skin. After a moment he drew the blade across. What he saw astonished him.

INTRODUCTION TO

The Avenger of Love

I n 2006 at the Nebula Awards in Tempe, Arizona I got a
little drunk on Kilt Lifter Scottish ale and asked Harlan Ellison if he planned to publish any more stories in science fiction
magazines. By then I'd met him once before, in Seattle in 2003.
We weren't friends or anything, but he knew who I was. I don't remember exactly what his initial response was, but I do remember
telling him that I had started selling stories late, in my forties, and
by then most of the writers I'd admired when I was a kid had died
or stopped publishing. One exception was Robert Silverberg. He
wrote a monthly column for *Asimov's*. When I saw my name in
the TOC my eyes always tracked to that one reliable byline from
the mythic past, linked across generations on cheap sf magazine
paper. I also mentioned Harlan's book, *Partners In Wonder*, and
how I disagreed with the critics who didn't like the Ellison-Silver-
berg collaboration that appeared in that book.

Somehow, by the end of that conversation, Harlan was saying he would collaborate with *me* on a story and we'd sell it to
Asimov's with my name appearing first. Not only that, we would
discuss the writing process live, or live-ish, on his website's message board. Here's the best part: our collaboration would be called
"Partners In Wonder Redux!"

I said I'd think about it.

Okay, I wasn't that cool a customer. The idea thrilled and terrified me in about equal measure. At that point I'd sold five or
six stories. A collaboration with Harlan Ellison was intimidating.
And doing it in public? I never talk about stories while I'm still
working on them. The potential for humiliation seemed high.

The next day I was talking to Sheila Williams, my new editor at *Asimov's*. I noticed Harlan holding court on the other side
of the lobby. After a while he came over, full of beans. He'd been

telling a story to a group of fans—a story about *me*.

"One guy was in tears," Harlan said.

"Really?"

What story could Harlan have told about me, based on our conversation of the previous evening, that could bring a grown man to tears? I do remember Harlan wincing when I mentioned I'd been working in an airplane factory to pay the bills while continuing to write. Well, as any reader knows, Harlan Ellison could really drill down on the pathos.

On the last day of the awards weekend I approached him at the table where he'd been signing books and told him that I'd decided to go ahead with his proposed collaboration. I knew it was risky, but I also knew I'd be some kind of coward if let the opportunity slip away. As my friend Daryl Gregory has said about writing opportunities: always say yes. Later on you can figure out how to do it.

So it began.

The morning after I returned home from Tempe, Harlan called and announced we would start right away. That call was on May 8, 2006. Great! But nothing happened. Then, on October 9, he directed a note to me on The Art Deco Dining Pavilion, which is what he called his message board:

> *I haven't forgotten. I'm cleaning up detritus. Soon, Jack. Be of good cheer . . . and stoic patience.*
>
> *Yr. pal, Harlan*

Alas, our story "Rust" never got written. Eventually, Harlan did post an opening sentence on the message board then promptly said I should take the first whack. I wrote six pages and faxed (yes, faxed) them to his house in Sherman Oaks—Ellison Wonderland, a.k.a. The Lost Aztec Temple Of Mars. Harlan phoned immediately and declared them not good enough. Probably so. This went on for about two years. I only ever saw that one sentence from him. I think in Tempe I had caught him in a manic period, but in those later years of his life he was frequently depressed and had trouble writing at all, or so I've been told. At the time I didn't know that. Eventually I talked to other writers, some quite famous, who had also been invited to collaborate with Harlan—with similar outcomes.

None of this is to knock Harlan Ellison. There are plenty of people, sometimes with justification, who are happy to do that. He crossed a lot of lines. But Harlan seemed always to make an effort with me. I don't know why. Once I was supposed to drop by Ellison Wonderland. I was in Los Angeles, getting my daughter situated for her first year at Chapman University. I was so nervous about not being able to find Harlan's house that I drove over to Sherman Oaks the day before, to get my bearings. He lived on Coy Drive in the hills above L.A. I got as far as the Coy Dr street sign and stopped. Around the next bend was one of the most famous dwellings in science fiction history: the Lost Aztec Temple Of Mars with its Watergate villains cast as gargoyles and Martian-themed frieze on the street-facing wall. For whatever reasons, now obscure in my mind, I decided I'd save my first view of the place for the next day.

The following morning I had a feeling something wasn't right. I called Harlan to confirm my visit. His assistant (probably his wife, Susan) told me to hold on. A few minutes later Death came on the line. That's how he sounded to me, like a man making a huge effort to speak from the bottom of a well . . . or an open grave. Somehow he managed to say he couldn't have anyone over that day, that he was unwell. I told him not to worry about it and to take care of himself.

A half hour later he called back. Sounding marginally better, he told me a few "old Jew" jokes to cheer me up. I replied with the only joke I could remember, which was one my daughter had told me the day before. It wasn't funny, but hey. We chatted for twenty minutes or so about depression and anger. He described a recent incident at home where he blew his top, and he sounded genuinely anguished that he didn't understand why he had done it. The point of this story is that he knew I was disappointed, and he made an effort to talk to me. It sounds like a small thing, but if you've ever been laid low with serious depression you know even a small effort—like picking up a phone—can feel like climbing Everest in the middle of winter.

Another time, and I can't remember whether it was before or after the L.A. visit, Harlan called me out of the blue to say that the collaboration wasn't going work—"No harm, no foul" was one of his standard phrases. Clearly he wanted off the hook, but I kind of pushed it and said I'd try again. I'm still shocked that he didn't flatly say no. Anyway, I went to work, plunging in with everything I had as a writer, and thus produced the first three pages, more or less, of the story that follows this overlong introduction. I faxed them to Ellison Wonderland and put the whole mess out of my mind, satisfied that I'd done my job. On February 17, 2007 he posted in the Art Deco Dining Pavillion:

> BIG J:
> *As you can see, there's a fahr in mah belly these days, amigo. In large part from our collaboration. Sit tight, I ain't goin' nowhere.*
>   *Yr. Pal, and Collabo, Big H.*

My pages had worked!

The next time Harlan called he sounded excited as a kid. "I'm writing," he said. "and it's good, a riff on the Jerome Bixby story, "It's A Good Life.""

"That's great, man!" I said. "Save a little for me to do."

Harlan's response (paraphrasing): "It's working now. I don't want to fuck it up."

Was he joking? My take all these years later is that he felt genuinely engaged with the story and was afraid to turn it back to me for fear of losing his own momentum. I can appreciate that. Harlan was battling demons, and writing meant life to him, as it does for so many of us ink-stained wretches. But maybe for Harlan, at that point in his fight against depression, it was especially vital. Looking back, I wish I'd told him I was cool with him finishing "Rust" on his own. Instead, I told him that I wasn't exactly planning to fuck anything up. I didn't say it in a pissy way, but I could feel the energy level drop.

I never saw what he did with my pages. The story must not have worked out in the way he thought it would, or it ran out of gas for him. I don't know. Months went by without a word. I still liked my three pages, so I wrote "The Avenger of Love" by myself, the title my own riff on Harlan's story "The Avenger of Death."

Preparing for the collaboration, I'd re-read all of Harlan's collections, including of course his personal introductions. I knew the basics of his life, and we shared some similarities. For instance, when Harlan was a young teenager his beloved father died at home, right before his eyes. When I was the same age Harlan had been, my mother died while I was down the hall. I didn't see it happen but I heard the thud when she hit the floor. I still hear it. There were other coincidences, but that's enough. I used all this stuff to write a story *he* might have written, oh, twenty years previously. "The Avenger of Love" really flowed. I was in the zone.

When Gordon Van Gelder bought the story for *F&SF*, that was a great day for me. It was my first sale to that magazine. I sat down and wrote a paper letter to Harlan, since he didn't do email (at least not with me). I told him about the story and the sale, and I thanked him because I would never have written this particular story if we hadn't first tried to produce something together. In that sense, I regarded the collaboration as a success. You're off the hook, I told him.

The last time I talked to Harlan was in 2009. He called to tell me he had received his copy of my *F&SF* issue early and was reading my story. Harlan sounded exhausted. He seemed to like it but of course, being Harlan, he had criticisms. Fifteen years later, based on something he pointed out about how a certain character would handle a valuable comic book, I've made a small change in the story.

Soon after that call a mailer arrived from the Coy Drive address. It contained the magazine and a request for a signature, which I was happy to provide.

"I'm preserving your Avenger," he wrote in the attached note, "in *my* Avenger file."

I suppose it's still there.

The Avenger of Love

Norman Helmcke, aging pit bull, pounded away at his keyboard in the law offices of Cohen, Helmcke & Melko. After another sleepless night his eyes were burning. Then it happened again. Norman stopped typing. He slumped, pulled off his glasses. The Wakita brief went blurry. Norman himself felt blurry, contingent, as yet another hole opened within him.

This one was big.

Though sixty-two and divorced three times, Norman had always remembered his first love. He recalled her by the scent she had worn in high school: *Bon Nuit.* Associational memory. Like a sensory switch in his mind, lighting up secret chambers, illuminating innocent preoccupations he hadn't experienced in decades. But now it was as if someone had crept into his memory vault and stolen the bottle of amber-gold perfume. And with the scent gone, so was the girl. Oh, he could *remember* Connie; but her vital presence was faded—a departing shadow.

It wasn't early on-set Alzheimer's; it was thievery.

And he could sense the other holes without knowing exactly what had caused them. More and more gaps occurring over the last few weeks, undermining his identity. Killing off what he was to himself. He squeezed his eyes shut and rode out the intense, drilling pain in his head. When it was over Norman called forth his rage. His rage had never failed him, and it didn't fail him now. Instantly his attention sharpened. He flung himself out of the leather office chair, grabbed his hat and overcoat, ran through the rain to Macy's and demanded a bottle of *Bon Nuit.* The saleslady, a dishwater blonde half his age, passed it to him as if she feared he might bite her finger (that cornered look he'd seen so many times in the eyes of witness-stand victims of his cross-examinations). He snatched the bottle, twisted the cap off and sniffed. Pale attar of roses. His frown deepened.

"It's just perfume," he said.

"Sir?"

"It's *nothing* to me." The memory association was dead. She was gone. First love.

Stolen.

Norman and his rage and his Swiss cheese psyche strode up Fifth Avenue in the cold rain. The wind flapped his unbuttoned London Fog out behind him. Head down, fists balled, he shouldered people out of his way, spoiling for a fight. The quadruple bypass was eighteen months old. They had taken twenty-seven and a half inches of vein out of his left leg. He had been on the table for nine hours and almost died. After the operation, he had been required to give up many things that he was disinclined to give up. His rage, for instance. Right now Norman didn't care; all he wanted was the thief. He was his rage.

A whispery voice that might not have been a voice at all but an instinct cut through. *This way, then.* And Norman turned aside into the little urban park he passed every day on his way to the firm.

The park became . . . wrong.

He stopped and looked up. The rain, now warm and needling, rattled waxy leaves the size of elephant ears. Vines, thick and black and braided like chains, hung from shaggy monsters of trees. Steam rose from the ground. It was like something out of Tarzan. For a moment Norman was transported back to an almost pre-conscious state, and he was a little boy snuggled under his father's arm, that lost voice speaking Burroughs's words, and Norm doubly cozy occupying two worlds, the safe, comforting place beside his father's breathing presence and the wild, unpredictable jungle.

Three worlds, now.

Directly before him stood a storefront. A sign over the door proclaimed: NORM'S JUNK.

"What the hell?" Norman said.

He looked over his shoulder. Fifth Avenue traffic crawled behind a gray veil, almost invisible. The cement walkway blended seamlessly into brown earth.

Norm approached the store. Another sign, this one taped

crookedly in the window: BIG GOING OUT OF BUSINESS SALE!!! He used his hand to shade his reflection in the glass. The shop was empty—except for a comic book in the window display. *The Shadow*, 1940s vintage, with a great Charles Cole cover and a dead fly beside it on the dusty drop cloth. Vol. 5, issue 6: *The Death Master's Vengeance*.

He *knew* that comic.

It had been part of his father's collection. Something about the pulp hero especially appealed to Norm's sense of injustice avenged. Two years after Norman's father disappeared in Korea, Norman's mother remarried. His stepfather, Steve, had soldiered with Bernie Helmcke. He came, ostensibly, to console the widow. Steve was hell on defining his territory. He showed Norm a picture of Norm's mother, a wallet-sized studio shot that Bernie used to keep tucked behind his driver's license. *When I was over there,* Steve said, *this picture kinda kept me going.*

How did you get it? Norman wanted to know.

Steve just smiled. He burned all the comics, Norm's and his father's. With the ashes cooling in the fireplace (the flames had turned colors, fed by the alchemical ink of glossy covers), Norman had lain awake staring at the ceiling. It was *The Shadow* he remembered, the bold avenging hero.

A figure moved out of the gloom at the back of the shop, reached into the display, and snatched the comic book.

"Hey—"

Norman slapped the plate glass with the flat of his hand. The figure retreated to the rear of the shop. Norm ran inside. His head immediately began to throb. He rubbed his eyes, squinted at the man standing at the back of the shop. The man was holding up the comic book.

"Doesn't feel so good in here, does it, kid?"

Norman pointed at the comic.

"That's mine. Give it to me."

"Naw. You want it, you'll have to come and get it."

Norman lurched across the empty shop, the pain in his head growing more intense, almost blinding him. He stopped, pressing the heels of his hands against his temples.

The man, now a vague, pulsating shape, reached back and opened a door.

"You have a choice," the pulsating shape said. "It's fair I tell you that. You can stay here, or try to go back, or follow me. You know what's back. Stay here and you're finished. If you follow me, there's another story. I don't guarantee you'll like it."

Norman lurched toward the shape, and found himself plunging over the threshold into darkness . . .

. . . to land on a broken tongue of pavement, wet after a recent rain.

It was night.

The yellow moon warped into black puddles. He heard the hissing of rolling wheels on wet paving. His heart was pounding. Norman pushed himself up on his knees and waited, catching his breath. After a while, he turned his head and looked back. The sidewalk ended a couple of feet behind him in jagged vacancy. The shop was gone, the jungle was gone. It was as if the sidewalk—maybe the whole world—had been bitten off by some unimaginable thing that had then recoiled into space, stranding Norman and whatever else remained to drift in a void.

Norman stood up and faced—the dark city.

Neon blinked and shifted, making paint-splash patterns on the wet street. Towers twisted into the sky, their points tearing at scudding carbon-paper clouds. Norman tilted his head, trying to get his mind around the architecture.

A dog appeared. It stood at the mouth of an alley between a diner straight out of Hopper and a pawnshop. It was an undersized, scruffy thing, a Puli. There was a red scarf tied around its neck.

The dog started walking in his direction. Norman watched it. The dog halted before him.

"Good boy," Norman said.

"I'm good," the dog said in a female voice, "but I'm not a boy."

"I don't believe it," Norman said.

"Check under the hood, if you want."

"I don't believe you can talk."

"I can't. It's telepathy. I'm projecting the words inside your head. Try not to look so stupefied. I'm thinking about getting a bite to eat. Let's sit down, and I'll give you the big picture. I'm Scout, by the way."

The dog turned and started toward the diner. Norman stood where he was.

"Come on," Scout said. "I can't open doors by myself."

After a moment he followed the dog to the diner and opened the door. The inside was long and narrow, like the inside of a rail car, and bright with fluorescent tube lighting. The counterman was Norman's age, beefy and balding, a blue tattoo of a Marine anchor-and-world like a stain on his hairy forearm.

"They let dogs in here?" Norman said.

"Please. The rules aren't the same as what you're used to."

Scout jumped onto the red leather bench seat of a booth. Norman hesitated then sat opposite the dog.

"Just where is 'here'?" Norman asked.

"You wanted to catch a thief," Scout said. "This is where the thief currently dwells."

"Yes, but where *are* we?"

"The best diner in town. You want to read the Night Owl Specials to me? I can't quite manage the menu. Old war wound, you know."

"What?"

"That was a joke."

"Hilarious," Norman said. He was looking at Scout's scarf. It bothered him. "Who tied that thing around your neck?"

"A former companion."

"What happened to him?"

"Nothing good. Night Owl Special?"

Norman glanced at the menu. "Hobo Scramble . . ."

"Say no more."

"I know that scarf."

"Do you."

Norman stared over the top of the dog's head at nothing in particular. "I've had a stroke or something."

"Welcome to non-sequitur theater," Scout said.

"My neurons are misfiring. This is some kind of hallucination."

"I can't decide on a beverage," Scout said. "I'm thinking cranberry juice."

Norman stood up. "It isn't real," he said.

"Do you want the Hobo Scramble, too?" Scout said.

"You can't die in dreams, and that probably goes for hallucinations, too. I'll walk off the edge, and that'll wake me up."

Scout yawned and when she shut her mouth her teeth clicked
like billiard balls.

"I wish you could keep your mind on breakfast."

The voice was centered in Norman's head, even though he
was already at the other end of the diner stiff-arming the door.
Thought projection. Once outside he headed straight for the
edge. He didn't slow down when he reached the jagged, broken-
off place. His vision hazed over briefly, and his stride carried him
forward—in the opposite direction, back toward the diner. He
stopped, looked over his shoulder, turned and tried again, attain-
ing the same result.

When he returned to the diner a plate of steaming hot scrambled eggs and a cup of coffee was waiting for him. A second plate
was set before Scout. There were chopped onions, crumbled ba-
con, and cheddar cheese mixed in with the eggs, all of it heavily
peppered.

"Have a nice walk? I waited for you."

Norman picked up his fork. He didn't want to be, but he was
starving. The Hobo Scramble smelled almost orgasmically deli-
cious. Naturally he wasn't allowed to eat anything like it, not since
his surgery.

"You don't get to go back," Scout projected. "You made the
choice, remember that."

Norman slipped a bite of scrambled eggs into his mouth,
washed it down with coffee, and said, "I know who you are. And
your name isn't Scout."

"Isn't it?"

The dog started lapping and chewing at her plate of food,
making wet-slurping sounds.

"That's disgusting," Norman said, though he didn't really care;
the Hobo Scramble was igniting his pleasure centers.

Scout looked up. "Maybe the way *you* eat disgusts *me*, ever
think of that?"

"No. Why'd you change your name, anyway? Your name was
Mona when I was a kid."

"Scout," the dog said, "was your private name for me. "You
don't remember, do you."

"Everybody called you Mona, including me."

"Sure, while I was alive. I'm talking about after I died."

Norman put his fork down.

"You used to pretend I was still around," Scout said. "I was like your imaginary friend. And you called me Scout, after the girl in that movie. Really, you wanted a father like Gregory Peck. Instead you got Steve."

Norman rubbed his forehead. All his life he'd had a picture in his mind of Mona dying. He had watched from the front yard, paralyzed. His mother sat in the middle of the street in her green housedress, the little dog cradled in her lap, Mona coughing up blood in thick gouts, as if she were expelling whole organs. And, of course, Norman *had* forgotten the rest. The way he used to imagine Mona still existed as an invisible dog that only he could see. And in her new state of being she had been named Scout. Norman had been smarter than the other kids, and he made sure they knew it. So Mona had been his only friend, and the same situation obtained with Scout.

"The thing is," the dog in the diner said, "I wasn't an imaginary friend. I was really there, and I was really invisible. Life is strange, huh? It's whatever you believe it is, even if you stop believing later on."

They caught a yellow cab in front of the diner. It looked pre-World War II vintage, a Hudson or something. But it wasn't that normal. The windshield was so narrow that it was barely more than a slot. Climbing in, Norman noticed the driver's side wing mirror looked like a big human ear cast in silver. The driver wore a visored cap pulled snug over his eyebrows. He stared at his lap while he drove.

"So, you know who the thief is," Norman said to the dog. They were sitting together in the back seat.

"Yes."

"Well?"

"It's one man."

"Who is he?"

"You'll know him when you see him."

"When I see him I plan to knock his teeth down his throat.

That is, after he gives me back my property, my memories."

"It isn't memories that he's stolen. Look inward. There are no gaps in your memory."

It was true. Norman remembered everything about his first love, for instance. Nevertheless she was gone.

"Well he took something. A lot of somethings. And I want them back. My mind is full of holes."

"I know. But really there's only one thing missing, trust me." Scout barked twice, and the driver tucked the cab into the curb. "This is the place," Scout said in Norman's head.

Norman leaned over and looked out the passenger window on the dog's side of the cab. A brick hotel, six stories high, loomed over the sidewalk. A sign above the lobby entrance said: THE MIDTOWN. Norman threw the door open, and Scout hopped out ahead of him. They stood together on the sidewalk. THE MIDTOWN leaned so much it appeared in danger of tumbling its bricks into the street.

"Top floor," Scout said. "Room 606. Lots of luck."

"You're not coming?"

"Confrontations give me a runny stool. Also, I'm a pacifist at heart."

Norman looked up at the cockeyed face of the hotel. A raft of clouds drifted under the moon.

"I won't really hurt him," Norman said, "not if he returns what's mine."

"I'm not worried about you hurting him. Watch yourself, Norm. This is a rough town."

Scout started walking away, nails clicking on the paving.

"Hey, where are you going?"

"Lady's Room, sugar. I'll be here when you get back."

"You mean *if* I get back, is that it?"

"Fiddle-de-de."

The lobby smelled like boiled cabbage. The desk clerk had a Poe forehead and dirty cuffs. He leaned on his elbows, reading a newspaper, and never looked up. A ficus drooped on the brink of death in a cracked terracotta pot. Dry, crumbled soil littered the carpet. An OUT OF SERVICE sign hung on the elevator cage.

The door to the stairwell bent noticeably to the right. Norman regarded it, head tilted. He entered the stairwell. It appeared to corkscrew into infinity. He started up, counting floors as he went. On the sixth he stopped, even though the stairwell continued.

Standing outside Room 606, Norman hesitated, then knocked. Nothing.

He knocked again, harder. Waited. He could hear movement on the other side. A minute passed, then the door opened. A man in a sleeveless white undershirt and suspenders stood before him. The man's huge gut stretched his undershirt out like a beach ball.

"What?" he said around the dead stub of a cigar. Behind him a ratty easy chair angled toward a television set with a screen that bubbled out like a fish bowl. The current program was a distorted test pattern.

"You have something of mine," Norman said.

"What is this, a gag?" the man said.

And that's when Norman noticed the comic book rolled up in his fist. Norman couldn't see the cover, but he *knew* it was *The Death Master's Vengeance.*

"Let me see that," Norman said, pointing.

The man acquired a cagy look. "Who says I got to?"

"I'm a lawyer," Norman said. "You can be charged with receiving stolen goods. Did you know that?"

"This ain't stolen goods, shyster!"

Norman, who stood several inches taller than the man and besides was now in full possession of his most reliable rage, grabbed the comic book and unrolled it with a snap. It wasn't *The Shadow*; it was *Betty and Veronica.* The issue was titled *The Sirens of Riverdale* and featured a cover illustration of a nude, dog-collared Veronica Lodge reclining on a golden throne reading Sartre's Being and Nothingness.

The fat man snatched the comic back.

"I told you I ain't got your *Shadow*," he said, and slammed the door in Norman's face.

Or tried to. Norman blocked it with his foot, then shoved it open with both hands, sending the fat man reeling into the room.

"Who said anything about *The Shadow*?" Norman said.

"You got nerve busting in here!"

The room smelled of ancient farts. A fly-specked fixture dimly illuminated the mess of beer bottles, dirty clothes, news-papers—and comic books. The comics were the only neatly ar-ranged objects visible, stacked in orderly piles on a gate leg table in the dining alcove. Norman strode over. On the top of the first stack was The Shadow, vol. 5, issue 6: *The Death Master's Ven-geance*. Norman's fingers trembled over the cover.

"Not so fast!"

Norman spun around in time to block the fat man's attempt to brain him with a beer bottle. He knocked the bottle away and grabbed the man's undershirt in his fists and gave him a hard shake. The man's face bunched up, red cheeks popping out like cherry apples all webbed with an alcoholic's burst capillaries.

"I don't know from lawyers, mister, but I'd say you're a *thief*, for sure."

Norman pulled him close, nose to nose. "We'll see who the thief is."

He released the man and picked up the comic. "My father wrote his initials in every book he ever owned."

"So?"

Norman peeled back the cover of *The Death Master's Ven-geance*. On the first page, in the upper right hand corner, in blue ink faded into the ancient paper: B.H.: Bernie Helmcke.

And Norman felt . . . nothing.

Holding the impossible artifact in his hand, a comic book from his father's lost collection, burned by his stepfather more than forty years ago, Norman felt absolutely *nothing*. Whatever hole its absence had made in his psyche remained unfilled. Nor-man started for the door.

The fat man grabbed his arm. "Hold on—"

Norm jerked his arm loose and shoved the man over the back of his chair. His legs stuck up in a "V" capturing the fish bowl pic-ture tube, where a blurry Indian Chief's head wobbled.

Scout was sitting in front of the hotel licking her butt when Norman came out. She stopped, and stood up on all fours.

"I see you survived."

"Yes."

"And you got your *Shadow*."

"Right."

"But you don't feel any better, do you?"

"Look, Mona—"

"Scout."

"Look, Scout. Do you know something I don't know? And besides that, what made you think that fat nitwit was going to hurt me?"

"I just like to keep you on your toes, Norm. Also I didn't know he was going to be a fat nitwit; this is a very dangerous place, generally. And yes: I know something you don't know."

"Would you like to share that information?"

"Perhaps."

"Has anybody ever told you how annoying you can be?"

"Is that what *you're* telling me?"

"Perhaps."

Scout put her nose up in the air. "Well. I'm glad to see your sense of humor is showing at least feeble signs of recovery."

"There's never been anything wrong with my sense of humor."

"On the contrary, it's been dead as a crate of door nails, as Dickens might have said. What you refer to as your sense of humor has really been bottled vitriol. Would you like me to tell you why the retrieval of your dad's comic book failed to fill in any of the gaps in your windy head?"

"You talk too much."

"I'm not talking at all, if you want to get technical. Anyway the reason you can't fill gaps with comic books, or anything else, is that there is only one absolutely essential element, and without it all you are is a gap. Everybody has a portion of the essential element. In your case you decided to bury it deep. Hey, nobody's blaming you; you got a rough shake. It was this element that the Thief had been after from the very beginning. He only took all that other stuff because he couldn't *find* the damn thing."

"Are you going to get to the point one of these days?"

Scout started walking. She tossed her head and thought-projected: "Love."

Norman caught up with her. "What about love?"

"Without it, nothing is vitalized—that's what about it."

"*Bon Nuit*," Norman said.

"The perfume doesn't matter. It's about your ability to experience love at all."

Norman halted at a bus stop, inspected the bench for filth, sat down. He opened the comic book to the first page. His father's initials were barely visible in the cold glow of the street lamp. *The Shadow*. His dad had been a collector, but not like the fat man in the Midtown Hotel. As a small child, Norman had longed to be a hero. A mysterious one, of course. Striking down Evil and injustice wherever he encountered it. Instead Evil struck down his own father. MIA. No one knew how he died. In Norman's mind the death wasn't real, not like Mona's bloody end. He had seen Mona die. Years later Norman read a *Life Magazine* article about American G.I.s who had defected to the North. He knew his father hadn't done that, he *knew* it. But the idea grew bitter roots in him, from a seed planted by Steve.

Plenty of guys defected, kid. They were scared, and they loved their chicken asses more than they loved their country. I'm not sayin' that's your old man for certain. Hell, Bernie seemed like a decent guy. But there's plenty of guys living up there north of the dmz with gook wives that left more than their country behind. All I'm saying is, I never saw Bernie go down. All I saw was him running.

When Steve kissed Norman's mother he liked to squeeze her ass. The first time Norman witnessed this he almost started crying. Almost. Even then, at age eight, he was past crying about anything. It stuck in his head, though. Steve's big ape's paw grabbing a handful of his mother's ass, the way her housedress bunched up. And Steve looked right at Norman, letting the kid know who owned what in that house. Who was boss. It was the comic burning thing all over again, but worse.

Norman wiped his eyes with the heels of his hands. The buildings leaned and twisted over the sidewalk. Brassy jazz issued from nightclub doorways. Mutated simulacrums of vintage Detroit steel rounded city blocks, headlights aimed at unaligned angles, as if searching for something. A girl screamed his name, and Norman stopped. He squinted, listening. Scout looked up at him.

"Was that real?" Norman asked.

"The girl? Absolutely."

"Where—"

"What am I, your guide dog?"

"*Where*?"

"Okay, okay. Sheesh. Follow me."

Scout turned and trotted back to the last nightclub they'd passed, Norman stepping quickly after her. Red neon tubing pretzeled into a symbol unrecognizable to Norman. A black man of sumo proportions lounged in the doorway with his arms crossed. He wore a leather vest and small, round, perfectly black sunglasses.

"Yeah?" he said.

The girl screamed again. She screamed, and Norman *knew* who she was.

First love.

He started to go inside, but the bouncer or whatever he was stepped in front of him.

"You aren't on the list."

"What the hell's going on in there?"

"Nothing of interest to you." The bouncer dropped a huge hand on Norman's shoulder and squeezed, not too hard, but hard enough to indicate it wasn't a friendly gesture.

Norman slugged him.

It was a reflex, and his rage was behind it, and it surprised him as much as it surprised the bouncer, who fell back clutching at his gut. His face clenched in an ugly knot. He started to reach out, and Norman side-kicked his knee. The bouncer hit the ground and did not bounce. Norman stepped over him. Scout followed at his heels, thought-projecting:

"Nice work."

The interior of the club was dark. Smoke layered the air in noxious strata. It wasn't all cigarette smoke, either. The trio on stage were smoldering, the trumpet player in particular. Or was it a quartet? The chanteuse in a black dress lay sprawled at the front of the stage, and she was the smokiest of them all, like a thing burned out of the sky by lasers. Norman pushed forward between the crowded tables. When he got closer he saw that the chanteuse was just a kid, a teenager. In fact she was the girl he used to hold hands with in high school. Connie.

Somebody grabbed his arm and yanked him around.

"You're not on the list." It was a different guy, but he shared dimensions similar to those of the toppled sumo, not to mention the same one-track mind. Before Norman's new-found reflexes could assert themselves, sumo number two slapped him hard across the jaw with an open hand that felt like a mahogany plank. Norman staggered back, upsetting one of the dinner plate-sized tables. A glass tumbler broke on the floor. A man sitting at the table yanked on Norman's lapel and snarled an obscenity. Scout bit the man's ankle. The man yelped, and Norman pulled free.

"That dog's not on the list, neither," the new bouncer said. He was now holding an automatic.

Norman hit him squarely on the nose. The bouncer dropped the gun and spun away, spraying blood through fingers cupped over his face. Norman retrieved the automatic and tucked it in his belt.

The trio kept playing.

Norman approached the stage. It was Connie, all right. Around the girl's neck there hung on a fine gold chain a vial of amber liquid. Norman glanced up at the trumpet player, who continued to blow, his round face streaming sweat, whiffs of smoke lifting from his hair, his shirt collar, even the bell of his trumpet. His eyes, rolled down to meet Norman's, seemed to be mostly egg-white sclera. Norman looked away, back to the fallen chanteuse, his lost first love, from whom he now derived only righteous anger. He closed his hand around the vial and tugged it once, breaking the delicate chain.

Connie wavered, like a body seen through disturbed water, and then she vanished.

The music stopped. For a moment the musicians looked confused, directionless. The horn player wiped his mouthpiece on the sleeve of his white jacket. "That kid was good," he said, then caught a new tempo with his snapping fingers, brought the horn to his lips, and resumed something bluesy, sans smoke.

"What have you got there?" Scout said.

Norman twisted the stopper out and sniffed. "*Bon Nuit.*"

"Naturally."

Norman replaced the stopper. He slipped the vial into the inside pocket of his overcoat next to the carefully folded comic.

"You!" someone shouted.

He turned, his London Fog sweeping over the crowded tables like a cape but never upsetting a glass. The bouncer with the squirty nose had found some friends. One looked like a stick figure in black tie. The stick figure was smoking a cigarette in a long, onyx holder. He gestured, briefly, and one of the big boys next to him pointed a gun at Norman. The music halted for the second time, and patrons evacuated tables. Norman grinned. He snatched the automatic from his waistband and triggered it rapidly. The big man's gun sparked and spun out of his hand. A second slug struck his gun arm. Norman glided across the room. The unwounded bouncer made a grab for him, and Norman chopped at his windpipe, sending him gasping to the floor.

The stick figure casually removed the cigarette holder from his thin lips. "I could use a man like you."

"I bet."

"I assume there is some purpose in your chaotic visit to my establishment."

Norman produced the vial of perfume. "This. Don't lie. I can see you recognize it."

"I do indeed."

"Well?"

"A trifle purchased from a military gentleman. I thought it might improve the band. It did."

Scout lunged past Norman and latched onto the throat-chopped bouncer's arm. At the end of the arm the recovered automatic went off, sending a slug into the ceiling. Norman twisted the gun out of the man's hand, tucked it away next to the other gun, then moved in on the stick figure, lifting him up and throwing him back against the wall. He knocked the cigarette holder away then pulled one of the automatics and pressed the barrel against the little man's very pale forehead.

"This military gentleman. Where can I find him?"

"I wouldn't—"

"Where?" Norman pressed harder with the barrel. The manager grimaced.

"He used to run a shop on the outskirts. Now he does business out of the Bijou on 52nd Street. That's what I understand. Now please leave."

Norman put his gun away. There was a red circle third eye in the middle of the manager's forehead.

"Come on, Scout."

"We shot that place up pretty good, and I still don't hear any sirens. You've got lazy cops around here."

"They aren't lazy," Scout thought-projected. "They don't even exist. This is a lawless place. No attorneys, either, by the way. Except in comic books. There's the theater."

At the end of the block, golf ball-sized light bulbs raced each other around a marquee: RONALD COLEMAN IN LOST HORIZON. Smaller letters crawling along the bottom of the marquee spelled out: OPEN ALL NIGHT, CONTINUOUS SHOWS PLUS NEWS REELS.

"They're a little behind around here," Norman said.

"Progress is relative."

"Let's get this over with," he said, striding toward the Bijou. "I want to go home."

The ticket window was unmanned but the doors stood open. Norman and Scout entered the lobby and discovered it empty and redolent of hot buttered popcorn.

"Will you kill him?" Scout said.

Norman gave the dog a dirty look. "Hell no."

"Because you could get away with it here."

"I said no."

"Why not?"

"Because." Norman swallowed. "Because I'm the good guy."

"I'm sorry," Scout said. "I just thought you should say it out loud."

It was easy to spot the thief. There was only one head visible in the sea of theater seats.

"Wait here," Norman said.

"Check."

Norman walked down the center aisle and stopped at the end of the thief's row. On the big screen Ronald Coleman desperately searched a frozen wasteland for signs of Shangri-La.

"Do you even know who I am?" the thief said, without looking at Norman.

"Yes."

The thief turned away from the screen. Bernie Helmcke's face was young and smooth, the face of a man in the last blush of youth. Movie light shifted over his features. Norman collapsed a little inside but fought not to show it. At that moment he realized he had been fighting his whole life not to show it.

"Why'd you do it, Dad?"

"I was compelled. Do you know what the most valuable commodity in the universe is? The greatest binding force? The Universal Integument? Do you know what it is?"

Bernie had to raise his voice to be heard over the swelling musical score as the end credits began to roll. Norman stared at him.

"Love," the thief said.

They walked up the aisle together. Bernie was wearing an olive drab infantryman's uniform. Norman was taller than his father, but he felt reduced, a child. He tried to make his hands into fists, but his rage had deserted him at last.

"Come on," Bernie said, patting his back, "I'll buy you breakfast."

"No, thanks. I already ate with the dog."

Norman, his dead father, and his imaginary dog walked toward the edge of the world.

"What time is it?" Norman asked.

"There isn't any time here."

"What about the dawn? When—"

"There is no dawn. Don't ask me how that's possible. All I know is this. We're here to serve the ultimate proliferation of love, which vitalizes the universe. There are beings who see to this. I don't know what they are. I wouldn't call them angels. They look inside us, and they spin out these worlds. They tell stories, give us roles, harvest the vital end product; I believe they must be insane. I mean, look around. You see, son, death isn't what we thought it was."

They arrived at the edge of the world. Beyond the jagged paving, stars suggested themselves out of the void.

"I'm going home," Norman said.

"Son—"

"Look, I don't believe it. I can't. And if this is a dream I want out. I want to feel normal again."

Norman stepped off the edge, blurred briefly, and found himself walking toward his dad and his dog. He stopped.

"Bottom line, Norm," Scout projected, "the way you feel is normal."

"True," his father said. "This is the place that hurts, son. The place where love resumes."

A car that looked like a De Soto with great, oval headlights on flexible stalks screeched around the corner and braked sideways in the middle of the street. The doors flung open, and men with guns piled out.

"Dat's him," the biggest one said, pointing at Norman. Norman's reactions were unconscious and lightning quick. He filled his hands with the twin automatics and brought down two of the armed men before either of them could get a shot off. Unfortunately the third man was fast enough to fire a Tommy gun burst before Norman could drill him.

The Tommy burst stitched across Bernie Helmcke's chest.

The De Soto squealed away, leaving bodies behind like bales of newspapers.

Norman dropped his guns. He sank to his knees at his father's side.

"I'm finished," Bernie said. "Again."

Norman felt it coming—the flood he'd dammed a lifetime ago.

"In my right pocket," Bernie said. "Keys for my apartment. Scout knows where it is." He coughed, misting the air with blood. "You'll need a place."

"Dad—"

"I'm sorry, son. I love you."

A savage coughing fit took him, and when it was over, so was the thief.

The world contracted into a throbbing locus of pain under Norman's heart.

"The apartment," Scout said. "—it isn't much. Deli on the ground floor. A *noisy* Deli. Two flights up to a hot plate and a smelly carpet. Of course, I have a sensitive nose."

Norman sat down in the street.

"At least you don't have to worry about anybody finding you there," Scout said. "But you'll need some kind of disguise when you go out. You could use my scarf, if you want."

Norman closed his eyes, the flood all through him now. The terrible thing. The love.

Scout bit his ear.

"*Ow!*"

The dog backed away. "You better get off your dead ass. This is a tough world. And as of today you're the only lawman in it. Norman, *there are innocent people here*. You can do something."

Norman fingered his lobe, which was not bleeding. "You're a real son of a bitch, you know that?"

"You're half right, sweetheart."

Norman found the key in his father's pocket. He lifted the body in his arms and carried it to the edge of the world and held it a moment longer before letting it roll away into the star twinkle. He waited, but it did not roll back. After a while, compelled, The Avenger of Love turned toward the City of Endless Night.

For Harlan

Author's Notes

The oldest story in this collection is "Double Occupancy." Technically, it was my first sale, and occurred in 1995—seven years before Gardner Dozois bought "Dead Worlds" and made me a household name—even if it was only in my own house. I say "technically" because, though I received a check for $150, the story didn't appear in print.

If anyone's interested, here's how publishing works sometimes: Back in the early 1990s I saw a listing in *The Gila Queen's Guide to Markets*. It was for a new magazine called *A Different Beat*. They wanted genre stories with a law enforcement element. Beyond that, anything went. I gave it a try, writing an old school Stephen King-influenced horror story about a couple of state troopers encountering Lovecraftian monsters in the Cascade Mountains. The assistant editor, an MIT student named Michael McComas, worked with me over a period a few months to accomplish several re-writes. I felt optimistic. I felt this was my lucky story, the one that was going to make it, the one with legs.

After completing the last rewrite request I sat back and waited, fairly certain I had a sale. A year later I wasn't so sure. I wrote to Mike and asked him what was up. My letter was a little cranky. When he got back to me he seemed surprised that I didn't know they had bought the story. And by the way, *A Different Beat* was no longer a magazine but a trade paperback anthology. Wow! I was in! Another year or so passed. I wrote to ask how it was going. Mike informed me that the senior editor was having personal problems and no one could get at the manuscripts for the book, which were locked away in her house. Eventually the other senior editor, and earthbound angel, Dawn Albright, took over the project. She made sure all the contributors got paid, but still the book didn't appear.

Years slipped by . . . and I felt that defeat had been snatched from the jaws of victory. I had a first sale, but it didn't feel anything like what it was supposed to feel like. During this period I was still writing stories, a few of them good, but I was running out of optimism. Even the gloomiest writers flourish only because of a fundamental and largely illogical optimism. When the optimism runs out, so do the stories—and occasionally the writer.

Jump ahead a few years. Stephen King publishes his book *On Writing*. In the middle of it he invites readers to try an exercise in writing from a situation. The situation was simple and appealed to me, so I gave it a shot. I have no idea why. By this time I was out of optimism. Like dead out. A year later I get an email from Marsha DeFilippo, King's personal assistant. I was one of five winners. Stephen would like to post your story on his website . . . Optimism raised her weary head and attempted a smile.

I got organized.

And I returned to an old love—science fiction. The first new story I wrote was "Dead Worlds." Right before Gardner picked it up for *Asimov's* in August of 2002, I received a couple of other acceptances from a guy who ran Undaunted Press, a small publishing concern somewhere in the Midwest. But Gardner's acceptance was the Big One. I worked nights, and when I returned home, weary and discouraged after nine hours in the factory, I stood in the kitchen and opened the mail. As I read Gardner's letter, which was all of two sentences, I got teary. That's how a first sale is supposed to hit you, I think. At the time, I was married to my first wife, and she asked me what was wrong. I told her a letter I'd been waiting for finally arrived. It was twenty years late, but nothing's perfect, and the twenty years were my fault, not anybody else's.

The newest story in this book* is "The Avenger of Love," which started out as a collaboration with Harlan Ellison, though I ended up doing this version by myself and selling it to *The Magazine of Fantasy & Science Fiction*, which I'd been trying to crack since, roughly, The Dawn Of Time. Most of the other stories were written and sold after "Dead Worlds," but a few, "Reunion," "The Tree," and "The Apprentice" are from the period of disorganization and diminishing optimism. They are survivors.

Interestingly, right about the time Gary Turner accepted this collection for Golden Gryphon, I heard from Dawn Albright. It had been years. She was starting an online magazine and wanted, at long last, to publish "Double Occupancy"—twice! First in the online mag, then in a print anthology,** due out about the same time as *Are You There and Other Stories*. I cleared it with Gary and signed a new contract with Dawn. Gary claims that "Double Occupancy" is his favorite story in the book. For all I know, it tipped the scale in my favor when he was deciding whether or not to make my agent an offer. I guess life, or the writing life, anyway, is circular.

I'd like to thank the editors who have bought stories from me over the years. In chronological order: Sandra Hutchinson, Dawn Albright, Cullen Bunn, Gardner Dozois, Diane Walton, Sheila Williams, Rich Horton, Patrick Swenson, Shawna McCarthy, Lou Anders, George Mann, Gary Turner, and Gordon Van Gelder.

I'd also like to thank Nancy Kress, who surprised me when she offered to write the introduction to my as-yet unsold collection.*** And John Picacio, who created the cover art. He went the extra mile, because that's what John does, and he totally nailed it. I count myself almost preternaturally lucky to have these two lauded and accomplished pros participate in the project. Finally, I want to thank Christine Cohen, my agent on this book. She took a chance on me years ago when I barely knew anyone in the business. I'll always remember that.

These stories kept me going through some dark stretches, which may account for the tone of many of them. Certainly the stories have changed my life, given me a new world to inhabit, populated with friends and colleagues. The dark is in retreat. Writing is magic.

Jack Skillingstead
February 15, 2009
Seattle, Washington

* In the Fairwood Press edition "Free Dog" is the newest story.
** Actually, the anthology never happened.
*** A few years later I surprised her back by asking her to marry me.

If you're interested in my story-writing process, this essay I wrote in support of Marty Halpern's Alien Contact *reprint anthology gives insight into my admittedly quirky approach. The story "What You Are About To See" first appeared in the August 2008 issue of* Asimov's.

THERMALLING

I used to fly airplanes. I didn't do it professionally but as a private, recreational flier. All through high school I rented Cessnas and gave my friends scenic, and on some occasions hair-raising, tours of the airspace over the Puget Sound Basin. Eventually, I think I was twenty-two, I decided to try gliders. I had the idea this would be more "pure." On my first instructional flight I learned something invaluable about staying up in the air without an engine—and about writing.

Heat rises. Everybody knows that. But for glider pilots the rising columns of air called thermals are like free gas stations. Really good glider pilots can stay aloft all day and even conduct cross-country flights by "thermalling" across the sky. It's a matter of skill and luck. So is writing. And it's a matter of being keenly sensitive, or I would say, intuitive. Which is also true of writing.

There's an instrument called a variometer. It's a highly responsive vertical speed indicator. This helps in identifying the presence of thermals, which are invisible and can be subtle. But the best glider pilots have their own built-in variometer, much like Hemingway's "built-in, shock resistant shit detector." The pilot feels the slight updraft of air—sometimes barely perceptible—and banks steeply into it, climbing hundreds or even thousands of feet, pivoting on the long, elegant wing of the airplane. The first time my glider instructor handed the controls over to me I cluelessly soared through multiple thermals without even realizing they were there.

I used to do that with story ideas, too.

Really, calling them "ideas" is overstating the case. With "What You Are About To See," the first thing I had was a short, declarative sentence, like a stubby knife: *It sat in a cold room.* This sentence lifted out of my unconscious like a thermal seeking my attention. By now I was experienced enough as a writer to recognize that the sentence might be a valuable skyhook that could carry me into a story, or it could be nothing more than a bump in the air. It was far more likely to be a bump.

I was writing very fast that summer. At least, very fast for me. I wanted to emulate some of the more prolific writers from an earlier era, writers like Ray Bradbury and Harlan Ellison. At the Nebula Awards in Tempe, back in 2006, Harlan had suggested we collaborate on a story. As part of my run up to that possibility I spent the summer writing short stories as fast as I could. When I felt the updraft of *It sat in a cold room* I banked steeply into it, without hesitation, without thinking—and at once ascended vertically into a story. If I'd been more methodical and slow, as was more usual for me, I probably would have missed it altogether.

I had been thinking about desert landscapes. I find them evocative, and they were on my mind because of Tempe. But the next thing that came to me in my rising column of warm air, after that first sentence, was the smell of cigarette smoke. My parents had both been smokers. My father eventually quit but my mother never did and she died young—younger than I am right now as I type these words. I think I got to the cigarette thing by way of a tough-talking clichéd picture of a hardened government agent. *That* was a conscious image, something no doubt received from the pop culture universe of movies. Certainly I didn't *know* any government agents. I looked at the image and asked myself what was in it that I could relate to personally, and it was the cigarette, the way different people hold them, the whole ritual of tamping the tobacco and lighting up, the way my mother, who had only one arm, could light a match one-handed, the way she let me help her change the flint in her classic Zippo, replace the fibrous cloth wick and saturate it with lighter fluid. As a little kid I did that many times. It was fun. It was something I did with my mom.

Now I had a desert landscape (conscious intention) and cigarettes (gift from the thermal). I made it night time under a nearly full moon—and suddenly there was a 7-11 store standing by itself in the middle of nowhere with its glaring bright fluorescent lights. The desert ran right up to the double glass doors. I got to the 7-11, probably, because I associate it with cigarettes, with customers asking for a "packa Marlboros" or whatever. I once worked in a 7-11 store in Portland, Maine. It was not a good experience.

And by now I was rising rapidly in my little thermal and I knew what my story would be about. All I had to do was go into the cold room and see what was waiting for me.

At the time of its writing I didn't view this as a particularly personal story but re-reading it today, after a number of years, I was struck by a couple of obvious things. My narrator, Brian Kinney, is a guilt-stricken "extractor of information from reluctant sources." He was hurt as a child, which drove him inward and estranged him from everyone, and this provided sufficient detachment so that, for a while, he was able to be a not very good guy. To say the least. Pretty simple character sketch. But guilt was the hot spot informing the whole thing. The world had gone all wrong, and Brian was part of that wrongness. And I remembered helping my mom with her cigarettes and lighter. As an adult I don't see myself as culpable in any way for the havoc—for the *wrongness*—that my mother's early death visited upon me and my family. But the child I had been felt plenty of guilt, and that child never really disappears. He lives down there in the unconscious and sends stuff up the thermals now and again.

The other thing I noticed was how political the story is. The fearful climate of the times is reflected in almost every paragraph. No doubt, that's why I saw the clichéd government agent, this caricature that represented my general unease. Suffice to say writers are creatures of their times, as much as anyone else, and are likely to express opinions, even when they don't realize they are doing so.

The collaboration, by the way, never panned out. But in the year or so it went on I learned a ton about being my own writer and trusting myself beyond my influences. Really, that was the best possible outcome. Life itself follows its own quirky story process for each individual. Tempe changed my writing life and, eventually, my real life. But that's another story. Suffice to say, a thermal rose up, and I banked into it.

About the Author

Jack Skillingstead has sold more than forty stories to markets including *Asimov's*, *Clarkesworld*, *F&SF*, and *Lightspeed*, as well as various Year's Best volumes and original anthologies. In 2004 he was a finalist for the Sturgeon Award and in 2013 his novel *Life on The Preservation* was a finalist for the Philip K. Dick Award. In 2019 *The Chaos Function*, a science fiction thriller, was published by Houghton Mifflin Harcourt/John Joseph Adams books. Jack has taught writing classes onboard ship in the Bahamas and in Seattle for Clarion West's one-day workshop series. He lives in Seattle with his wife, writer Nancy Kress.

PUBLICATION HISTORY

"Reading Jack Skillingstead" © 2009 by Nancy Kress | "Dead Worlds" first appeared in *Asimov's Science Fiction*, June 2003 | "Life on the Preservation" first appeared in *Asimov's Science Fiction*, June 2006 | "Double Occupancy" first appeared in *Polu Texni*, September, 2008 | "The Chimera Transit" first appeared in *Asimov's Science Fiction*, February 2007 | "Overlay" first appeared in *Asimov's Science Fiction*, October/November, 2005 | "Scatter" first appeared in *Asimov's Science Fiction*, October/November 2004 | "Bean There" first appeared in *Asimov's Science Fiction*, April/May 2005 | "Girl in the Empty Apartment" first appeared in *Asimov's Science Fiction*, September 2006 | "Rewind" first appeared in *Asimov's Science Fiction*, February 2004 | "The Apprentice" first appeared in *Whispers From The Shattered Forum*, Fall 2003 | "Everyone Bleeds Through" first appeared in *Realms of Fantasy*, October 2007 | "Reunion" first appeared in *On Spec*, #56 Spring 2004 | "Strangers on a Bus" first appeared in *Asimov's Science Fiction*, December 2007 | "Free Dog" first appeared in *Asimov's Science Fiction*, October/ November 2011 | "Thank You, Mr. Whiskers" first appeared in *Asimov's Science Fiction*, August 2007 | "The Tree" first appeared in *On Spec*, #62 Fall 2005 | "Are You There" first appeared in *Asimov's Science Fiction*, February 2006 | "Transplant" first appeared in *Asimov's Science Fiction*, August 2004 | "Here's Your Space" first appeared in *Are You There*, first Fairwood Press edition, 2009 | "Cat in the Rain" first appeared in *Asimov's Science Fiction*, October/November 2008 | "Alone With an Inconvenient Companion" first appeared in *Fast Forward 2*, Pyr, October 2008 | "What You Are About to See" first appeared in *Asimov's Science Fiction*, August 2009 | "Rescue Mission" first appeared in *Solaris Book of New Science Fiction*, Vol 3, February 2009 | "Two" first appeared in *Talebones* #35, Summer 2007 | "Scrawl Daddy" first appeared in *Asimov's Science Fiction*, June 2007 | "Human Day" first appeared in *Asimov's Science Fiction*, April/May 2009 | "Introduction to 'The Avenger of Love'" appears here for the first time | "The Avenger of Love" first appeared in *Fantasy and Science Fiction*, April/May 2009 | "Thermalling" © 2013 by Jack Skillingstead.

OTHER TITLES FROM FAIRWOOD PRESS

Liberty's Daughter
by Naomi Kritzer
trade paper $18.99
ISBN: 978-1-958880-16-6

The American Writer
by Jack Cady
trade paper $19.99
ISBN: 978-1-958880-17-3

Whispering Wood
by Sharon Shinn
trade paper $19.99
ISBN: 978-1-958880-13-5

Two Hour Transport 2
ed. by NIB, Ramona Ridgewell
& Keyan Bowes
trade paper $18.99
ISBN: 978-1-958880-20-3

Egyptian Motherlode
by David Sandner & Jacob Weisman
paperback $18.99
ISBN: 978-1-958880-21-1

Storm Waters
by Kat Richardson
trade paper $18.99
ISBN: 978-1-958880-22-7

Beyond Here Be Monsters
by Gregory Frost
trade paper $18.99
ISBN: 978-1-958880-15-9

Substrate Phantoms
by Jessica Reisman
trade paper $18.99
ISBN: 978-1-958880-23-4

Find us at:
www.fairwoodpress.com
Bonney Lake, Washington